GRACE NOTE

THE CAKE SERIES

J. BENGTSSON

Grace Note

Edited by Dorothy Zemach

Cover art copyright Michelle Lancaster www.michellelancaster.com

Cover Model David Bodas

To my cherished Kollyns Rae
I hope someday my stories will make you proud.
Love you forever, Grammie

HE WAS THE ONE WHO GOT AWAY, THE
OG OWNER OF MY FORMER LOVESICK,
TEENAGED HEART.

CONTENTS

PART III
THE BRIDGE

PROLOGUE

G race note
      (grās ˌnōt)
noun

    1. An extra note added as an embellishment or
       decorative flourish; not essential to the main melody

I was sixteen years old the day I discovered nightmares were just memories in disguise. The truth had always been there, lying dormant, waiting for the right trigger. It came in the form of a boy daring me to dive deeper, to find the place inside me where the darkness cowered. I found it, all right—poked it with a stick and made it sing. My songs would never be the same after that, carrying me to new and unimaginable heights,

But at what cost? I could never go back to the naive girl I once was. Every effort had been taken to shield me from the horrors of my brother Jake's kidnapping, as well as the "nightly news" madness that followed. It took a village, literally. Community leaders along with good-hearted citizens banded together to create an alternate universe for me—and to a lesser extent, my slightly older brother Quinn—to live in. Gifted with scholarships to an ultra-private K-8 boutique school where the other kids were as clueless as we were, Quinn and I were allowed to grow up without the pollutants our older siblings breathed in.

Yet it would be wrong to assume I had been untouched by the tragedy that befell my family. I still grew up with the nightly screaming, with the stress, with the conversations that hushed when I walked into a room. I developed an aversion to all things kidnapping-related. If a news article or social media post popped up about Jake's abduction, I kept on scrolling. If kids at school tried to engage me in conversation about the crime, I walked away. The gory details of my family's past were not my own. I'd chosen to live in the light.

You know what they say: what you don't know won't hurt you. My god, why had I tested the theory? It took me all of two minutes to discover the explosive truth and then another five to throw it up in the toilet. Of course, I knew there were things my family hadn't told me, but I never could have imagined that the biggest secret of all—the smiling face, the sinister whisper— lived inside my head.

PART I

THE BOND

1

GRACE: NOT MY HERO

PRESENT DAY

A hand jostled my shoulder, startling me out of a restless slumber. I gasped, jolting upright as confusion took hold.

"Shhh. It's all right, Grace," Elliott soothed. "You were whimpering in your sleep. You're safe. It was just a dream."

"It... it was?" I asked, my voice almost childlike in its optimism. If Elliott was to be believed, then the horror in my head had never happened, and Quinn was not currently lying on an operating table with doctors diligently working to save his life. "It was all a dream?"

Elliott's eyes widened, and he stuttered, "No, I mean... it's not, um... no... it did happen, but... uh..."

I snapped back into my hard plastic chair, the events of the evening flooding back with a vengeance. What was I thinking? Of course it was real. I'd watched it happen with my own two eyes. The first pops had gone largely unnoticed. Concerts were deafening beasts to begin with—the music, the high decibels, the screams—some so piercing they rang in the ears for days. From where I'd been seated, alongside the stage in an area reserved for family, it made sense that I was unaware of the horror unfolding behind me... until it arrived at center stage. That was when the crowd surged forward, when the music abruptly cut out, and when my absolute favorite brother in the entire world went down in a hail of gunfire.

"...but Quinn's a fighter," Elliott said. "He'll pull through this. You know he will."

No, I didn't. This wasn't a sprained ankle. The blood I'd been covered in earlier was Quinn's, and while I'd gratefully accepted the change of clothes from my sister, Emma, Quinn's girl Jess had respectfully declined. Like Jackie Kennedy before her, she had chosen to remain in her blood-soaked clothing to show the world what they had done. Not that anyone would blame her for her defiance given that Jess had just gotten engaged to my brother as he lay dying in her arms.

Elliott continued to try and comfort me by massaging my neck and speaking soothing words of reassurance in my ear. Normally, I appreciated his calm, cool head but not today. Even his touch made me squirm.

I held up a hand. "No offense, but please stop talking."

Elliott stiffened as he took immediate offense. "I'm just trying to be supportive."

"Well, you're not," I clipped, scowling as my lower lip began to shudder. This wasn't like me. I was known for being easygoing and weep-resistant. I had never found tears personally beneficial. It came down to the whole quantum theory—if a tree falls in the forest and there's nobody around to hear, does it make a sound?

Well, the same could be applied to lastborn children. While firstborns were falling off the jungle gym into the arms of their protective parents, I just fell. By the time I was born, the last of seven children, there just wasn't a lot of sympathy left for my scrapes, bruises, and tears. As a result, if little-girl me face-planted or scuffed my knee, there would be no fussing over the wound. No Hello Kitty Band-Aids. No kissing and making it better. Instead of first aid, I got... well, a standing ovation.

Oh, the attention I would receive for a sniffle-free ounce of blood! My father would beam. My brothers would line up to slap me some high fives. No wonder I began to equate pain with a jolly good time. Sometimes I even purposely wiped out just to feel the love.

No doubt that early indoctrination inspired the daredevil in me. I was the tiny girl with loose strawberry-blonde curls spilling out from under her helmet dropping into a half-pipe at the skate park while dressed in a pink tutu and camouflage kneepads. The wide-eyed kindergartener who stayed up way past her bedtime to watch scary movies with her older siblings. The determined kid sister who stood on her tippy-toes at the amusement park in hopes of clearing the height restrictions to ride the roller coaster with the rest of her long-legged family.

But right now, I was none of the above. I'd been backed into a corner, and if anyone dared cross me in this state of mind, they could expect me to come up slashing. And that included my boyfriend of six months. He was one bad decision away from living a lonely, sterile life.

The wounded expression on Elliott's face forced me to clamp down on my lower lip which, quite honestly, was the only thing keeping me from biting his head off. I knew I was being unreasonable—mean, even—but I just couldn't with him. Not right now. Not after his tone-deaf comedy act earlier in the day—throwing shade on Quinn right before the start of the concert.

"*Watch him choke,*" he'd said. "*Get up there, open his mouth, and be like uh... uh... uh.*"

Elliott had thought he was so funny, cracking himself up, but I hadn't found it hilarious. Normally, I was up for a good laugh, but not at the expense of my family. And talk about a joke not aging well! An hour after the callous comment was made, Quinn was up on the same stage Elliott predicted he'd choke on—lying in a pool of his own blood.

"Hey," Elliott said, drawing in a breath to get him through the chore of dealing with little ol' unreasonable me. He entwined his fingers in mine and gave them a reassuring squeeze. "I know you're scared, but everything will be all right. I promise."

He leaned in and kissed my cheek. It was meant as a sweet and reassuring gesture, but again, I wasn't feeling it. A shiver of fury swept through me. How dare he offer his upbeat support? His empty promises? I knew I was being irrational and that I might even owe him my life—he'd covered my body with his when the shots rang out—but I still felt a strange disconnect. Like he was somehow trespassing on this intensely personal moment in my life. Like he shouldn't even be here, taking part in my family's misery. It was ours alone, for no one else to see. Playing hero didn't earn Elliott his stripes. If there was one thing us McKallisters did well, it was to close ranks when tragedy struck. You were either in by way of DNA or you were in by holding on to your chosen McKallister for dear life. My sister-in-law Casey was one of those hardened survivors. She'd outwitted, outplayed, and outlasted my labor-intensive brother Jake, thereby paying her dues and earning her place in the inner circle. And then there were Finn and Kenzie and Sam and Jess, all had taken on a sibling and lived to tell about it. They could stay.

But what about Elliott? Where were his bleeding knuckles? His tested soul? Yes, he'd protected me in the arena, but I hadn't asked him to. Hadn't even wanted him to. Yet, once my father discovered what he'd done, he'd proclaimed Elliott king and now I'd have to deal with the trickle-down effect of my entire family bowing down at his feet.

Meeting Elliott's eyes, I calmly untangled my fingers from his and used the back of that same hand to wipe his kiss right off my cheek. He winced, clearly shocked by my vindictiveness. Not that I blamed him. I'd never given him any indication that, during times of stress, I might shape-shift into a honey badger. Yet here we were, the truth finally revealed. I was a self-serving carnivore, and if he didn't get out of the way, he'd become my prey.

Elliott shook his head, confused. "Why are you acting like this?"

Why? Why was I acting like this? Did I need to spell it out? Did I need to remind him that a disgruntled employee of the music arena Quinn was playing at tonight had taken out his rage on both concertgoers and the band performing up on the stage —the band my brother was fronting. Elliott couldn't understand the glue that bonded my family. He was lukewarm with his own. Their suffering was not his. But for me, my family was my whole world, and Quinn was at the center. He was the scared little boy who'd huddled under the bed tent with Emma and me when Jake's nightly screams wouldn't let us sleep. And he was the big brother who'd vowed to keep me safe by not letting go of my tiny baby hand when we were out in public. Quinn had grown into my confidant. My protector. My biggest fan, always seeing the potential in me, in my music, even when I doubted myself.

And I might lose him tonight.

Shivers rocked me. Quinn couldn't die. I had no roadmap to follow without his haphazard navigation skills leading the way. Why him? Why now? It was all so senseless. This was supposed to be Quinn's big break, his chance to prove to the world he was every bit as good as the legendary brother he'd been chasing after his whole life. But now he might never get that chance. He might very well die in his prime. Forever young. Forever talented. Forever missed.

I lashed out at Elliott for his insensitive question. "I'm acting like this because I'm angry and irrational, and I'm going to take it out on whoever ventures into my space. I warned you, Elliott. I put myself in a time-out away from everyone else for a reason. You're the one who followed me here, so now you can't complain when you get clawed."

Elliott leaned away, unfamiliar with this deviant version of me. Most people were. I put on a good act. Honestly, it wasn't even an act. Ninety-nine percent of the time I was a rough and tumble, bubbly little sister with the world's best hug. When I was a baby, my older siblings lined up to get a piece of the cuddle action. I was like a human sloth, and when I wanted, I could go from one person to another with my feet never touching the ground.

My reputation for purity and light followed me into adulthood, no one remotely suspecting that I was hiding one tiny percent of pitch darkness inside. That was what fueled my writing and what sparked the anger I'd just unleashed on Elliott. Every developing talent needed an origin story, and oh boy, did I have one. Sometimes I wondered if Fate had never linked eyes with mine, had never exchanged a friendly wave, and had never patted me on the head and spoken those damning words, would I be the songwriter I was today?

With a swiftness that startled me, I could barely breathe, and teardrops slipped down my cheeks faster than I could wipe them away. I turned my back on Elliott, not wanting him to see my pain. I didn't do heartbreak in the company of others... unless those others shared my last name.

I felt a shadow fall over me. Elliott was on his feet.

"Right. Obviously, you don't want me here, so I'll give you your space," he said, averting his gaze like a browbeaten dog.

I watched him weave a path around the seats in the waiting room and exit out the glass door. I knew I should go after him, let him try to comfort me, but shamelessly, I was happy he was gone. A weight had been lifted off me, though really, I shouldn't have felt that way. Elliott was my boyfriend, the man I'd fallen for at the little corner café in London. Our first meeting had cliché TV-movie cuteness written all over it. I was the newly arrived American starting her semester abroad, and he was the awkwardly charming Brit five years my senior. Elliott had accidentally grabbed my coffee off the counter, and seconds before pressing it to his lips, I'd playfully stopped him with my best *Law and Order* impersonation. *'Sir, put the coffee cup down and slowly step away from the counter.'*

We'd shared a good laugh—a great one, even—and that led to a common table at the café followed by a dinner invitation. Elliott wasn't the sporty type of guy I normally gravitated toward, but his unassuming confidence and quick wit had won me over that day. I came to adore his out-of-fashion, round-rimmed glasses and the tousled, floppy brown hair he was constantly redirecting off his face. What made our instant connection all the more meaningful was that he'd fallen for me even before knowing my last name.

Everything had been damn near flawless until the two of us flew back to Los Angeles and took up residence in my parents' house. I'd noticed a change in Elliott almost from the beginning. Or maybe it was me? Whoever was to blame, our downward spiral had begun then, even if I hadn't been willing to admit it to myself. Elliott was textbook perfect for me. At least, that was what every person in my family was saying. He was a man to settle down and start a family with. I'd never said that was what

I wanted, but still, the implication was there. If I couldn't hold on to a guy like him, what hope was there for me?

Needing to clear my head, I zeroed in on the most perfect distraction a girl could ask for—my famous brother, Jake. There was no one more fascinating to me. Not only was Jake a world-renowned musician, he was also a warrior of the highest degree. The survivor of a childhood stranger abduction, he'd been imprisoned in hell and had resorted to extreme measures to save himself—only to spend the years following trying to silence the horror in his head.

He'd always been a mystery to me. Bits and pieces of our lives intersected, but we'd never really connected. Of all the siblings, we were the furthest apart. With nine years and a kidnapping between us, Jake and I were like two parallel lines moving in tandem. While he'd left the nest early to begin his celebrated music career, I was still at home honing my culinary skills on an Easy-Bake oven. While he was amassing a fortune, I was earning the majority of my income from the tooth fairy. And while Jake traveled the world in customized tour buses, my main mode of transportation was in the back seat of Mom's minivan strapped into a forward-facing booster seat.

Yet despite the distance between us, Jake was the only person in the world who knew about my one percent darkness. Not that he remembered. I'd confessed it to him on what I'd believed to be his deathbed. Weeks into a coma, Jake had served as a silent, nonjudgmental sounding board for me to unload my ultimate truth. And while Jake had not retained any of the one-sided conversation, I was comforted just knowing my secret was in his head somewhere, relieving me of having to carry the burden alone.

Jake shifted his gaze, catching me in the act of shamelessly invading his privacy. Fringe strands of hair tumbled over his famous eyes, partially shielding them from view. He was still wearing his stage outfit: black leather pants, a black tank that clung to him while showcasing his tatted arms, and a silver chain that dipped from his belt buckle to the back right pocket. In a catastrophic turn of events, Jake had been performing on his own stage in Arlington at the exact same time that his newbie rocker brother, performing in Los Angeles, got gunned down on his.

Neither brother finished their concert tonight.

To my surprise, Jake held me in his stare, and because it was such a rare occurrence, I didn't dare look away. Slowly, his eyes shifted to the door Elliott had just walked out of and then back to me, openly letting it be known he'd seen the kiss-wiping fiasco. I offered up a weak smile and shrugged, too emotionally drained to make excuses for my behavior.

An endearing lopsided smile hitched the corner of Jake's lips as he subtly brushed the tip of his nose with his pointer finger two times. My eyes widened and then I laughed, actually laughed in the midst of all the misery. See, before tragedy ripped his world apart, Jake had once been a typical big brother who teased his little sister. When we were just kids, he'd convinced me that tapping the tip of the nose twice meant "I love you." I'd apparently started double-tapping my nose to family members and strangers alike, forcing my worried parents to take me to a child psychologist and have me evaluated for a disorder.

Our double-tap had become family folklore, brought up now and again for a good laugh, and it just occurred to me that it might've been the last time Jake had told me he loved me. His simple gesture settled my aching heart and gave me the strength I needed to see this horrible day through. I smiled and double-tapped my nose right back at him. Jake nodded once before returning his head to his hands and resuming the restless leg bounce.

A movement at the door caught my attention, and I looked

over, expecting Elliott to walk back through. But it wasn't him. My back straightened into a steel rod.

Oh my god. It was him.

I bolted to my feet, a breath catching in my throat. In shock and awe, I stared at the man standing on the other side of the doorway. That was the place he'd always been: on the other side. Alone. Cast out by society. But I'd taken him in. I'd loved him and nurtured him and given him a home inside my heart. I'd given him others things, too—like, all of me. He was my first love, and if my heart had only had its way, he would've been my last.

He was the one who got away, the OG owner of my former lovesick, teenaged heart. Our eyes locked from across the room, and instantly, those long years of pining over a man I couldn't have came to a screeching halt. He was here, in the flesh. Somehow, the universe had understood what I needed at the exact moment I needed it.

I barely recognized the intoxicating boy he'd once been. It was as if the years had zapped him of his originality. He looked like a neglected flower pulled from the dirt and tossed in the trash. His hair, once the most vibrant and unique part about him, was long and soiled, dangling over his handsome face like a curtain, the only openings where the strands caught in his overgrown beard. His normally sun-scorched skin was so pale it appeared almost translucent under the harsh florescent lighting. And his eyes—his beautiful, soulful brown eyes—were nothing but sunken, red-rimmed misery. I thought I'd seen him at his worst—a streetwise runaway surviving with only the clothes on his back—but I was wrong.

He was worse off now. So much worse. Yet despite his obvious unraveling, he'd still come for me, and I knew why. He'd seen what happened on the news. He was checking up on me, making sure I was alive. Because he loved me. He always had.

We could've been so good together had he not chosen her over me. But I was willing to overlook the past because I needed him now. Not Elliott. Not my mom or my dad. Not even Jake and his love taps.

No, I needed *him*. Rory Higgins.

My drummer boy.

2

GRACE: THE COUNTDOWN

I don't even remember getting to the door. My sole focus had been the guy on the other side of it, the one who disappeared from view the second our eyes met. I should've expected it. Rory never stayed in one place for long. He'd never really trusted me; not fully. I knew it in the way his body tensed when I hugged him or the way his eyes would leave mine to scan the perimeter behind us. He was always watching. Always preparing for the fall. Maybe he'd known something I didn't because the fall did come. And it wiped us both out.

Skidding out into the hall, I whipped my head around looking for him, but he wasn't there. I stood in the center of the wide, sterile corridor, my pulse racing as I turned in circles, scanning every closed door in my search. I cursed under my breath. Had he really come all this way just to dodge me now? The coward.

"I swear to god, Beats, you have ten seconds to show yourself before I start screaming."

I waited. All the doors remained frustratingly closed.

"I know you're here," I called out to him, understanding that if Rory didn't want to be found, there was little I could do to unearth him. He was damned near an expert at disappearing. A life of running had prepared him well. But I knew Rory. He was always contemplating his next move. Always ready to bolt or hunker down, whichever benefitted him in the moment. But if his current plan was to wait me out, my ex would be sorely disappointed because I had plans of my own, and they included flushing his ass out.

"Ten. Nine." I started the countdown, my voice shrill with indignation. "Eight. This isn't gonna be pretty, Rory. My screams will be so piercing they'll bust the windows off their hinges and set the fire alarms shrieking. Good luck escaping unseen then, Houdini. Seven. Six. My brothers are in the waiting room. They're going to be *real* unhappy to see you."

A door cracked open down the hallway, just a sliver, but I knew it was him. I could feel his magnetic pull.

"Five. Four..." I continued my countdown ultimatum for no other reason than it made me feel like I was in control, when in reality, he held every bit of my sanity.

A hand emerged from the door and I stepped forward, laying mine in his open palm. His fingers, long and nimble, closed around mine and the familiarity sent a wave of heat through me. My god, it was Rory Higgins. These hands were the first to ever touch me. They'd awakened me. The things he'd done, the way he'd made me feel... it wasn't an exaggeration to say he'd ruined me for all others. I might have moved on, but my body never did.

Rory pulled me into the family-style bathroom, locking the door behind us. And then there he was, an arm's length away, the talented boy who'd managed to shake the ordinary right out of me. My blustery countdown came to an abrupt halt. The air between us stalled as we stood staring. He'd managed to pull the hair out of his face and secure it into a knot on the back of his head, but that only served to highlight the deepening creases in his forehead. His intense gaze dragged over me, rendering me immediately insecure. What was he thinking? Did he not like what he saw? I wasn't the trusting, wobbly colt he'd once loved, but whose fault was that?

Painfully self-conscious, I slid my thumbs under my eyes and wiped away any mascara residue in a last-ditch effort to preserve what was left of my dignity. I hadn't been good enough for him once, and this current state I was in would not bolster my chances now. But then, time had hardened Rory too—maybe even brought him to his knees—so he really shouldn't be casting those deep creased forehead wrinkles at me.

Rory closed the distance between us, his proximity made all the more shocking when his fingers skipped across my skin. It took me a second to realize he was performing a full-scale physical, frantically checking me for injury. If I'd been of sound mind, I would've slapped his hands away, or at the very least, his worry. He didn't get to be my protector anymore. That was Elliott's job, and tonight, my boyfriend had proven he was up to the challenge even if I'd given him no credit for it.

Yet Rory's fingers felt so familiar, so comforting, and I stood motionless as he surveyed my brows, my cheeks, the nape of my neck. But his newfound interest in my flesh must have been driven by fear for my safety rather than lust for my body. My heart sped up as his hand moved downward, past my collarbone and over my bloody arms to my trembling hips, where his probing fingers sent trembles cascading through me. I hated that my body reacted to his touch like nothing had ever happened.

Anger reared its aggrieved head. How dare he rev my heart for no good reason? This time I did slap his hands away, but like a pesky fly, they immediately returned. I shoved Rory back. He barely moved, his long, solid frame more than a match for the exhaustion in me. But my anger evened the score. I advanced upon him, slapping the remainder of the countdown into his chest one rage-filled word at a time. "Three. Two. One. Where. The. Fuck. Have. You. Been. Rory. Higgins."

The object of my animosity batted his way through my wrath before grabbing my wrists and holding them steady. I fought free of his restraint, spewing obscenities. Hitting. Accusing. Someone needed to pay for this. For Quinn's undoing. For Elliott's unreturned devotion. For Rory's long-ago betrayal.

Someone. Needed. To. Pay.

Rory kept his composure through the barrage of my rage.

Finally, mercifully, I burst into tears, dropping my head into his chest. So tired of the fight. Rory's strong, capable arms wrapped around me, offering me the rest I so desperately needed.

"I'm here," he spoke in a heartbreaking whisper. "I'm here, Grace."

Yes. Rory was here, towering over me, so gentle as he murmured sweet everythings in my ear. *I'm here, Grace.* Did he have any idea how long I'd waited to hear those words? Pressed against him, I could feel his heart speed up for me, and I squeezed tighter. We stood there for the longest time, no words passing between us. Eventually, my tears subsided, and only then did the reality of our clandestine meeting take hold.

Oh god. Elliott. My boyfriend.

I unfolded myself from the hug and took a giant step back. This was wrong. The man I was supposed to take my comfort from had been banished and humiliated. What would he think if he found me here in another man's arms? And not just any man, but the one I'd never been able to let go of. The one I'd never even told him about because the memory of our last parting still tore at my heart. This secret rendezvous with Rory made me wonder if Elliott and I had been doomed from the start. The whole thing tonight, our fight, my behavior... I'd pinned it all on him. Yet it had always been me. Me and Rory and our promised life together that he'd thrown away. I knew he'd been lying to me that night—that he didn't want to go—and yet he'd still walked away. Rory had done this to me, stunting my growth and seeing to it that I could never fully love another.

Perhaps sensing I was pulling away, Rory swept me up in his stare, his deadened eyes roaring back to carnal life. Ours had always been an animal attraction. A primal urge. He was forbidden fruit, always had been. I'd wanted him from the very first time I'd watched him drum. I'd been too young and naive to fully comprehend what it all meant, but he'd shown me. Oh yes, he had. And in the process, he'd set in motion an obsession that still lived inside me today.

"Grace..." he said, so alluring with his broken tenor.

My breath quickened. I wasn't over him. Had I ever claimed to be? No. But seeing him now solidified what I'd always known. Rory was my toxin. If he allowed it, I'd drop everything—destroy my life—just to have him ruin me again.

Rory closed the gap between us, and that cavernous wrinkle in his forehead was back and so were his hands on my body.

"The blood," he said, elevating my splattered arms to look for the source of the injury. "Where's it coming from?"

"It's not mine."

"But..." He pulled up my shirt to expose the smear of red blotting my skin. So familiar was he with my body that Rory hadn't stopped to consider it might be an invasion of my privacy. And I didn't tell him because when his hands skated across my abdomen searching for the nonexistent entry wound, they sent shivers right down to the tips of my toes. "You're covered in it."

"Listen to me," I said, commanding his attention with the tip of his chin. "I'm okay."

"You don't look okay." He frowned. "I've seen dead people with less blood on them."

He said things like that sometimes, and I'd never known how to respond. He'd always kept the realities of his past life far away from me. "It's not mine," I repeated. "It's Quinn's blood."

A muscle pulsed in his cheek. He was angry... for me, as if the world had bobbled and knocked both of us off our axis. Rory understood my reliance on Quinn. Never questioned our connection and never made me feel shame for needing my brother close by.

"I don't know what to say," he muttered, despite his empty expression saying it all. "Sorry isn't enough."

No, it wasn't. Rory got it. Sorry wasn't nearly enough.

"I tried to wipe it off," I said, my whispered hysteria building. "But I just ended up spreading it around, and now I'm splattered in my brother's blood and I can't hardly think straight."

He lowered my shirt, smoothing it out. "Sorry, I shouldn't have been touching... I thought you were injured."

I shook my head, both in response and exasperation. "Why did you come here?"

"You know why I came here."

"No, Rory. I don't."

"You. Quinn."

"But why do you even care? You walked away."

"Because you were once..." Rory stopped himself, looking away.

"Once what?"

His voice crackled as he finished the sentence. "...my family."

The sincerity in his admission broke me. We were the family he'd never had, not just Quinn and me but the rest of them too. And yet he'd given it all up... for her? I would never understand.

"I couldn't just"—he blinked heavily, his eyes lowering—

"just sit at home and watch it on TV. It's the same shit over and over. No updated information on Quinn at all."

I felt sympathy for him. How could I not? So much had happened between Rory and Quinn, so much animosity, that it was easy to forget they'd once been friends, bandmates. They'd made plans to ride the crazy train of fame together... until Quinn caught him in the act of betrayal, blowing Rory and me to smithereens. To my knowledge, they'd never spoken since, but if the pain that shrouded his features was any indication, he still cared about my brother... and that touched every raw nerve in me.

"There's nothing to report. Quinn's in surgery. It's been hours, and we still haven't heard anything yet. I'm scared he's not going to make it through," I said, trying not to wince at my own words. "The blood you see on me wasn't even half of it. Me and his fiancée, Jess, were trying to slow it down until the ambulance arrived."

Rory listened. Nodded. Cringed. His fists curled into knots.

Unlike Elliott, he didn't offer up empty assurances or tell me everything was going to be all right. He didn't rub my shoulders or make uncomfortable small talk in an effort to soothe me. Rory was a realist. He'd seen the dark side of life and didn't believe in happily ever after. He would never sugarcoat the truth for me or promise me a bright future, but what he would do was suffer alongside me. Really, that was all I'd wanted from Elliott —someone to mirror my rage and justify the horror I felt inside.

Rory's jaw steeled at the injustice of it all as I told him what had happened inside the arena and of a heroic but wounded Quinn coming to our rescue and leading us out of harm's way through a hatch under the stage. Once I'd run out of words, Rory lowered his head, slipping his fingers through my hair, cupping the back of my neck and laying his forehead against mine in a show of solidarity. We stood like that, his hands caressing, and then he drew his head back and stared me in the eyes.

He wore a brooding look that tugged at his eyebrows and tapered the bones in his sculpted face. I swallowed hard, burning to touch his whiskered cheek and pepper kisses on his mouth. But I didn't dare. Rory was one giant danger sign. He couldn't be tamed. If I didn't heed the warnings, it would be my own damn fault. I had Elliott, a man who loved me. A man who would never leave me screaming in the driveway. No, I thought. If I continued down this path, I'd be the Rory in Elliott's and my story. I had to immediately extract myself from this very precarious situation.

But before I could act rationally, Rory glided his thumb along my wanting lips. I sucked in a breath, my heart flapping like a mama bird's wings after her baby fell out of the nest. Closing my eyes, I valiantly tried to summon up Elliott's face, but Rory was making it so damn difficult. He knew me so well, could read the conflict written across my face. If I did this, if I fell back under his spell, I would lose Elliott and the life he promised. Stability. Family. Happiness.

"Grace." Rory's ragged breath exhaled my name. A storm brewed in his eyes. God, why was he always so damn conflicted? So primal and unstable. I couldn't do this with him again, put my life on hold while I waited for him to get a handle on his. He wasn't going to. He was never going to... as much as my heart desired it.

"No." I snapped awake, pushing him. "No. I can't do this again."

He took a step back, shaking his head. "I know... I wasn't thinking. I'm sorry. I don't blame you. You deserve so much better."

Oh, hell no. Rory wasn't going to play that game with me. I'd offered him unconditional love. He was the one who couldn't accept it.

"Stop it. Just stop. I deserved *you*, Rory. And you deserved me. It never had to be more complicated than that. You chose someone else, and now I've moved on. I have a boyfriend. I'm"— I swallowed the word down hard—"in love with him."

He studied me with laser-focused eyes. "You're not. I know you."

"You knew me before. Past tense. You don't know present tense Grace, the one you created when you abandoned me. I'm not going to risk a sure thing on the off chance that you might want more than a hookup."

His eyes flickered with anger. "Like you were ever just a hookup to me."

It was a mean thing to say. I knew that. We'd been so much more. But that didn't change a thing. I couldn't go back and end up with nothing.

"You know I'll always love you," I said, my broken words barely audible. "I'll always want you. I'd always put my life on hold for you. But don't make me do it, Rory. Don't make me choose because I can't survive you again."

A sharp knock on the door jolted us both apart.

"Grace, are you in there?"

It was Elliott.

I glanced at Rory, witnessing the defiant anger in his eyes and knowing he was one irrational decision away from blowing up my entire world. I placed my finger over my lips, nonverbally begging for his compliance.

Hastily clearing my voice of heartbreak, I replied to my boyfriend, "Yes, I'm here."

"Well, shite, Grace," Elliott said. "I've been looking every-where for you."

"Oh god." A breath caught in my throat. "Is it Quinn?"

"Yes. But good Quinn news, not bad. He's out of surgery. Doctors have repaired the damage, and your badass brother is expected to make a full recovery. Now get your tush out here! Everyone's celebrating."

My legs instantly turned to jelly, and I would've crumpled to the ground in relief had Rory not been there to catch me.

"I... I..." My heart pounded viciously in my chest as I tucked my shirt back into my jeans and fluffed out my tangled hair. "I'm so relieved. I'm coming out. Just give me a second."

"Take your time. I'll be here waiting."

Of course he would be. Elliott was dependable like that.

"Is that him?" Rory whispered.

"Yes."

"He sounds"—a muscle danced in his cheek—"nice."

I ignored the contempt. "He is, actually."

Rory watched as I checked my reflection in the mirror for any telltale signs of cheating.

"And he's good to you?"

It was none of his business, but since he asked... "Yes."

Rory nodded and toed the ground. "Then I'm happy for you, Grace. I know you don't believe me, but that's all I've ever wanted for you."

Wrong choice of words. I swung back around, furious. "Oh, but that's a lie. I *was* happy... with you. I would've floated down your lazy river forever. You did this to us, Rory. You. And don't ever forget it."

The force of my words gutted him as surely as if I'd taken a knife to his abdomen. He looked stricken, and rightfully so. My heart still hurt for him, and I feared it always would, but I was done comforting him.

Avoiding eye contact, I turned for the door.

"Goodbye, Beats."

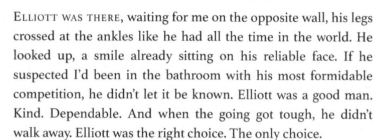

ELLIOTT WAS THERE, waiting for me on the opposite wall, his legs crossed at the ankles like he had all the time in the world. He looked up, a smile already sitting on his reliable face. If he suspected I'd been in the bathroom with his most formidable competition, he didn't let it be known. Elliott was a good man. Kind. Dependable. And when the going got tough, he didn't walk away. Elliott was the right choice. The only choice.

So why did I feel like I'd swallowed a cleaver?

No, I just had to get my head back in the game. Rory always did have a way of derailing me. But not this time. This wasn't about Rory anymore. I had to make it right with my boyfriend so that I could return my focus to the man who needed me most: Quinn.

Walking straight up to Elliott, I grabbed his smooth, whisker-free face and planted a kiss on his lips. He eyed me with a wicked grin before taking his revenge by wiping my kiss away with the back of his hand.

"Oh, no, you didn't." I laughed, swatting his chest playfully. "How dare you wipe my cooties away!"

"Just evening the score, sugar."

"And so you should." I kissed him again. "I'm so sorry. I was a bitch."

"Nah." He shook his head. "You had good reason. That joke I made about Quinn earlier was tasteless, and then, in the scope of what happened later, just really horrendous. I was such a fucking idiot. I deserved everything you gave. Forgive me?"

A huge weight lifted off me; I wouldn't be forced to dig deeper for the apology because I wasn't sure I could.

"Forgiven," I said, reaching my hand out and we shook on our shared guilt. "Now, tell me everything you know about Quinn."

Elliott pushed off the wall and snagged my hand, walking and talking as he filled me in. Basically, everything he knew had already been communicated through the closed bathroom door, but no matter. I hung on his every word because it meant my brother was on the road to recovery, and this night would soon be in the rearview mirror—the same mirror I was forcing myself not to glance back in for any sign of my drummer boy slipping out of the bathroom door.

3

RORY: UNLIKELY ALLIANCE

I was in destruction mode, thundering around the bathroom trying to find something to ravage. Something to satisfy the fury in me that Grace had left behind. But the bathroom was battened down tight, almost as if it had been constructed with this very tantrum in mind. The toilet paper holder was caged in plastic and drilled into a stud. The titanium hand dryer needed power tools to dislodge from the wall. Even the soap dispenser required a full-on cabinet disassemble to squirt that shit around the room. With no other outlet for my rage, I gripped the edge of the sink and roared.

"Arrggg!"

Forcing my eyes up, I cast flitting glances at the saboteur in the mirror but was careful not to catch his eye. I hated him for what he'd done to me. For what he'd done to Grace. I could feel his deadened glare, daring me to look. I faltered. God, what was wrong with me? If I couldn't meet the eyes staring back at me in the mirror, how could I ever be good enough for her?

And Grace wondered why I'd walked away.

I'd had to do it—for her.

Slowly, my eyes scanned upward, over my neck, up my chin,

along my nose, and then finally locking eyes with the child I'd once been who was staring back at me through a camera lens, accusing me. He had every right. I'd let him down, and so much more. I'd ruined his life. My life. But what did he expect? I was just a child. I was once him. The boy in the mirror. Gripping the sink tighter, I held the boy's gaze and wondered which one of us would blink first. But I knew who'd win—who always won. The kid with the condemning stare.

The door handle jiggled, indicating that there was a line forming just outside. I needed to get the hell out of here. Go home. Drink my night away. Reluctantly, I broke the morbid connection with the image in the mirror. It was further than I'd gotten in years. Give me another fifteen and we might actually get somewhere. Grabbing my beanie out of my pocket, I shoved it down over my head and lifted the hood up and over to protect my identity. For obvious reasons, I'd revealed myself to Grace, but I wasn't feeling generous with the rest of her family. One restless breath later, I opened the door and could instantly feel the opposing weight, the force of it pushing me back. I offered up a fight, but he was inside the bathroom and blocking my exit before I even knew what was happening.

"Not a word," he demanded, using the back of his foot to hasten the door's closing. Only then did I see who I was dealing with, and it wasn't the assassin I'd been expecting.

"Jake?"

It had been years, but it wasn't like I could forget his face, not when it was consistently in the media. I stood my ground despite knowing I had very little bargaining power against this formidable opponent. Jake McKallister really was in a class all his own. Not only did he command respect for his fame alone, but he also held a secret for me that even time and estrangement hadn't tempted him to spill. We hadn't even really been friends, not like Quinn and I had been, but we weren't enemies either. And I trusted him, which was a feat all itself, considering that if Jake wanted to, he could totally and completely destroy me.

He asked the same question his sister had before him. "Why did you come here?"

"I saw it on the news. I had to be sure she was okay."

"You could've contacted me."

"You? Yeah, I don't have your direct line."

Jake's eyes narrowed at my thinly veiled accusation. "Is that my fault?"

Indirectly, yeah, but I wasn't going to tell him that because I believed his heart had been in the right place that night and he hadn't purposely led me astray. Plus, Jake was as close to a hero as a guy like me got. He was the frontline warrior who'd paved the way for us wounded souls, proving you could always rise above. At least in theory.

"Look, Rory, I've got nothing against you, but if I'm going to pick a side, it's going to be my sister's every single time."

I didn't fault him for that. How could I? Knowing Grace had a support system many bodies deep had helped make the decision for me years ago, the one that still pained me today. The one he'd helped push me to.

"And I haven't asked you for anything since…"

There seemed no reason to finish the sentence. We both knew what I was referring to. The reason he now held my trust for the secrets he hadn't betrayed.

"I wasn't talking about that. I was talking about Grace. Dude, you destroyed her. What was going through that head of yours, making her think you left for another girl?"

I clenched my jaw shut. He was seriously asking me this after the pep talk he'd given me just before my life forever changed?

"What was I supposed to do? Tell her the truth? Or worse, disappear? She never would've stopped looking for me."

Jake seemed to consider my words before replying. "You're probably right. Hating you kept her away."

"You see?" I threw my hands up in barely controlled anger. "I'm a fucking genius."

"Where do you live now?"

"As of a few months ago, I'm back in LA."

Jake tipped his head in surprise. "That's permitted?"

"I wasn't in prison," I sneered. "I fulfilled my duties, and then, after a while, I decided I was done hiding. And now I'm back."

He nodded in that deliberate way that let me know he'd been following the case. "How was it?"

"How was what?"

"Testifying?"

"It was super fun," I said, pushing through the bitterness. "Got to relive it all, piece by piece. Too bad you never got the chance, but then you skipped right over the trial part, didn't you?"

Jake immediately retaliated. "There was a trial. I found him guilty as charged."

Oh, he'd definitely found the defendant guilty, and the whole world knew how Jake had chosen to sentence him. An uncomfortable laugh passed between us. Honestly, I couldn't believe I'd just said that to him. More shocking was his reply. There were clear lines with Jake that most people didn't dare cross; the kidnapping was at the top of that list. But I wasn't most people, a fact that became evident years ago when the similarities between the two of us came to light.

"So, you're back, then," he said matter-of-factly.

"I mean, yeah."

"Now what? You're going to start right back up with my sister like nothing ever happened?"

"Like it would be that easy."

"It shouldn't even be an option. You can't just pop into her life whenever you feel like it."

"Whenever I feel like it?" I bristled at his depiction. Everything I'd sacrificed had been for her. To give her a better life, away from me and the kid in the mirror. "I've stayed away for years. I did my part. She graduated high school. Went off to college. Met that bespectacled nobleman that she claims to be in love with. I'd say she was doing just fine until tonight."

"Until you show up and make things so much worse."

"Hey, she got every last thing she ever wanted. If one conversation with me knocks her out of alignment, then that's her own fault. Not mine."

Jake didn't have an answer for me because, ultimately, he was the one who'd sent me down this path. He'd faced the same dilemma I did once, only his conclusion had veered drastically in the other direction. He'd gotten everything he ever wanted. I'd lost everything, right down to my very identity.

Jake's fingers, coiled into my clothing, loosened. I hadn't realized he'd been holding me against the wall. I straightened up, and he took a step back.

"Sorry," he said. "Had a steroid moment there."

"I noticed."

His stand down signaled we'd come to an impasse, and the tension between us eased. I took that moment to look him up and down, and for the first time, noticed what he was wearing. He was decked out in head-to-toe rocker apparel. Despite that being what he was, Jake had always been unassuming. On multiple occasions, I'd seen him walk through a crowd of people in jeans, a t-shirt, and a baseball cap and go completely unnoticed.

"Dude. Are those leather pants?" I asked, the slightest smile ticking up my lips.

He matched my grin. "Fuck you."

"Hey, I'm not judging," I said, holding up my hands. "I've just never seen you looking so... fancy."

"I was on stage when I found out. Didn't have time to change," Jake said in defense before looking me up and down. "What's your excuse?"

I glanced down at my mismatched ensemble, as dull and rumpled as his were crisp and smooth.

"I have none. These were the only pieces of clothing in my overflowing stack of laundry that were clean enough to make the trip to the hospital."

"How does that not surprise me?"

We shared a quick laugh.

"Seriously, though, Rory." A tremor of concern furrowed his brow. "You look rough."

I was fully aware of how I presented, and dirty clothes weren't the half of it. I hadn't shaved or cut my hair in a long damn time. In fact, the last time I'd looked halfway presentable had been at the trial. Even then I hadn't wanted to, trusting my rough exterior would serve as both a defense to keep people away and a cloak to mask the shame. But the prosecutors had pleaded with me to freshen up—they wanted a choir boy on the stand, not the man that innocent boy had become. In the end, I gave them what they wanted: me with a close-cropped haircut and a smooth, hairless jawline. The day the trial ended was the day I stopped trying.

"Yeah, well, I've been a little preoccupied with the whole starting my life over again thing. You'd think I'd be used to it by now."

"Are you using your real name again?"

"Yes."

"Is that safe?"

"At this point, I don't really give a shit. If someone wants to take me out, more power to them."

"That's the spirit." Jake grinned.

I couldn't help but return the gesture. Jake had never been one for sympathy, and I could understand why. Anything anyone else had suffered, he'd been subjected to double or triple the pain.

"Is there anything I can do to help? Without my sister finding out?"

"No, but thanks. I know I don't look it, but I actually have a job. Been working as an auto mechanic for a couple of years now."

"That's good. What about music?"

"Nah. Gave that up."

"Why? Plenty of bands are looking. Hell, I'd replace Trent with you right now if I didn't think he'd murder me in my sleep."

I smiled at Jake's joke, but we both knew I wasn't a fair trade for his world-class drummer. "I was asked not to play by the US Marshals Service. Drumming puts a bull's-eye on my back, and since I was supposed to be lying low…"

"Right, but you're not lying low anymore. Isn't that what you said?"

I frowned. "I haven't picked up sticks in years."

"A waste, if you ask me."

I agreed with him, not that I was going to verbalize as much. "Yeah, well, whatever. No band would pick me up anyway. I suck."

Jake leaned in, patting me on the chest. "Definitely not with that attitude, they won't."

"Oh, and Rory?" he said, backing off and heading for the door. "Stay away from my sister."

I waited until his hand was on the doorknob before testing his allegiance. "Maybe I don't want to anymore."

He stopped, his body visibly tensing.

"Maybe I'm tired of hiding. Of worrying what everyone

thinks. Maybe I want to take back what was mine. Give that posh prince of hers a run for his money. What do you say about that?"

Jake slowly turned back to face me. Our eyes locked in a showdown, both of us understanding that if I let my pieces fall, part of his wall would be coming down with it.

A slow smile hitched the corner of his lips. "I say bring it on."

4

GRACE: MCKALLISTER STEW
THE PAST

I peeked around the corner and breathed a sigh of relief. Quinn's door was shut, and the music was blaring. Just as I'd hoped. I tiptoed past his room, watching for shadows under the door, before sprinting down the hall to the front room. Hudson would be arriving soon, and as long as Quinn stayed put, I'd be out of here before my brother ever knew I was gone. Quinn and I didn't have a lot of secrets between us, but boys were one of them. Basically, he didn't want me anywhere near the male species, and I was... well... obsessed with them. It was a delicate balance we struck between him being an uptight prude and me sneaking out the front door with his arch enemy.

That's right. I was going on a date with Hudson Cowell. Yes, *the* Hudson Cowell. Not to brag or anything but, um... yeah... this was sort of a big deal. Hudson was top shelf. A dream date. Any girl would be lucky to get asked out by the studly all-state defensive tackle on track to a Division II school. That he'd chosen me for this date would open all sorts of doors, making me hopeful that my three years of desperation were finally coming to a close. Really, it couldn't get much worse. I was a junior in high school and had never been on a date, never held hands with a guy who wasn't a big brother, and most frustratingly of all, I'd never been kissed.

Quinn insisted he had nothing to do with my loser streak, but I wasn't so sure. I had a good sense of humor, could perform an ollie off the curb with a skateboard, and I was the baby sister of a rock star. You'd think that would buy me some credit with the boys in school. But no. The closest I ever got to actual interest was if a new boy at school flirted with me before he knew the law of the land or the occasional infidel absently commenting on my ass. But when it came time for promposals or an invite to a once-in-a-lifetime party, I was sitting at home... or rocking it out in the garage with my dude pack.

Correction—Quinn's dude pack. I'd just sort of inherited them. They'd saved me from a fate worse than death: sitting at the lunch tables alone. I'd started off strong the first day of freshman year, the sheltered private school girl with a major claim to fame arriving at the neighborhood public school to a whirlwind of activity. Everyone wanted to be my friend—until they realized my aversion to discussing the one thing that made them spin. Jake.

Actually, it wasn't Jake himself I refused to talk about. He was, honestly, my favorite topic ever. I was so proud of him and loved talking about his music and his fame and his good looks. But that wasn't what most kids at school wanted to discuss. Sure, they'd start out all excited about his music and his fame and his good looks, but then the narrative would inevitably change. They'd adopt that all-knowing concerned presumption on their faces and dive right into discussion about Jake's famous kidnapping. What did I know? What had I seen? What had Jake said about this or that? Even if I knew, I wouldn't tell them.

Did no one consider that such a topic might be sensitive to

members of my family, akin to bringing up a very recent death? Did they think that because Jake was a public figure who'd become famous for his music only after being the central player in a sensationalized news story that it made him less susceptible to the effects of personal attack and speculation? Did they think those who loved him had also developed that same thick skin, allowing them to freely gossip about his torture and near murder as if it were a made-for-TV movie?

I, for one, had not developed that thick skin. Quite the opposite, really. As a child, even the slightest mention of the kidnapping was enough to provoke instant, cartoonlike tears to burst out of my eyeballs. Even with early childhood therapy, no one had ever been able to explain the terror it induced in me nor why I couldn't look my brother in the eye during those early years without running away screaming. Maybe it was the trauma of being so young when my life turned upside down that led to this exaggerated response, but all I knew was exposure to details of the kidnapping often set off a post-traumatic stress type reaction in me that took days to recover from. I'd found it easier to walk away from the trigger.

Unfortunately, doing so had given me the reputation in some circles of being a snooty brat, which wasn't me at all. I was the resilient, self-sufficient baby of my family, known for conflict resolution and my love of animals, romance, and underdogs. Yet nobody at my new school seemed interested in knowing that side of me, which led to my banishment at the lunch tables. It was also what prompted Quinn and his dude pack to swoop in and rescue me from social oblivion. I'd been with them ever since.

I loved my boys, but my god, they were such horndogs. All they did was talk about music, compose music, or try to hook up with girls who thought they were cool because they made music

—and not very good music, I might add. The horndogs never hit on me, though. Half the time they seemed to forget I was female at all.

I chose to believe it was Quinn and his not-so-subtle intimidation techniques that kept the boys away. I couldn't prove my theory, but certainly I preferred it to the alternative—that the problem was me. And, honestly, it very well could be. I just didn't stand out. It was like I'd been crafted for life on a Monday. Tired after a long weekend, my creator had taken the easy way out, and instead of bestowing on me my own individual uniqueness, he'd simply lifted a hodgepodge of personality traits from the family members who'd come before me. I was a sliver of my father's kindness. A splash of my mother's refinement. A dollop of Mitch's athleticism. A sprinkling of Keith's quirky charm. A shaving of Emma's independent spirit. A speck of Jake's undisputed courage. A morsel of Kyle's sense of humor. And a smidgen of Quinn's attractiveness.

That was me. McKallister stew.

My phone pinged, startling me to the point that I nearly fumbled it to the floor. Recovering at the five-yard line—thank you, Mitch, for that tiny bit of athleticism—I took a quick look around for Quinn before clicking on the surveillance app, which brought up a video image of none other than my studly date, Hudson, at the front security gate of our Jake-bought family home.

"How the hell does she expect me to get through this damn fortress?" Hudson's grumblings reached me through the microphone. Clearly he didn't know I was listening in, and his tone low-key irritated me. He knew very well how to get through the gates of my "fortress" because I'd given him detailed written instructions in a text. Was it my fault he hadn't read them?

Hudson let go a string of profanities before pushing random

buttons on the security screen. My eyes doubled in size. If he managed to punch in an actual code that was not mine, someone else in my family might get the video image of my unannounced visitor on their phone, and that would not bode well for me, considering none of my next of kin knew I had my very first date with a local legend.

"Hudson," I said, all chirpy in the delivery. "Hello, I'm here."

I watched from the small screen on my cell as Hudson looked up, down, and all around.

"Oh, um, no. I'm still in the house. I can see you through the security camera."

Again he looked up, down, and all around.

"To your left," I said, directing him to the overhead camera recording him. "No, to *your* left... then up. Um... just a little more to the..."

"Grace!" he bellowed. "Just let me in! Jesus Christ. I don't have all day!"

I was taken aback by his brashness but then reminded myself of his overall hotness and let it pass. Still, what was his hurry? The concert didn't start for another three hours, and we had priority parking and backstage passes. But again, he looked nice in a pair of jeans, so who was I to complain?

I remotely opened the gate and watched through a slat in the blinds as his black Mercedes crawled up the driveway. The magnitude of the moment wasn't lost on me. I was going on a date with Hudson Cowell. Me. Grace McKallister. Holy crap.

"What are you doing?"

I jumped in surprise, hastily letting go of the blinds, which snapped back into place with a loud clap. I twirled around, coming face-to-face with the first date killer himself—Quinn.

"Nothing," I responded, positioning my body in front of the giant picture window like a scarecrow with all of my digits pointed outward.

"Nothing?" Quinn repeated, squinting despite there being no bright light entering through the blinds. "What's out there? Is someone out front?"

"No." I wiped the sweat from my brow. "I already told you no."

"Right, but your aggressive body language tells me you lie."

"There's nothing to see here, Quinn. I suggest you walk away."

"You suggest?" His eyes narrowed even further. "Why do I feel like you're using the Force on me?"

I shrugged, my lying lower lip performing the tiniest little wobble.

Quinn moved toward the blinds and I jumped into action, boxing him out with my hip. We tussled.

"Fucking hell, Grace," he blasted, trying to move between my flailing arms. "That better not be Hudson out there."

I flushed. How did he know?

As if reading my mind, he replied, "I overheard you telling the Terminix guy out back baiting the rat traps that you had a date with Hudson, but I just thought it was you role-playing."

Role-playing? What a dick. As if I couldn't land a guy like Hudson outside of Fantasy Land. And, how dare Quinn eavesdrop on that special moment between me and that Terminix guy, whatever his name was? He'd been so happy for me.

"Keep your voice down, drama queen," I whispered, my hands now on his chest, pushing him back. "None of this is your business."

"I'm babysitting you, so yeah, it sort of is."

"No, you're not. We're babysitting ourselves."

"That's not what Mom and Dad told me before they left. They clearly said I was in charge."

"...of turning off the lights, removing any dead animals the cats drag in, and locking the door," I replied, my voice ticking up a notch. "I'm in charge of like literally everything else. They even asked me to feed you because they know you would starve otherwise."

"Well, at least I'm not the one lying to them and sneaking out on a date with a convicted felon."

"It was a misdemeanor," I scoffed. "And I'm not lying to Mom and Dad because guess what? They already approved it."

"Did they?" Quinn replied, his brows shooting skyward. "And if I were to call them now and interrupt their anniversary weekend in Monterey, they'd corroborate your story, would they?"

I averted my gaze, knowing he had me cornered. I *had* actually asked my parents for approval, but only just... sort of. They knew I was going to Jake's concert with a "friend," they just didn't know exactly which "good buddy" I was going with. And for good reason. See, while Hudson was the coolest thing on two legs at school, he didn't have the best reputation in the community, after setting fire to the ag building. But it was all a giant misunderstanding; he'd said so himself. How was he to know hay was so highly flammable?

"Uh-huh, that's what I thought." Quinn nodded knowingly. "I don't like doing this, Grace, but I'm pulling rank. You are not going out with Hudson Cowell! I told you he was..."

I pushed Quinn out of my way before he could get out words that I didn't want to hear. I knew Quinn's opinion very well... because he never shut up about it. My brother was single-handedly trying to ruin my nonexistent dating life. Quinn would've preferred I stay in diapers the entirety of my existence rather than grow up and date. To him, any guy who got near me reeked of Ted Bundy and had a similar-colored Volkswagen Beetle idling out back. He really was worse than both our parents combined, and that was saying something given the sheer number of true crime documentaries my family had starred in.

"Think, Grace. Hudson's only using you for the concert. For the backstage pass."

My temper flared. "So what you're saying is I'm such a hideous creature that no guy would want to date me without a dowry attached?"

"I literally said none of that."

"Yeah, well, it was implied," I spat back.

Hudson honked.

Quinn's thermostat cranked higher. "Seriously? The shithead can't even come to the house to get you?"

"I told him not to because you're such a colossal douchebag."

Not offended in the least, Quinn smiled, backing himself up against the door and folding his arms in front of him. "I don't want to do this, Grace, but you leave me no other choice."

His lower half was left wide open, and I knew just where to land the punch, but I stopped myself at the last second. I wasn't a child anymore, and it was no longer acceptable to use his dangling parts to get my point across. Besides, I had way more damaging dirt on my brother, an arsenal of misdeeds committed by him and his randy pack of band geeks that I could leverage against him.

"Aren't you cute?" I smiled, waving a hand in front of him. "Now, step aside."

Quinn offered up his own counterfeit grin. "Yeah, I don't think so."

That response prompted the inner animal in me. With a low, menacing growl, I replied, "No? Okay. But I do wonder what Mom and Dad will do to you when they find out about your encounter with police at the Hollywood sign. I know you had to take a piss, but really, Quinn, on a national treasure? Also, I think you might forget I have access to your toothbrush... *and* the toilet, should I decide your baby-soft bristles need to go for a swim."

"You wouldn't."

I squared my jaw. "Oh, but I would."

Quinn hesitated, clearly giving my threat some serious consideration. I could almost see the wheels turning in his head as he decided whether eternal grounding and good oral hygiene were more important than cock-blocking me on my first date. In the end, good old-fashioned blackmail won out.

"Fine." He threw his hands up. "Go to the concert with the arsonist. But don't say I didn't warn you."

"Playing with matches does not make him an arsonist."

"Yes, Grace. It actually does."

"Whatever you say. Are we done here?"

"Not so fast. If you turn off your location and I can't track you, then I'm coming after Hudson... and I won't be responsible for rearranging his face."

I rolled my eyes. Quinn was not exactly the MMA fighter he fancied himself. But I allowed him his tough guy persona today for no other reason than I wanted out the door with as little fuss as possible.

"Yes, fine." I performed a little curtsy. "You may defend my honor if Hudson steps out of line. Will that make you happy?"

Quinn's bravado faded, replaced with acceptance and maybe even a little anguish. My heart softened just a smidgen. This was hard on him. Quinn still carried the anger from the days when Jake and, to a certain extent, the rest of the family, had gone missing. That was what had prompted Quinn to vow to be my protector. And he'd been a good one. The best. I had no qualms with the way he loved me; I just needed him to understand that I'd grown up and could now take over that role for myself.

"Stay home with me." He made one final push. "We can watch a movie. I'll order a pizza. Just us, like old times."

A part of me wanted that—to escape into a place of safety with my big brother by my side—but Quinn had always been my umbrella and I'd never been allowed to feel the raindrops on my head. I needed to venture out on my own and risk the storms that might follow.

"How about tomorrow night?"

"How about tonight?" he countered, a convincing smile slanting his upper lip.

"If you're so worried about me, come to Jake's concert."

The same smile faded. "Nah. I'll just stay home and stalk you."

I figured that would be his response. Only Quinn would pass up the hottest ticket in town—Jake's last show before surgery on his knee would sideline him for at least a year. The tickets had sold out within minutes of their surprise release, and now, everyone and their mother was trying to score secondhand tickets.

Except apparently for Quinn, who couldn't be bothered.

"Fine," I sighed. "But you're wasting your time. Hudson is the perfect gentleman."

Quinn scoffed. "And that naivety, right there, is why you need to skip out on this date, Grace. Everybody but you knows that Hudson's a shithead."

"I'm sure he's said the same about you."

"No doubt, but the difference is you know me. Do you really know Hudson?"

No. I didn't know him at all because he'd never talked to me until last week when the ticket feeding frenzy was in full swing. I wasn't dumb. I knew Hudson was using me for a ticket, but I was using him too for the exposure. For a chance to finally matter at school. So we were even.

Of course, I couldn't admit that to Quinn.

"Isn't that what a first date is for? To get to know him? Look," I said, pulling my phone out of my pocket and holding it up to prove my tracking was on. "All prepped for stalking. Are we good?"

He stood there, deciding, before finally stepping aside. I didn't give him the chance to change his mind—or mine— before blowing past him and out the front door.

5

RORY: THE STREETS HAVE NO WALLS

They knew me now. The kid with cash. That was what they called me the last time they chased me through the alleyway and beat me to the ground. After that, I was the kid with *no* cash and a possible concussion. My new handle might've been flattering had it not been the furthest thing from the truth. I lived on the streets, same as them. But unlike my strung out tormentors, I had a paying gig, one that didn't require me to shake others down, drop my jeans, or eat three meals a day out of the trash bin.

Too bad integrity meant nothing out here. Neither did possessions. They were here one day and gone the next. I wore what was left of my measly clothing selection either on my person, in bulky layers, or tied around my waist. Not that clothing mattered all that much to me. The only thing I really, truly cared to hold on to was my collection of five gallon paint buckets, which served as a makeshift drum set. They went everywhere with me, threaded through a bungee cord and slung over my shoulders like a cape.

Fitting, I'd say, considering drumming was my superpower

and the only thing I'd ever been good at. When I played, I was special. Talented. Going somewhere. Little did they know I was going back to nothing. I had no family. No friends. No roof over my head. But I had my buckets and a dream. One day, I'd have the best drum kit money could buy—even better than the one I learned to play on when I was a kid. Someday I'd be sitting on my throne at center stage, throwing it down like a pro, and the crowd, yeah, they'd be on their feet screaming my name.

Until then, I honed my drumming skills on the buckets or just any surface that could handle the beat. It was a double-edged sword, though. To make the money for the junkies to steal, I had to pound on my bucket drums for hours on end, and that, in turn, put a huge target on my back. The vultures could hear me playing from blocks away. They'd just wait in the wings, salivating as passersby dropped dollars into my tip bucket, and then, once my set concluded, me, my buckets, and my cash were on the run. Sometimes I made it to safety with the money still in my pocket and sometimes I didn't. It was the price I paid for existing.

Going it alone was a dangerous risk. Last time I was out here, I'd run with a pack. We were the leftovers, the kids thrown out with the trash. Our numbers ebbed and flowed, but at one point we were a baker's dozen. It wasn't like we sought each other out. We sort of just found one another, slipping into the group unannounced and then effectively being absorbed like amoebas. The misfortune that brought us together—abuse, neglect, drug addiction, foster care—also bonded us. We all understood the life-and-death stakes and that joining forces greatly improved our chances of surviving the turbulent nights.

While some of the kids bonded like blood, I stayed along the perimeter—partaking in the comradery but prepared to run if things went wrong. I knew better than to get attached. Nothing had ever been permanent in my life, and our ragtag unit was never meant to last. One by one, we got picked off. Some by drugs. Some by arrests. Some by injury or death. And some, myself included, finally just gave up. I turned myself back into the Department of Children and Family Services, naively believing that as bad as life often was inside the system, the streets were worse.

But it wasn't true. Sometimes running away was my only option—a decision forced on me by caretakers like Lucinda and her adult son, Brawley, predators who saw opportunity in my misfortune. I'd rather take my chances on the streets than try to keep those sick fucks out of my room at night. The first time Brawley tried making it past my bucket barricade was the last night I had a roof over my head.

This time around, I walked alone, preferring solitude over losing my pack all over again. Watching us go down the drain, one jaded duckling at a time, fucking sucked. I couldn't do it again. Sometimes I ran into one of them in a group home or out on the streets. We were older now. Harder. Less trusting. Less willing to give each other the shirt off our backs or to split the profits from our peddling. Even back in the system, finding each other was near impossible considering none of us used our real names on the streets. It was an unwritten rule. Nicknames were not only useful in protecting our identities but also excellent masks for those who just wanted to forget.

I did miss the others. I missed not having people to watch my back out here, but then I'd remind myself that I couldn't lose what I didn't have. What I'd never really had. Growing up in foster care, I'd been forced onto the defensive line before I'd even finished teething. Innocence was for kids with families, those whose survival didn't depend on how well they behaved, how fast they could run, or how skilled they were with their fists when their backs were up against the wall.

Today I'd gotten lucky, having made it through the night

totally unscathed, but I knew not to get cocky. Lasting from dusk to dawn was only the beginning of a long and treacherous day. Take my daily commute, for example. I had to dodge the mentally insane, the meth heads, the dealers, and the sex traders just to make it to the business or tourist areas of the city where people still had jobs and homes and beating hearts. I would have been happy to stay where I played, too, but people like me weren't welcome in the general population. We could wander the streets. We could perform for the public. But when it came time to lay our heads on the pressure-washed asphalt, we were shooed away like mangy strays.

"Hey, kid."

Shit. I lowered my head and picked up the speed. I had no friends out here. Only enemies with bloodsucking souls.

"Hey, you wanna make some money?"

I didn't even afford the dude a sideways glance, having no interest in becoming his drug mule or whatever other nefarious thing he had to offer. I broke into a jog and crossed the road. It wasn't until I was safely on the other side that I glanced over my shoulder to check his position. He'd stayed put. I let out a breath and moved on. Downtown was full of these opportunistic preda-tors. These were the real hunters—cruel and ruthless, they prowled the street for the weak, the innocent, the defenseless. I wasn't any of those things. Not anymore.

I winced, shaking those thoughts right out of my head.

With my eye on today's prize, I followed the sidewalk toward the towering bowl-shaped building up ahead. Because predictability was the kiss of death out here, I alternated where and at what time I set up my bucket drums. Sometimes I played during the day and other times at night. Sometimes I took the bus to perform on the Hollywood Walk of Fame, and other times I set my buckets up in the shopping districts or outside of trendy bars. Only one thing remained a constant, one event I never missed: concert nights at the downtown amphitheater. Me and every other musician within a twenty-mile radius. We all showed up, vying for a few prime spots. For me, it was doubly important that I staked my claim early because my musically inclined competition had a tendency to band together and try to run me out of town.

They assured me it was nothing personal. And really, I wouldn't want to be playing next to me either. My drums drowned everyone else out. Not by sheer volume, either. When I played, I was in my element, my head held high. I knew how to draw a crowd. How to keep them riveted. People gravitated toward me. They saw me. They respected my talent. They wished they were me. For a small period of time every day, we were equals. But when the show ended, they went back to their comfortable lives, and I went back to the giant game of whack-a-mole on the other side of the tracks... where I was the mole.

Blazing down the street with my trench coat billowing behind me, I could always tell the moment my competition saw me coming. Not that I was hard to spot with all my accessories. Add to that my very long six-foot-three-inch body that no amount of food could ever hope to fill, and I probably looked like an underweight circus performer.

Activity doubled as two talentless singer-songwriters jumped into action upon my approach, trying to make themselves look bigger and more spread out. "Uh-uh, Beats. Not here. Move on."

I contemplated whether the spot was worth a fight. It might be, if I was forced to circle back around, but at this point I still had other options to check out first. That said, I wasn't one to leave without a parting gift. I lifted my fist in the air and flipped them the bird.

The next corner was more of the same, only this time a

group of them were working together to keep me away. Dammit, I should've arrived earlier, even if that meant I had to sit around for a while or play much longer. I knew better. Every musician would be out in force tonight. Earning potential was never better than when big-name artists were inside the stadium performing. And it didn't get much bigger than Jake McKallister. I was sure his fans in particular would appreciate my unusual party trick, and that would translate into a windfall for me.

The goal was always to make enough to rent a room for the night at some sketchy skid row motel, a place where the addicts went to die. Motels were hit and miss. Technically, to rent a room, I needed an ID to prove my age. Without it, I had to rely on a pocket full of green to persuade the managers to relax their rules. God, I hoped they would tonight. I really needed a respite from the streets, a place to wash off the grime of the city and to sleep with both eyes shut.

With that goal in mind, I kept pounding the pavement and scanning the perimeter, but it seemed like all the premium performance sites adjacent to the arena had been taken. Until I saw it. Way down the street, one golden nugget of land, an outcrop of sidewalk on the main pedestrian thoroughfare, and it looked to still be available. This was a huge score. I sped up, my eye on the concrete prize.

Entirely too preoccupied, I failed to see the brick wall with feet and a letterman's jacket standing in my way. We collided with a heavy thud.

"Watch where you're going, asshole," the jock blasted, shoving me aside.

The front-loaded buckets dangling around my neck nearly toppled me over. What the...? Why the manhandling? So fucking unnecessary.

Too bad for him, I didn't take my orders from a privileged

frat boy. I pushed right back. "Well, then maybe don't block the sidewalk, dickwad."

He sneered, puffing his chest out. "Maybe take a shower, vermin."

A moment of uncompromising silence settled between us before the girl beside him grabbed his arm forcefully to pull him away. His large frame didn't budge, causing her to ricochet back like she was in a real-life Wile E. Coyote cartoon. I would've laughed had I not been so incensed.

Her eyes flared. "Stop being a jerk, Hudson!"

"A jerk?" He jolted his head in her direction. "How I am I a jerk for not wanting to catch whatever disease he's carrying?"

The girl huffed her disapproval. "If you don't know the answer to that, then no one ever taught you manners."

The dude's fists hardened into knots. Ah, shit. I'd seen this show enough times to know it wasn't going to end well for the girl. My defensive instincts kicked in. Reaching for her arm, I pulled her away. She seemed stunned when she was suddenly behind my Gumby-like body, like it had never occurred to her that she might be in danger.

"Did you just touch her?" the dude growled, advancing on me.

I sighed, knowing the routine and readying my fists. Dammit. What the hell did I do that for? This totally went against two of my steadfast rules on street living. One, walk—no, run—away whenever possible, and two, never insert myself into a fight that wasn't mine. Now I was going to have to drum with a broken nose, all because I'd gotten into the middle of a domestic dispute between two entitled richies.

"Don't you dare," the girl said, fearlessly advancing from behind me and shoving her boyfriend back. "If you touch him, you can find another way into the concert."

Whoa. Damn. I couldn't have been more shocked by the turn of events if I'd tried. This feminine whiff of fresh air had just defended my honor. Me. The vermin. Well, shit. That was hot. Her boyfriend appeared as stunned as me, offering no protest as she led him away. I watched her go, admiring the uptown girl's spunk... and her ass. Just as I was about to go claim my little piece of land, she whipped her head around and zeroed in on me like I was the target for her missile attack. I wasn't sure what to do. Us vermin didn't get a ton of eye contact from girls in Lululemon leggings, if you know what I mean. But things went from uncomfortable to flat-out bizarre when the girl's eyes widened in what could only be interpreted as a sign of recognition.

Wait. What? I blinked.

Clearly this girl was mistaken because there was no chance in hell she knew me. We weren't just from the other side of the tracks; we were on different halves of the urban equator. I raised my brows and challenged her recognition. Only instead of her backing down, those sunny blue eyes of hers clouded over with a hazy layer of sadness.

Again. What the actual fuck?

The girl ultimately broke contact, grabbing her tree trunk of a boyfriend and steering him away. I stood there dumbfounded, my uber-cool five-gallon paint buckets hanging there limply around my neck like the world's worst wingman. I couldn't take my eyes off her. Something supernatural had just happened between us, something I couldn't explain.

I watched her walk straight over to the VIP entrance like she owned the place. How did that not surprise me? It certainly answered one of my burning questions. I was definitely not suffering from a severe case of amnesia because no old acquaintance of mine would ever be let through the concierge doors of a Jake McKallister concert.

The arena staff waved her in, and just before disappearing

inside, the girl turned her head and looked back at me. I blinked. I swallowed. I flushed. What the hell did she see? Why was she acting like she knew me? The hair on my skin prickled. Did she have her own boy in the mirror? No, it couldn't be. She was too pretty and polished. Too valuable and virtuous. No way had the hunters gotten to her too.

If they had, she'd be just as messed up as me.

6

GRACE: NEPO SISTER

"Grace?" Hudson snapped his fingers in my face. "Hello? Are you listening to me?"

I'd heard him all right, but he was throwing a lot at me in one go. I was still processing the whole sidewalk horror show, where he'd called some unsuspecting stranger vermin, and now this. These popular kids really didn't understand the concept of subtlety. Even my brother Kyle, who arguably had very little going on in that shaggy-haired head of his, knew enough to sugarcoat information that might require a hard landing. How exactly was I expected to respond to Hudson's request? I knew how I wanted to respond—with a swift karate chop to his nuts—but then how would that make me any different than him and the fistfight he'd tried to instigate outside?

But this.

Hudson had just asked if I wanted in on the ground level of a three's-a-crowd type throuple. The players? Hudson. Me. And obnoxiously beautiful homecoming queen Mia. But Hudson and I were on a date, right? Granted, I was no expert, but I was under the impression that a date implied two people. Alone together.

You know, a *date*.

I nodded in response to Hudson's question only because I wasn't entirely sure what else to do or if I even wanted to be on a date with him after what he'd just done to that kid on the street.

"So, yes then?" Hudson perked up, exchanging a relieved glance with Mia—my sister wife. Number three in our throuple. Or, wait, was *I* the third wheel?

Clarification was definitely in order because whatever was happening here predated the tiff Hudson and I had just had out on the sidewalk. This seemed previously planned. Meticulously calculated.

"Oh, um, wait... are you saying you want me to give my backstage pass to Mia?"

"My god, Grace. Yes. I've said it like four times already. Give her your pass, and then we can all hang out backstage."

There it was again. *All.* As in the three of us. I sighed inwardly; maybe outwardly too. Hudson was single-handedly ruining my first date experience. There was no good way to spin this in my milestones book... no way to strategically crop Mia out of the picture.

"It's just... I didn't realize Mia was going to be joining us."

Hudson buried the knife a little deeper. "The more the merrier, right?"

What? No. Not merrier. Not at all. Didn't Hudson know that plenty of wonderful things came in twos? Eyebrows. Pot holders. Electrodes. I wasn't looking to be part of his tripod, especially not with Mia Lorenzo, one of the founding members of the 'nepo baby' hate club.

Oh, god. This was my scarlet letter, the unflattering nickname I'd acquired day one of high school, through no fault of my own. By definition, a 'nepotism baby' was the child of a famous actor or celebrity who became famous through no discernible skill of their own. Technically speaking, I was a 'nepo sister,' since my claim to fame came from Jake. But that didn't much matter to the trendy kids in school who used both derogatory terms interchangeably in an effort to shame me for having the good fortune of being related to a superstar.

Somehow, Quinn, only sixteen months older than me, had escaped the unflattering label. He claimed it was because no one dared mess with him, but he was giving himself way too much credit. The simple truth was, Quinn escaped the scrutiny because he was cute and all the girls loved him, including those who'd come up with my title in the first place. But Quinn was fooling himself if he thought he wasn't benefitting from nepotism too. In fact, with his resemblance to Jake as well as their shared musical talents, Quinn would be the one voted "most likely to coast his way to stardom on the back of our brother's fame."

Don't tell him I said that.

Up until freshman year, I'd had very little exposure to petty classmates, since the private K-8 school I'd attended was bursting at the seams with nepotistic little freeloaders. You'd be hard-pressed to find anyone at that school who wasn't six degrees of Kevin Bacon. Quinn eventually rebelled against the exclusivity of the school, leaving it in sixth grade, but I rode it out to the end, more than happy in my fairy-tale world where I could feel good about being a privileged parasite.

But life inside my educational la-la land was never meant to last, and by the time middle school came to an end, the donors' memories had faded and the money ran out. And so, while my friends all moved on to the ultra-private 9-12 boutique high school, I joined Quinn at the neighborhood school, packed with kids who treated me like a foreign exchange student—weirdly curious but not enough to stake their reputation on.

And, look, maybe I wouldn't have minded being reduced to the sum of Jake's massive accomplishments... if there had been something in it for me. My old private school classmates raked in the nepotistic rewards by pimping out their connections for modeling contracts, record deals, and roles in their daddy's movies. Me? All I wanted was a date. Was that too much to ask?

"I thought we were..." I let the sentence trail off because it really didn't matter what I thought. They were ruling class seniors, and I was nothing but a powerless junior with a notable last name. "I'm just a little confused. If I give Mia my pass, wouldn't it be just the two of you hanging out backstage? Because I wouldn't be able to get in."

Mia and Hudson's eyes connected, and they lingered there a moment before shifting their attention back on me. Ah man, they were a thing. Hudson and Mia. Not Hudson and Grace. I was definitely the 'spiritual' wife in this polygamist trio.

"You're Jake McKallister's sister. They'll let you in with or without a backstage pass," Mia said, speaking up for the first time in that smooth-as-butter, right-out-of-the-flapper-twenties voice she was known for. With my perpetually raspy, three-pack-a-day smoker voice, I was the flip side of her fake sweet-as-pie coin. When I was young, my aunt Mel used to insist I'd damaged my vocal cords because of all the yelling I had to do to be heard over all my siblings, but I'd had my distinctive, gravelly voice since I'd first begun to talk.

"That's not true," I argued. "I need the pass in my possession for the security check."

Mia sighed as if I was such a chore. "Aren't you the one always blabbering on and on about Jake and how you are best friends with his bandmates and with the backstage staff and the roadies? All you have to do is tell your buddies you lost your pass and they'll get you a new one, no questions asked. Stop being selfish."

Blabbering on and on? Her words were a slap to the face, not only because she'd called my bluff on obtaining another backstage pass but also because I was now worried that people thought I was leveraging my famous brother to earn favor with the popular crowd. And if that was what they all thought of me, then it should come as no real surprise that Hudson was now flipping the game in his favor. A flush burned through my cheeks. Quinn was right. I should've stayed home with him and shared a bowl of popcorn on the couch. I didn't belong with these people.

"I'm not being selfish," I protested, even though I knew I was. I could secure another pass if I really wanted to. One call to Kyle or Jake's manager Sean or even Jake himself would do it. I just didn't want to. Not for Mia. Not for Hudson. Certainly not for them together as a couple. Even if I no longer wanted Hudson, I absolutely did not want him to be happy. "It's just Jake... he wouldn't like for me to give away a pass. There are rules..."

Mia cut me off. "So don't tell him. It's not like he'll even know, with all the people backstage."

He'd certainly notice if I didn't show up... actually, on second thought, he probably wouldn't.

"Fine, whatever." Mia reached over and bopped my shiny curls with her freshly manicured fingers. "Take the pass for yourself. It's just Hudson and I thought you were cool... I was even going to invite you to my birthday party next weekend."

No. Way! The *Call of Booty Birthday Bash*? Mia's parties were legendary. I had a chance to make the guest list? My mouth watered. So much for shunning popularity. So much for Quinn and that heaping bowl of popcorn. I was weak. Needy. Maybe if I could be seen at the party, I wouldn't have to rely on Jake to supplement my social resume. Maybe I could stand on my own two feet for a change.

But I understood Mia's invite came with conditions, and I had to ask myself how far I was willing to go to grab the goodies being dangled in front of me. I could almost hear Quinn's disapproval, but again, he'd never been forced to make this decision. His name was at the top of every guest list, whether he chose to attend or not. I didn't have that privilege, and that was why the devil was now tapping me on the shoulder.

"Do I have your word?" I looked Mia in the eye, ready to make a deal with this fashion-forward devil but only if I could get it in writing. "If I give you my backstage pass, you'll invite me to your party?"

Mia smiled, knowing she had me in her clutches now. "Consider it your RSVP."

That was good enough for me. I lifted the lanyard over my head and handed it to her.

"You're the best," she said, wasting no time hanging my pass around her own neck. "You won't regret this."

I didn't intend to.

"Oh, and Grace?" Mia called over her shoulder as she headed for the priority gate. "Try to get Quinn to come to my party. He's turned me down twice already. He's such a turd sometimes. Anyway, text us once you're inside. Can't wait for you to introduce us to Jake."

My smile faded. Jake? Since when had an audience with the king become part of the deal? My soul was one thing, but offering up my family for sacrifice was quite another.

Oh, god. I was so going to hell.

7

GRACE: FEED THE BEATS

Things took a turn for the worse almost immediately after watching Hudson and Mia walk off without me. I realized a minute too late that Hudson had my phone, and with it, all the contents inside its protective case—my ID, my cash, my debit card—that I could use to prove my identity. Not a problem if I was dealing with Jake's own security team, who knew me and could easily usher me backstage, but to get to them, I had to clear the first line of defense, the arena staff, and they were not willing to entertain me. With no way to call someone to save me and no backstage pass, or even a general admission ticket in my possession, I was escorted straight out the side door.

And that was where I was now. A sheltered suburban girl on the streets of Los Angeles alone. Worse still, I couldn't even text or call anyone from a borrowed cell because I was a Gen Zer and had no flippin' clue what anyone's actual phone number was. Why would I, when every number of importance was permanently programmed into my phone like a reliable friend?

The sound of violent shouting turned my head.

"I warned ya, Shirley! So many times, I warned ya. But you gotta keep bitchin', don't ya, Shirley? Don't ya?"

This. I thought to myself. This was why you memorized phone numbers.

I sidestepped my way along the outer wall of the arena, putting distance between myself and the whacked-out-of-his-brain Cro-Magnon man who was kicking poor Shirley in her alloy core. "Shirley" was a trash can, and as such, remained silent, absorbing each swift kick with a sickening thud.

As if all this wasn't already totally disturbing, the disheveled man began to disrobe right in the middle of the one-sided domestic dispute. It was like an episode straight out of *Cops*. He was the first naked man I'd seen in the flesh, and I now sorta hoped he'd be my last. This, right here, was the consequence of the deal I'd made with the devil: I'd been preemptively sent to hell.

Ugh, if only I had my phone! Hudson had taken it right after we'd entered the arena. I'd placed it in a bowl and sent it through the screener at security, fully expecting to be reunited with it on the other side, but Hudson had rushed through the metal detector two people in front of me, and by the time I got there, he'd already pocketed my phone and was on the move. I hadn't realized at the time, trot-walking behind him, that it was Mia he was eager to see. And once she'd come into play, my phone was the last thought on my mind.

Now it was all I could think about. The only way to get my phone back was to wait around for Hudson and Mia to finish my date and drive me home. The humiliation. I'd considered hitching a ride home with Jake after the concert, but that would involve intercepting my brother's escort vehicle as it exited the venue through a sea of females desperately vying for his attention. I'd also contemplated borrowing a phone and sending a message to one of my lifelines through social media. Any one of my siblings would rush to my side and bring me home. But I was embarrassed. I'd done this to myself and felt stupid. The fewer people who knew of my humiliation, the better. Whether I liked it or not, I was dependent on Hudson for the remainder of the night.

Cheers lit up the darkness, and I twisted my head in the direction of the applause. That was where I wanted to be—wherever that drummer was. He'd been playing since I got out here. At least an hour and still going strong. He'd been the only positive part of my banishment. Even from this distance, I could tell the dude was seriously shredding it. I'd considered abandoning my post outside the venue more than a few times tonight just to watch him drum, but I knew my parents would want me to stay put in this well-lit area with plenty of people milling around. Safety was paramount in my family after everything we'd been through.

But what happened when the safe place became dangerous? What if the naked garbage man decided to go in search of a new Shirley—one with a beating heart like mine? Suddenly, waiting around the venue didn't seem like the smartest idea. I pushed off the stadium wall, giving a wide berth to the man and his trash can, then headed down the street to chase the cheers.

ON MY WAY, I passed a handful of street musicians who were performing to very little fanfare, but it wasn't until I arrived at the semicircle of people formed around the drummer that I realized why. The powerhouse performer was going full force to keep his crowd motivated and entertained, siphoning off everyone else's customers.

I squeezed through the onlookers to get a better position and wasn't surprised to find him playing on an assortment of overturned paint buckets, with a bronze cymbal plate resting on his foot and a pair of drumsticks in his hands. From down the street,

I could hear he wasn't playing on a regular drum kit, but it shocked me all the same that he was able to get these results on dirty, dented paint buckets. Yet this guy shined above the simplicity of his equipment. His whole sound just hit differently, like he was pouring his soul into every nuanced note.

Weaving around a few more people, I finally claimed a spot in the front row. The streetlights working as his own personal spotlight, the drummer lifted his head and made eye contact with the crowd before diving back in. It was in that split second of audience acknowledgement that I made the connection. A breath caught in my throat. The teen Hudson had called vermin was my talented drummer boy.

It all made sense now. The buckets. The raw, gritty emotion. The turmoil behind his weary eyes. He was the homeless-looking kid from the sidewalk—the one who nearly stopped me in my tracks with his Jake-like eyes. The parallels between my brother and him extended to his talent as well. Like Jake, he played with such confidence, such rage. A boy existing on a razor's edge. There was something so tragic about him, yet also hopeful in a strange and regressive way.

I was instantly struck. Shaky, even. He was a teenager like me, but there was no comparing us. I'd never seen anyone my age as wild and unrestrained, a lightning bolt of electricity that never hit the same spot on his bucket drums twice. I had to know who he was and where he'd learned to bang drum solos out like he owned the night.

No doubt he'd recognize me from the confrontation, and I was sure he wouldn't remember our interaction fondly. I couldn't blame him. Just the memory of Hudson being such an elitist jerk made me cringe. How hard would it have been to just let the drummer walk on by? He hadn't been looking for a fight. His attention had just been focused elsewhere.

I'd seen him coming toward us in the seconds before the

collision. He'd been hard to miss, with those buckets hanging around his neck and cold weather clothing layered over every inch of his body despite it being early fall in balmy Los Angeles, his beanie drawn down over his forehead shielding almost the entirety of his face. But it was his filthy lady's brown puffer trench coat reaching all the way to his knees that was the real star of the show. He wore it like a cloak, billowing out behind him as he trudged forward in a pair of severely scuffed Doc Martin-like black boots.

I never would have guessed under all that layering he looked like this—long and lean and tanned like he'd been resurrected from the seventies skateboard scene. I might even concede he was the sexiest musician I'd ever seen, and that was saying a lot because I'd been hanging around backstage most of my life. I'd seen a lot of hot musicians.

The drummer boy was thrashing his head too fast for me to see his face, but I remembered it from the sidewalk when I'd looked into his defiant, soulful eyes. He'd caught my attention then but nothing like he did now. The boy was an oddity, all right. An oddly striking one, and it all started with his hair. No longer contained by a beanie, it was now flying free and a show all its own. The geometric masterpiece of knots, all joining forces with other uncombed strands, created a fusion of tangles that could almost be confused with shoulder-length ringlets. Nothing short of a head shave would tame that snarled brown, sun-streaked mane.

And if that wasn't enough to command my attention, his distressed black Metallica t-shirt with sleeves rolled up to his shoulders did. The worn fabric clung to his sweaty body, show-casing every hard-earned flex. He was perfectly flawed. Even the strips of black leather wrapped all the way up and around his long, drummer-toned arms were squeal-worthy. I watched in awe as he brought the song to its fiery conclusion, banging out those last exaggerated beats for the crowd.

"You want more?" he called out, his voice the perfect pitch of virile male everythingness. And they reacted with cheers. I noticed women twice his age had joined me in lustfully eyeing the young musician. Like me, they wanted more. A whole lot more.

Giving his buckets a momentary reprieve, the drummer focused on the sticks spinning in his hands. Starting off slow, he gradually picked up the pace until they were rotating at such dizzying speed they disappeared in a blur of motion.

"More?" he teased, flipping the drumsticks in the air and catching them like it was no big deal. The display of showman-ship wowed his crowd. Sweat dripped from his hair onto his face and neck as if he had his own personal rain cloud dumping precipitation down upon him. He was working so hard, and he deserved the riotous applause. "Yes? You want more?"

He waited for the whoops and cheers to die down before speaking again. "Okay, I hear ya. How about an encore? Anyone want a little..." The sticks instantly stopped spinning so the drummer could bang out the first beats of "We Will Rock You." It drew a thunderous response.

But it was just a tease. He pulled the sticks away from the buckets and began spinning them again, spinning and flipping them in the air, only this time in the opposite direction. Damn, such a performer. Drummers tended to be in the background, out of the spotlight. With all eyes typically on the lead singers and guitarists at center stage, it was easy to overlook the hardworking percussionist in the back. But I never did because I knew what most didn't—a good drummer was worth his weight in gold. Much like the FedEx guy, he was expected to show up on time. Every time. There was no room for tardiness when the fate of a song rested on his shoulders.

But this drummer was different, born for the stage. He came alive with those sticks in his hands and entertained like a young Tommy Lee. Within seconds, his sticks were again lost in a high-velocity centrifuge. The cheering continued, louder and more explosive than before. I was swept up in the thrill of the moment, feeling as if I was witnessing the birth of newborn baby star. Then, as swiftly as it had started, the drummer's sticks came to a swirling, twirling halt, and with his foot, he thrust an upright bucket toward the crowd.

Written across the front read, "Feed the Beats."

There was a moment of pause as those in the audience tried to catch up to the abrupt transition, but then the light bulb went off. The drummer expected, and rightly deserved, compensation for the show. His worshipers did not disappoint, stepping forward and dropping dollar bills into the collection bucket. I would have been right up there with the rest of them had I any money to give. But I didn't, so I stayed put and kept my eye on the resting drummer.

Lifting the hem of his shirt, he bent over and wiped off his face, exposing a generous expanse of stomach. Sweat carved trails of dirt into his skin, almost like his perspiration had gone off-roading and hadn't had a chance to stop by the car wash on its way home. More notable was his concave abdomen. There wasn't an ounce of fat on his lengthy body, making me wonder if it was genetics at play or if he was going to sleep hungry.

It felt criminal to profit off his sweat without giving something in return. All night I'd bemoaned being parted from my phone and my money and my identity, but it was only now, when I desperately wanted to give something to this talented boy, that I felt its profound loss. I didn't deserve to be standing in the front row, taking up space from those who could help him fill his belly. I had to fall back, lose myself in the crowd. But before I could slip into the background, the drummer shifted his eyes in my direction, and his head instantly cocked. That slack jaw of his was indication enough that he recognized me.

Our eyes locked, just as they had earlier on the sidewalk, and I was again immediately drawn in, free-falling into the depths of his misery. Dark and fiery, it was Armageddon down deep in his soul. What had happened to this boy to cause such despair? I'd been there before, staring into the eyes of a wounded boy who'd gone to war with himself right before my terrified eyes. My brother had needed me then, but I'd forsaken him. The regret stuck with me, and I'd made a promise to myself: never again would I abandon another lost soul.

Shifting uncomfortably from one foot to the other, I was unsure what to do with his undivided attention, so I faked it and forced a smile. He didn't reciprocate, responding only with a scowl. But I didn't shy away, allowing him to study me as I'd done him, waiting on him to blink and break the spell. But he didn't. The sidewalk percussionist kept that deep focus on me even as he extended his arms straight out in front of him and pointed the drumsticks directly at me.

I scrunched my forehead, looking over my shoulder to see if there was another girl behind me more worthy of his attention. But no, it was me he was pointing at. His eyes sparked with a sudden playfulness as they registered my 'Who, me?' antics. With the slightest smile on his face, he began alternating the sticks back and forth like an air traffic controller motioning an aircraft to the gate. I took two cautious steps forward, stopped, and looked up at him. Was I good?

He shook his head, not satisfied with my minimal progress. The drummer ramped up the back-and-forth motion. I took another step forward. Then another. He was strangely mesmerizing as he continued to lure me in. I feared if he wanted me in his lap, I might jump right on. It was only when I was within a few feet of him that he halted me with his sticks, now upright and parallel to his face. There was clear expectation in his expression, but for what, I didn't know.

And then he showed me.

Tapping the feed-the-beats bucket, he said, "I don't work for free."

My cheeks ignited, totally on fire. I'd been busted for free-loading and had nothing in my pockets to prove him wrong.

"Oh, I... I'm sorry," I stuttered. "I totally would, but I don't have any money."

His jaw steeled, his playfulness erased. "No, of course you don't."

"No, really. I don't. Remember that guy I was with? The one who called you..." I bit down on my lip, preventing the word from escaping. *No, Grace, don't bring up unpleasant experiences when you're trying to get him on your side!* "Er... um... anyway, that guy dumped me for another girl, and now he has my phone and all my money."

The drummer blinked. Then stared. Then blinked again. Clearly, I'd provided too much information in too short a time. The other possibility was he just didn't care about my suburban drama.

A quick pop of annoyance skipped over his face.

"Whatever," he said. "Step aside, 90210. I've got an encore to do."

What the...? Was he shaming me by zip code?

"Oh, I don't... I don't live in Beverly Hills."

Although to be fair, I didn't live that far off. Undeterred, I continued. "I'm going to come back tomorrow and bring you some money. Then you'll know I'm telling you the truth."

No emotion registered on his face. "I won't be here tomorrow."

"You won't? Why not?"

"Because I don't plan my gigs around you, Gucci."

His words hit with a punch, and after holding it together all night, the stress finally caught up to me. I punched back.

"You know what? I've had a really crappy day, and I'm sure" —my eyes scanned him—"you have too, but if you could just tone down the dickery for, like, two seconds, that would be swell."

Several beats passed before I added my own insult to the mix: "Bam-Bam."

The drummer took a moment to digest the information I'd provided as well as to, perhaps, internalize his own nickname before shocking the hell out of me by checking the time on his imaginary watch and performing a mime where he turned down a pretend dickery dial.

A grin broke across his lips. "Better?"

"Well... yes," I laughed, the stress instantly dissipating. "I could tell the difference immediately. Thank you."

He tipped his head, peering up at me under his wet, clumped lashes. I'd never seen anyone as attractive as him in all my life. It wasn't just his unruly looks that had me hopelessly fawning, but also his talent and the way he spoke to me with edge and a whole lot of mockery. He reminded me of a mish-mash of my brothers, only hotter and cooler and every temperature in between. I wanted so badly to get to know him, but I had a feeling he was already done with me.

Or not.

"What a relief." Bam-Bam's words reeked of sarcasm as he wiped the sweat off his forehead sitcom-style. "I don't think I could sleep on the concrete tonight just thinking about how crappy your day has been."

Was he joking, or was he, as I'd suspected earlier, actually homeless? His wardrobe suggested he was sleeping with rodents, but wasn't he too young to have fallen through the cracks? There were services available to him. Why didn't he use them? If he truly was out here all alone, then I felt like a chump because his crappy days trumped mine by a thousand.

I averted my gaze, embarrassed. He must think I was the most cliché basic rich girl. And he'd be right... almost.

"Hey," he called out. "Girl with no cash."

My eyes swung back only to catch his mischievous smile and the sticks that were again spinning in his hands. "Stop being so dramatic. I was kidding. Now, can you please step off my stage? I really do have an encore to do."

"Oh, right. Sorry." I hurried back to the front line. "Do you want me to leave?"

The drummer held me in his stare as he righted the spinning sticks in his grip and let loose the opening beats of "We Will Rock You." It ripped across his assembly of makeshift drums... all without him once letting go of my eyes.

He said, "I dare you to try."

8

RORY: ON THE FRINGES

So much for my dare.

The girl stayed through the encore but not a second longer, taking her exit when the rest of the crowd dispersed. I looked for her, naively assuming she'd circle back around, but she didn't. Don't even know why I was surprised. It wasn't like I had the best track record when it came to holding on to things that weren't mine. Besides, I knew the game. People with options like her didn't wait around for dead ends like me.

Still, it took courage to stand up to her douchebag boyfriend and pluck to withstand my Richie-Rich name-calling. If anyone could take me up on my dare, it would be her. And if anyone would want to stick around at the end, it seemed like it would be her too, considering how engaged she'd been in my performance. I'd fed off her energy, my tired arms swinging overtime in an effort to impress her. And for all that, I got nothing. It wasn't like I was asking for the unattainable. I just wanted her to stick around long enough so she could... what? Compliment me? Say goodbye? I mean, what exactly did I think was going to happen? It wasn't like I could take her back to my place. Get her number. Buy her a meal.

I shook my head, pissed at myself for thinking I had
anything of value to offer a girl like that. Besides, if she knew the
truth about me, she'd run in the other direction. Frustrated, I
turned to the only thing that could cheer me up. Money. Pulling
out wads of cash from my beater bucket, I quickly counted out
eighty-six dollars. Not bad for a few hours' work. Enough to
bribe my way into a motel room for the night. With no fake ID to
prove my age, legally I wasn't allowed to buy myself a roof over
my head. But money talked, and I had a pocket full of cash. Hell,
if the girl had stuck around, I might've even had enough left
over to buy her a meal. At a fast-food joint. If she didn't
supersize.

Not that it mattered now anyway. In a few minutes' time, I'd
make my way back to the seedier side of life, never to see her
again. I gathered my belongings and tossed them up against the
closest building before sliding down the wall myself. The slick
metal siding of the high-rise cooled my fevered skin. It was hot
outside, and this was as close to air-conditioning as I got. A few
minutes of rest was all I needed to tackle the perilous journey
ahead. Taking the walk at night was like trekking through a
series of downed power lines: you had to be hyperaware and
watch every step. I wasn't in that headspace yet.

Raking my fingers through my slippery hair, I tipped my
head back, longing for a quick nap but knowing that dropping
my guard with money in my pocket was inviting armed robbery.
So I kept my eyes open and moving, scanning the perimeter
with a sniper's focus. It was during one of those surveillance
passes that I saw her walking toward me, the streetlight illumi-
nating the wholesome shine of her beachy curls and the glow of
her lotioned skin. She was the picture of health, while I was
slowly dying. Tension coiled in my stomach as she approached.
I'd wanted her to come back, but now that she had, I didn't
know what to do with my good fortune.

"Surprise," she said, tucking a strand of freshly conditioned hair behind her ear. It was the only indication she might feel as uneasy in my presence as I did in hers. "It's me again. The girl with no cash."

"Oh, I remember." I nodded. "How's your night been going? Better?"

"Honestly, it's looking up." She brightened, her eyes passing over me and letting it be known I was the source of the uptick. "I'm young and free and hanging out with a wicked cool drummer."

I smiled, liking the sound of that. The girl had been here for less than a minute, and she was already restoring bits and pieces of my battle-tested ego. I drank her in, a ray of sunshine in the drab, gray landscape. Confident yet cautious. Sweet but tough. This was a girl not ruled by fear. I couldn't imagine her ever being forced to booby-trap her bedroom door before going to sleep just to give herself a head start when the sun went down.

I'd never seen anyone of her caliber in the flesh. She was like a girl in an ad campaign for Martha's Vineyard, or maybe sailboats. Classically pretty. Crisp. Clean. She probably even had a spattering of nose freckles under that tastefully applied layer of foundation. Wearing a formfitting white tank top, a crocheted light-gray sweater, white Converse, and a pair of black leggings, the girl's clothes were carefully chosen to give her a casually cool vibe. It was a conservative outfit, for sure, at least in comparison to her peers who preferred to showcase considerably more skin. Not that I was complaining. Exposed flesh made me look, but only skin deep. I had to wonder if this girl was less influenced by trends or if someone was checking her outfits before she walked out the door. I decided on the latter. This girl had parents who feared for her safety. The kind who would be horrified to know their little precious was talking to me now.

"I thought you left," I said, trying to keep my need for her companionship from infiltrating my voice.

"No, I was hanging out over there behind the planter." She pointed in the direction I'd scanned multiple times. So much for my surveillance skills. No wonder I got jumped regularly.

"The planter? No one hangs out by planters unless they're peeing in them."

"Well, that explains the smell. But no, I wasn't peeing in them." She smiled. "You do understand that plants are useful for other things too, right?"

"Are they?"

"Mm-hmm... I mean there's that whole thing with them oxygenating the planet and keeping us all alive."

I shrugged, letting her know I wasn't hugely impressed.

"They feed cows," she tried again.

Still not impressed.

"They can be rolled up for a good time."

Now she had me. I smiled. "You don't strike me as a do-it-yourself joint girl."

"I'm not. I was simply stating the useful properties of a plant."

"Ooh. Fancy words. For a fancy girl."

"If you think I'm fancy, you don't get out much."

"I live outside," I said, my voice tipped in amusement. "How much more 'out' can I get?"

She seemed to falter at my words, and I had to remind myself I wasn't dealing with an anything-goes street girl here. I needed to ease her in.

"So, again, why were you hanging out over there by the planter?"

She dropped her gaze, suddenly timid. "I was hiding."

"From who?"

"From you, of course."

That admission came as a surprise. Just the fact that she saw me as an apex predator told me this girl wasn't from around here.

"Me?" I dismissed with a wave. "I'm a fucking delight."

"Okay, well, you and I have different definitions then," she said, raising a brow before clearing her throat and attempting a deeply layered impersonation of me. "*Step aside, Louis Vuitton. I don't plan my gigs around you, Priss in Boots. Get off my stage, American Express.*"

"Well, shit," I said, enthralled by her prickly characterization. "I gotta remember those for next time."

"Next time? How often do you get freeloaders like me?"

"Freeloaders? All the time. Girls like you? Not very often."

Her smile grew to epic proportions, completely transforming the concrete jungle around us and letting it be known she wasn't holding past grudges against me. In fact, my earlier behavior might actually be working in my favor.

"Anyway, I know you're probably busy, and I don't want to bother you," she said. "But I had to come over and tell you what mad skills you have. I mean, that was some straight Nirvana-era drumming there."

If I could have handpicked the perfect compliment, it would have been that. Praise always hit differently when it came from someone in the know, and the way she delivered it with such conviction convinced me that the girl spoke from a place of authority.

"You think I'm good?"

Any of her earlier uncertainty melted away. "I don't just *think* you are. I know you are. I come from a family of musicians."

"Yeah? Anyone I would know?"

She toed the ground, not answering the question. "Are any of them looking for a drummer who can play a mean bucket?"

"Buckets? Not so much. Maybe try the Blue Man Group for

that. But I might be able to help you out if you know your way around a drum kit."

"I didn't learn to drum on paint buckets, if that's what you're asking," I replied with the slightest edge. Was she seriously questioning my versatility? "Buckets became a necessity once I discovered drum sets don't fit inside black plastic garbage bags."

"Plastic bags?" she replied, wrinkling her nose. "I don't get it."

No, of course she wouldn't. Moving from place to place with only what fit in a plastic bag was a uniquely foster kid experience.

"Plastic garbage bags are like luggage for the poor," I stated matter-of-factly.

The quizzical look I got back told me she had no idea what I was talking about. Definitely not from around here.

"I'm a ward of the state," I explained in more easily understandable language. "Meaning that my mommy and daddy are the State of California. And we all know how dysfunctional that can be."

She flinched, and why not? It wasn't a lineage to be proud of.

"I'm sorry," she said, peering down at something that was suddenly very important on the sidewalk.

"Don't be. I've had a lifetime to come to terms with it."

"Is that why you ran away? You had a bad foster home?"

"Something like that," I replied, feeling instantly anxious. I tapped out a song onto my boots to give my jittery hands something to do.

Tipping her eyes back up, she watched me curiously. "You're always moving."

"Yeah. I'm hyperactive. Or at least that's what they tell me. To be honest, I don't even know what it means. All I know is I can't sit still long enough to satisfy the requirements of most potential caretakers."

"So, you get whatever's left over?"

Damn, she was catching on. In foster care, there were no permanent placements. No settling in. No guarantees.

"The worst of the worst." I nodded, stretching out my arms to encompass the landscape. "Hence why I'm out here."

"Aren't you scared?"

"At first I was, yeah, but the beauty of living on the streets is it zaps you of emotion to the point where you simply don't care what happens anymore. I'm there."

"That makes me sad. You're too young to be that jaded. What are you, sixteen or seventeen?"

"Nineteen," I answered without a moment's hesitation. I was so used to lying about my age it came naturally now.

She called my bluff. "Liar."

"I'm not lying."

"Well, you're not nineteen."

"How would you know?"

"You don't even have peach fuzz on your chin."

"Because I shave."

"Oh, do you? Where do you keep the razors? In your buckets?"

"Yes. A whole pack of them. I also use them to shank my enemies."

"Hmm," she said, tapping her lips. "I don't believe you."

"Hmm," I tapped back. "That seems like a you problem."

She smiled. "Let me search your buckets."

I slid one over and hugged it to my chest. "No."

She bent down, I grabbed for her hands, and she swatted me away. We both laughed at the unexpected contact.

"Fine," I relented. "I shave in the shelters."

"Wait—you have access to shelters?"

"Everyone has access to shelters. It's sort of in the name."

"Why don't you sleep there, then?"

"Spoken like a person who has never slept in a shelter."

"I don't have to sleep in a shelter to know it's better than sleeping on the streets."

Oh, how wrong she was. Shelters had four walls and one exit. I'd argue they were the most dangerous living situations of all. Not to mention filthy and filled with the mentally deranged. There was a youth shelter for the under twenty-one crowd, but age was just a number and in no way precluded a person from doing horrible things.

"I tell you what, Saks. Why don't you give one a try sometime and then let me know how you like it?"

Her lively gaze dropped to the ground. Shit, I'd embarrassed her. Sometimes I could be too blunt, forgetting that not everyone had grown up on the same evil merry-go-round that I did.

"Is it time for me to dial down the dickery again?" I asked, hoping to ease the tension.

She stole a glance. "Maybe you should just set a timer at regular intervals. But you're right. I shouldn't be talking about stuff I know nothing about."

I shrugged, not sure how to reply. I wasn't used to people taking my feelings into consideration.

"Can I ask? Who taught you to play like that?"

"No one," I said. "I taught myself."

"Seriously?"

"I had a foster dad who was a drummer. Piece of shit, that one, but he used to play in a band, and his drum set took up most of the living room. He found me playing on it one day—actually I wasn't interested in the drums at all, I was just watching TV and there was nowhere else to sit. Anyway, he taught me the basics. The high hat, snare drum, bass drum. Stuff like that. I took to it instantly. The constant movement appealed to me, you know?"

I stopped, remembering the scene as if it were yesterday. It was one of the few memories I could look back on without wanting to blow my brains out.

"So what happened?"

"With what?"

"That family?"

"I don't know. I never know. Social worker just shows up, hands me my black garbage bag, and I move on."

I thumped out a quick rhythm on the sidewalk, my feet getting in on the action. Bad memory. That was why I hated looking back.

"So, wait. You haven't played on a drum kit since then?"

I looked up, shaking my head. "I'm not completely feral, Patagonia. I go to school."

She seemed stunned, like the thought had never crossed her mind. "You do?"

"I mean, not currently, but I've played in a couple school bands. It's just not easy to hone your skills on an instrument you don't have access to on a regular basis, so I started playing on buckets instead."

"Dang. I'm so impressed. How has no one discovered you yet? You should be in a band."

"Yeah, well, not many bands are looking for their next drummer in the gutter."

She opened her mouth, then shut it again, no doubt to stop herself from asking sensitive details about my situation. Being a foster kid. A runaway. A homeless teen. Those weren't topics for the faint of heart, so instead, she just stared into the darkness and pretended she wasn't dying to ask.

"You're not in the gutter," she said, in a possible attempt to bolster my self-esteem.

"That's not what your boyfriend said."

"Okay, let's get something straight. He's not my boyfriend. He was a date. And now I hate him."

"You should." I spun my sticks, flipping them in a series of threes. "He's a dick. You really need to start making better choices."

"Yes, complete stranger guy." She smiled down at me.

God, she was pretty.

"You're right," my dream girl continued. "I definitely need to make better choices. But at least it led me to you."

"See, now..." I winced for effect. "There are plenty of people who would look poorly on that decision as well. Your parents, for example."

"Eh." She waved off my observation, as if it were beyond ridiculous. "What they don't know won't hurt them."

"Careful there. Those are the famous last words of many murder victims, and you're standing on prime hunting grounds. I think maybe it's time for you to scuttle on back to the safe side of town."

"Don't you think I've been trying?"

I scanned her from top to bottom. "No." My voice pitched an octave. "Not real hard."

"What do you want me to do? I don't have a phone or my money, and I can't remember any numbers to borrow a phone and call someone."

"That's it? Those are your obstacles? Shit, if I had only twice as many, I'd be halfway to Cancun by now."

She laughed, her eyes taking me in. "Who... are... you?"

"They call me Beats."

"Who does?"

"Anybody who asks my name."

"But that's not your name?"

"No."

"And you're not going to tell me what it is?"

"No. That's the whole point of running away." I lowered my voice to get her to lean down. She did. "If you don't want to get caught, you don't tell anyone your real name. So, yeah. The name is Beats."

"Okay, then, I'm not telling you my real name either."

"It doesn't work for you."

"Why not?" She nudged me with her foot. "Why do you get an alias and I don't?"

"You gotta earn it. Sleep with the rats."

Her face told me what she thought of that idea. "Never mind. I don't want an alias that bad."

"No, I didn't think so."

"I'm Grace. It's on my birth certificate."

Her near perfect moniker tumbled through my brain. Not only did her temperament fit the refinement, but it spoke to the musical side of me too.

"Like a grace note," I said.

"Wait." Her mouth dropped open. "You know what that is?"

"Uh, yeah. Did you not hear me playing? I use them all the time."

"It's just really weird you'd say that because I'm actually named after a grace note. My mom's a music teacher. It wasn't until I was older that I found out what it meant—an added note that's not actually part of the song. So, evidently, Mom envisioned me as a sad, two-sentence side character and not the star of my own show. Not cool."

Her wide eyes shone with amusement. I hung on Grace's every word, mesmerized by the way she lit up in her retelling.

"Obviously, I wasn't entirely thrilled when I found out. To try and convince me that a grace note was actually a good thing, my brother played two versions of the same song. The first he performed strictly as it was written. Bor...ring. The second was performed with added grace notes. I don't think I need to tell you which one sounded better."

"No, ma'am, you do not."

I could almost picture that heartfelt scene in front of me: her brother taking the time to make her understand and feel better. It was like something out of a television show. Normally, I hated hearing warm and fuzzy stories of the privileged growing up in loving homes, but for whatever reason, Grace seemed worthy of an ideal life.

"The way I see it"—I stopped talking momentarily to perform a ten-second drum solo on the concrete—"you can never have enough grace."

"No, I don't believe you can," she agreed, beaming. "Can I sit?"

I squinted up at her, genuinely curious. "Now, why would you want to sit here?"

"Well, I asked the ukulele guy around the corner, but he turned me down."

"Fucking Ronald." I palmed my forehead. "He makes us all look bad."

Grace didn't wait for my approval; she dropped down onto the concrete beside me and pointed at my hands. "Can I borrow your sticks?"

"I'd rather you didn't."

"You'd rather I didn't?" she mimicked, seeming suddenly very comfortable in my presence.

"You heard me." I tapped a stick on her leg, getting some-what more comfortable myself. "I'd honestly rather share a Q-tip with you than hand over my sticks."

She laughed, pushing against my shoulder. "Come on. What do you think I'm going to do with them? Break them over my knee? I just want to look."

"Then look," I said, holding them up to her eyes.

Her lips formed the most perfect pout, slaying me with cuteness. "Please."

I could not withstand such manipulation, especially when that little crease formed on the bridge of her nose. She was deceptively pretty, and it weakened me. Reluctantly, I handed them over.

"Thank you," she said. Such manners.

Grace turned my sticks in her hands before testing out her grip. I swallowed hard. She was holding them like she was about to dive into a steak dinner. I had no choice but to correct her.

"Don't tighten your grip. That requires more energy, and the sticks won't rebound like you want. Like this..." I said, reaching over and placing the sticks into position on her lithe hands. Gently, I folded each of her lean fingers inward to hold them in place. Her head dipped as she followed my instructions, enticing one long curl to untuck from behind her ear and spring to life like a gleeful music note.

Common sense escaped me—completely. I swept the strand back, returning it to the obedient others who had remained tucked in place. She seemed as surprised as I was, shyly looking up at me from the shade of her lashes. I swallowed hard. The freshness of her. Such innocence. Even as a young child, I didn't remember ever being so shiny and new.

The slightest tremor rippled over her skin as her eyes connected to mine, and like she'd done numerous times already, her gaze burrowed into my soul. We both hung there in that pulsing limbo. Grace's chest rose and fell in time with my drumming heartbeat, and I resisted the urge to pull her to me and kiss those glossy lips. But I didn't have the nerve. The risk of rejection was too high. That was until she tilted her head to one side in what looked like an open invitation. No way could I be reading her cues right. And even if I was, I'd be a fool to act on them. The optics alone of a sweaty street kid macking it out with a certified American Girl doll was sure to lead to a citywide pitchforking.

I cleared my throat.

She dropped her gaze.

We both ricocheted back into our own space. Sanity restored.

"Sorry," I said, swirling my finger in the air to mimic her curls. "Your hair fell out of place, and I..."

"Oh, I know. It does that all the time," she answered, swirling her own imaginary lock. "Bad curl."

I croaked out what I'd intended to be a laugh, but it came out all sexually frustrated. You'd think I was an inexperienced middle schooler the way I was acting around her, and I hadn't been inexperienced even *in* middle school.

"Hey, focus," she said, snapping me out of my head. "Back to the lesson. Are my hands still good?"

She lifted them up to show me that the sticks were still properly positioned.

I gave her a thumbs-up. "You're a natural."

"I have a good teacher. Now what?"

"Now, you show me what you've got."

Grace let loose, wild and out of control. If I didn't know better, I'd think she'd overdosed on bath salts.

"You know what..." I grabbed her hands. "Why don't we try a beat?"

"I thought that's what I was doing."

"No. No. That's not what you were doing at all," I said, not even attempting to sugarcoat the rhythmic atrocities she'd just committed. "Try alternating your hands. Right, left, right, left."

"Ah, good idea. Okay. Hang on. Let me just..."

I watched her mime writing with her right hand and could not, for the life of me, understand what ritual she was performing.

"Uh, Grace?"

She waved off the question I'd yet to ask. "Don't mind me. Sometimes I get confused by what's right and left, so I pretend to write something to remind myself."

"That's just... really concerning."

"Stop." She laughed, tapping the beat into my leg. Entirely incorrectly. Left, right, left, left, right.

I gripped my damp hair, tugging it at the roots. "You're killing me."

"Fine," she sighed. "How about we try it my way?"

Using my thighs as her drum kit, Grace dropped into an actual beat, one without an ounce of that right and left bullshit. She lifted her eyes, and the shine that radiated off her blew my mind. This girl knew exactly what she was doing.

My little Grace Note was actually a damn good percussionist.

9

GRACE: WHEN THE SAVING HAPPENS

His shock was duly noted. I fed off of it, copying some of his performance mannerisms to fully engage my audience of one. Sure, I wasn't as dynamic as he was, the guy who'd managed to command a small army of musical recruits with the swing of his mighty arms, but I was holding my own in the eyes of the only one who counted—Beats—the hottest street guy in Los Angeles County.

I couldn't believe I'd just formulated those thoughts in my head. Holy hell, what was I doing? In every single safety-first bedtime story my mother had ever read to me growing up, this very scenario existed. Do not... I repeat... do not go off with a strange man. First chance I got, what did I do? Went off with a strange man. Granted, I hadn't actually gone off with him. No, it was worse; I'd sat down beside him and made myself comfy. I'd let him tuck a strand of hair behind my ear with such smoldering intensity that I nearly forced my first kiss on him. And if all that wasn't bad enough, I was now drumming a Shinedown song onto his open thigh.

Mommy would not be pleased.

I wasn't sure where I thought this whole pop-up shop tryst

with the sarcastic, sexy drummer was going, but I sure hoped it wasn't into some true crime annals. If he wanted, it wouldn't take much for him to off me—I was making it oh so easy for him. But no. I was going off the assumption that he was too good-looking to be hiding bodies in the freezer.

Looking up from the beat, I found him staring. Oh lord, he was dangerously delicious. Like a young Kurt Cobain before the drug addiction engulfed him. Actually, that was maybe not the best comparison, considering how that all worked out for him and Courtney Love. Still, I smiled at Beats cunningly, my lids fluttering. Shamelessly flirting. And Beats—oh yeah, he was soaking it up like a sponge.

I really needed to stop. Go back to the parking garage and wait for *my* date to finish *his* date and drive me home. That was the smartest thing to do. The safest bet. And I totally wasn't going to do it. Because I liked Beats. Like really, really liked him. Like butterflies in the chest and a whole bunch of other places liked him. Like getting my fingers stuck in that mangled mess of his hair liked him. I'd never experienced such unquenched thirst. If this was lust, sign me up. I wanted whatever he was offering. And I could have it, too... if I was bold.

"Hold on there, Grace Note," he said, using my adorable new nickname. "Have you seriously been fucking with me this whole time?"

I smiled, concentrating on my drum solo. "Just about the drumming."

"So, no issues with your right and left then?"

"Uh, you know, sometimes. But everything else..." I winked, feeling like I could be my goofy self around him. "Totally factual."

"Right," he said, keeping an eye on the sticks as they whomped his thigh. "What song is this anyway?"

His question was valid, given the surface I was playing on

had no range, but I pushed out my lower lip anyway. "Oh my god, soo... offended."

"Don't be. The only sound I hear is of my flesh crying."

"Such a baby. I'm barely touching you."

"My thighs do not agree."

"The song I'm playing is actually inspired by you."

"By me? I've known you for fifteen minutes."

"That's how inspiring you are."

He laughed. "Okay."

"I'm playing 'I Dare You' by Shinedown. Have you heard of it?"

"Because of my whole daring you to stay in the front row thing?" He grinned. "Very clever."

"I thought so. Hold on. I'm coming to the end of my masterpiece."

His eyes followed the sticks as they inched nearer to his sensitive triangle. It occurred to me then that I was just a hop, skip, and a jump away from his dick and balls. Holy shit, was that a bulge?

"You're getting a little close there, don't you think?" he asked, understandably concerned for the viability of his future children.

"It's creative license," I explained, finishing off the last two beats of the pantleg version of one of my favorite songs before taking a well-deserved bow. "And fade."

"Wow." Beats clapped, so moved by my performance he even pulled out a dollar bill from his pocket and flicked it at me. Turning it into an airplane, I flew it back to him. He wadded it up and lobbed it at my head. I ended our game of hot potato by taking it entirely too far, rising to my knees and shoving the dollar bill—and my hand—into his front pocket. He actually grunted like he was in pain, but the look on his face said other-wise. I felt something churn inside me, a new feeling but one that begged to be explored. Just not here. Not on the sidewalk. Not with a homeless runaway boy that my parents, if they found out, would murder me for.

I rocked back onto my butt, returning to my safe space, which wasn't safe at all because I couldn't keep my hands to myself. Beats was like quicksand. On the surface he looked solid, but the minute you stepped in, you sank to your waist in submission. *Think, Grace. Think.* How was I going to pull myself up and out of this gelatinous thirst trap?

I picked his precious sticks up off my lap and presented them to him in my opened palms. "Sir."

Beats reclaimed his property, turning them to check for damage.

"What did I say? Not a scratch on them."

"You said; I just didn't believe you."

He smiled. I smiled. The air around us smiled.

Beats reached over and tapped me on the nose with a stick.

"You," he said, watching me intently.

I got a little lost in the curiosity of his eyes. His heavy-lidded squint could easily be mistaken for a sultry gaze, but upon closer examination, Beats seemed to have a sensitivity to light or some other outside element that forced his lids to overcompensate by half closing. A slight dark tinting under the eyes only drew more attention to them.

"What about me?" I asked.

"You're not all you seem to be."

"Neither are you."

"I don't know about that. Look at me. I've been stripped down to the bare minimum. But you... you're all decorated up, looking like you just stepped out of the Hamptons, and then BAM—there you are knocking out a hard rock drum solo like a gift from the musical gods."

My heart fluttered at the compliment. It was like he saw me.

Not who I was supposed to be but *me*. Even the ones I was closest to, Quinn and Emma and Mom and Dad, didn't really know me. They thought they did. But they didn't.

Beats seemed to instinctively get that I was more than my exterior. More than my last name. And it was the highest compliment coming from someone as dynamic as him. Someone who had no choice but to live in the moment. The guys at my school tried so hard to be relevant and cool, but meeting Beats convinced me that it was an internal state of being and couldn't be forced. You either were or you weren't. Beats *was*, a thousand times over.

"You know what I think?" he said, smiling slyly.

"No."

"I think you've been sent here to destroy me."

I almost laughed in his face. No one would ever accuse me of being a femme fatale. I wore bunny slipper-socks to bed.

"Or..." I offered up a more complimentary scenario for myself. "Maybe I've been sent here to save you."

A muscle in his cheek twitched, and I caught the faintest dash of despair pass through his eyes. "I wish. You're about a decade too late."

I could tell the minute he said it, Beats regretted the words, and I watched him regress right before my eyes. The conflict. The indecision. My god, he was giving off such strong Jake vibes that I placed a hand to my chest to calm my beating heart. It was then that I realized why I was so drawn to Beats. He was my do-over. My chance to right one of life's biggest wrongs. I could save him, and in the process, redeem myself.

"I don't know, Beats," I said, touching his leg with my sneak-ered toe. "Isn't that when the saving happens—after the deed is done?"

Slowly, his gaze lifted until his eyes were focused on mine, imploring me to look beyond the obvious. Beyond the dirty clothes. Beyond his terrible housing predicament. Beyond the hopelessness of his situation. Beats wanted someone to see him. A long-ago scene flashed before my eyes, of Jake being rolled into the house in a wheelchair. It was the first time I'd seen him since the kidnapping over two months earlier. He was so broken and beaten. I was so frightened. Jake's eyes followed me around the room until they hit their target. He had me locked and loaded. I stared straight into his shattered soul that day, and my toddler brain had no idea how to comprehend what it was seeing. Clearly, he wanted something. Somehow, I'd convinced myself that my brother was trying to suck the life right out of me. Instead of showing him the mercy he desperately needed, I screamed in his face and ran the other way.

Beats unleashed a very slow series of nods. "Yeah, I guess *after* does make more sense."

He averted his eyes then, resuming the unsettled movements of his hands and feet. Those sticks were in constant use.

"I always wanted to be a great musician like you," I admitted.

"Like me?" He huffed. "That's yet to be determined."

"You will be. I can feel it."

He shrugged noncommittally. A little of that confidence of his had faded. "You look like a pretty great drummer to me," he said.

"Ha! We both know I'm nowhere near your level. That's okay, though, because drumming isn't a passion of mine."

"What's your passion?"

"Songwriting."

He pondered a moment. "Like pop songs?"

"What makes you assume that?"

"Songwriters write what they know, Miss Swift." He grinned.

"And you assume all I know is the upbeat stuff?"

"My assumptions are strictly evidence based. You went on a date with a frat boy punk. You walked into the VIP entrance at the arena. And you own a cell phone and credit cards. All I'm saying is you don't appear to be too angsty."

Of course, Beats would view me like that. Light and airy. A pop princess. Miss Swift. That was probably the vibe I was giving off, but there was more to me than that. I mean, there were documentaries made about my family, for god's sake. If that didn't give me the required street cred, I didn't know what would.

"You don't know anything about me," I replied.

"Don't get mad. It's what my eyes see." He smiled, so sure of himself. "Although there is one bit of evidence that doesn't fit with the rest."

"What's that?" I asked, shoving aside my irritation out of curiosity.

"The look you gave me before disappearing into the arena. I know you saw something in me. Something you didn't like."

Didn't like? No. Shivers instantly prickled my skin. Jake. I'd seen Jake in him, that was all. But it didn't feel that way. It felt like he'd picked up on some trigger of mine that I didn't know I had. I drew in a sharp breath. "That's not true. I like everything about you."

He sat, silently studying me before finally shrugging. "Maybe I was wrong. Maybe you don't have any secrets in you. In which case, you might want to stick to pop songs."

I bristled at the smugness in his tone but couldn't let the conversation go. "Why don't you tell me, Beats? What do you think I saw?"

"Why should I do the work for you? Everyone knows that what makes artists great is unleashing whatever it is inside that scares the shit out of them. If you want to go beyond the ordinary, then you've got to dig down deep."

He leaned forward, dropping his voice to a whisper. "But only if you dare."

My blinking game was off the charts. I had no rebuttal. Nothing to say. He was right, of course. Look at Jake. He'd exploited the hell out of his tragedy and found the pot of gold at the end. But me? I avoided all mention of the thing that scared me most—the kidnapping. Why? Why couldn't I read an article about it or scroll the web looking for clues? Was there something I was afraid to see? I'd always told myself the reason I kept talk of the kidnapping at bay was because I chose to live in the light, but what if there was more to it? What would happen if I unleashed whatever it was I feared inside me? Would it become my angsty muse... or be the death of me?

RORY: AFTER DARK

There were times when being an untouchable worked in my favor. The trip back to the arena, traveling upstream through thousands of exiting concertgoers, was one of those times. The normal people saw me coming, and like the hull of a ship carving through a school of fish, they parted down the middle, allowing Grace and me to sail on through.

Even she noticed the phenomenon. "Wow. It pays to carry a lot of baggage."

"In more ways than one," I agreed, relieved she'd seemed to bounce back from the stupidity of my words. What the hell had I been thinking, accusing this girl of having some unspoken secret when I knew nothing about her? More importantly, why did she react the way she did if I wasn't right?

But all was forgotten when we walked back to the arena, that easiness between us restored. There was a weightlessness with her that I hadn't felt in years... maybe ever. If Grace was embarrassed to be seen with me, she didn't show it, and that meant a lot to me. If someone like her could accept me, were there others?

"Speaking of baggage," she said, "you want me to wash your clothes for you?"

I stopped walking to gawk at her offer. A few minutes earlier, she'd watched me gather up all my clothes, limp with grime and inattention, and shove them in my buckets. I'd tried to keep the stench from reaching her nose by turning my back to her, but it was no use. My clothes were pungent, like overripe fruit that had plunged to the ground and split wide open with rot.

Poor hygiene was my biggest shame. Of all the shit I went through out here, being dirty and covered in filth hurt my pride the most. But washing my clothes always proved a huge ordeal. Laundromats required a full day commitment of travel, wait times, and judgment as I tried to wash as much of my wardrobe as possible with just enough of my body parts covered to keep me from being arrested for indecent exposure.

Some shelters offered washers and dryers, but most of the time they weren't working. On the off chance they were, I'd have to drape my body over the machines to prevent my clothes from being forcibly adopted. For those reasons, I tended to put off washing my clothes until they were walking to the laundromat themselves.

"Seriously? You would do that for me?"

"It's the only thing I can think of to extend our one day into two."

"All you had to do was ask."

"Really?" She blinked, like she couldn't believe my time could be bought so easily, when in reality, I had nothing better to do. Ever.

"Yes. Why wouldn't I want to hang out with you?"

"I don't... know."

"But no takebacks on the clothes," I quickly followed up. "You already offered."

"I'm not taking it back," Grace replied. "I want to wash them for you."

"You *want* to? Are you a sadist?"

"No." She twirled her locks. "I like you."

Oh, my damn! Girls like her didn't happen to guys like me. "Why?"

"I just do."

"Huh, well, I like you too."

"But, do you like me as a friend, or..."

"I like you as anything you'll allow me to be."

She smiled. "Just for that I'm going to add fabric softener."

"Don't fucking tease me, Grace."

"And those little dryer sheets."

"Stop." I grasped my chest. "I can't take anymore."

Grabbing my arm, Grace playfully steered me to a side entrance of the parking garage, and we started down a row of cars. "I'm just not sure how to explain the, uh... odor to Hudson when I get in his car."

"Just tell him while he was in the arena enjoying the concert like an asshat, some homeless dude shit on you. He'll totally buy it."

Her eyes widened before she burst into a fit of giggles. I joined in, the two of us bonding over... well... my dirty laundry.

"I hope he didn't leave already," she said, nibbling on her bottom lip.

"He wouldn't do that, would he?"

"Well, let's see." Grace rolled her eyes as she kept walking. "He did double-book our date and then fail to realize I was missing for hours, so yes, I definitely think he'd leave me."

She had a point. The dude was slimy, and as much as I hated the idea of him driving her home, the alternative was worse. Grace might have effortlessly survived a couple of hours on the streets, but downtown after midnight was another story altogether.

"Oh, whew. This is it," she said, stopping at the black Mercedes and kicking its back bumper with more than a little force. "The douche."

"Okay, girl with the dragon tattoo, let's not damage Hudson's ride before he gets you home safely."

"Once he gets me home, can I smash a tire jack into his window? Pretty please with sugar on top?"

I smiled, her spunk and resilience a constant form of amusement to me. "Knock yourself out."

During those times when I'd gone to school regularly, I'd avoided the rich girls whenever possible. My swap meet attire and unstyled hair sticking out every which way were ripe for their mockery. But if I'd known there were ones like her, I might not have been such a savage in my approach to socialization.

"Probably not a good idea for Hudson to see me," I said, guiding Grace behind a concrete pillar within eyeshot of Hudson's car. I wasn't afraid of him. He might've been bulkier than me, but I was scrappier, and I knew how to both give and receive a punch. If I was going down, he was coming with me. But I didn't want to risk Grace's ticket home, so I kept us out of view.

Spotting a few empty plastic store bags in a garbage can, I shoved my clothes inside three bags and tied them all off before dropping them to the ground at her feet.

"For you." I bowed.

"Wow, such a gentleman. So, where is our clothing exchange taking place tomorrow?"

I thought for a moment. It had to be somewhere out in the open, somewhere her safety wouldn't be compromised. I couldn't tell her the things that lurked in the shadows. It would break her trust in humanity, and she deserved to keep her innocence for as long as time allowed.

"There's a shopping center down the street," I answered.

"The one with that huge furniture store?"

"Yes. Meet me at noon in the last parking spot on the row directly in front of the entrance to the furniture store."

"That's oddly specific."

"You asked for a place." I shrugged. "I gave you one."

"I know, but I wasn't expecting such precision. What happens if I park in, say, the second to last spot?"

I shook my head, smiling. "I wouldn't do it."

"I mean, maybe I park, like, one row over. Or sideways. What happens then?"

"You'll get stuck behind people driving slow in the fast lane forever."

"Oh." She laughed. "That's not good. I suppose you're right. We'll go with your obsessive-compulsive spot then."

I saw Hudson approaching his car and gestured toward him with my head. "Your ride is here."

Twisting her head, Grace spotted him and stomped her foot like an insolent toddler. "Ugh, don't make me go."

"You have to," I whispered, placing the bags of my dirty clothes in her hands, turning her around, and scooting her toward him. "Who else is going to wash my clothes and bake me cookies?"

She barked out a laugh. "I never said I was baking you cookies."

"You never said you weren't."

She turned back around, her nose crinkling. "Are you going to be all right out there all by yourself?"

All by myself? Hell, I wished. When the sun went down in Los Angeles, the cretins crawled out of their holes and I was very much *not* alone.

"Don't worry about me," I reassured her. "I know how to disappear."

She nodded, nibbling on her bottom lip. "But you won't disappear on me, will you?"

How could I explain to her that she was the power player in this pairing? She was the one with the life to live. I had nothing. I'd always show up. I wasn't sure she could say the same. "No. Now go. Don't miss your ride."

"Okay," she said, walking away backward so that she was still staring at me. "Tomorrow. Noon. In that ridiculous spot of yours. Don't be late."

"I won't. Oh, and Grace? That stuff..." I pointed to the plastic bags in her hands. "It's all I own."

"I got you, Beats." She lifted the bags up to show me as she continued walking backward. "I promise I won't let you down."

I stayed behind the pillar, watching as Grace approached Hudson. The two exchanged words, and then she slipped into his car and away they went. A moment passed. And then another. I couldn't seem to move my feet from this spot after she'd disappeared from sight. I'd watched people walk away plenty of times before, but it had never felt like this. As illogical as it seemed, I knew this privileged, inquisitive girl would come back for me. I couldn't say how I knew; I just did.

Somewhere on a desk at The Department of Children and Family Services was a file with my name on it. Inside of that file was a psyche evaluation with a fancy diagnosis stamped on it: Reactive Attachment Disorder. An inability to show affection for others. To trust. To bond.

Grace had just proven the experts wrong.

～

STANDING ALONE in the parking garage, I had a decision to make. Walk the four miles back to the part of the city I knew well, the part where cops didn't bother the squatters and where the motel management was a little less beholden to the state ID laws, or find myself a place to crash around here for the night. Both held their risks. Remaining in an area I was unfamiliar with was dangerous but it would avoid me having to make the same trip back in the morning. I glanced around the garage, wondering if maybe I could get away with crashing here. I wandered the different levels until I found an out-of-the-way nook and settled in.

I must have fallen fast asleep because I had no idea where I was or what time I was awakened by the man in a security sweatshirt. "This is private property. Gotta move."

I jolted upright, my heart racing at the unexpected intrusion. "Okay, I'm going."

Grabbing my buckets, I was already walking away when he called to me. "How much?"

Slowly, I turned my head in his direction. "What?"

"How much?" he repeated, his eyes lingering on me. "I get off in thirty minutes."

I hated the assumption that I could be bought. "Fuck you."

Exiting the garage, I moved through the night, looking for another place to lay my head. The zombies were out roaming now, making finding a suitable spot more difficult. I made a few turns until I arrived in the area known as The Stroll, where scantily clad female sex workers peddled their wares. The women wouldn't bother me; it was their pimps that gave me pause. But I felt safer in a busy area, so I decided to stay. Stashing my buckets in the bushes, so passersby wouldn't use them for toilets, I found my myself an empty wall along the alleyway of a building and slid down it, preparing for a long night.

I was just dozing off when I heard my name being called. Not Beats. Not Stretch. Not Ringo. Not any of the names I, or others, had given to me. No, she'd called me by my real name.

"Rory."

Knowing the voice well, I reluctantly lifted my head off the wall to find my sister Nikki walking toward me, looking like life had severely beaten her down. It was hard to believe she was only three years older than me and already sucking at adulthood. The dress that barely covered her assets told me all I needed to know about her current occupation. Before I could rise to my feet and shake some sense into her, Nikki sank down to her bare knees and wrapped her arms around my neck, burrowing her head into the hollows. It had been a long time, and we hadn't left on the best terms. Actually, we'd left on the worst of them.

We didn't speak. Just hugged. She was so thin—skin and bones. Growing up, that hadn't been the norm for her. Nik had always had a thickness to her—a feature she'd hated with a passion, but I bet now wished for a little of it back.

"Ah, Rory," she said, stroking the back of my neck. "I hate that it's you."

"Right back at ya, Nik."

"I thought maybe things were going better for you."

"Well, you thought wrong."

"What about Patty?"

"What about her?"

"Didn't you go back to her after we were separated?"

"No. She had other kids by then. I went back into the round robin rotation. Got spit out into the worst placements the county had to offer. Needless to say, my life went to shit."

She pulled out of our hug and tucked an errant breast back into her dress without an ounce of embarrassment. "And you blame me, right?"

"I didn't say that."

I didn't have to. We both knew I blamed her for everything bad that had ever befallen me. But still I loved her and worried about her.

"You're working the streets now?"

"What was your first clue?"

"The tit peekabooing out of your dress."

"Like you haven't seen it before."

I wasn't sure if the words just slipped out of her mouth or it was somehow intentional, but it made for a supremely awkward moment of silence between us.

"Why are you out here?" I finally asked.

Her brows shot up. "I think you know why I'm out here. After what... happened, I wasn't quite able to make the transition to law-abiding citizen. I tried for a hot minute. Moved to Seattle for a fresh start. Even got a legit job. You would've been so proud of me, scrubbing toilets with the best of them. But it turns out I couldn't pay my rent on a hotel maid's salary, so I started turning tricks again. And then I thought, 'Hey, if I'm gonna be sucking dick anyway, might has well do it in the sun and not in the pouring rain.' So here I am, back in the land of sunshine and dreams."

She fashioned a gun with her fingers, aimed it at her head, and blew herself away. I winced at her brutal, unapologetic honesty. If ever there had been someone who owned her lot in life, it was my sister. Actually, foster sister. We were siblings in oath alone, brought together when I was five and she was eight. She took to me instantly, the two of us becoming so inseparable that social workers noted in our charts that placing us apart would be detrimental to our development. How were they to know that the very bond they were protecting would destroy me?

"So, here you are," I repeated. "What's your plan, then?"

"My plan? Were you not listening, Rory? That was the plan."

"I'm talking more long term. Where do you see yourself in five years?"

"With any luck, six feet underground."

Sadly, she was probably right.

"What about the mansion in the hills?" I asked.

Her smile wilted. "No more Disney films for me."

I frowned, taking in her emaciated body. I hated that she had nothing left to live for. We'd both had dreams once. Maybe hers had died, but mine were still alive and kicking, and as long as there was a flicker of hope, I was hanging on.

"How are you, really?" I asked.

A shiver rocked my sister, making me wish I hadn't given Grace my jacket to wash. "Not great."

"Are you still using?"

"Just enough to get through the day, nothing more."

I wasn't sure I believed her but she wasn't crawling through the streets with the other whacked-out zombies, so maybe she was telling the truth.

"What about you, Rory?" She glided her fingers over my face, with the intimate touch I'd always hated. I tipped my head away. "How are you holding up?"

"I mean..." I opened my arms to my reality.

Nikki nodded, looking past me before redirecting her focus. "You hate me, don't you?"

"I don't hate you."

"But you don't forgive me."

I wondered which incident she was referring to because there were plenty to choose from. Had I never met her, had she never led me into darkness, maybe I wouldn't be out here on the streets today. But then again, maybe I would. The truth of the matter was my life had started on the streets and would probably end out here too.

Nik drew in a breath, and I could see her emotions getting the best of her. "You wanna hear something stupid?" she asked.

"Always."

"The only thing that keeps me going on my bad days is wanting to see you up on that big stage proving everyone wrong. Just you and your drums." She smiled up at the stars. "Yeah. That's all I want. To watch you shine. And then you can drop me in the ground."

"Don't say that."

"It's true. You're still drumming, aren't you?"

"I am. I got my buckets over there." I pointed to the bushes. "I'm drawing big crowds every night."

Nikki's brows indented. "Where are you playing?"

"Around. Mostly tourist areas. Played near the arena tonight."

"How long have you been doing that?" she asked, the alarm on her face prompting some of my own.

"Since I got out here. Why?"

She lowered her voice to a barely audible whisper. "What if they find you?"

"Why would they? No one knows I'm a drummer."

"Rory, they know everything about you. At least they did when you were in foster care. You're their biggest liability. A loose end they want to tie off. You being in foster care was the only thing protecting you."

"How would you know?"

"I don't... I just..." Nikki couldn't meet my eye.

"Foster care didn't save us the first time around, so I'm not betting my life on that."

"Rory, this isn't a joke. If they know you're on the street, they'll..."

"They'll what?"

"They'll..." She hesitated, glancing around for spies. "Just trust me. Get off the streets and stop playing the damn drums where they might hear you."

"Why would they hear me?" The fear in my sister's eyes sent me straight to my feet. "You didn't! Tell me you're not working for them. Tell me."

Her lips quivered. "Rory, I..."

That was all I needed to hear. I rushed for my buckets and swung them over my shoulders, preparing to flee.

She grabbed my arm. "Please believe me. I didn't have a choice."

I ripped my arm out of her hold. "Yes, Nik, you did. Your choice was to suck dick in Seattle, but no, you had to choose the fucking sunshine. You know what? I take it all back. I do hate you... with all my fucking heart."

Nikki's eyes flooded with tears. "Good. Now run."

11

GRACE: LAZY RIVER

I t was times like this I wished I had a female friend. Someone I could share all the meet-cute details of my time with Beats. Someone who would take the information at face value and actually be happy for me. I loved my sister dearly, but she was not the right person for this job. Emma had my best interests at heart and would definitely not be excited that I'd spent the evening with a hot drummer. She'd be even less thrilled to discover he was homeless and had hair like a circus performer. A girlfriend, on the other hand, wouldn't care about pesky little safety issues. She'd be cheering me on, asking when I was going to see him again. Tomorrow, fictional friend. I was going to see him again tomorrow, I squeed. Yes, I definitely needed to get me one of those.

"What's the code?" Hudson asked, pulling up to the security gate in front of my home.

"Just let me out here," I replied.

The two of us had barely spoken on the way home, not after he'd accused me of purposely sabotaging his and Mia's night by not showing up backstage like they'd apparently pre-planned.

Even after I explained to him what had happened, he remained pissed for the rest of the drive.

I opened the door and grabbed the plastic bags with Beats' clothes.

"Goddamn, what the hell is that smell?" he grumbled. It wasn't the first time he'd asked. I had half a mind to shove one of Beats' socks into the seat back pocket and let it be the gift that kept on giving.

"A homeless guy shit on me," I replied, slamming the door shut behind me.

QUINN WAS out when I returned, having left a note that he was hanging out with our horndog musician friends and to text him when I got home. Not that I needed to, with him tracking my every move. Wouldn't he be surprised to discover my phone had been inside the arena all night but I had not?

With my brother gone, I had time to prepare for my day with Beats—because that was what I hoped it would be. A day of fun where he could feel like a kid again. I knew just the place. But first, I had a promise to keep.

Dumping the first load of laundry into the washer, I used extra of all the good stuff Beats wanted on his clothes and then went to the kitchen and made him cookies. To cover my tracks, I made a double batch. One would be for Quinn when he returned home because there was no disguising the wonderful aroma, and he'd pull the kitchen apart looking for the chocolate chip cookies. The second batch would be for Beats. I smiled just thinking about him enjoying a comfort from home.

It was pushing one in the morning when I changed into my pajamas and got ready for bed. Something was nagging at me.

What Beats had said. *Digging deep.* I grabbed my laptop and sat on the bed, staring at the closed cover. My hands began to shake. Did I dare? I opened the cover and typed "Jake McKallister kidnapping" into the search engine. My finger hung over the return button. The blood in my veins turned ice cold. I backspaced and shut the lid. Setting my computer aside, I got under the covers and tried to fall asleep, but my eyes remained wide open.

Sitting back up, I opened the cover again and typed in the same three words. This time I hit return. A seemingly endless supply of articles appeared for me to scroll through, but that wasn't what I was looking for. I changed the "ing" on "kidnapping" to "er" and pressed return again. A series of images populated my screen, one specific one catching my eye. My heart beating out of my chest, I enlarged the picture and then audibly gasped.

"Oh my god!" A sob burst forth. "Oh my god!"

I slammed the cover shut, but it was too late. I'd found the darkness hidden inside, and a flood of memories came roaring back. I made it to the toilet just in time to purge my gut.

HE WAS LATE. Eleven agonizing minutes, to be exact. I wasn't sure why I was so nervous. People were late all the time. It was a daily occurrence. You waited, they came—or didn't—and you moved on. But Beats' absence seemed more ominous. Less under his control. But then, maybe I was looking at the world differently after what I'd discovered last night. I pushed that aside. I wouldn't let it ruin my day. This was about Beats and me and no one else.

Still, the longer I waited, the worse my worry got, my brain conjuring up a whole array of horrors that could've befallen him since we'd parted in the parking garage last night. I'd seen him as we were driving away, camouflaged behind the concrete pillar. How was it fair that I was going back to everything while he had absolutely nothing? Where would he go? Would he be cold? Hungry? Would rats be nibbling at his toes?

I'd wanted to scream at Hudson to stop the car so I could get out and rescue my drummer boy. But then what? What would I do with him after that? I couldn't just pick Beats up and bring him home. He needed long-term help. He needed off the streets. Would he even go? Beats put up a good front, the picture of confidence riding atop his drummer's throne, but there was a fragility to him too, like a teacup dangerously close to the counter's edge. One small bump and over he'd go. Someone needed to help him, and as much as I wished that someone could be me, I was a teenager with limited resources. What Beats needed was a village.

My phone buzzed, and for a split second, I thought it was him letting me know why he was tardy. But then reality snapped me back. Beats had no way to call me or even to tell time. If he didn't show up today, there was a good chance I'd never see him again. A sick feeling twisted in my gut as I glanced down at my phone.

UNKNOWN

Hey. It's Mia. Hudson gave me your number

I made a face. Not now. I already knew I'd been uninvited to her party. Hudson had informed me on the car ride home last night. And honestly, I didn't care. I had bigger things to worry about now.

GRACE

Hey

Mia got straight to the point.

> Super disappointed I didn't get to meet Jake

I stared at her words, wanting to blast her but choosing restraint.

> I couldn't get backstage. Hudson had my ID and phone

There was a long, dotted wait for her response and then a series of lightning-fast texts.

> Yeah, he told me what happened

> I suppose it wasn't really your fault

> You can still come to my party

> With conditions…

Conditions? The nerve. I wanted to block her right then and there, but curiosity got the best of me.

> GRACE
>
> ?

> Ask Jake to record me a birthday message

> Something I can play at the party

> Think of it like a goodwill gesture

> A way to gain back my trust

I laughed. She couldn't be serious. Like Jake would even do that. My fingers hung over the keys, undecided how they wanted to address her conditions. Yesterday I probably would have catered to them, scrambling to make amends. I might even have begged Jake to make all my tormentor's birthday wishes come true. After all, Mia had the means—and the mean spirit—to socially destroy me. But somehow, none of that mattered to me anymore. It was as if I'd grown up in a day. Beats' plight had put my own life into perspective. I was done being a follower. From now on, I made my own rules, and if that meant I'd spend the rest of high school on the couch eating popcorn with Quinn, so be it.

> You still there?

She typed.

> Yes. Still here

It occurred to me then that I had something she desperately wanted; what all the kids at school craved from me. Access to Jake. And that was mine alone to give or take.

> GRACE
>
> No, I'm sorry. I can't ask him that.

> Why not?

> Because Mia, Jake is a worldwide celebrity. He doesn't make housecalls and he certainly doesn't record birthday greetings to girls who call his sister a nepo baby. And don't bother uninviting me. I already removed my name from the guest list. Have a great birthday, Mia

My face flushed with both terror and thrill as I pressed send and mentally prepared for the world as I knew it to end. And, strangely enough, I couldn't wait to reclaim the part of me who had been a slave to their whim.

Turning off the phone, I tucked it into the cupholder just as movement caught my eye. I looked up to see Beats striding toward me, naked from the waist up and those buckets swinging with each step he took, like some hatless urban cowboy heading for a standoff.

Holy, holy hell. My untrained teenage eyeballs popped from their sockets upon his approach. What had I stumbled upon last night? I mean, Beats had been hot under the street-lights, but seeing him blazing in the sun was a whole new experience, one that every nerve ending in my body was screaming for.

My overstimulated brain focused in on his torso. So long and lanky and tan and sweaty. And dirty. Those off-roading trails cutting swathes over his stomach had now reached up to his chest and circled around his neck. And there were bruises mixed with road rash, like maybe he'd been dragged along the concrete at some point. If I hadn't been so preoccupied by the needle pierced through one of his nipples, I might have questioned him on that as well. I wasn't sure I liked the piercing, but I certainly didn't hate it. That sort of summed him up. I shouldn't like him. I shouldn't lust after him. I shouldn't invite him into my car. But I did like him. I did lust for him, and I was absolutely going to invite him into my car.

He approached with that squint in his eyes and that sly smile on his face. Oh wow, the tousled bad boy was on full display. I'd always fancied myself a clean-cut kind of a girl, but Beats was calling my bluff. He was a kind of sexy my racing heart had never experienced before, one of those rare breeds that looked better grubby and all scuffed up. Yet I was convinced Beats had the goods to transcend his setting. Drop him into my high school with a shower, a haircut, and some clean clothes, and every girl in school, including Mia, would be throwing themselves at him. He wouldn't even look my way. But on this side of the tracks, with my trunk packed full of goodies to buy his love, I just might have a shot.

A dreamy smile jumped to my lips as Beats came to a stop at my passenger side window. I rolled it down, trying to remain calm. "You're late."

"You'd be late too if you had to tell time by the placement of the sun and the moon."

"Wait, seriously?"

He smiled. "No."

I laughed, his sarcasm easing my nerves. "Where's your shirt there, Beats?"

"I was hot. I took it off. I didn't think you were an establishment that required it."

Yep. A sharp-mouthed cowboy.

Beats slid a hand over my freshly painted ride.

"Really, Melrose?" He grinned, waggling his brows. "You drive a Bronco?"

"I can explain."

"Go ahead then. I'll wait."

He dropped an arm onto the roof and leaned his head into the open window, still grinning. Oh boy. What had I been thinking coming here alone? Last night, under the streetlamps, he'd seemed manageable, but in the daylight, Beats was clearly way more than I could safely handle. And what the heck was up with his hair? It was like the sweat from last night had dried into a cone on top of his head and then began to peel back like a jester's hat. He was seriously the unruliest guy I'd ever laid eyes on, and all I could think was, where do I sign up?

"Before you assume I'm a spoiled rich girl, this Bronco is not straight off the production line. My dad has had this thing since the early nineties. He insisted on keeping it after the notorious sixty-mile long slow-speed car chase down the Los Angeles freeway, convinced it would one day become a collector's item. But in the process, he basically drove it to the ground. Anyway, long story short..."

"Oh good," he said. "It took two to three business days just to get to this point."

"Shut up," I laughed, speeding through the conclusion which included the car lasting long enough to become cool again and my dad putting in a new engine and giving it a fresh coat of paint so I would have a car to drive.

"The end."

"So... just a piece of advice. If that's the story you're rolling with to prove you're not a spoiled daddy's girl, you might want to tweak the ending."

That smirk—it was enough to lose my train of thought. "Do you want your underwear or not?"

He leaned all the way in. "I want."

I drew in a gulp of courage. *Ask, Grace. Just ask him.* "Hey. You wanna get out of here for a while?"

"Uh..."

With his head still fully inside my vehicle, Beats took a quick scan of the area. Where was this hesitation coming from? Last night, he'd said he'd take anything I had to offer. Well, I was offering, and he wasn't taking.

"Or... you don't have to," I said, giving both him and me an out.

"Where are you planning on taking me, Grace Note?"

"It's a surprise."

"Just a little heads-up—I'm not a huge fan of surprises."

"You'll like this one, I promise."

There was something bothering him. Something holding him back. My only chance of wrangling it out of him was to get him into the car, but that required being bold. Yesterday's nepo baby was not today's leading lady.

"Get in, Beats. Let's go for a ride."

A SMILE LIT up my passenger's face as we stepped out of the car. He was looking up at the monstrosity of slides crisscrossing in all directions. I followed his gaze, gulping. I didn't mind roller coasters or rides with straps on them, but free-falling in a bikini had never been my idea of a good time. *This isn't for you*, I reminded myself. It was for Beats and my quest to give him a day he'd never forget.

"Oh, shit." His mouth was open wide. "You go big with your surprises. I thought you were taking me to a fast-food joint or something."

"I considered that, but then I thought, 'Where can I take Beats that will meet all of his needs in one place?'" I gestured toward the waterslides. "There you go."

"How does a water park meet all my needs?"

"Well, first, you get a shower." I held up a plastic bag full of mini toiletries, plucked from every hotel my father has ever stayed at. "Then food and entertainment and an adrenaline rush. And then, as if all that isn't awesome enough, you get to follow it all up with a nap on the lazy river."

"Sounds amazing. What's the catch?"

"The catch?"

"Yes. What do you want from me? Nothing is free."

He was so jaded. Not that I blamed him, but it screwed up my plans of springing the 'catch' on him until later in the day once I'd buttered him up.

"I'm going to try to convince you to go inside," I admitted.

"What does that mean?"

"Don't you ever get tired of just surviving, Beats?" I asked, choosing my words carefully. "Don't you want more?"

He averted his eyes. "I mean, ideally, I'd like a roof over my head, but it's not that simple."

"What if I could help you?"

"How are you going to do that, Grace? Hide me in your shed?"

"I don't have that part all planned out yet," I said, walking around to the back of the car and opening the trunk. "But I'm working on it."

"So, you're telling me that a teenage girl is going to fix the entire foster care system that has taken years of dysfunction to get to where it is today?"

"I don't have to fix the entire system, Beats. I just have to fix your situation. Baby steps, you see."

His eyes lingered on me for the longest time before finally reconciling with whatever was circulating through his head. "Okay, then. Fix it and I'll come inside."

I didn't believe him. "That seemed a little too easy."

"Because I know you aren't going to fix it."

"Watch me. And once we have you situated, I'm going to help you get auditions. That much I know I can do."

Beats shook his head, appearing more surprised than anything else. "Why? What's in it for you?"

I forced my eyes up, embarrassed. "Isn't it obvious? If you're off the streets, we can hang out together."

He stared at me. "And that's what you want? To hang out with me?"

"Only if you want to."

He didn't answer. I wasn't sure why.

"What's in the box?" he asked, flipping the lid to look. Inside were men's swim shorts in every conceivable waistband size. My mom kept a supply in the pool house for the occasional brother who forgot to bring his over, although she also kept sizes that went all the way back to their childhood. With Beats being so long and lanky, I wasn't sure what would fit his waist, so I brought everything.

"Take your pick."

I watched as he rifled through the lot, holding some up to test the waist. "Does your family own a surf shop or something?"

"I have five brothers... and a pool," I said by way of explanation.

Beats finally settled on a pair of Kyle's old trunks—no surprise considering the two shared a similar body type. We walked side by side to the park's entrance, casting furtive glances at one another as we went. Without his buckets and clothes and baggage to weigh him down, Beats could have passed for any other teenager. And that was the point—to make him feel like a kid again, if only for one day.

My DRUMMER LAY on his back, his eyes closed and his head floating in the water. With his face angled up toward the sun and his body soaking in the rays, Beats was in the REM portion of the afternoon. He'd earned it. From the minute he'd stepped out of the water park bathroom freshly showered and wearing my brother's brightly colored swim trunks, it had been a whirlwind of activity. We spent the time running from one waterslide to the next. Some we rode alone, while on others his arms were firmly around my waist, keeping us locked when we hit the water.

While we waited in the long lines, we got to know each other. I told him all about my family, though leaving out the single most noteworthy bit. It wasn't that I actively wished to deceive Beats, but keeping our budding relationship Jake-free allowed him to focus solely on me, and not what my brother brought to the table. I knew how musicians were, and Jake would be a huge lure.

I might've felt bad about keeping that information away from him had Beats been an open book about his own life. But he wasn't. Not even close. I had to fight and claw for every tiny piece of information, and even then, most of it I suspected wasn't true. See, according to Beats, he had no parents 'that he knew of,' but actually, he might've known who they were. *Huh?* Oh, and he had a sister. Kinda. Sorta. But not really. Couldn't remember her name either. *Okay.* He was a junior in high school; but wait, he was also a senior. And he was born and raised in Los Angeles, although he might've also lived out of state... but probably not. You get the idea.

Beats was lying so hard about his past that I half expected his head to blow off partway through his fictitious storytelling. But I wasn't offended. If Beats felt the need to keep his history close, there had to be a reason, and it wasn't my place to force it out of him. He didn't trust me yet; I got that. He barely knew me. But he would, and someday, I'd be the person who knew all his secrets. And he'd be the one to know all of mine.

There was something else I noticed about Beats as he lied his way through the afternoon. He would alternate from being the animated, flirty smart-ass from our conversation last night to losing himself in thought. I asked him once if everything was okay, but that only led to him playing the finger drums all the way up the staircase to the Aqualoop, and that was a long-ass line. Obviously, something was stressing him, but I knew if he couldn't even get his story straight about what grade he was in school, he certainly wouldn't be spilling the dirt on whatever was bothering him.

Thankfully, all the lying was behind him as he floated down the lazy river with seemingly not a care in the world. For the first time all day, he was still. No tapping of his fingers. No bouncing up and down on his toes. And the stress line between his eyes—the crease that deepened as he scanned the periphery with an eagle's eye—had completely vanished. I thought this might be as close to peace as this boy got, and I felt a sense of victory being the one who gave it to him. Beats would soon return to his world of stress and worry, but for one short, lazy afternoon, he could take a well-deserved breather.

I turned to my side on the inner tube and watched him. God, he was attractive. They say beauty is in the eye of the beholder, but I wasn't going out on a limb here by saying that most people would find him striking, with his medium-length hair, lanky build, and half-naked body. Of course, he came with a few modern upgrades, like a nipple piercing and a bucket lei.

I was used to the guys at my school who were beholden to the norm. Someone like Beats, who was unapologetically himself, was cool without even trying, and I, for one, appreciated his lack of effort. So, it seemed, did many others. I'd noticed girls staring, and I felt a sense of pride being the one walking beside him. If he was aware of how popular he was with the ladies, he didn't let it be known. His focus was on me... and the lies that carried him through the day.

Perhaps sensing me staring, Beats stirred on his inner tube, raising an arm to block out the sun before turning his head and squinting over at me.

"A picture will last longer."

"I know. I've already taken a few."

"You have?" he asked, not seeming entirely thrilled.

"No."

That wasn't true. I'd taken some.

His eyes narrowed. "You're lying."

"You would know."

"What does that mean?"

"Have you said one truthful thing to me all day?"

A smile swept his face as he cast his gaze downward, hair falling over his face. I gulped. "One."

"One? You've said one truthful thing? Wow, Beats, such a

good start." I laughed. "Okay. Let me guess. Was your favorite dog named Bruce?"

"No. I've never had a dog. I've had other people's dogs in houses I've lived in, but none named Bruce."

"So why'd you say that?"

He kept his eye on the water, swirling a finger through it. Apparently, he wasn't going to answer.

"Okay. Can you speak Spanish?"

"No."

"Are you vegan?"

He smiled. "I lick discarded pizza boxes. I'll eat anything that doesn't move, and even a few things that do."

"I'm just confused as to why you're lying to me about your life."

He shrugged. "I thought that's what you'd want to hear."

"Lies? That sort of defeats the purpose of getting to know *you*. So, what was the one truthful thing you said?"

"I actually haven't said it yet," Beats replied, keeping his gaze lowered.

"You can say it. This is your safe space," I said, opening my arms to encompass our surroundings.

He looked up. "You hurt my eyes."

"I what?"

"You hurt my eyes because you're so pretty. That's fact."

His one truth blew me away. And that he'd saved it for me... my heart fluttered.

I wanted so badly to reach over and brush the hair from his eyes, but I didn't dare. "Really? You think so?"

"Like you don't already know."

"I don't. I think you might have an overinflated idea of me, Beats. I'm not a hot commodity at school. Far from it."

"Not possible."

"Uh, very possible."

He arched his brow. "What kind of freaky institution do you go to?"

"One where the girls are way prettier than me."

"Impossible."

"Again, very possible. And they're mean to me."

A slow head shake accentuated the furrows in his forehead. "Because they're jealous. They know you're someone special. One day, Grace Note, the world will fall at your feet."

He sounded so sure of his prediction that he almost made me believe.

"I'd settle for one drummer boy."

Beats' eyes lingered on me before he dropped his hand into the water, midway between our tubes. An invitation. I reached over and accepted it, our fingers lacing together perfectly.

We floated. Just the two of us. The real world felt so far away.

"Someday," Beats said, "I'm going to build a lazy river in my backyard and float all day."

"I like that. Can I come over and visit?"

"No."

"No?" I laughed. "You have this whole make-believe world and you won't let me be a part of it?"

"You don't need an invitation, Grace. Because, in my future world, you live there with me."

I yanked his hand, sending his inner tube careening onto mine, and I kissed him on the cheek. Just a quick peck, but I didn't dare steal more. And then I pushed him away, our inner tubes again a handhold apart.

Beats smiled; no, it was more of a smirk. He knew I wanted him. That I wasn't afraid to take a test ride on his lips. Reaching for the side of the wall, he pulled us both over to the edge, and we discarded our inner tubes. He grabbed my hand and led me out of the lazy river. He seemed to be on a hunt, his head swinging from side to side until he found an acceptable place to ravish me. And I was a willing participant. An outcrop of trees served as our make-out spot. It wasn't ideal, in eyeshot of moms and their toddlers, but what were we supposed to do, wait till the car? Beats' hand flattened onto the small of my back, pressing our bodies together. I felt like a different person with him. Sexual. Desired. I wrapped my arms around his neck, and he lifted me right off my feet. I straddled his waist. His face was right there, water droplets trickling off the strands of his hair, then rolling over his parted lips like an open invitation. Our mouths were so close, the breaths between us hot and ragged.

All this time, I'd waited for a boy to give me my first kiss, but in the end, it was I who took it. Rushing his mouth, my lips crashed into his. There was nothing nice about my first kiss. Nothing sweet and loving and romantic. No, this was... insane. Hot and crazed and wild and wet. Every single thing I'd never, ever imagined. And it was perfect.

Sensations like I'd never experienced flicked some switch inside my body. My nipples hardened, and that dry riverbed between my legs—the one that had long laid thirsty—suddenly swelled with wetness and threatened the levees. As it turned out, kissing was instinctual for me; primal, even. Beats, who probably thought he'd be leading the way, was now simply reacting, fervently trying to keep the clinging feline he'd just inherited from using his body as a scratching post.

Not that he needed sympathy. Or guidance. With my body shaking in his arms, Beats slid a hand down and hooked it under my ass. His thumb absently slipped between my legs, over my bikini bottoms. I tipped my head back, and my lower body convulsed. Beats took advantage of my vulnerable neck, sliding a tongue along it in such a sensuous glide that blood flooded my core and I ground myself into his thumb. The levee had been breached.

"Grace..." His breathing was coming out in ragged grunts,

and I could see him scanning the area behind us, only this time he wasn't on the lookout for an enemy ambush but for a place to bring his unexpected find.

We were making a scene, but I didn't care. Beats could have me here, against a tree, if he wanted to. Thankfully, he had more sense than me, lowering me to my feet and nearly dragging me behind him like a Tarzan with his Jane. We both spotted it at the same time: a towel hut that appeared to be abandoned. I don't think either one of us thought it would open, but when Beats tried the door, it was mercifully unlocked. He looked at me. I looked at him. Then I pushed him in.

Beats shut the door behind us by pushing me up against it. Suddenly, I was back in his arms, my legs wrapped around his waist, and his palm was on my breast, under my bikini top, massaging. Pinching. If I hadn't been a hot, trembling mess of need before this, I was now. Especially when his thumb found its way back to my core, sliding over the thin cloth of my bottoms. His fingers never invaded. They didn't have to. He was taking me to a place I'd never been by way of touching. Manipulating. It came with little warning, a rush of gratification that contracted every muscle in my body.

My drummer boy silenced my moans with his lips on mine, his body moving to my beat despite not riding that wave with me. It was more than I could've imagined. *He* was more than I could've imagined. Once my body had shaken loose from its quaking, Beats wrapped his arms around my back, taking his pleasure in mine. He kissed my nose, my chin, my cheeks. My lips. How could someone who lived so rough be this kind and gentle?

I decided right then and there that I loved this boy. I didn't care that I'd only known him for a day. I didn't care that he was living hard on the streets. I didn't care that he'd lied his way

through the day. All I cared about was the way he made me feel
—like I was the only one for him. The girl who hurt his eyes.

"I've decided," he said.

"What have you decided?"

"I've decided to let you save me."

12

RORY: LIGHTS OUT

To be saved. I didn't even know what it meant. No one had ever attempted it before. At least not anyone who had my best interests at heart. I'd once thought Nikki would be that person. When we were little, she'd tuck me into bed and whisper, *I'll always protect you, Rory.* I'd believed her. With everything in me, I believed her. And then she'd led me straight to hell.

But Grace wasn't Nikki. She wasn't promising me protection. She was promising me a way out. A future. And I'd be a fool not to take it. Especially after last night. If what Nikki said was true, and they were looking for me, it could mean only one thing: they didn't want me talking. But who would I even tell?

"I don't like this," Grace said, keeping her car idling as she pulled into the well-lit parking lot of a fast-food restaurant. This had been our compromise; I'd told her to drop me off where she'd picked me up and I'd walk the rest of the way, and she'd wanted to drive me right up the motel's front door.

I pointed up at the sign. "Don't be hating on Colonel Sanders."

"Never. I'd just feel better taking you directly to a hotel."

I smiled at her word usage. As if I were staying at a hotel.

Any place that I could bribe my way into tonight would have a crooked *M* in front of it.

"I'm not letting you drive to that part of town. It's too dangerous."

"But it's fine for you?"

"I live there. I survived without you worrying, Grace. And I will continue to survive even after you've bit off every last one of your nails."

She slowly removed her finger from her mouth and smiled. "Just don't forget to at least use their phone to call me when you get there."

I patted my pocket with the number she'd given me along with the wad of cash. I hadn't wanted to accept it, and probably wouldn't have had I not been worried about retribution from my past. Holing up in a motel and staying off my drums until Grace could help find an acceptable foster care solution for me seemed the safest bet. I'd told her about care facilities that catered to at-risk kids like myself. They were more like centers than homes, but they offered both school and vocational studies, and I could stay in them until I aged out of the system. So, yes. I'd agreed to her loan, knowing one day I'd pay her back in full, and then some.

"I will. As long as the room has a phone."

"What kind of hotel doesn't have a phone?"

There was that word again. Hotel. "The kind I stay at. But I promise, Grace. I'll find a way to contact you."

"Tonight?"

"I'll try. Otherwise, tomorrow I'll find a shelter and use their phone."

"Tomorrow," she repeated, laying her head back against the seat and pretending to cry. "Tomorrow is so far away."

I leaned over the console, just staring at her. She was so beautiful. So much more than I should be allowed. I couldn't help but flash back to that moment in the towel hut, her moaning in my arms. I could have had her right there, but I knew well that once innocence was gone, you could never get it back, and I didn't want her to have any regrets. But I also wanted to give her a taste of what to expect when we finally became one.

Grace turned to the side, allowing me full access to her pouty mouth. I closed the gap, sliding my fingers around the back of her neck and pulling her to me. Her lips pressed into mine, and without hesitation, her fingers glided along my bare chest. I hardened at her touch. She noticed, pressing her palm on me.

"No." I moved her hand away.

"I want to."

"Me too, but we can't. Not here."

I kissed her, deep and long. Her mouth parted, and I swiped my tongue along her lips. Tentatively hers touched mine, testing. Curious. We stayed locked like that, our bodies reacting to the heat, and despite my warnings not to touch, I slid my own hand up her shirt and under her bikini top. She gasped when my fingers traced around her nipples. My touch ignited her, like little blasts of static electricity. It was power like I'd never felt before. I had the ability to take her down to the studs, and while I reserved the right to do it sometime soon, it wouldn't be today.

I removed my hand and sat back up. "Jesus, Grace. The things we could do."

She nodded, a dribble of my spit clinging to her swollen lips. "I'm not stopping you."

"I know. That's why I have to leave."

We sat there a second just staring, neither one of us wanting to end this thing we had going but both knowing we had to.

"Meet me around back," Grace said, opening her door. "I've got your clean clothes and a few other things for you. I didn't know what you needed, so I brought everything."

She wasn't kidding. Anything that might help me survive on the streets was in her trunk. Boxes and boxes of supplies. She moved the one of camping gear out of the way.

"You won't be needing this in the hotel. And some of these clothes can probably wait."

A shirt caught my eye, and I slid the box back to rifle through it. It was like stepping into a skater shop—all the brands the kids at school wore that I could never dream of owning. But as much as I wanted these things in my wardrobe, so would everyone else. I'd been jumped for my Goodwill duds. I could only imagine the beatdown her brand name stuff would get me.

"Save these for me," I said, knowing once she got me off the streets, I'd very willingly accept the donation.

"I will. Honestly, Beats, none of this stuff is really necessary, since you'll be sleeping inside, but I do have one thing..." Grace made a show of hiding whatever it was behind her back before whipping it around and dangling it in front of my face. "The holy grail."

I gasped, ripping the Ziploc baggie out of her hands and wasting no time shoving the homemade cookies into my mouth.

"Slow down," she laughed. "There are more where those came from."

I looked around her trunk. "Where?"

"No, I meant like me. I'm your cookie dealer. You stick with me and I'll hook you up like the sugar junkie you are."

This all felt too good to be true; like I would close my eyes and it would have all been a dream. Like when I was a kid and a small bit of fortune would come my way, in the form of a good, loving foster home. But they never lasted. Just as I'd get attached, Nikki would do something shitty and a garbage bag would be thrust in my hand. And away I'd go. What if this thing with Grace was just as fleeting? The fear made me want to back away from her, to protect myself from the losing like I always did.

Grace handed me my laundered clothes, now in gray tote bags.

"It's going to be a long couple of days without you," she said, her words sounding almost ominous. "I wish I didn't have school or I'd come hang out with you."

"I know what we could do if you hung out at my motel," I said, hooking my arm around her waist and pulling her in for a kiss. Her tongue slipped right in. From 'never been kissed before' to this. Damn, Grace was a quick learner.

I walked her to the driver's side door and opened it for her. She slipped into the driver's seat and secured her belt before gripping my face and kissing me again.

"Stay safe," she said between kisses.

"I will."

And I meant it. As soon as I was safely inside my motel room, I wasn't leaving until Grace got me the hell out of here.

MY PROMISE to Grace had been delivered in good faith. In a perfect world, things would have gone according to plan, and I would've stayed safe. Of course, I should've known promises never panned out in my world. They wouldn't this time either. Ten minutes into my trek to the motel, a car screeched to a halt. A man jumped out and pushed me into the alleyway. Pain exploded on the right side of my face. I saw stars just before landing on my back.

"Remember me?" he asked, suddenly straddling my waist. His large hands circled my throat and black dots instantly swarmed my vision. But I saw him. I hadn't forgotten his face. Or his name: Hartman. The hunter who'd destroyed my life before it had ever really begun.

Hartman shook me by the neck, the pressure slowly squeezing out my last remaining air.

Out of nowhere, Nikki latched onto Hartman's back, her screams slicing through the night. "Noooo! Get off him."

Hartman swore, removing one hand from my throat to pitch her off him like she was nothing more than a rag doll. Her scrawny body skidded across the asphalt. The pressure on my throat temporarily subsided, and I forced air back into my lungs. For that split second, I was free. But it didn't last.

"Don't let her fool you, boy." He grimaced, his grip back on my throat and squeezing it tighter. My hands tore at his in a desperate attempt to restore my breathing. "She ratted you out for three capsules of oxy."

"I didn't, Rory," she said, crawling toward me with blood trailing down her face. "Don't listen to him. One of the girls saw me with you last night, and she heard me say your name…"

Nikki didn't get the chance to finish her rebuttal. Hartman backhanded her to the ground with his one free hand. The other one he was continuing to use to crush the life out of me.

"I heard you've been talking."

He let up on my throat long enough for me to answer him.

"I haven't…"

It was the truth. I'd never told a soul what had happened to Nikki and me. Whatever source he had was lying.

"Oh, but you have. We warned you, didn't we?"

Hartman and the men he worked for were so damn arrogant. Did they really think they could operate with impunity? You didn't dabble in the shit they dabbled in and not have people poking through it.

"No, you actually didn't," I dared to defy only to be stopped mid-sentence when my head was lifted from the asphalt and then smashed back into the ground.

"Yeah, well, it was implied," Hartman said, lifting my head up again. The next time it connected with the concrete, darkness shut me down.

PART II

THE BREAK

13

GRACE: FALL IN LINE
PRESENT DAY

We'd formed a line in order of importance. Nothing formal, just a general acceptance of where each of us fit into Quinn's life. Mom and dad were first in to see him after he woke from surgery. They'd birthed him, so I had no real qualms with that. But after them, I came next. And I dared any one of my siblings to contest it. Yes, even though the typical line of succession in our family went something like this: everyone else, then the dog, then the parade of cats, and then me.

Not this time. Quinn and I were a package deal. Had been ever since the day he angrily declared at six years old that the rest of the family wanted us to starve to death. He'd always been dramatic that way, but who could blame him? We had sort of been left on our own. Not dissing Emma—she'd come in the clutch after Jake went missing, taking care of our basic needs. More importantly, when he returned, she hugged us through the turbulent nights when Jake wreaked havoc on our sleep. But the vast majority of each day was spent with just Quinn and me entertaining ourselves.

He was a little dictator back then. Only his play choices were allowed. God forbid I suggest dress-up or Candy Land. He'd fall apart, throwing himself to the floor like a lunatic when he didn't get his way. I learned real quick that Teletubbies was out of the flippin' question. Being his second-in-command during this time must have made me a more compassionate person because every time he shoved a sword in my hand and made me wear an eye patch to play Captain Hook, I didn't kill him. So, yes, I'd paid my dues and earned my spot in the line of succession.

The rest of the family regularly called on me to tame Quinn's combustive personality. The Quinn-whisperer, they called me, but really, he was easy to manage. Quinn didn't want solutions; he just wanted someone to listen, to be patient and understand where he was coming from. That was where my Captain Hook training came in handy. I knew just how much to poke him before he totally shut me down.

It made me sad to think that after what had happened in the arena, my Quinn whispering might not be enough. Once my brother discovered the true toll this night had taken, he might require help of a more professional nature. While he was in surgery, news began arriving of the losses. Concertgoers and stadium staff alike had gone down. But it was the identity of one specific victim that would punch the biggest hole in Quinn's heart. It was tragically revealed that my brother was not the only member of the band felled on the stage tonight. Brandon, Sketch Monster's drummer, was gone before his head hit the floor.

I cringed to think of what that loss would do to my brother. But I could handle it. I'd take an active role in his recovery, putting my own suffering aside to be the support he needed. It was the least I could do after he kept me from starving to death all those years ago, even though his hot dog bologna sandwiches still haunted my dreams. So yes, I could confidently claim to be number three on Quinn's guest list.

Only to my shock and horror, I wasn't.

It was Jess. I watched as my mother went straight to her after leaving Quinn's room. My mouth dropped open. He'd requested her. Of course he had. What had I been thinking? Jess was his fiancée now, the new most important woman in his life. A lump formed in my throat. I wasn't sure my heart could take the bump in numbers. She'd just replaced me at number three. Wait, no—Mom and Dad, going in to see him first, had assumed wrong. Jess was number one. Goosebumps sprouted up over my forearms as if the tiny muscles under my skin were also coming to terms with the loss.

Don't get me wrong—I loved Jess and she was the perfect match for my thorny brother—but Quinn had always been mine. I wasn't ready to give him up, even though I had no choice in the matter. The last thing I wanted was to hold my brother back. He'd found this beautiful, spunky woman and inherited an adorable built-in son. They were his destiny now, just as building a life with Elliott was mine. I blinked. And blinked again realizing at that moment I didn't want Elliott at the top of my post-surgery list. But who? I manually ran the alternates through my head, and literally every member of my family came before him.

What? No. That couldn't be right. I recalculated, but came to the same total. It was then I knew—Elliott would never be my Jess.

And the goosebumps spread.

I glanced in his direction. Elliott was way ahead of me, already smiling as if he'd been waiting for his chance to cheer me up. I left him hanging, shifting my gaze back to Jess and my mom, watching from my place of utter insignificance as they spoke and then hugged. But instead of heading straight to my brother's hospital room, my future sister-in-law took a detour toward me. I didn't know why I wanted to hide.

Stopping at my seat, she held out her hand. I took hold, and

she pulled me to my feet. She must've seen the tears of acceptance welling in my eyes. Like me, she understood the impact of
the moment. This was the passing of the torch. From today
forward, she would replace me in the most significant moments
of Quinn's life, and I would allow it to happen because I loved
him. I loved him so much that I would not hold him back no
matter how much it hurt my heart.

Jess drew me into a hug and whispered, "Do you want to go
first?"

"Yes," I admitted with a shallow giggle-sob. "But it has to be
you."

She leaned out of our hug and looked me in the eyes. "I want
you to be okay with that, Grace."

Tears now slid down my cheeks. "I am. But only for you."

She wiped my tears away, then kissed my cheek before she
carried the flame into my beloved brother's hospital room.

I'd just slipped into Quinn's fourth position, and somehow,
I'd survived.

NOT LONG AFTER, I pushed the door open to Quinn's dimmed
room. Machines were moving and humming, but my brother
looked surprisingly strong and whole. I wasn't sure what I'd
been expecting, but Quinn had always taken the role of hero for
himself and, of course, he would claim it now.

"Hi," I said, stopping at the foot of his bed.

He got right to the point. "I heard my fiancée made you cry."

"Right? What's up with that? You need to have a talk with
her."

As if it took all his resolve, Quinn smiled and opened his one
good arm for me. I slunk over to him and laid my head on his
chest.

"Thank you," he whispered into my hair.

"For what?"

"You know for what."

I nodded. I'd relinquished control without a battle. If the roles were reversed, Quinn would've pushed Elliott aside... and I would have wanted him to. Those pesky tears I never cried came roaring back. I wasn't used to being so delicate, like sand falling through an hourglass.

"Sorry," I said, sitting back up and wiping away the tears. "It's been a rough day."

"Mine hasn't been great either," he replied.

"I know. But mine was worse," I hiccupped out a laughing cry. "I even wiped Elliott's kiss off my face."

"No, you didn't." He winced through the hard-fought chuckle.

"Oh, but I did."

"Why?"

"Because I was mad at him."

"How'd that go over?" he asked.

"Oh, you know, about as well as can be expected."

Quinn croaked out a laugh. "It's that evil streak. You might have everyone else fooled, but I've got your number."

I raised a finger to my lips. "Shhh. That's our secret. You don't want me to reveal yours, do you?"

"Oh my god, Grace. When are you ever going to shut up about that?"

"What? It doesn't make you less of a man for liking *Bridget Jones*."

Quinn attempted to protest, but that led to him wincing.

"Is this morphine?" I asked, pointing to the clear bag hanging from a hook. "Are you in pain? Do you want me to squeeze it? Because I will. I'll strangle the little sucker until you're high as a kite."

"No, just stop making me laugh."

"Would you prefer I make you cry? Because I can do that too."

"I already did."

"Cry?" I cocked my head into the dog-shock position. It wasn't often I saw my brother cry. Tantrum crying, yes, but real, emotional tears were something he avoided at all costs. Quinn had always been stoic like that.

"I told you I had a bad day."

I smoothed down his hair, my face twisting at the memory. "Bad day doesn't quite describe it, does it?"

"No," his voice cracked. "No, it doesn't."

"I'm so sorry about Brandon."

His jaw clenched and he looked away, but that didn't stop the words from coming. "I can't get it out of my head, Grace. We were all talking backstage, and he was being a punk like always, trying to embarrass Tucker with his request for anal beads after the show. How can he be gone?"

Quinn's hands trembled, an indication of his profound shock. I grabbed them both in mine and held them steady, tipping my head to his and allowing him the time to mourn for his friend. I might not be Quinn's plus one anymore, but I still knew him better than anyone else in this world, and I knew he would suffer this loss for a long time to come.

"I have so much anger right now," I admitted. "Like I'm going to explode. I watched you go down, Quinn. I could see you lying up there on the stage. I tried to get to you, but Elliott..." I clenched my teeth. "Elliott held me down. He wouldn't let me climb onto the stage to help you."

"Good."

"No, not good. Do you have any idea what I would have done to him if he'd prevented me from saving you and you'd died?"

"That didn't happen."

"But it could have. I was already plotting Elliott's murder under those chairs when I heard your voice. There you were stumbling over to us with a bullet in your chest and then somehow, you go into commando mode and save us all through an exit under the stage. You did all that and I couldn't even shove one machismo hero off my back."

"You always were a weakling."

"Hey," I laughed.

"Seriously, though, don't be pissed at Elliott. He was just reacting. We all were. There are a lot worse things than a guy's instinct kicking in to save his girl."

"I didn't ask him to."

"You didn't have to. He did it because he loves you, like I love Jess. I'd do anything to protect her. And Elliott proved he'd do the same for you."

The whole left side of my face went numb, like I'd stroked out at the very thought of Elliott and Jess being in the same category. She was going to marry Quinn and be by his side the rest of his life. I couldn't imagine holding Elliott's hand on the day I died.

I loved him; I did. But not the way Quinn loved Jess. Or any of my siblings loved their significant others. Elliott and I were friends. Lovers. But we weren't soulmates. Not like Rory and me had once been. Did it matter?

"You all right?" Quinn asked.

I nodded.

"No, you're not. What aren't you telling me?"

"You don't need to hear my petty concerns."

"No, but I want to. Unless it's about frappuccinos. I don't want to hear about that."

"Right." I smiled. "Of course not. Okay, here it goes. What if I don't actually love Elliott in an 'all or none' sort of way? Is it wrong for me to build a life with him knowing it's the best my heart will get?"

I'd already lost Quinn. Totally blank stare. Honestly, he probably would've preferred a conversation about a caramel skinny vanilla decaf frap.

"Hear me out. I'm just being realistic. Lightning almost never strikes the same person twice, so if I've already been struck, then Elliott's not my bolt of electricity. But that doesn't mean I can't build a loving, stable life with him and be happy that way. Right?"

He stared back with a glassy-eyed expression.

"I think so too." I breathed in deeply, allowing a sense of calm to fall over me. "I've already experienced true love, so there's no sense in waiting around for it to happen again. Don't you think?"

Quinn slowly nodded, like he wasn't quite sure what he was agreeing to but instinctively understood the direction I was heading.

"I feel better now," I said, leaning over to kiss his cheek. "Thank you."

"On second thought, Grace. Can you give the bag a little squeeze?"

14

RORY: OLD FRIENDS

Three simple words. That's what they were. Apart, they meant nothing, but together they were a rallying cry. *Bring it on.* I couldn't sleep that night, nor the night after. My brain held on to the words, repeating them over and over even during the most mundane of tasks. Washing dishes. Eating dinner. Fixing cars. *Bring it on.*

Only problem—I wasn't sure what my subconscious mind was telling me. Was I supposed to move forward or circle back? Maybe for some it would be an easy decision but not for me. Hell, I couldn't even decide who I was. Even though I'd told Jake I was using my real name again, I was straddling between my old identity and my new. For work purposes, I was still Rory Robinson, the son of a welder and his occupational therapist wife but only because all my job experience went through him. For everything else—which was nothing really—I considered myself Rory Higgins. Yeah, I know. It was confusing as shit.

I probably should have kept hold of my picture-perfect past, the one that had been specifically crafted for me courtesy of the US Marshals Service. In that fictional world, I'd grown up in a sprawling ranch house with a brother and a sister and a trampoline out back. We were a happy family, or so it had been written. None of it existed, of course, but I'd had to memorize the details all the same.

The first day under my new alias, I remember sitting at the round four-person dining table by myself and staring at my updated ID card, thinking that at least they'd given me a false identity I could be proud of. A dad I could watch the big game with. A mom who'd bake me cookies. A home to celebrate Christmas in. I'd never had that. No parents. No siblings. The closest I'd ever come to a real family was the McKallisters, and, well, that did not end well. Not that I'd had much of a choice once my past came for me and threatened the ones I loved. I'd given them up but not easily.

For years I lived in limbo as Rory Robinson, working an unassuming life as a mechanic while quietly being prepped for trial as the star witness for the Department of Justice. There were supposed to be two of us, but Nikki skipped out well before the trial began, leaving me to testify alone. I bared my soul and gave those who deserved it a one-way ticket to life in prison. I'd kept my word. My job was done. And everyone was happy but me. I wanted my old life back, the one with Grace and the McKallisters, even if I knew it would never happen.

I clung to Rory Robinson as long as I could. But it got to the point where everything felt wrong, like an alien assuming control of me. I was now nothing but the host human. I didn't see the point of pretending anymore. Alias me had nothing to offer. It was like my fake life dissolved after my real one settled the score.

Asking for my old identity back, such as it was, I returned to Los Angeles with nothing to show for my twenty-three years except the clothes on my back. Not because I couldn't have taken Rory Robinson's things with me; I just didn't want anything that was his. If I was going to shed his skin, I had to leave every part of him behind.

This was me moving forward... or was it back? I still wasn't sure. But I was tired of both. What I wanted was to carve myself a new life free from the spoilers of the past and the nothingness of my future. I wanted to drop myself back into the only time in my life when I had been happy and loved. A time when a bright future seemed all but guaranteed. I'd had that once, and I could have it again... if I brought some old friends back from the past.

I stood up and walked into the bedroom, circling the mattress on the floor until I arrived at the only piece of furniture within these four walls—a side table with a broken drawer that I'd thrifted from beside a dumpster. One man's trash was another man's treasure, and this one served just one purpose. I forced the drawer open and stared down at a pair of well-worn sticks, the ones Michelle McKallister had gifted to me that night in the rec center. The ones she'd used to train the bad habits right out of me. The ones I'd been clutching like a security blanket the night the black van picked me up and whisked me away from the bright future I was forced to give up when the past came knocking at my door.

During all the security briefings, I'd been "strongly advised" to abandon the drums because they would attract too much attention and put a target on my back. I understood, yet it had pained me all the same. In the early days as talentless Rory Robinson, I'd sometimes bring my sticks out and draw out a beat on a table or chair, but soon, even that thrill was lost. With no dream to carry me through, drumming was just a hobby, and hobbies were things people did as a mental escape. And since there was no escaping my crucified brain or the trial that loomed over me like the mother ship, I just stopped playing.

These abandoned sticks were the key to it all. With them I could take back what I'd lost. The life I'd always wanted came at the end of these sticks. The career I dreamed of. The respect and adoration I craved. The redemption I'd paid my dues to gain. And Grace. Yes, I heard what she said—that she was in love with another—but it wasn't true. No matter how brutally she'd annihilated me in that bathroom, I knew it was her anger talking. If I could explain to her why I'd left, why I'd made the choices I did, and who the girl was she thought I was cheating on her with, then maybe I could make her see.

But first I had to win her back, and the only way to do that was by resurrecting the boy from the past she couldn't resist. I could be *him* again if I just picked up the sticks. Yet there was some invisible force holding me back. Since when had they become my kryptonite? They were just sticks, nothing more. The power in them came from me. From what I could do with them. I alone could bring them back to life.

Reaching down, I snagged my old sticks from their dusty coffin.

Bring it on.

15

GRACE: CURB APPEAL

Elliott and I didn't make it through the night of the shooting. That was when I officially clocked out of the relationship. Not that he knew at that point, but I did. I just needed to figure out a way to break it to him. It was easy to blame our demise on the visit from Rory, but the truth was I'd had doubts well before his reappearance. Moving into my parents' place was the beginning of our end. Rory just closed the door behind us.

But breaking up with Elliott in my mind was not the same as breaking up with him in person. It took weeks for me to summon the courage. Weeks of getting my talking points in order. Weeks of watching him grow closer to my family. But I finally gathered up my bravery and did it. I sat him down and told him the truth of how I was feeling, that the relationship just wasn't working for me, and that I wanted to go our separate ways. Elliott was quiet. Emotional. He fought for us. And then, in the end, he said he wouldn't accept the breakup.

Like, he totally refused.

I'd had a few of short-lived boyfriends in college and had become familiar with the breakup process. From what I could recall, it had been fairly straightforward. One of us said we weren't feeling it. The other left. The end.

But Elliott? Oh no. He wasn't leaving until certain demands were met. The main one was that I had to give him a month to win me back. Why a month? Because that was when his visa ran out and he had to return to England anyway. So romantic. The original plan had been that I would return with him, and we would travel through Europe until the waiting period was over and we could fly back to the States and get an apartment together. Now he would return home alone on his nonrefundable, unchangeable plane ticket. When his visa ran out.

And when that time came, he insisted, I'd be on that plane with him. I was adamant I wouldn't.

That was when the games began.

"No, no, no." Elliott swooped in to grab the platter of fruit and cheese out of my hands on his way back from the bedroom where he'd gone to change into basketball shorts. "Graduation girl doesn't need to lift a finger on her special day."

My college graduation fell during Elliott's grace period. Actually, it was an informal graduation, as I'd completed all my courses in the middle of the year and had to wait until the summer to actually walk. But that didn't stop my parents from prematurely celebrating my accomplishment anyway.

It was a festive affair. Quinn had been out of the hospital for well over month and was recovering in the pool house at our parents' home. It wasn't what he'd wanted, but the little apartment he shared with Jess and her son was wholly inadequate for the deluge of reporters and fans that descended upon him. Sketch Monsters, a new band before the shooting, suddenly saw its songs soar to the top of the charts, including the one I'd written. Quinn had everything he'd ever wanted—fame, fortune, and his name in lights beside our brother's—but the sacrifices made to get the band there were also tearing him apart.

Elliott might still be hoping to win me back and take me on that trip to Europe, but there was no way I was leaving Quinn in his current state. Or mine. Nightmares plagued my sleep, making returning to a normal routine nearly impossible, but I kept my own issues at bay to be a rock for those who really needed it.

"Ah, thanks. Are you sure?" I cooed to Elliott, not waiting for the answer as I relinquished the fruit platter to him and slid back onto the bar stool next to Emma.

"Of course, anything for you, luv," Elliott cheerfully replied. "I'm heading outside anyway. Stay and chat with your sister."

Balancing the tray, he winked at Emma, then bent down to kiss my cheek.

"You're the best," I said, trying not to laugh at the absolute, over-the-top show of awesomeness he was displaying for my family's benefit. They didn't know we were broken up—another one of his demands. I suppose his plan was to make them adore him so much that if he was going down, I'd be right there with him.

"Oh, and babe?" I stopped him in his mid-jog out the door. There was a game of pickup basketball about to start, and I knew he didn't want to miss it. "Did you get me my lip gloss?"

"Your what?"

"My lip gloss," I repeated patiently. "You know, the one with the cute little bear holding a clover. I asked you to get it for me when you ran by on your way to the room."

He stopped, tray in hand, his eyes narrowing. "No, I don't recall you asking."

"Oh, I did. Remember, Emma?" I turned to my sister but didn't wait on her reply. This was the first time Emma was hearing the request too. But if Elliott was going to kill me with kindness, I would ricochet it right back at him. "I really do need my gloss."

"Right. You want some lip balm featuring a bear holding a meat cleaver, am I hearing you correctly?"

"Not quite." I was overly patient in my reply. "It's a clover. You know, like a four-leaf one?"

"And you need it right this instant?"

"I mean, my lips are really chapped."

He glanced out the large opening, where accordion doors had been pushed aside to make for a true indoor-outdoor living space. From Elliott's vantage point, he could clearly see my brothers practicing their shots. It was a place he desperately wanted to be.

"Right, I get that," Elliott said. "But it's upstairs and on the other side of the house. The schoolyard pick is about to start."

"Oh." I cast my eyes down. "Okay. Never mind."

Elliott shifted his feet, deciding. "No. I'll do it. Where is this lip balm you speak of?"

"In my bathroom. The cabinet to the right when you first walk in. Left side of the double vanity. Second drawer down. You might need to rummage a bit."

A flash of irritation passed over his features before he steadied his reaction and set the tray of cheese and fruit back down.

"Actually, Elliott"—I made a whole show of grimacing—"my mom wanted that tray right away. Can you take it outside to her first, and then go get me the bear with the cleaver... I mean, clover?"

He sucked in a breath before responding with a bow and all the gallantry his British accent afforded him. "As you wish."

"Ah, thanks, Pooh bear." I matched his game and raised him one.

Emma waited for Elliott to walk out to the back patio before she threw a chunk of bread at my chest. "You diabolical bitch."

I laughed, throwing the chunk back at her. After a quick scan for spies, I lowered my voice and addressed the only member of the family who knew the truth. "Hey, this isn't my fault. I broke up with him. He's free to go at any time."

"That's not usually how breakups work. You say bye, and then..." Emma waved her hand. "He goes bye-bye."

"But, Emma, he has"—I changed my voice to mimic Elliott's oft-used line—"a nonrefundable, unchangeable plane ticket."

"Yes, I know. But there's this thing called a hotel. It's where ex-boyfriends go when they're waiting out their visas. This is not a democracy, Grace. He doesn't get a vote. Unless..."

Just by the hesitation in her voice, I knew what she was going to say.

"No," I stopped her. "Don't say it."

"You don't want Elliott to leave."

She said it. I dropped my head onto the kitchen island and rolled it around. "Emma," I whined.

"What? It has to be said, Grace. The dude's likeable. I mean, even I like him, and I hardly like anyone."

"Ugghhh, stop making me feel bad."

"I'm not trying to. But I think maybe with all that's happened in the past two months, you're struggling with your emotions, and this could be a decision you regret later. If you take a step back, you'll see that Elliott's a catch."

"I know he's a catch." I sighed. "Don't you think I wanted this to work? Here, let me put it a different way. How do you feel when Finn walks in the room?"

She thought for a second. "Like I can't believe he wanted me."

I lifted my head and blinked. "I was thinking more along the lines of you wanting to push him into the pantry and have your way with him, but we'll go with your very sad self-reflection instead."

Emma laughed, pushing me. "Sex in the pantry? Are you crazy? What if any items inside were to get misaligned, or worse, soiled?"

That was where my sister and I differed. She needed sterility and candles and soft music and gentle foreplay. I'd started my sexual explorations with Rory Higgins. We went right for the action, so for me, any old car or shed would do.

I sighed. "Now I don't even remember what I was asking."

"You wanted to know how I felt about Finn walking into a room, and my new answer is—I can't imagine loving anyone more."

"Bingo. That's the problem, Em. I'd love to be friends with Elliott, but as far as the love part, I don't."

"Well, I love Elliott," Emma said. "And so does the rest of the family."

"Then you marry him."

She flashed me her wedding ring. "See that guy out there hanging off the basketball rim? I got my hands full with him."

That she did. Keeping Finn on solid ground couldn't be easy. He was her stuntman turned actor, known for his high-flying antics and the best head of curls on the planet. He was my sister's opposite in every way, yet still, they'd found each other.

"Shhh," I whispered. "Elliott's coming back."

"One cheese platter delivered." He jogged through the door and right past me, yelling out on his way down the hall. "Your mother says hi. Now I'm off to retrieve the fucking bear with a cleaver because I certainly don't want my pookie's lips to slough off."

I held a finger in the air. "Clover."

Once he was gone, I turned to Emma. "There's no lip gloss. That's my tampon drawer."

"You're a terrible human," she replied, laughing. "Just truly awful."

"Hey, if he insists on staying, then let's see what he's made of."

Emma shook her head. "Please tell me he's not still sleeping in your bed."

"No, he's on the chaise longue."

"Okay, but he's still in your room."

"Yes."

"Talk about sending him mixed signals, Grace."

"There are no mixed signals. I've been very clear with him. No intimacy. And honestly, Emma, I don't think he's all that into me anyway. I think he just wants to be part of the family. Hell, he'd marry Dad if he could. Have you seen their secret handshake? It's got fourteen components to it."

"Dad went through that shiny, new son stage with Finn too."

"Not the same thing. Finn didn't save your life. Finn doesn't have a British accent. And don't forget, Finn knocked you up repeatedly."

"I've been pregnant twice."

We halted our conversation when the sound of panting drew closer. Elliott rounded the corner, slid to a stop in front of me, and instead of placing a tiny tube of chapstick in front of me, handed me the entire bathroom drawer.

Bending over, he grabbed his knees to catch his breath.

"There is no bear." Pant.

"There is no clover." Pant.

"There is no meat cleaver." Pant.

"There is no lip balm." Pant.

"Can I go play now?"

Our eyes locked. He smiled, and I instantly recognized that Old World charm I'd fallen for in the café on the corner. He was trying to win me back, and if I wasn't careful, he'd do it. Shit. I had to stop being so adorable or I'd be right back where I started.

"Sure," I said. "Go play."

He grabbed my cheeks and planted a sweaty kiss on my lips before racing out the back door.

I turned back to Emma, who resembled a wide-eyed emoji.

"What?" I shrugged.

"You think he's leaving, Grace? He's never leaving."

"GRAB A DRINK EVERYONE. A toast to Twinkle," Dad said, using an old nickname of mine. "Oh, and Quinn, no alcohol. I think we have an IV bag lying around here somewhere for you."

"Where did that even come from?" Quinn asked, lifting his hands in protest. "I've taken three ibuprofen in the past week. God, you're such an ass."

Giggles erupted out on the patio where we'd all gathered after dinner to celebrate my sort-of graduation. Currently, I was snuggled up against Elliott, but not by choice. He'd forced himself into the wedge between my hip and the armrest of the outdoor sofa. He was sitting sideways, his arms at his sides like a rocket ship. I could scoot over, but his comfort was no longer my concern.

"Why are you called Twinkle?" Elliott asked.

I glanced over at my brother. "Kyle? You wanna take this?"

"I was like ten. Grace was maybe two. I was trying to concentrate on a show, and she stood right in front of the TV and sang 'Twinkle, Twinkle, Little Star' over and over. I threw the remote at her and screamed, 'Would someone shut Twinkle up?' It stuck."

"Ah, yes." I grinned. "A living reminder of your impatience.

And now, whenever I'm slightly louder than the accepted norm, he calls me Twinkle."

His wife Kenzie elbowed him. "She was two, you jerk."

"What?" Kyle defended himself. "Keith called me Velociraptor until I was twenty."

"Hey," Keith jumped in. "That was totally justified. You got sent home in kindergarten for chewing the buttons off your shirt and spitting them across the room."

Elliott's head volleyed back and forth between my brothers. He loved this. I knew my family was one of the reasons he was holding on to me so tight, but that wasn't enough for me to keep him.

My mother ignored the malicious nickname game as she passed out juice packets to all the kids so they too could participate in the toast. Jake's son, Slater, had other plans. He always did. Immediately, the adorable terror squeezed his juice packet like a liquefied bomb, forcing the built-up pressure up through the straw and sending a geyser of fruit punch into the air. Casey sprang into action, sacrificing herself for the good of the others. While she did manage to redirect most of the flow, it was too late for Keith, who had droplets of juice dripping off the ends of his surfer dude hair. If anyone had to take a direct hit, Keith was the best man for the job. He was totally unfazed, shaking it off like a dog in a downpour, in the process soiling his wife. Sam didn't blink.

As Casey cleaned up the mess, Slater inexplicably began stripping. Her eyes widened. "Oh my god, Slater, no. Put your pants back on!"

She then turned on her unresponsive husband. "Jake!"

My brother shot up on command, grabbing his half-naked son and throwing him over his shoulder.

Slater made his argument from his upside-down position. "My wiener wants to come out and see people."

A smile swept Jake's face. "Yeah, well, it's a little early for your wiener to be thinking for you, bud."

"Slater," my dad called. "Why don't you come over here and help me with Auntie Grace's toast?"

Jake walked him over to our distracted dad and waited to pass him over.

Dad glanced up. "Just drop him anywhere."

"On his head?" Jake responded with amusement. "Not sure Casey would allow it."

"I dropped you boys on your heads all the time. Which, in hindsight, might explain why none of you graduated college."

"Mitch graduated," Jake said.

"Right, but Mitch only lived with us half-time, so I dropped him on his head fifty percent less than I dropped you boys."

"Only us boys?" Quinn asked. "You didn't drop Emma or Grace?"

"God, no. I wouldn't do that."

"Don't listen to your father," Mom said, taking Slater out of Jake's hands and flipping him upright onto her lap. "I can assure you he didn't drop any one of you. If he had, he wouldn't be alive today."

"Wait." Kyle cut into the conversation. "Is that why it took me four tries to pass my driver's test at the DMV?"

"Let me just put it this way, son." Dad could barely contain his amusement. "You know the old saying, 'If you put your mind to it, you can do anything'? Well, you can't. None of you boys can."

Keith rolled his eyes. "You talk an awful lot of smack for a guy who falls over while he's putting on his underwear."

"I fall over because I have big feet."

"Then angle your damn foot." Keith laughed. "It's not rocket science. Jesus, old man. Don't make me put you in a home."

The laughter was like a rolling thunder, getting louder and

louder as it traveled through the gathering of my relatives. The key to Dad's humor was to never take him seriously. He was as good as a stand-up comedian in our family. Clearly Elliott, laughing beside me, didn't take him seriously. It was one thing I loved about my counterfeit boyfriend—soon to be ex-boyfriend once his visa expired. Elliott's lightness was what had attracted me to him in the first place. He was fun and easygoing, like my father.

Wait. Oh, shit.

Was he... was he... my father? Had I picked a man just like him? If so, that wasn't so bad. My dad was the best man I'd ever known. Loving. Kind. Funny. And despite his jokes to the contrary, he would never do anything to put his kids in harm's way. Ever. I should be so lucky to have a man like him.

"To answer your question, Kyle," Jake said, returning to his seat after being relieved of his childcare duties, "you kept failing your driver's test because you couldn't get out of the parking lot."

"The curb!" I yelled, giggling.

"Not the curb." Keith palmed his face. He was the first to discover it, failing his inaugural driver's test because his tire went up and over the concrete edging. The raised sidewalk at the right turn out of the DMV parking lot had been the killer of thousands of teenage cruisers' dreams. If your tire even grazed it, you were done for. Automatic fail. It got Keith twice, Emma once, and Jake once. But Kyle... Poor Kyle. He hit that curb over and over and over, forcing my father to drive him to another city where he could at least get out of the parking lot. After Kyle, Dad took Quinn directly to a curbless DMV in the other city, and he passed on the first try.

Me? I didn't want to take the easy way out. I wanted to be the first McKallister to conquer the curb. I'd always been determined like that, making decisions quickly and sticking to them. Which explained Rory and the risky choices I'd made right after meeting him. Sometimes, I looked back and wondered what I was thinking, if it had been worth the risk. An image of Beats in his youth popped into my head—that wild hair, that confident smirk, those sticks spinning in his hands—oh yeah, he'd been worth it.

"I don't think Grace gets enough credit for passing the curb challenge," Emma said.

I raised my hands in the air and did a little victory dance.

"She brought it for this family," Keith agreed. "I wish we had an old participation trophy we could offer her. Quinn, you probably have a few."

Quinn scoffed, flipping Keith off with his good arm. Even he knew not to verbalize his displeasure with the scores of my siblings' kids running around. I glanced around at the hectic scene. Once my siblings started having kids, it was happy chaos all the time. I loved being Auntie Grace to the rowdy pack of rug rats, but I loved just as much to shut the door behind me at the end of the night.

I think maybe that was the first sign that Elliott might not be compatible for me because as soon as he saw my siblings with their kids, he began talking about ours—the fictional ones he seemed convinced we would have. It made me realize that the two of us were at very different places in our lives. While I was just starting out, Elliott was ready to settle down. It was true he was still in college, but he'd been a successful day trader for years, earning a strong income right out of high school, and only later enrolled in college to bolster his resume. By then he'd already set himself up nicely, owning a home back in London and even contributing to a retirement plan like such a big boy.

If anyone was ready to settle down and start a family, it was Elliott. But I wasn't there yet. Songwriting was my passion, not marriage and kids. I wanted to work with other musicians. Travel with the band. All I knew was I wanted to be free. And I couldn't do that with a husband and kids waiting back home for me.

Dad tapped a spoon to his glass to get the room's attention.

"Everyone, raise a glass to my baby girl. Or a Capri Sun—except for you, Slater. You lost your juice packet privileges." Dad cleared his throat, sincerity taking hold. "Grace, honey, I think I speak for all of us when I say how proud we are of you. You always work hard and never need congratulations. You just put your head down and make it happen with a smile on your face. It's hard to believe my baby is old enough to hold a diploma in her hand—or I guess you won't get that until May—anyway, my point is, you make all of our lives better. You always have. From the moment I laid eyes on you in the hospital, I was a goner. So, to my precious daughter, always keep your spirit burning bright because that's how good things will find their way into your light."

Dad nodded his head toward Elliott before redirecting his gaze to me. "Congratulations, honey. I'm a proud, proud man."

I dislodged from Elliott and crossed the room, flinging myself into the arms of the best man I knew. But as I buried my head in his chest, a frown took hold. How could I love this man so much, yet not his doppelganger over there on the sofa? Maybe I was making a mistake. Maybe I needed to try harder to love Elliott.

"Wow, as always, your father upstages me," Mom said, laughing. "I can't follow that, but I can second the motion. You are everything your father says and more."

The rest of her speech was blubbered into my ear as she hugged me to her. I understood none of it, but the message was clear: I was loved. The rest of my family piled on the affection until it dissolved into a roast of sorts, with a smattering of favorite memories to make it somewhat nice.

"Okay," Emma laughed. "Remember the time she sneezed

and then looked up at me with her innocent little eyes and said, 'Emma, I think I have the bless yous'?"

"My favorite Grace memory was the time we were watching *Avatar* and she asked how the Smurfs grew up so fast." Keith reached over and punched my arm. "God, you were so dumb."

"Okay, but in her defense," Quinn said, "I actually had the same question. She just beat me to it."

"And what was up with that imaginary friend of yours?" Kyle asked. "What was his name again?"

My throat tightened on a sharp inhalation.

"Oh, yeah. The Reindeer Man. Where did *that* come from?"

I cast an unintentional glance in Jake's direction. Don't know why; I just did. To my shock, he was staring back. Our eyes met for a split second before we both looked away. A chill rattled my bones. Did Jake know who the Reindeer Man was?

If he did, then he'd heard me.

And he knew what I knew.

16

RORY: A BAND WITH NO NAME

The stakes couldn't be higher. This was the fourth band I'd auditioned for this week, and I already had two offers and one callback. The original idea had been to take whatever opportunity came my way, but after posting a highlight reel of my skills on a musical matching app, I was flooded with interest from local bands and even some from out of state. Suddenly, I found myself in the enviable position to pick and choose.

This was my best prospect yet: a rock band being formed by the lead singer of a semi-successful band that had recently broken up. This guy already had contacts and an actual shot at getting his foot in the door. I wanted this bad, but I wasn't the only one. I arrived hoping it would just be me auditioning, as it had been at the other tryouts, but that was wishful thinking. Four others were ahead of me and one behind. I waited out in the hall, forced to listen to my competition.

I wondered what my chances would have been against this talented group if Mrs. M hadn't gotten to me when she did, correcting all the quirks I didn't know I had. I was eighteen and full of cocky swagger, believing in the hype of the crowds that gathered around me when I played my buckets on the streets. Mrs. M saw my talent but knew I had so much more to give. She brought me back to earth and made me work for every victory. Any magic that came out of my sticks now had her stamp of approval on it.

The guy in front of me in line was on the drums now. Shit, he was good. But I was better. It had been a couple of months since I'd rescued my sticks from the drawer and walked straight to a home improvement store to buy some buckets. That night I was on Hollywood Boulevard, testing my wings. By the end of the night, I was owning my performance and could feel everything falling back into place.

Every night after work, I played, sometimes on the streets and sometimes at my old stomping ground—the recreation room where I'd first met Mrs. M. Not that I knew who she was at the time. All I knew was she volunteered with a music therapy program for foster teens and young adults who'd aged out of the system. I had no interest in the therapy part. What drew me there was the drum set.

The staff at the transitional housing center where I'd once lived had welcomed me home, opening the room for me when it wasn't in use to practice. And I'd pushed on, feeling Grace and Michelle in that room with me as I ramped up my skills in preparation for an audition just like this one. So, yes, I was better because none of these guys had been taught by the same woman who'd molded a superstar.

When it was my turn, I played with ferocity, energy emanating from every pore. I was swinging from the rafters on this one, knowing if I didn't get the gig, I'd be pissed. I needed a win. Something. Anything.

Applause followed my set. The lead singer, Cap, approached, reaching out a fist, and I bumped it.

"Nice."

I grinned, remembering when Mrs. M had said that to me

the first time I played for her, only her *very nice* wasn't as complimentary as Cap's.

He nodded, looking me over. "You primarily play buckets, is that right? On the streets? You said on your reel that you read music and use a click track, too. I wouldn't think it necessary to know those skills for bucket drumming."

"I've had professional training on a kit. It's just been a few years since I've had one to play on."

"Why is that?"

"I have a one-room apartment in a shitty area. If I assembled a drum kit in my living room and started playing it, I'd definitely get murdered."

The other guys in the room laughed, but Cap stroked his jaw, analyzing me.

"And you've never played in a band before?"

"A garage band, but that was almost five years ago, and we never actually had a gig."

"Where have you been since then?"

I wasn't sure what to make of Cap's questioning. It was almost as if he were trying to catch me in a lie, but my answers were getting shorter and less accommodating. I could feel the opportunity slipping away from me.

"Just... around," I said.

The guys exchanged looks with one another.

"Did I say something wrong?"

"No, dude, sorry. It's just... you seem too good to be true. You show up on the scene out of nowhere, and everyone's buzzing about you. We're curious how a percussionist of your caliber, who has no on-stage experience and hasn't played in five years, comes in here and slays it, that's all."

I needed to get my damn story straight. Figure out a plausible reason to explain my absence. But until then, I'd go with the bare minimum. I wasn't getting the gig anyway, so who the hell cared?

"I gave up drumming for personal reasons."

"What made you want to start up again?"

This was a question I could answer with honesty. "You know, man. Just chasing the dream."

Cap smiled. Then nodded. "When can you start?"

I ARRIVED HOME SOMETIME LATER, adrenaline pumping through my veins. I got the job! I got the fucking job. To hell with my neighbors. I sat down at my buckets and banged out a few songs, ignoring the pounding on the walls and the threats to call the police. Really? Like I hadn't had ample opportunity to get the boys in blue involved in their questionable lives. When I first moved in here, I was the quietest person in the complex, going about my business while shit was constantly going down around me. Did I complain when Ralph had his psychotic break and smeared his genitalia along every window in the complex? No. Did I call the police when Lori took the Nintendo away from her eight-year-old daughter Serendipity and the girl screamed and screamed like she was being slowly dismembered? No. Did I report the couple "borrowing" other neighbors' cats so they could make TikToks about saving the "strays" and getting millions of views and packages from their Amazon wishlist? Actually, I did point the cat owners in the right direction on that one.

No one could say I wasn't a good neighbor... until I took up drumming again. Now I was public enemy number one. But since I was already going to jail, I might as well make it count. I smashed out the last thunderous drum strikes. That oughta make 'em squeal.

Flush with the thrill of accomplishment, I raised my arms in the air and silently cheered my good fortune in getting the job. It was one of those "Do you believe in miracles?" moments. I'd been sinking for so long, I'd almost forgotten what it felt like to stand on solid ground. No—to soar.

Heading to the bathroom, I ran my cracked and bleeding hands under the water. Long training sessions had not been kind to them. Nor had they been kind to my overall appearance. Without even looking in the mirror, I knew my hair needed something drastic. I looked like the stringy-haired bad guy in every drug movie. When I was working and playing the drums, I pulled it back to minimize the off-putting aesthetic, but that made me only slightly more palatable, like a dirty Viking just back from plundering a village.

And the beard. Oh, man. I was embarrassed for myself. It should've been gone long ago. I opened the medicine cabinet, looking for razors before remembering I didn't have any. Yeah, that wouldn't do. I'd stop by the store after work tomorrow. This was a whole new beginning, and I needed to look the part.

Grabbing for a towel, I caught my reflection in the mirror. Typically, I tried to avoid a direct stare, but I couldn't resist checking in on the boy in the mirror. Would he be proud of me? Not only had I realized a dream, but I'd also gone to great lengths to vindicate him, testifying for three full days to give him his justice. Yet he showed me no mercy.

"What more do you want from me?" I whispered to my biggest critic. No matter how high I climbed, I could never make him happy. My jubilant mood faded as I left him there to judge.

There was a knock at the door.

"Shit," I grumbled under my breath, turning my music down as a small concession to the complainer. Steeling myself for a confrontation, I walked to the window next to the door and lowered one slat of the blinds with my finger. The guy on the other side was cloaked in a hoodie and dark sunglasses. Expensive stuff. He was no neighbor of mine. Ice filled my veins. Had I not gotten them all? Had one come to finish me off? It was only when he removed his sunglasses that I realized who the visitor was.

"Surprise," Quinn said.

Surprise didn't begin to describe it. What was he doing here? Had Grace told him about my visit? Had he come to defend her honor like the attack dog he'd always been? I let go of the blinds and checked the lock. No way was I opening the door. If Quinn took a swing, I'd be swinging back, and the last thing I wanted to do was to send him back to the hospital.

"You've got thirty seconds to open this door," Quinn said, "before I start blasting an Oingo Boingo song and telling your neighbors you're the lead singer."

He wouldn't. He knew I hated eighties pop. "Go away, Quinn."

"No can do, bud."

"I've got nothing to say to you."

"Fair enough. Just open up and listen, then."

I stood with my forehead against the door, deciding what to do. I was curious. Quinn was big-time now. There was no reason for him to be at my door. Yet he was.

"Fifteen seconds," Quinn threatened. "Let's see, should I play 'Weird Science' or 'Just Another Day'?"

Gah, such a dick. I opened the door. He jumped back, seemingly surprised that his intimidation tactics had worked.

"What do you want?" I asked.

My former friend looked me up and down, an amused grin sweeping across his face.

"There's this thing called a razor, dude."

How did I know he'd instantly start picking on my hygiene? Sure, I'd already decided it send it all to hair heaven, but no way would I give Quinn the satisfaction. "I like my beard."

"Ah, high self-esteem. Way to go. Just one question: isn't your beard annoying in the summer?"

I fought a smile. "No, Quinn, manliness is not seasonal."

He laughed. "Can I come in?"

"I'd prefer you not."

Quinn paused, his eyes narrowing, and his amusement turned to concern. I couldn't blame him. Hair aside, I was rough. I just hadn't cared about my appearance in years, and it didn't hurt that I'd had so many enablers. I got hired on the spot at the dealership looking like this. Of course, they were like twenty mechanics short and were careful to keep me in the far back garages, away from the customers. The bands I'd auditioned for hadn't seemed to care either. That was no excuse. I needed to take an active approach, not only on my looks but on my health too. I'd been lazy for way too long.

"This is actually really important," Quinn said. "You'll want to hear it."

What would he have to say to me now that was 'actually really important'? My blood froze. Not...

"Grace?"

Quinn rocked back, surprised. I wasn't sure why. Did it never occur to him that I might still have a thing for his sister?

"No. She's fine. Great, really."

There was a hesitation in the way he said 'great,' leaving room for interpretation. Was she great because her relationship with Elliott had progressed to an engagement, or was she great because she'd wisely kicked him to the curb?

"I've got things to do," I said. "I'm shutting the door now. Say goodbye."

"Come on, man. I drove all the way out here. Aren't you the least bit curious what I have to say?"

"I think last time we talked, you said everything I wanted to hear. Look, I'm really sorry about what you went through, and I wish you luck, but you and me shouldn't be alone together."

"All right. Then talk to me here."

I looked behind him, concerned that Ralph might have another psychotic episode or that Serendipity might lose her internet connection right in the middle of our conversation. Nah, a hallway chat was too risky. I opened the door wider and he stepped in, his eyes darting around the room at all my dumpster dives. Quinn wasn't used to no-frills living. It wasn't that I was necessarily poor; I made a decent paycheck. I'd just learned to live with the bare minimum and preferred it that way. Less stuff to gather up when I needed to disappear in a hurry.

I followed his gaze to my buckets, feeling the need to explain despite having nothing to atone for. "I can't afford a set."

"But you still play." He almost sounded relieved.

I looked down at my wrapped hands. "I still play."

"Good. I need you."

"For what?"

"To take Brandon's place at the drums."

My first reaction wasn't gratitude. In fact, it was the complete opposite. He was making fun of me. Dangling a piece of steak in front of my ravenous eyes and jerking it away just before I had a chance to sink my teeth into it.

"Fuck you, Quinn. I don't know what your angle is, but I don't appreciate you coming here and messing with me."

"Look, I'm sorry for anything I've done to you. Obviously you hold a grudge, and that's something we'll have to work on, but I'm not kidding. I want you to join Sketch Monsters."

"Sketch Monsters?" I asked, skewing my lips in irritation. "You want some guy who plays buckets to join your Grammy-winning band?"

"Yes."

"Why?"

"Because despite everything, you're still the best drummer I've ever seen. Sketch Monsters needs you, Rory."

LIKE A STUNNED WOMAN whose man went down on one knee, I accepted. Yes, I'd marry Sketch Monsters. Yes, I'd take them in sickness and in health until death did us part. Yes, I'd live happily ever after in their awesomeness. And to think only a few hours ago I'd considered giving my verbal commitment to Cap's band to be the pinnacle of my career. But this? This was the opportunity of a lifetime. Things like this didn't happen. Not to me. I was the mole.

Wait. Shit!

Everything came to a screeching halt. I stumbled back, gripping the edge of the sofa for support. What was I thinking?

"I fucking can't, Quinn. I'm already in a band."

"What? Which one?" He looked every bit the jilted groom.

"We don't have a name yet," I replied.

"You don't have a name? How long have you been a part of this band?"

"Since this afternoon."

"Have you signed a contract?"

"No, just a verbal."

Quinn let out a sigh of relief. "Well, shit. You scared me. A band with no name is no band at all."

"So, what, I just bail on them? That's shitty. What do I even say to them?"

"Tell them you got a better offer from a band that already has a name *and* a sold-out stadium tour coming up. You don't have time to feel bad. Now, text your little playmate and let him know you've joined Sketch Monsters. See what he has to say about that."

"Like right now?"

"Do you want to wait until you're in Vancouver? Yes, now."

Snagging my phone off the table, I pulled up Cap's contact and started texting my resignation.

RORY

Hey Cap I'm really sorry to have to tell you this...

"I swear to god, Quinn, if you're messing with me..."

"I'm not. I had a vision."

I sighed, backspacing out of my resignation. No way was I betting my future on a premonition. "Dammit, Quinn. I don't have the luxury of playing this game with you."

"I dreamed you were in the band, shithead. Hear me out. Way back when we were putting Sketch Monsters together and were auditioning drummers, I thought you'd be perfect, but I didn't know where you were, and I didn't have time to search for you because it was a time sensitive situation. So, we hired Brandon. And he was great, but after he died, the label has been pressuring us to hire a new drummer. As a band, we've been struggling to find someone who meshes with us. Then, a couple of weeks ago, I had a dream. We were playing in front of a massive crowd, and I turned around and saw you sitting there behind the drums. It was a sign. No disrespect to Brandon, but you were always supposed to be in the band. That's the truth."

"You might want to leave that out of the introduction speech during shows."

Quinn grinned. "I will."

"What about the other guys? Are they dreaming about me too?"

"You're so conceited."

We had a good laugh over that, like old times—before he'd become sheriff and run me out of town.

"The other guys are in. I showed them video of us playing together years ago. They see it. But we have to hurry."

"For what?"

"We've got to go to Mike's garage. Make you an official Sketch Monster. We've got a whole blood-swapping, cattle-prod ceremony planned. You don't want to miss it."

I didn't. The truth was I'd happily take a brand to my ass cheek if it meant I could be that guy in Quinn's dream—an official member of a headline band. "Let's go!"

"Hold on there, bud. We're going to head to Mike's so you can practice a few songs before we introduce you to our manager, Tucker Beckett. Here's the thing about Tucker: you cannot meet him looking like this. I can't stress this enough. You need to take a bush whacker to your, well, everything. The dude created AnyDayNow, and while he's relaxed his boy band beauty requirements, we at least need to be able to introduce you in the light of day."

"You're such a dick, Quinn." I shook my head, suppressing a smile. "I almost missed it."

"Almost?"

"I missed it," I admitted.

"Me too," he said in a conciliatory tone. "I'm sorry. After everything went down that night, I did try to find you. Bring you back and give you a chance to explain. But you were nowhere to be found."

"I left town."

"You did more than that. You *disappeared*. My mom went to your apartment complex. The staff there was worried about you. You left everything behind."

Thankfully, Quinn said it as more of a statement than a

question, so I let it be. But I should have known the follow-up was coming.

"I have to ask. Be honest with me. Did you cheat on Grace?"

Withholding the truth about my disappearance was one thing, but leaving Grace in the driveway with that lie had eaten away at my soul for years. I looked my old friend in the eye, and after a tense moment between us, I shook my head.

"Fuck," he swore. "Fuck. Are you saying I ruined your relationship for no reason? If that's true, why didn't you fight for her? Why didn't you prove me wrong?"

"I couldn't."

"Why?"

I took a step back. And then another. Ready to run like I always did. But then I thought better of it. From this day forward, I was standing my ground.

"Here's the deal, Quinn. I'll join the band. Be your friend. Tour the world. And I'll be grateful to you every day for that. But I don't trust you. At least not enough to give you access to my personal life. Maybe someday. But not today."

"Okay. Fair enough."

I woke my screen and began texting Cap again.

RORY

Hey Cap I'm really sorry to have to tell you this...

"Before you send that," Quinn said, "we've got one more thing to discuss."

I looked up, knowing what he was going to say before he said it.

"It's about Grace."

17

GRACE: A DIFFERENT KIND OF THRILL

I sat limply on the edge of the bed as I watched Elliott pack. I'd known the day was coming and thought I was prepared, but it was very clear now that I wasn't. If anything, we'd grown closer during the breakup, rediscovering the friendship lost when love got in the way.

"That's it," Elliott announced, zipping up his suitcase with a gloomy sigh.

"That can't be it. Keep packing."

"I probably have room for Luke Skyhopper?" he teased, reaching for the stuffed rabbit with long ears and big fluffy feet sitting center stage on my bed.

"Touch my Lukey and you won't be leaving here alive."

"Well, I'm done, then. The only other thing I want to pack is you."

Sigh. Elliott had been hitting me with these little gut punches all day. And all yesterday. And all the days since I'd broken up with him. It was wearing me down. I either needed to send him on his way or reinstate his boyfriend status.

"I don't think me and Luke Skyhopper will fit in that suitcase."

"I'll throw everything out to make room for you," Elliott said, grabbing my hands and pulling me to my feet. He smoothed his hands over my hair and kissed my forehead. I wrapped my arms around his back and buried my head in his chest. We both stood there in suspended misery. *Be strong*, I pleaded with myself, all while preparing my heart for the next round of punches.

Elliott was the angel on my shoulder in this battle of good versus evil. I could play it safe with "good" and be happy with the guy I already had, or I could throw the dice with "evil" and see where life took me. I'd picked the devil the day I broke up with him, but damned if the angel didn't keep reminding me it was there.

"Come with me," Elliott said, perhaps seeing my hesitation as his chance to sway my decision. "You don't have to worry about leaving Quinn anymore. He's doing great. And the trip is already paid for. The flights. The trains. The hotels. You should know—you planned it. It's just two weeks. All the places you wanted to visit. All the restaurants you wanted to try. Don't make me go alone because you know I will. I hate throwing money away."

Oh, I knew. Elliott was a money man through and through. The idea that he would blame me for the loss of a good chunk of it haunted me enough that I'd slipped an envelope into the cowboy boots he'd meticulously budgeted to buy. It wouldn't make up for what I'd done, blowing up not only his vacation but also his life, but at least he wouldn't be out monetarily.

"I know," I said. "But what message would it send to our breakup if we shared a vacation? It's already confused as hell."

"Our breakup will learn to deal with it, as it has everything else that's come its way."

"We'd be in the same hotel room, and it's Europe, so we'd be on top of each other."

"Our breakup sincerely hopes so."

I smiled. "Our breakup is going to be sorely disappointed."

"You underestimate our breakup. It has survived without sex for what seems like decades, and you don't hear it complaining."

"You're right. Our breakup has been very patient."

Our smiles dissolved into frowns.

"I'm so sorry for putting you through this," I said for the umpteenth time. "I know it's confusing."

"I'm not confused. I know what I want."

Squaring up, I held his determined stare. "And I'm not confused either. I know what I want too."

"And it's not me?"

My lip wobbled. How was I supposed to answer that without severely wounding his pride? I took several steps back, giving myself the space needed to be honest with him... and myself.

"I want *me*, Elliott. Just me."

"What does that even mean? I'm not holding you back. I've always encouraged you to be who you are."

"I know, but what I want for *my* future is not what you want for your future. You're ready to settle down. Have a family. I see the way you look at my siblings' kids. You want all that, and I... I don't know if I do."

"You act like I have some grand plans, Grace. I don't. I just want you. The rest will fall into place."

"That's just it. I don't want my life to fall into place. I want it to be big and messy and chaotic, even if just for a short time. I've been sheltered my whole life. I don't remember life before Jake was kidnapped, but after, it was like being preserved in an airtight mason jar. Only one time in my life did I get to live like the lid was off. And, oh my god, Elliott, the thrill. I've been chasing after it ever since."

"I don't do that for you? I don't give you that thrill?"

"You're a different kind of thrill."

Resolve hardened his face. "Great. Wonderful. Just what a guy wants to hear."

"You're the thrill of getting everything all wrapped up into one. And if I was at a different place in my life, we probably wouldn't be having this discussion. But after what happened in the arena, I can't see myself moving in the same direction only to wake up in twenty years and realize that the lid is still securely fastened."

"Then I'll wait... for as long as it takes."

Slowly, I made my way back to him. "No, Elliott. I don't want anyone to wait for me. I don't want to feel like I have to come home. And I especially don't want you to wait for something that might never happen. That's why I broke up with you. The last thing I want is for you to gamble your future away and then end up with nothing to show for it. I'm a bad bet, Elliott. I'm going to break your heart."

My ex sat on the bed, dropping his head into his hands. "You already have."

"I know."

There really wasn't anything more to say. I was ready to get him in the car and go. Take him to the airport. Say goodbye. This time for good.

"Be honest with me, Grace. Is there someone else?"

I was stunned. No, flabbergasted. "What? No!"

"Then tell me—who's Rory, and why haven't you mentioned him before?"

I blinked until I thought my eyelids would fall off. "Who told you about Rory?"

"Your dad. Accidentally. He called me Rory one day."

I closed my eyes, sighing. *Dammit, Dad!*

"You'll be happy to know he tried to cover it up, but good god, that man is a terrible liar."

"I'm aware."

"I thought at first he just called me the wrong name, but then he started stuttering and backtracking, and when none of that worked, he challenged me to a burping contest."

Palming my forehead, I asked, "When did this happen?"

"A couple of days after arriving to the States. Remember when I was moody and told you I had jetlag? It was then."

I nodded. I remembered that day. Something had been off, but I'd thought he was just tired. Yet if I thought back, that was the day doubt had begun forming in my mind. That was how powerful a presence Rory still was in my life. All it had taken was a mere mention from my father to drive a wedge between Elliott and me, and we'd been losing air ever since. "Why didn't you say anything?"

"Because you didn't. We talked about all our former flames, and his name never came up. Not once. Obviously there's a reason you failed to mention him."

Oh, there was a reason, all right; one that Elliott would definitely not want to hear.

"He's the thrill you're chasing, isn't he?" Elliott asked, and the words were sour coming out of his mouth.

Elliott and I had reached the end. There was no reason to hide Rory now. No more secrets.

"Yes. He's the thrill."

18

RORY: THE REPLACEMENT

The middle-aged man ambled in with a cane, trying to move faster than his limp would allow. Dressed in a sharp suit and tie and looking deceptively younger than the years he'd been rumored to live, Sketch Monsters' manager, Tucker Beckett, was the type of guy who didn't have time for injuries. Yet they'd made an exception for him. He was one of the arena victims, having taken a bullet to the thigh in his attempt to rescue his charges and get them off the stage. Not a bad guy to have around.

Tucker's reputation in the business had made a huge turnaround after that night. To be fair, he'd already been a legend, having made his name and fortune as the manager and creator of the boy band AnyDayNow, but the fallout of that band's demise had made him a dirty word in the music business. Sketch Monsters was his redemption, and from what I could see, he'd more than earned his comeback story.

I'd gotten the lowdown on Tucker Beckett at lunch with my new bandmates. They'd arrived an hour earlier to the barber shop where I was getting my makeover. By the time we left, three quarters of my hair was gone and my skin was as smooth as newly poured concrete. My beard had been so thick, I now had a tanline that marked its former location. Although I looked undeniably better, I was going to miss the mask that had shielded me.

During lunch, I discovered how Sketch Monsters had come to be, formed after Quinn's ill-fated turn on a reality singing competition shot him to unexpected fame while simultaneously making him a pariah in the music business. That was where Tucker Beckett had come in and built a band around the youngest McKallister boy. He was the one who'd booked Sketch Monsters for the opening show on the night of the shooting. It was supposed to be their big break, and in a roundabout way, it was. With the notoriety that came with being on stage during a tragedy, they'd shot to fame. And now here I was, taking the throne of the member of the band who didn't survive.

"What time does practice start?" Tucker barked, as he sailed through the rehearsal studio without noticing me on the drums. It was like the cane was a motorized scooter.

"Fifteen hundred hours, sir," Mike, the bassist, answered in his best militarized response. He even added a crisp salute.

"That's correct, Michael. And what time is it now?"

"Fifteen and oh five?" Mike guessed. "I don't know how to tell military time past the hour."

"It's fifteen five. And what does that mean, boys?"

Matty, the guitarist, tentatively raised his hand. "We're late?"

Tucker clapped his hands once in an aggressive gesture that left no room for interpretation. "It means that every single minute that passes is coming out of my pocket."

"Isn't the studio paying..."

"Quinn!" Tucker cut him off. "I swear to god. Shut it. This tour starts in five weeks, and we're still playing with a sideman drummer. Do you have any idea how much it's going to cost to pay a short-term replacement? Do any of you care?"

The guys all shook their heads. I sat there in silence, having no say in the decision-making.

"Just pick a drummer, any drummer, and let's get..." He glanced over at me for the first time. Then did a double take. "Who the fuck are you?"

"Rory Higgins." I paused before adding, "Sir."

"And I repeat. Who the fuck are you?"

"He's our new drummer," Quinn said.

"We already have a new drummer. He came on last week. His name is..." Tucker raised his eyes to the rafters in an attempt to bring forth his name from somewhere deep in his brain. "Busch."

"No, Busch was a few weeks ago," Quinn informed. "Then we had Woo. Followed by Denyer."

It was the sigh heard around the room. "You told me the last drummer was the last one."

"No, Tucker, *you* told us that. We never agreed."

"Are you trying to kill me? Is that it?"

"We told you from the start that we weren't going to replace Brandon until we found the right drummer."

Tucker threw his hands up, the cane whizzing through the air. "The three of you are never going to find the right one because you're thinking with your hearts and not your heads. You have no time left. None!"

"Tucker," Quinn yelled over his tirade, "Meet Rory Higgins. He's not a session drummer. He's the final member of the band."

Tucker blinked, looking around. "You all agree?"

The consensual nods brightened his mood. "You're sure?"

More nods.

"And he's the one you want to go on tour with?"

Verbal assurances followed.

Tucker appeared momentarily speechless before wiping a fake tear from his eye. "Well, hallelujah. And Higgins? I don't care if your drumming makes me want to dive headfirst into a steamy pile of poo. You've got the job."

And with that vote of confidence, practice started at fifteen ten.

THREE QUARTERS of the condensation in the room came from me. Every song had to be played over and over as I learned the rhythms and beats. When the others took breaks, I stayed. Like Tucker said, the tour started in five weeks, and not only did I need to know the songs, I also needed to fill the shoes of a ghost. I'd never known Brandon, but I knew I'd have to walk a fine line between staying true to his beats while adding my own unique style to the songs. I'd go easy on them at first, only adding subtle changes. The remaining members of Sketch Monsters weren't ready for more than that. Not yet, anyway.

Tucker caught me on my way out; more like poked me in the back with his cane.

"Higgins," he huffed. "We need to talk."

Ice replaced the blood pumping through my veins. I'd never heard that line spoken without hellfire coming my way. Dropping my head, I followed him back into the empty room.

"Was I shit?" I asked, once the door was closed behind us.

Tucker's forehead wrinkled. "No. Quite the opposite, which makes this all the more difficult."

Fucking Quinn. He'd promised I had the job, but clearly he wasn't in charge of Sketch Monsters. That was Tucker Beckett, and I was about to get fired. Dammit. I'd already texted Cap and told him I was out of the band with no name. Would they accept me back? Did I even have the balls to ask?

"Quinn said the spot was mine," I protested. "I quit another band for this."

"It's not about that." Tucker grimaced, sweat pouring down his face. He swayed in place. "I've got to find a place to sit."

I could clearly see his pain, and despite the fact he was about to let me go, I strode over to my stool and dragged it across the room for him. Even helped him onto it. He grumbled the entire time but accepted my assistance.

"Thank you," he said, looking embarrassed. I could imagine this wasn't the type of guy who asked for help very often; but then, he also hadn't asked to be wounded on stage. "When Quinn told me you two played together as teenagers, I wasn't hopeful. Figured you'd suck. But I'm pleasantly surprised, and typically I'm not either of those things."

No, I didn't think he was. I stood there, hands crossed in front of me, waiting patiently for the firing. But then I thought better of it. The least I could do was put up a damn fight.

"Mr. Beckett, I know what you're going to say, but I'll work harder. Stay later. I'll do whatever needs to be done to have the set down in time for the tour. Just give me this chance. I promise I won't let you down."

"That's good to know, Higgins. Although this is of a more personal matter. What's the situation with you and Grace?"

There was no hiding my surprise. "Quinn told you?"

"No, I overheard Tweedledee and Tweedledum in the bathroom."

Mike and Matty, I assumed, but I didn't know the band well enough to confirm the validity of those nicknames.

"We dated as teenagers," I said.

"And it didn't end well?"

"It did not."

He nodded. "She's been hired to work with the band to write songs for the second album. We've got her traveling on the tour bus, so work can get done on the road."

"I know. Quinn already told me."

Quinn also told me he wanted to keep my involvement in the band a secret from Grace. No issue for me since I had zero communication with her. According to him, Grace was out of town and dealing with some "issues," and he didn't want to stress her out. He'd made the decision to tell her when she returned in two weeks. The way he explained it, it didn't seem like a big deal. The way Tucker was obviously perceiving it, it did.

"My question for you is, will that be a problem?"

"No. It's been five years. We've both moved on."

"You sure about that?"

I may have blinked one time too many, and Tucker picked right up on it. He sighed. "That's what I thought. This whole thing is too much of a liability. I can't risk the band imploding because the two of you can't get along."

"So that's it, then? I'm fired?"

"You? I've been trying to get those fuckers to pick a drummer for months. No, Higgins, your spot on the bus is safe. It's Grace who has to go."

Time slowed as I processed the gravity of his words. For my dreams to come to fruition, Grace's had to die. She was going to lose her job because of me.

"No, really, she and I..."

He raised a hand to stop me. "Normally, I never mix the sexes on a tour. In those tight quarters, it's ripe for drama. The only reason I got the studio to bankroll Grace was because she wrote the biggest hit song the band has had, and she's Quinn's sister. The others wouldn't dream of touching her. But you"— Tucker eyed me skeptically—"you're going to be a problem."

"No, I promise. I won't touch her."

But Tucker wasn't listening, instead talking strategy to himself out loud. "We'll make it a budget cut issue. She doesn't have to know the real reason."

Oh, she'd know. Grace would take one look at who was sitting behind the kit and know why she'd been expelled.

"No one has to go. Can't you at least give us a chance to prove we're professionals and can handle being in close quarters without killing each other?"

"It's the not killing each other part that worries me. What happens if Quinn finds the two of you banging in the bathroom? Or worse, Grace finds you hooking up with a groupie in the bunk right next to hers? I tell you what: Arma-fucking-geddon. But that's not your problem, is it? No, it's mine. I'm the one who'll have to clean up the blood. Cover up the crime."

"Nothing will happen."

"Right, because in all my years of working with musicians I haven't heard that before."

"This time it's true. I promise you. I'm going to friend-zone Grace so hard, before you know it, she'll be wearing oversized volleyball sweats with a hole in the crotch and stains she can't explain."

Tucker sighed like a man who'd seen it all before. But it was also a sigh signaling he was going to reluctantly allow it to happen again.

"Okay," he relented. "One chance. But if you so much as touch her..."

"I won't," I interrupted him, eagerly jumping all over his change of heart. "You won't regret this."

"Oh, I already do. I've bet my whole career on trusting good-looking, young talent like you."

"Well, there you go."

"It wasn't a compliment, Higgins."

19

RORY: IN MY FILE
THE PAST

I could see the light flashing in my eyes. Could hear a calm female voice beckoning me back. Instinctively, I knew I was safe in this place with no pain. Which could mean only one thing: Hartman was gone. Nikki too. I fought through the haze, knowing full well that outside of my head was safer than inside, but the bad memories kept sucking me in.

~

Rory, ten years old

I was bored. Nothing to do but toss a small rubber ball at the ceiling after the morning supervisor took my sticks away. She said I could get them back if I apologized, so I did... and then she didn't give them back. I asked the night supervisor, and he said I was destructive and that I'd caused dents on the refrigerator after I used it for a drum solo. That was a lie. Not the drum solo part—the dents.

This morning I told one of the social workers who stopped by that they'd stolen my sticks, and she promised to get them back, but before she left, she told me I couldn't have them until I learned to be still and to not drum on every single surface.

So I was never getting them back.

I hated this place. Nikki said I should feel lucky because this group home was meant for younger kids and brothers and sisters like us. She pointed to the colorful walls and the toys and the extra staff that she said were for kids like me, but I didn't feel lucky. I was mad because they took my sticks away. And I was mad at my sister. Nikki was the reason we got kicked out of the last foster home, and wherever she went, I went. It was in my file. This was the first time I wished it wasn't. If they split us up, then I could go back to my last foster home, where there was a mom and not a bunch of supervisors. I was the youngest kid in here, and Nikki was never around anymore. She was always out with her friends, and I was stuck in here without my sticks and nothing to do.

I didn't want to cry, but I did anyway. I missed Patty. She was my last foster mom, and Nikki and me lived there for eight whole months. A record, Nikki said. A miracle, I thought. Patty was strict but not mean. She made me go to school and do chores and finish my homework, but she also read me stories and cooked me dinner every night. And she had Riley, the floppy-eared brown dog who liked to sleep in my bed at night. Patty didn't hate when I made noise. She even let me practice my drums on some old buckets in her garage.

I would've stayed forever, but Nikki hated her. They got in fights all the time, and then one day Nikki hit Patty, and a social worker came and made us pack up. Patty wanted me to stay, but the lady wouldn't separate Nikki and me. It was in my file. So, I had to say goodbye to Patty and to Riley and to my drum buckets in the garage. I wiped the tears off my cheeks. Nikki said I shouldn't cry. That the bigger kids might hurt me for it. But she wasn't here now. So I cried.

The door flung open, and Nikki pirouetted into the room, the giant smile on her face making my tears instantly dry up.

She jumped on my cot. "Guess what?"

"You got stuck in a revolving door?"

She giggled, smacking my face back and forth between her hands. "Try again."

"You cut the tag off the mattress?"

"Ugh. You're so annoying, Rory. I'll just tell you. I'm going to be a star."

"Like in the sky?"

"No. You're not very smart for a ten-year-old, are you? Like in Hollywood, I mean."

"How?"

"I met a producer outside the sandwich shop."

"What's a Hollywood producer doing at a sandwich shop?"

"They have to eat, dummy. Anyway, he's making a film, and he said they're casting an older teenage girl for the part, so I told him I was sixteen."

"He believed it?"

"He believed these." Nikki squished her boobs together.

I turned my head away, tapping out a beat on my knee.

"Stop interrupting me, jeez. What I was trying to say is, they already picked another girl, but the producer's going to ask his part-ners if they can audition me instead."

"Oh," I said and kept drumming.

"Don't you get it, Rory? I'm going to be famous, and that means someday I'll buy us a big mansion in the hills. We can even get married if you want."

"To you? No, thanks."

"What? We're not actually related, so it's legal."

"It's gross. I'm not marrying you."

"Fine. Whatever. You can still live in my mansion."

"I don't need to live in your mansion because I'm going to have one of my own... if I can get my drumsticks back."

"They haven't given them back yet? Those fuckers."

"Nikki, you can't swear like that."

"Why? What are they going to do, kick us out? News flash: once you land in group homes, you never get out."

"What? I don't want to stay here. I hate this place. I want to go back to Patty's. I wanna play ball with Riley."

"You think Patty is your new family? That she loves you? You're money to her, nothing else. Patty is not taking you back, Rory."

"Why?"

"Because I can't go with you, and they aren't going to separate us. It's in our files. Besides, she already has new kids. She doesn't want you around anymore."

I hated when Nikki said stuff like that. She wasn't nice to me like she used to be when we were younger. She used to take care of me and protect me. Now she was just mean most of the time.

"Maybe I don't want it in my file anymore." It was the first time I'd said the words out loud.

Nikki looked like she might cry. "You want to leave me?"

"No," I lied. "I just don't want to stay here."

Nikki was quiet for a long time before she said, "If you leave me, I'll have nothing. I might as well kill myself."

"No!" I grabbed her arm. "You can't."

"Yes, I can. And I will. If you leave me, Rory, I'll kill myself, and you'll be all alone because no one loves you but me."

Tears rolled down my cheeks. Nikki was all I had. She was all I'd ever have.

"No," I cried. "I'm sorry."

"Then stop being mean. Stop saying you're going to leave me. And stop crying."

"Okay," I said, wiping any lasting remnants to cover my tracks. "I stopped."

"Good, 'cause I told you that you gotta stop acting like a baby."

"I'm not acting like a baby. I'm mad."

"Why are you mad?"

"Because they took my sticks and I hate this place and you're always gone. Why do you have to leave all the time?"

"Because I'm a teenager now. I want to hang out with older kids like me."

"You don't like me anymore?"

She hooked an arm around my back. "I love you, Rory. You know that. You're my best friend in this whole world. How about this? How about you come with me when I meet the producer tomorrow. When he sees how cute you are, he might have a part in the movie for you too."

"You think so?"

"I know so, and then we can be stars together. Everyone will know our names."

MY LIDS LAY heavily over my eyes, protecting me from the vertigo that ascended any time I tried opening them. I couldn't remember where I was, but I knew where I needed to be—on the phone with Grace, letting her know I was okay and that I was coming back to her as soon as the world stopped swaying.

"There you go. Open your eyes."

The female voice was soothing in tone, and I struggled to follow her instruction, but as I cracked my eyes partially open, the room spun. Nothing was stationary. Flashes of light and white. A woman with black hair and a white coat. I was in a hospital.

"Right here. Focus on my light."

Gradually the spinning stopped as my eyes rallied, working together for a common good. The woman came into view—a doctor, I assumed—and she was standing over me.

"Welcome back," she said, checking my pupil reaction. "We've been worried about you."

"What...?" I tried formulating words. "Where...?"

"You're in the hospital. You were brought in with a head injury, among other issues."

"How... how long... am I...?" I knew what I wanted to say but nothing was coming out of my mouth the way I wanted it to.

"You were brought in a little over a week ago. You've been sedated most of the time due to brain swelling."

A heavy knot twisted in my stomach. I never called her. I never called Grace. She was going to think I'd been lying to her. That I didn't care. I needed to find her number and call her. Where were my things? I tried to get up, but the spinning in my head wouldn't allow it.

The doctor laid her hand on my shoulder and eased me back down. "We're weaning you off the sedatives, but you need to stay as still as possible. You have a skull fracture. A concussion. Some broken bones."

"My stuff. Where is it?"

"As far as I know, you weren't brought in here with anything but the clothes on your back. No wallet or bag to help us identify you. Can you tell me your name?"

Nothing? I had nothing at all? No buckets. No sticks. No backpack or the money Grace had given me for the motel. And if all that was gone, no note with Grace's phone number written on it in bright-pink Sharpie. That had been my only connection to her. Without it, she was as good as gone.

I squeezed my eyes shut, wishing death would just come for me and get it over with. "I'm no one."

Rory, ten years old

We stood on the sidewalk outside of the sandwich shop with Nikki's producer guy, Mr. Hartman. He wasn't sure about me and got on the phone with another producer guy. I was all ready to go back to the group home when he motioned me over with his finger.

"How old are you, kid?"

"Ten."

Mr. Hartman squinted down at me, shaking his head. "You gonna be a problem, aren't ya?"

I blinked up at him, not understanding what he meant. "No."

"He's a really good actor, and he doesn't talk back," Nikki said. "I know he looks scrawny, but he's actually really tough."

I stood up a little straighter, puffing out what little of a chest I had to bolster Nikki's claims.

"Yeah?" Mr. Hartman said, looking me over. "You gotta do what we say and you can't be going around telling people. This is a secret project. Can you keep your mouth shut?"

"Yes."

A bunch of swear words tumbled out of Mr. Hartman's mouth, and then he shook his head and said, "I'm gonna go to hell for this."

Nikki giggled. I didn't. I didn't like him, but I couldn't say why.

"Fuck it." Mr. Hartman opened his car door. "Hop in. Both of you."

Nikki and me sat in the back seat and watched the landscape go by. It was only later when Mr. Hartman pulled into the driveway of a house with fields all around that I realized we weren't going to a studio. We weren't even going to a fancy mansion. I looked at Nikki, but she was talking to Mr. Hartman, so I just sat back and sipped on my milkshake as he drove us through the squeaking security gates and up to the one-story house. But inside wasn't a home at all. It was all cameras and lights and racks of clothes everywhere. My eyes widened at the sight of men and women walking around with hardly any clothes on, but Nikki didn't seem to care.

"This is so cool." She tugged on my arm. *"It's like a real movie set."*

I didn't think so, but I didn't know a lot about making movies either. Nikki was more an expert at that.

A man wearing shorts and a tank top like he'd just come from the beach walked out of one of the rooms. *"Are these our new stars?"*

"They are," Mr. Hartman said. *"This is Nikki and her brother Rory."*

The man looked at Nikki before his eyes landed on me and he stared.

"Damn," he said, *making a weird clicking sound with his tongue before walking away. I'd seen that kind of look before and knew something was wrong. I grabbed for Nikki's hand but she swatted it away, giving me a warning glare. She wanted to stay. I wanted to go. But she was always the one who got to choose. It was in our files.*

"This way," Mr. Hartman said, *putting a hand on my back and leading Nikki and me down the hall and into a space that looked like a kid's bedroom except one side had only cameras and lights.*

The man who clicked his tongue was in there waiting. So were others.

"Shut the door."

～

TIME MOVED DIFFERENTLY UNDER SEDATION. I drifted through the hours... or maybe it was days. People came and went, including detectives trying to identify me, but I barely acknowledged them. Nor did I reveal who I was. If they didn't already know, what was the point? I was effectively dead to anyone who mattered.

Maybe it was depression talking, but there was a hopelessness that had settled over me. It wasn't so much the beating itself but what happened in the moments after police interrupted the attack after hearing Nikki's screams. Instead of choosing safety in the back of a police cruiser, my so-called sister left me lying near death in the alley as she ran off with the man who'd stolen our childhood. No matter how I tried, I couldn't get over her betrayal. I'd forgiven her once, but never again.

I was moved to a rehabilitation center about two weeks in, and here I'd lingered ever since. Not really *lingered*; I was in physical therapy, and my body was slowly healing. But in the process, thoughts of the past slowly overwhelmed me. I withdrew further into my mind, replaying the most horrible moments of my life. I'd always been able to separate the abuse from my conscious mind but no longer. It consumed me now. What they'd done.

At some point during my stay at the rehab center, I had an unknown visitor. Actually, I had two, but one of them was well known to me, a crusty, frizzy-haired social worker named Mary. She had been assigned to me not long after I'd turned thirteen, and we'd had a combative relationship ever since. I was a number to her, nothing more, nothing less. There were two types of social workers: the idealistic, fresh, unjaded ones who still believed they could make a difference, and those like Mary who knew they couldn't fix things, so they didn't even try.

Assigned to those of us past our prime, Mary was where teenage foster kids went to die. Her job was to shuffle the unwanted ones around. A bed was a bed no matter where it existed, whether in a debatable foster home, in a rough and tumble group home, in a nondescript office building, in detention centers. Even warehouses were not out of the scope of her bed hunting. When you got to my age, it was all about quantity over quality, and in that respect, Mary was an expert at packing the bodies.

"Yes," she nodded, her frown deepening. "It's him. Rory Higgins."

Mary didn't bother acknowledging me despite our rocky

four-year relationship. Her presence in the room was for nothing more than to identify the body. Such a disappointment. I'd given those detectives a run for their money. The mystery of who I was had persisted all this time. Of all the people to crack the case, did it really have to be Mary Sutlidge?

"He ran away from a group home on July seventh," she said, all accusatory in her tone as if it were my fault she'd placed me with pervs.

"Why was no report generated?" the man asked. "We've been trying to identify this kid for almost two months."

"He runs away multiple times a year. You try keeping up."

Actually, I'd run away twice in my lifetime, both times because of her shitty placements. The other times, I'd just been hiding.

"It's November twenty-eighth, Ms. Sutlidge. Are you saying you didn't know he was missing for nearly five months?"

The accusation was clear, and that royally pissed Mary off. She used her pointer finger to talk the suited man down. "I knew he was missing. I just hadn't gotten the report filed yet. I really don't appreciate your tone, Mr. Dutch. I'd like to see you have the workload of three social workers and still get your reports in on time."

"Actually, it's Special Agent Dutch, and I have quite a workload myself."

"Are you insinuating I wasn't doing my job, Mr.... Agent... Dutch?"

He held his ground. "In this particular situation, I believe there's considerable room for improvement."

Despite my head injuries, I had no problem following their volley like a spectator at a tennis match, and I took great satisfaction in watching Mary squirm. She'd stolen my voice years ago, and no one had ever called her out on it—until today.

"Yeah, Mary." I jumped into the fray. "Do your fucking job."

Mary pinched her lips, so bent out of shape at the condemnation despite her negligence being undisputedly proven. The agent dude, on the other hand, was biting back a chuckle.

"I think that's all I need from you now, Ms. Sutlidge," he said. "I'll be in touch."

"Let's hope not," she huffed, pivoting on her heel and marching out, again without bothering to acknowledge me.

The man watched her go before turning back to me. "She seems nice."

"And they wonder why I run."

"They told me you didn't talk."

"It's not that I'm physically incapable. I just choose not to."

He nodded. "I do that with my wife."

I wasn't sure if he was trying to be funny but it was, sort of. I kept my poker face, though, until I knew what his angle was.

The man pulled up a chair and gingerly eased his body down onto the unforgiving plastic. "Hope you don't mind if I sit. I had a bonding-related injury last night. Was teaching my kid how to swing a bat, and he apparently got confused by the direction. Smashed me straight on the kneecap. I saw my life flash before my eyes."

"What'd you do to him?" I asked, knowing what would've happened to me if I'd been the one to reverse the bat.

"What do you mean?"

"Your son. What did you do to him after he hit you with a bat?"

"Nothing. It was an accident."

A momentary silence fell over the conversation as I pondered what it must be like to maim with impunity. In my experience, there were few things more terrifying than causing injury by accident and then awaiting the punishment that would surely follow.

"I'm Special Agent Daniel Dutch, but everyone just calls me Dutch."

He'd already established that with Mary, but I nodded anyway. I didn't know much about police work, but I was surprised they'd sent a special agent to investigate a "mugging," which was what Hartman's attempted murder had been labeled since I hadn't provided any details to dispute the police's findings.

"I've been looking for you for years, Rory."

The solemn expression on his face sent a chill straight up my spine. Fuck. This wasn't about the mugging at all. And Dutch confirmed it when he revealed himself to be a member of a special unit within the FBI investigating cybercrimes involving child assault victims. I'd always feared this day, knowing it was only a matter of time before my past caught up to me.

"Checking missing person databases. Following leads. Searching through foreign arrests. Interviewing other kids in your similar situation, hoping they had maybe met you some-where along the line. But I gotta tell you, Rory, your case has haunted me for a very long time. In recent years, we've been using facial recognition to try to match victims. Images of you after your 'mugging' made their way into our algorithms, which then matched up with images of you as a child. I went to the DCFS and showed your picture around until I was connected with Ms. Sutlidge, and here I am—almost six years later."

"Congratulations," I replied.

I mean, how else did he expect me to respond? Did he want a medal or something? Didn't matter whether he'd spent years of his life looking for me because by the time he saw those images online and started the search, I'd already been living with the aftermath for a year. So, in reality, he was more like almost *seven* years too late to save me now.

"I understand this isn't easy for you."

No, he didn't understand a thing. Did it not occur to him that I wanted to crawl into a hole and die, just knowing he'd seen me at my most vulnerable and knew exactly what had been done?

"No, I don't think you do."

Dutch laid out a series of mug shots, all of them men I knew. Men I hated. The visceral reaction in me did not escape him. "Obviously you recognize them."

Of course, he'd known I'd recognize them. He'd probably seen them all with me in multiple shots.

He placed another image onto the table. It was Nikki.

"And by way of deduction, I'm assuming this is Nicola Aldana."

"You seem to have all the answers. What do you need me for?"

"To help me get you and Nicola justice."

I laughed, but there was no humor to be had. No amount of justice now would change what happened then.

"I think I'll pass."

"They're still operating, you know."

"So shut them down. Arrest them. You don't need me for that." I pushed the images on the table away from me. "You have plenty of evidence."

"We've already arrested most of them, but they bailed out and are free men while we put together a case against them."

"Well, you better get going, then. Time's ticking."

Dutch eyed me wearily. "Trust me, we want these guys off the streets as soon as possible. The ones on camera are easy to put away; we have physical evidence against them. But what we're going for are the ones behind the camera. These guys"—he picked up the photos—"are the body. What we want is to cut off the head."

"By handing them mine? I don't think so."

"Do you know who the head is, Rory?"

Oh, I knew who the head was. I heard his clicking in my sleep. But there wasn't a chance in hell I was giving him up to *almost-six-years-too-late* Dutch.

"Just by your reaction, I can tell you do. We'd offer you protection. Change your identity. They won't be able to find you."

"They already have."

Dutch sat up a little straighter, his busted knee temporarily forgotten. "They did this to you?"

"The right-hand man of the head."

"Hartman?"

I didn't bother to confirm or deny, only to point out the obvious. "They already know you're digging into the operation. He accused me of being an informant. I'm guessing he's not too happy about me surviving."

"No, I can imagine he wouldn't be. All the more reason to get you under the protection of the US Marshal's department. To relocate and reinvent you."

"But only if I testify, right?"

"This is your chance to live a normal life, free from all this. You'll be off the streets. A new name and identity. A fresh start. We'll get you into a vocational program or college, whatever you prefer, so that you can provide for yourself and have security for your future."

"But only if I testify." I repeated the part he had totally ignored in his impassioned plea.

"That will be part of it, yes, but a small part in the scope of your life. And think about it. You'll get justice, and these guys will never be able to do this again."

"What about Nikki?"

Dutch jumped right on that. "She can come with you. Of course, we'd prefer to get both of you under our protection."

No, he wanted both of us to testify. He didn't give a shit about

Nikki or me. Just like she'd always said: no one cared about us. We were on our own. I'd have some respect for Dutch if he just admitted the truth—that he was using us as a means to an end, a way for him to close a big splashy case and be a hero.

"You can count Nikki out. She's with them again," I said, bursting his superhero bubble.

"Voluntarily?"

"Not sure. I think Hartman's been pimping her out on The Stroll."

He squinted, obviously not from around here.

"She's a prostitute."

"Yeah, I got that."

He pulled a small notepad and pen out of an inside pocket in his suit jacket and jotted a few things down.

I waited for him to finish before I spoke. "If I did this, if I accept protection, can I still play my drums?"

"Sure."

"I mean like professionally, in a touring band?"

He blinked, clearly surprised by the question. "You're a musician?"

"Trying to be."

Dutch shifted uncomfortably. "I'm not going to lie to you, Rory. That could be risky. There are certain restrictions for your own protection, and that includes not drawing unnecessary attention to yourself. So, yes, you can play drums, just not professionally. You need to understand—if you go into our witness protection program, Rory Higgins will no longer exist. But in exchange, whoever you become will be able to live safe and free."

How many years had I wished for this? To cease being me? But now that the choice was here, I wasn't sure what to do. Was I willing to give up the only dream worth living? The only thing that had even the slightest chance of getting Grace back? If I was famous, she'd see me. Yeah, giving up drumming would keep me alive, but was it worth it just to exist in a colorless world?

"Thanks for the offer, but I'm going to take my chances. I'm not ready to give up on my dreams."

Rory, ten years old

"I'm sorry, okay?" Nikki said just after Mr. Hartman dropped us off.

I didn't want her to apologize. I wanted her to make them stop. But she didn't, and they kept coming back. Making us go with them back to that house. Behind the closed door.

"Are you never going to talk to me again?"

I shrugged.

"You think I like this? What do you want me to do, Rory?"

"Don't make me go back." I burst into tears. "I don't want to go back there."

Nikki was crying now too. "I'm not making you. They are."

"You are! I wanted to stay at Patty's, but you got in trouble, and I had to leave. I don't want to go where you go anymore because you only go to bad places."

"You want them to separate us, Rory? Is that what you want? You want to be alone? Because that's what you'll be. Alone, like you were before. Alone, like I was before."

I could barely talk because I was crying so hard. "I want to go back to Patty. I want to play with Riley and get my sticks back."

"That's what you want?"

I nodded.

"Go, then. I don't care."

"I don't know how. How do I go?"

"Find the supervisor on call tonight. Tell them you want to talk to your social worker. Tell them you don't want to live with me anymore.

Tell them you want to go back to Patty. Tell them you hate me. Or that you're scared of me. Or that I hit you. Tell them whatever you have to. Just get out of here and leave me alone."

Nikki was bawling so hard I could barely hear anything she was saying.

"What if they come looking for me?" I asked.

"They won't."

"But how do you know?"

"Because I'm going to tell them the social worker moved you because you were such a fucking baby and crying all the time. It's not a lie."

I winced at her words but still needed answers. "Are you going to kill yourself if I go?"

"Maybe. What do you care?"

Tears rolled down my cheeks. I did care. But I had to save myself.

"Come with me," I tried. "We won't be together, but at least you'll be safe."

"I'm going to stay."

"You can't. What if they come back?"

"That's not your problem anymore. You hate me, remember? Besides, it's just sex, Rory. It's not like I haven't done it a million times before."

By eight o'clock that night, I was filling my black plastic bag.

Nikki didn't come to say goodbye, but she did lay my drumsticks on the bed with a note.

"I stole these back for you. You'll need them to buy your mansion in the hills. I love you, Rory. Even if you don't believe me."

～

20

GRACE: PLANTING A SEED

I'd known Beats for one day. One. Yet it had been enough time for him to put a dent in my heart. I'd waited for his call that night, and every night since. Four months had passed, and not an hour went by that I didn't think about him. What had happened to him? Was he hurt, or had he chosen to walk away? With no answers, all I could do was wonder and obsess—mostly about whether he'd found another girl to bring to new heights in the towel hut. God, I was so jealous and heartbroken. How could I have fallen so hard, so fast? And how could it hurt this much?

At first, I'd thought something bad had happened to him; that he was injured or even dead. But as time went on with no word from him, I began to wonder if maybe it was me. Had I not been enough? Too pushy, perhaps? It was possible Beats wasn't ready for the change I was proposing and hadn't wanted to let me down, so he'd left instead. It made sense. He wouldn't have been on the streets if the foster care system hadn't scarred him. Who could blame him for not wanting to return? Most likely he didn't know how to tell me to back off, so instead he'd skipped out into the night, never to be seen again.

In the weeks following his silence, when I still thought something terrible had happened, I'd done my best to search for him, but my youth and inexperience with bureaucracy was getting me nowhere. I had no choice but to turn to Emma for help. I knew it would take some convincing to get her on my side, considering the way Beats and I met, but I didn't take no for an answer. My persistence was what finally persuaded her. Well, that and the fact she'd actually plucked her own hitchhiking boyfriend, Finn, off the side of the road on the way to a musical festival. Apparently both McKallister sisters had a thing for wanderers.

Together Emma and I called or visited hospitals and police stations and even showed up at the local DCFS office to inquire about runaway foster kids. The answers were always the same: either they hadn't seen him, or they cited confidentiality rules. Eventually, we hit a dead end, and I had to accept the fact that I was never going to see him again.

It was crushing. All-consuming. The views from outside the window became my friend. But there was more to my melancholy than met the eye. The night I met Beats, the image on the computer, the deluge of repressed memories that had flooded back to me. I had a secret. A huge one. Who knew? I did, apparently. Either I'd just been too young to recall it or I'd suppressed it because my immature mind had no idea what to do with the information it had stored. The reason didn't matter; what did was that I might have had a chance to stop what happened. I might've been able to save Jake from a fate worse than death.

Go beyond the ordinary, Beats had said. *Unleash what scares you*. It was sound advice, as long as you didn't have a leering monster inside. Once he was awakened, I couldn't lull him back to sleep no matter what I tried. The songs born of angst that Beats had promised if I poked the beast didn't come. It was like the darkness was covering my eyes, trying to keep me from expressing my truth through song. There was some invisible line my mind refused to cross, and it wouldn't allow me to ask why.

Anxiety and fear took hold. I couldn't walk down the main hall without looking over my shoulder. Couldn't play the piano or guitar with crying. My family took notice of the change in my mood, yet no amount of prodding got the truth from me. What would it matter anyway? What was done was done. I couldn't rewind the past. No good would come with revealing what I knew; I'd just cause more heartache for my family. And it wasn't like revealing my secret to Jake would bring us closer together. If I had to guess, it would do the opposite.

I also couldn't share my heartbreak over Beats because the others wouldn't understand. They'd only chastise me for compromising my safety and act as if I'd done something wrong. But I didn't think I had. I'd attempted to help someone in need. In the end, he'd decided not to accept it, but I'd tried, and that was all I could have done.

My mother in particular took to nurturing me a little more snugly. It was almost as if she instinctively understood I was dealing with a broken heart despite there never having been a boy around. Little did she know! Mom and I spent a lot of time together, her teaching me the musicality of songs. Using poppy songs written before I'd slapped the devil, Mom and I tore them apart and put them back together again, structuring the songs by arranging sounds and notes to create verses, choruses, and all the other building blocks of a song. That was where my mother's expertise came in. She'd taught Jake to write songs that reached out and touched people's hearts, and with her guidance and training, my writing strengthened even without trudging through the murkiness of my mind. Slowly but surely, my sad heart healed.

It was during this time that I learned of my mother's own struggles as a young woman. Things I'd only known about her superficially before now came to light. Her early life as an heiress to a hotel mogul; meeting my dad; the disownment. But nothing rattled her until the topic came to Jake and the kidnapping and the things she'd done to help him survive, sometimes at the expense of the rest of us. She spoke with regret but also pride at taking the broken boy he was and making him whole again.

That was where we had something in common. Just as she'd helped Jake get through hard times, I'd wanted to do the same for Beats. Not that it mattered now. He was gone. But that didn't mean I couldn't advocate on his behalf and for those kids like him who might benefit from the same musical therapy Mom had given Jake. I pitched the idea to her—start a music program for foster kids—and it piqued her interest. Before I knew it, she was working together with other music teacher friends in the area to get a program up and running. I knew the class would be of no use to Beats, who I assumed had already aged out of the system, but his influence would benefit others in similar need.

"Psst. Grace." The kid directly behind me poked my back, waking me from my daydream.

I twisted my head to look over my shoulder.

"Check your phone," he whispered.

"Why?"

"Trust me."

As I turned back into my own space, I noticed kids around me staring. Whispering. I looked up at the teacher, who was continuing her lecture despite the low-rolling chatter. I slipped my hand into my backpack. Phones were not allowed during class, but when I looked again at my gawking classmates, each and every one of them had theirs in their hands.

Keeping it under my desk, I turned it on. Not knowing what I was looking for, I checked my messages first and clicked on the one from Quinn that read:

Holy fuck

It was followed by another text with a screenshot: a social media post from Jake, sent twenty minutes ago. A message to his fans. What? How could that be? He was in surgery. It was supposed to take most of the day, I'd been told. All I knew was that my brother was having surgery to repair damage to his knee, damage he sustained in the kidnapping. No further information was given, and I didn't ask. But I'd been under the impression it was fairly routine. No big deal. Jake had even encouraged Quinn and me to go to school. I'd gone, though Quinn hadn't. He was graduating in three months, he'd said, so any learning for him had already been completed. He was driving on fumes now. But not me. I had colleges I wanted to get into next year. I couldn't spend all day in a hospital waiting room.

Blocking out the activity around me, I read the heartfelt letter penned by my brother to his fans. In it, he gave some insight into the kidnapping, and surprisingly, I didn't shy away. It was like discovering my own truth had cured me of the fear. I read how the kidnapping and the media aftermath affected his life. It was honest. Heartbreaking. It was only when I finished that I realized what this was—a goodbye letter. Jake had written this thinking he was going to die. Chills swept through me, raising the hair on my arms. I didn't dare look up, knowing I'd have every set of eyes in the class staring at me.

Grabbing my backpack, I rose to my feet and walked straight to the front of the class.

"Did I excuse you?" the teacher asked as I approached.

"I have to leave."

"Do you need a bathroom pass?"

"No, I have to leave."

"Not without a hall pass. We have twenty minutes left. Sit down."

I dissolved into tears.

"Grace?" Mrs. Parker said, rounding the table. "What's wrong?"

"My brother. Jake."

"What about your brother?"

"I think... I think he's going to die."

21

RORY: A RAY OF GRACE

I had no faith in the system. That much had been established well before I ever stepped foot in Camden Place, a series of colorful buildings with a central hub that reminded me more of a college dorm than an upgraded transitional living center for aged-out foster kids. I'd heard of the place before—we all had—I'd just never given it much thought, knowing the utopian complex would never be for me.

The brainchild of wealthy donors who bestowed large endowments, Camden Place was the Harvard of placements, housing the best and the brightest of my kind—foster kids who'd survived the system with rosy cheeks and good grades and nary a trauma in their lives. They were the ones working toward degrees or being primed for apprenticeships in the trades. Every need was provided for them in an effort to turn the chosen ones into productive members of society and make the donors feel awesome about themselves as they wrote out their next check.

With my thick DCFS file, history of running away, and Mary as my social worker, I was all but disqualified from one of those coveted spots, so I'd regarded the place with nothing but disdain. Until the day the heavens parted and a corner room in building two of Camden Place opened up, and somehow, my name was at the top of the waiting list. There seemed only one explanation for my reversal of fortune, and his name was Daniel Dutch—the windmills, wooden clogs, and Vincent van Gogh special agent himself. Dutch had shown up for me in a big way, proving that it paid to have someone of power in your corner who had a vested interest in keeping you alive.

"Here we are, Rory," the woman said as she arrived at the yellow door in building two. "This is you. You're in Ryan Gosling."

I had no idea what she was talking about, but she was anticipating that, no doubt used to the questioning stares of the new tenants. She dropped into an informational narrative. "Every room is named after a Hollywood celebrity. Makes it more fun, and it's a nod to Los Angeles and Hollywood. Count yourself lucky—the last person I moved in got Kris Jenner."

"Honestly, I feel like it's a toss-up."

She guffawed, looking me over. She couldn't have been much older than me, a former foster kid herself, I guessed just by the telltale flicker of distrust in her eyes.

"Look," she said, "I'd take the Bill Cosby to live here. You hit the lottery. And a single room, even. Who sprinkled fairy dust on you? Someone usually has to die for one of these unicorns to open up."

Someone almost did: me, I thought to myself, as she turned the key in the lock and pushed the door open.

"It's fully furnished, and you have a starter kit of household items to get you through the first week. They already provided you with a phone, I see. Last thing. Did you go through orientation?"

"I did."

"Great! Then you know all about the facilities. If you have

any questions, the office is staffed twenty-four seven. All right, then, I'll leave you to it. Welcome home, Rory."

IT DIDN'T TAKE LONG to get acquainted with my new 500-square-foot digs. It took even less time to unpack. And then I stood in the middle of the space, unsure what to do. Where did I go from here? I couldn't go back to where I'd come from, but I didn't know how to go forward, either. No one had ever taught me. And now, no one ever would.

I was all alone. Just me, now, and what I made of myself. As the realization hit me, I sank down on the edge of the bed. Until now, there had always been that small part of me that still had hope. Hope that I would find a family. A mom or a dad. A place I could call home. A place to celebrate the holidays. I'd always imagined a father I could call for advice or a mother I could introduce my first child to. None of that would happen now. That portal had sealed, with me standing on the wrong side.

As grateful as I was to get this place, it came with independence and the expectation that I would need to become a man despite no one ever teaching me how. I had no life skills. No education. No money. No guidance. It occurred to me then that I was fucking terrified. I was in charge of the rest of my life. What the hell was I going to do now?

Beams of light crisscrossing the room drew my attention to the mini disco ball hanging from a hook above the window. Had it been left by the previous tenant, or did it come standard in The Gosling? I walked over to the window and examined the tiny mirrored tiles. Something about the ball captured my imagination, and as each facet reflected light back into the air, casting it into dozens of small beams that streamed out in all directions, I was reminded of Grace and her sparkling, sunny beauty. She lit up a space like a disco ball, only it didn't take thousands of tiny tiles to harness the effect. Her light came from the inside and illuminated everything in its sight.

I drew in a deep, lifesaving breath.

"Okay, Grace," I whispered, "I hear you."

22

GRACE: I HAVE A SECRET

Today marked the twenty-eighth day of Jake lingering in a coma, and I was on brother duty. We had a schedule. My time was every Tuesday and Thursday after school, as well as rotating shifts on the weekend. The idea was that Jake would never be alone in the solitary world he'd built somewhere inside his head. Each one of us pledged to keep his limbs moving and his brain stimulated. When he woke up—and we were convinced he would—such interventions would aid in his recovery.

Many of my Jake shifts were spent doing homework or reading from textbooks to him, but other days we worked through song lyrics, both his and mine. Pulling up his own extensive and award-winning discography online, I dissected his songwriting skills one track at a time with the slumbering master right by my side. Jake and I had full-on, one-sided conversations. Save for the occasional nurse or doctor visit during my shift, no one was around to hear me babble.

So many times, I'd wanted to tell him what I knew, and I'd come dangerously close a few times. There was nothing good that could come of it, I told myself. Nothing. Yet with each day that passed, the burden weighed more heavily on me. What if I just whispered in his ear?

I leaned over the bed and touched Jake's face, testing for a reaction. If ever there was a confession that warranted such precaution, it would be this one. He didn't stir, so I proceeded. "I have a secret."

I waited for a reply, my lips so close to Jake's ear I could feel the heat of my breath reflected back on me. Why was I so scared? It wasn't like I'd done anything wrong. I'd been a little girl at the time. How could I be blamed for things someone else had done? Yet the brutal truth was that Jake wouldn't be lying here in this coma today if I'd had the presence of mind to speak up all those years ago.

"I know what you're thinking, Jake. Who cares, right? What can your mundane little sister possibly have to say that would hold any interest to an icon like you?"

Jake seemed to agree as he remained perfectly still. I wondered every day what was going on inside that head of his. Doctors couldn't explain it. He should've woken up, they'd said. Every test had been taken, every X-ray performed, the consensus being that there was no obvious medical condition preventing him from opening his eyes, which begged the question—did he not want to come back to us?

No one would blame him if he chose to leave us all behind. He'd already suffered more than any one human should. But things were different now. He had Casey. She was the promise of normalcy that he desperately craved. With her in his life, he had a future. I couldn't fathom Jake wanting to leave her, not without a fight. So that led me to conclude this purgatory Jake was lingering in was something darker, something that held him like a vise.

"Here's the thing, Jake. What if my secret wasn't entirely mine? What if my secret was partly"—I let out the breath I'd

been safekeeping before whispering the final, scandalous bit—
"yours?"

That should do it. If Jake was listening, this would surely be
the moment he opened his eyes. Nothing. Really?

"I'd never tell you this if I thought you could hear me. It
would only bring you pain, and that's why I've never said
anything. I'm not even sure why I'm telling you this now, except
maybe I want to say it out loud. Acknowledge that it was real,
and maybe even relieve some of the pressure of knowing what I
know."

Jake neither confirmed nor denied receipt of my explanation, so I continued.

"I saw him, Jake. A couple of days before he took you, I saw
Ray."

There—I'd said his name. Ray. Jake's kidnapper. The man
my brother hated with every fiber of his being. The man he'd
battled in a fight to the death. Ray Davis. The monster who lived
in both our heads.

"He talked to me. I was four years old at the time and didn't
understand the interaction. I can't even remember his face. All I
remember was the baseball cap he wore and the words he spoke
to me. Growing up, I had dreams about the encounter, but I
never knew it was real until I got the courage to look up details
about the kidnapping a couple of months back. I'd probably
seen a picture of Ray before, but I hadn't made the connection,
not until I saw one specific image of him wearing the same baseball cap from my dreams. On the front was the logo of a
company: an embroidered deer.

It was then that the memories came flooding back. Of us at
the store. You, me, mom, Kyle, and Quinn. Mom was buying
school supplies for you boys, and she was distracted. She left me
sitting in the cart a few feet away, and the rest of you were
behind a display rack. I saw Ray peek around the endcap. He

smiled at me. We started playing this waving game, back and forth. And then he walked right up to me, so brazen, and whispered in my ear."

I stopped then, gulping back the horror. I couldn't tell Jake what he'd said. Even if he was asleep, I physically couldn't. The words wouldn't come. The cruelty of them. What I did know for sure was that Jake was never meant to survive. Yet somehow, at thirteen years old, he'd become his own hero, saving himself when no one else could do it for him.

"And then days later, he took you. No one told me what happened. All they would say was that you were coming home soon, acting like you were away at some really sad summer camp because everyone was crying. It didn't connect in my mind —the man with the deer on his hat, the words he spoke, and you suddenly gone. I'm so sorry, Jake. I wished I'd been older. Smarter. The interaction stuck with me through the years. I dreamed about it, sometimes waking up crying and trying to explain to Mom and Dad about the man with the green and white baseball cap with the logo of a deer on the front. Everyone thought he was a figment of my imagination. My make-believe friend. Eventually, I stopped remembering. Maybe that was why I didn't want anyone around me to talk about the kidnapping."

I drew in a deep breath, knowing I needed it for the final reveal, but if Jake was in there listening, then he surely already knew what was coming.

"Jake, Ray is the Reindeer Man. And when he whispered in my ear, he confessed to a crime that hadn't happened yet."

MY BROTHER'S eyes flew open.

~

DISORIENTED DISTRESS. That was the only way to accurately describe those split seconds after revealing my secret. Jake jerked upright, his eyes blinking rapidly and his hands clawing and ripping at anything in sight, sending tubes and wires flying. No joke, I thought I was witnessing a zombie uprising. I froze in place, my eyes wide open and suspended in horror. Slow and measured, his head turned in my direction, and I gulped. Audibly.

Jake's eyes narrowed in on me, his laser beam shrinking me down in size. Suddenly, I was my four-year-old self again, hiding behind Emma's protective leg as our dad steered a bruised and broken Jake into the house, proudly proclaiming that all was right in the world again. Um, no, it wasn't. One look into teenage Jake's lifeless eyes was all it took to convince me he was not all right. A ghost, Quinn had called him. A monster, I'd secretly thought.

And now he'd risen again, trying to speak despite no decipherable sound coming out. Jake seemed confused and panicked, dropping back onto the bed. With his pinpoint focus no longer paralyzing me in place, I sprinted for the door, away from him and toward the strength in numbers that would protect me. Running away like I'd done when we were kids. Like I promised I'd never do again.

"Help!" I screamed, swinging the door wide open. "Help me."

I meant him, of course. Help *him*.

HELP CAME RUNNING, nearly spinning me around like a revolving door as hospital staff dashed into Jake's room. I didn't follow them back in; I couldn't have even if I'd wanted to. My feet were glued in place, my mind a jumbled mess. It wasn't like they needed me anyway, I reasoned with my guilty self. They were the professionals, and I'd just get in the way. Besides, I'd done my job. I'd awakened the sleeping giant. My words had reached inside Jake's head and coaxed him out. That was a good thing. The world would rejoice and so would I, once the shock subsided. I loved my brother, and all that mattered now was that he get better. So why then did it feel like I'd just sacrificed myself to resurrect my superstar brother?

"Tell me again what happened," Kyle demanded, flipping around the chair he'd dragged from the nurses' station and straddling it.

"I already told you twice," I protested, hating to have to deceive my family. But what choice did I have? I couldn't very well reveal the truth, so instead, I spun an improvised, fanciful tale of Jake miraculously awakening to the image of Chuck the kitten, our new furry brother. As each new family member came to me for the story, I just kept repeating the same thin kitty lie over and over with such airheaded enthusiasm that I couldn't believe anyone would buy it. But they did. Each and every one of them... except for Kyle, who relentlessly attempted to poke holes in my story. Honestly, I wasn't sure what offended me more, that Kyle didn't believe me or that the rest of my family did. Who did they think I was, the Nickelodeon Channel?

"Again," Kyle repeated, beckoning my lie forward with the flick of his hand. "From the start this time. Speak slower, and please tone down the Minnie Mouse impersonation."

My lips flattened at his not-so-subtle insult. Kyle always let it be known that the pitch of my female adolescence got on his nerves, and normally, I fought back with a smear of my own, but I didn't have the luxury of a counterattack today, not when all of my brain power was going toward getting my story straight. Never a prolific liar, I could feel myself cracking under the pressure. I'd already whittled away three brightly colored nails, their tiny shards littering the floor below, and given that I still had round two with Jake to contend with, the odds were *not* in favor of the other seven making it through the day.

"Like I said before, I was showing him a video of Chuck..."

"Video? I thought you said picture?"

"Video. Picture. I showed him both," I said, throwing my hands up in frustration. "I don't remember which form of media interested him most."

"And he just woke up?" Kyle snapped his fingers. "Like that?"

I hesitated a split second before raising the pep level to throw him off course. "Yep, just like that."

Kyle shook his head, clearly not pacified by my lies. "And he didn't say anything to you when he woke up?"

Something in the way he asked the question gave me pause. Why was he so conflicted? Kyle had been in Jake's room not long before me. Had he seen something? It occurred to me then that maybe this had nothing to do with the kitten. Maybe Kyle had been the first one to jar Jake awake.

"No," I said, my tone softening for him. "He couldn't. Jake was too disoriented."

That seemed to satisfy Kyle, and he turned his attention away from me, deep in thought. I took the welcome hiatus to get a head start on nail number four.

Keith exited Jake's room, heading straight for me. "Grace, your turn. Keep it brief. He's really tired."

My siblings had all gone in to see Jake, and I was the only one left. I really didn't want to go in. I'd already said enough. "It's okay. I don't need to go in."

"No. I'm sure he wants to see you."

Uh, I was pretty sure he didn't. Even in best of times, Jake had never been eager to see me, and this was most definitely not the "best of times."

Pushing off the wall, I solemnly made my way to his door, stopping only to quietly address my sister. "Come with me."

"What?" she replied. "Why?"

"Because you know I get nervous around Jake."

If anyone knew, it was Emma. She'd spent countless nights holding me tight when I was a little girl as Jake worked through the trauma.

"Hey, I get it," Emma said, sweeping a wayward strand of hair behind my ear. "But you'll be fine, Grace. I was in there before Keith. Jake's weak. He can barely talk. Just go in, give him a kiss on the cheek, and leave."

"Come on, Em. Come with me," I begged. "No one cares if you do."

"Jake's doctor does. You heard him. One visitor at a time so we don't overexcite him."

Overexcite? A little too late for that, I'd say. Jake's doctor hadn't been there to witness me raising him from the dead.

"Go." My sister nudged me along. "I'll be right here waiting for you."

Right here wasn't *in there*.

Resigned, I dropped my head and walked the rest of the way alone. Was this what death row inmates felt like going to their executions? The lights were dimmed as I pushed my way in, such a contrast from the last time I'd opened the door when I'd been screaming and escaping. I couldn't tell if he was awake or sleeping because I refused to look in his direction, opting instead to stay along the perimeter of the room, as far a distance from him as I could get.

"Grace," his raspy voice whispered. Nearly a month on intubation was reason enough for his vocal cords to be affected, but the tube was out now, and he was doing the best he could with a raw and aching throat. That he could form words at all seemed almost like a miracle. He held his hand out for me.

I couldn't predict my fate by the tone of his whisper, but I knew there was no point in delaying. Slowly, I walked toward his bed, careful to keep my eyes averted as I gripped the railing on his bed.

"I'm sorry... if..." Jake stopped, wrestling with the words. "If... I scared you."

I looked up, more than a little surprised by the apology. "It's okay. I'm sorry about the... you know."

His brows furrowed like he had no idea what 'you know' meant.

"You know," I repeated, then followed it up with a whisper, "The Reindeer Man."

Jake was quiet for a long time, seemingly working his way through my words. I watched him, confused by his confusion. Finally, he replied. "Your imaginary friend?"

What the...? He had to be kidding me. There was no way. No way he didn't remember our conversation. I got that he'd just woken from a coma and things were foggy, but how could he forget the very thing that had awakened him from a twenty-eight-day sleep? Unless... he'd never really heard what I said at all. Maybe it wasn't my words that had woken him. It could have been my whispers triggering his brain to turn back on.

Who cared? He didn't remember, and my secret would continue to stay with me. I supposed it was a good thing, yet it didn't feel that way. For a very short period of time, I'd had an ally. Even if we never discussed it again, he knew, and I wasn't alone.

"Yes, Jake. My imaginary reindeer friend."

23

RORY: ON THE COUNT OF THREE

I sat in the back of the classroom, taking it all in. And it was a
lot; more than I'd bargained for when I'd seen the flyer for
the music class and decided to give it a try. At the very least, I
hoped to feel sticks back in my hands. At the very most, I wanted
to be playing again, on a drum kit like the universe had always
intended. But it was clear the minute the class started that I'd
been recruited to the minor leagues.

Yes, it had been advertised as a music class for all levels, but
from what I could tell, there was only one level—ground. Had I
not tucked myself into the corner and felt leaving in the middle
would be rude, I'd already have been gone by now.

My only consolation as I waited out the hour was watching
the teacher, a cultured woman in her forties, attempt to find
good in all the questionable performances, especially when
some of them were just messing with her. Wasting her time. And
she knew it. I had to hand it to her—she handled them well, like
she had some troublemakers of her own at home. This woman
was volunteering her hard-earned time for this shit. I had to
wonder what was in it for her.

After a particularly aggressive flute solo, the unflappable

music teacher cut a path in my direction and stopped directly in front of me. I quickly removed my propped feet from the table and looked up at her.

"I don't think I've seen you here before," she said, more a statement than a greeting.

I wanted to tell her to get a good look because it would be the last time she saw me in here, but the woman had already had a rough session and I was feeling generous.

"This is my first time."

"What brings you in here?"

"Just checking it out."

"That's it? No hidden talent you'd like to reveal?" She paused for a moment and then whispered, "Please."

I laughed.

She winked. "Let me guess—you play the drums."

I blinked up at her in surprise. What made her think that?

"You've been tapping out a beat with your fingers since you got here. Did you bring your drumsticks?"

"I lost them a few months ago."

"Well, that won't do."

She walked back across the room to her big bag of tricks and produced a set of well-worn sticks. My favorite kind. Instead of carrying them back to me, she stayed put and waved them in the air.

"Show me what you got and they're yours."

I smiled at her offer, then checked the clock on the wall... ten more minutes before I bounced. This place wasn't for me. I was too advanced, and really, I didn't *need* the sticks. I just wanted them. Like, really bad. I was tired of their subpar substitutes— pencils and spoons and Frigo cheese sticks.

Normally it would be a no-brainer. Get up and perform. I'd certainly never been shy with a pair of sticks in my hands. But her offer felt as if there were strings attached, like this woman would wrangle me into being the star of her dysfunctional school of rock.

"What's your name?"

"Rory."

"Nice to meet you, Rory, I'm Mrs. M," she said, and I could already feel her getting her claws into me. "So, what do you say? Are you ready to put some of that swagger to the test?"

Unable to resist the dare, I rose from my chair and ambled over to her. She held out the sticks, and before they'd even left her hands, I had them twirling through my fingers.

Her smile widened. "That's what I thought."

With all the confidence in the world, I walked to the drum kit and straddled the stool, taking a moment to glide my hands over the equipment. The tactile feel of the skins sent a thrill through me. It was like being back with old friends. It had been way too long. I'd wanted to pick up some buckets and sticks and start playing again, but then what? I couldn't go back out to the streets and busk, not with Hartman out there waiting to take me down. Had I known this drum kit was in here waiting for me, I would've been sneaking in through the back doors and playing while everyone slept, or tried to sleep.

Really, I should've known Camden Place would offer a class like this. They had something for everyone. Those wealthy do-gooders sure knew how to run a charity. And you wouldn't hear me complaining one bit. I was directly benefiting. With their paid and volunteer staff available to guide me, I got back on track with my education, choosing to go for my GED over being held back a grade in school, which was what I would've had to do to catch up after everything I'd missed. Tutoring was just one of the many programs offered. There were life skills classes and apprenticeship programs and group therapy sessions. Sports. Poetry. Art. Even goat yoga for the bougiest of us. And then there was Mrs. M and her sad little music therapy program.

Looking out over the class of underachievers, I decided they needed some Fireball in their lives, so I kicked it off with a single stroke, double kick pattern and some syncopated snare drum hits. With adrenaline pumping through me, I was a bit quick on the start but managed to bring the tempo back down and pace myself through the remainder of the song. It wasn't like any of these musical misfits would know the difference anyway. They were thrilled with my performance and gave me a roaring round of applause.

Curiously, Mrs. M did not. She watched. Studied. Nodded. But she didn't smile or clap. I couldn't read her expression, and she didn't give me much by way of verbal acknowledgement.

"Very nice," was all she said.

Very nice? Very nice! I had no conceivable way to interpret that.

Mrs. M dismissed the class soon after. I rose from the stool and followed the other students to the door, still clutching my sticks—they'd been part of the deal whether she liked my performance or not.

"Rory, can you hang back?"

Pissed at her lackluster reaction, I had half a mind to walk out, but I stopped in place and turned around, forcing the rest of the students to swerve in all directions to avoid a direct collision with me.

"You have a very interesting style, Rory."

Interesting? That ranked up there with *very nice* in the scope of unflattering compliments. With an abundance of adjectives to choose from, that was all she could think to come up with? Interesting didn't fill stadiums. Someday, Mrs. M would eat her words.

"I haven't seen someone with your talent in a long time. But what's interesting is you haven't even reached your full potential. You're like a raw, uncut diamond. You've got everything it takes to shine, but you need to be cut into the perfect shape and your rough edges smoothed out."

I frowned, irritation rankling my bones. As far as I was concerned—as far as the crowds who used to gather around to watch me play were concerned—I already was a diamond. Maybe I was rusty after not having played in a while, but I shone.

"You have a lot of bad habits," she continued, almost like she talking to herself out loud, so I could hear and get even more pissed. "But you're skilled enough to make it work."

"I'm rusty. I haven't played in months so..." I mumbled, letting my excuse trail off.

"You're self-taught, right?"

I almost didn't want to give her a reply. She didn't deserve one. People had always accepted my talent at face value. If she couldn't see it, well then, fuck her.

"Yes. I play on buckets mostly."

She raised a brow, tapping a finger to her lip. "Hmm. That's why."

"That's why?" I bristled. Mrs. M was wearing on my last nerve. "What do you mean?"

"You favor the rims, like you would on buckets. And the bounce is different on skins than on a plastic bucket surface, so it makes sense that your timing is slightly off. If you're just playing for fun, it's not a big deal..."

"I don't play for fun. I play for my survival."

"I hear you," she replied, her intense blue eyes studying me. "Can I ask you something?"

I laid the sticks on the stool and backed away, no longer wanting her gift if it came with condemnation. Who was this lady to question me? To judge me? To give me unsolicited advice. "Nah. I've got to go."

"Rory," she called to my exiting back. "How far do you want to take this talent of yours?"

I swung back around, squaring my jaw in defiance. "All the way."

"Then pick those sticks back up and I'll take you there."

ONE HOUR. I'd worked with her for one hour, and already my edges were softening. Mrs. M was no joke. This was not some bored rich lady trying to feel good about herself by giving an hour of her time a week to a bunch of misfortunate foster kids who had never been, and would never be, as privileged as her. Mrs. M had real knowledge to impart. A musician's mind. I was blown away by the things she knew about the instrument I considered myself an expert on. But I'd been self-taught; everything I knew about drumming had been learned through trial and error. While I'd had some training in school, it was only as part of the song we were performing and never as an individual musician. No one had ever sat me down like Mrs. M and shown me what I didn't know.

After our first of hopefully many sessions, I walked Mrs. M to her car and loaded her bags into the trunk. I still had a hold of the sticks she'd given me.

"Did you want these back?" I asked.

"No. They're yours to keep. I hope you'll return next week. I can work with you after the class."

"I will."

"I wasn't too blunt, was I? Sometimes when I'm super focused, I lose all social skills."

"Nah, it's all right. I did consider letting the air out of your tires at one point, though."

"Oh, no." She laughed. "It's just rare to find someone like

you. I know it's hard to hear criticism, but I can assure you, Rory, everything you need to be great is already there. I'm here to bring you to the next level, so you can excel like you were always intended to."

I could tell just in her tone that she believed every word she spoke, and that sparked something inside me. I wanted to make her proud, to prove to her that her faith in me was warranted. And I would make her proud. Someday.

"You know what, Mrs. M? No matter how I perform, I'm only *very nice* until I'm sparkling like a diamond."

She tipped her head up, smiling. "I'll see you next week, Rory. You did very nice tonight."

I found myself grinning as I headed back to my building. This felt like the start of something big. Like finally I had the upper hand. I had no doubt Mrs. M was going to get me where I needed to be, and when she was done, I'd have a real shot at my dreams. I'd only ever been good at one thing, and this was it. Drumming was all I had to offer. I'd do whatever it took to succeed.

Clicking my key fob against the pad, the outer door unlocked, and I was about to push it open when the flyer taped to the door stopped me dead. Flyers were all over the place, advertising different events, but this had just one phrase written across it. *On the count of three.* It hit me like a bolt of lightning. I swung around, my heart pounding in my chest as I scanned the area for the person who'd left the message. Because it was a message. And it had been left specifically for me.

Could it have been just a coincidence? Someone posting an inspirational quote? "On the count of three." But what else could that mean? Nothing that I could think of. There was no way this was a weird fluke. They had to be taunting me, knowing the sentence would instantly bring me back to the times spent in front of their lens. It wasn't just that they'd used the phrase often, following it up with a command and a three-finger count-down, but that I'd made my stand on those five words.

No, I'd bravely challenged.

No?

That message could mean only one thing: they knew where I was, and they wanted me to know it. Camden Place, my safe sanctuary, would never be safe again.

24

GRACE: THE START OF US

"So, how did it go with Kenzie's siblings at the beach?" Mom asked, passing me the salad bowl. She was so innocent in her query. If she knew anything about Kyle's girlfriend's triplet siblings, the three C's, as they were known, she wouldn't have asked in the first place.

"It..." Quinn paused, exchanging an amused glance with me. "Went."

Like pretty much every other teenager on earth, I loved the first days of summer. The sun, the surf, the freedom from studies. But after a difficult junior year where I'd lost Beats, almost lost Jake, and then had to watch every last member of my Dude Pack walk across the graduation stage, I was counting on this summer to bring some welcome relief. That was not going to happen with Kenzie's siblings attached at the hip.

"What's that supposed to mean?" Mom asked, seemingly surprised though I wasn't sure why. She'd seen them in action. Last night after dinner, she'd watched the water line in our pool drop to drought levels when the two boys got into a competitive belly flopping contest. "They seem fun."

"Let's just say I understand why they live in a cabin in the deep woods," Quinn said.

"You cannot tell me you didn't enjoy Caroline attached to your back in a bikini all day."

"I wasn't talking about Caroline. She can ride me like a fashion statement anytime. I was talking about your two homicidal admirers."

"Uh-oh," Mom laughed. "What did Colton and Cooper do?"

"They got into a fistfight over who would build me a sand castle. I would've accepted two." I shrugged. "And then they used their spilled blood as the liquid in their moats, each one trying to fill theirs the fullest. Sand play should not be so bloody."

"Those boys can be a little intense." Mom's diplomacy surrounding Kenzie's younger identical brothers did not fully depict the reality of spending a day with them. Of course, I'd heard the stories. The afternoon Kyle and Jake had spent with the Williams triplets at their home in Northern California was seared into my memory forever. But I'd never experienced them myself until they came to visit their sister at the start of the summer break. And today on the beach, their dysfunction was on full display.

"I knew those two were up to no good," Dad said, taking a break from his lemon chicken dinner to participate. "Last night, I caught them in the backyard workroom, and when I asked what they were doing, they said they were looking for a circular saw. What do you need one of those for on vacation?"

"What do you need one of those for in general?" Quinn asked.

"I hope you didn't give them one," Mom said.

My father held up his hands and wiggled his fingers. "You think I'd still have these if I had a circular saw?"

"Good point." She laughed, grabbing her plate and standing up. "Anyway, I've got to run. I have a private lesson tonight."

"Private lesson for who?" I asked.

"One of my students."

Dad swallowed a bite. "The free ones?"

"The ones I volunteer with, yes."

"Oh." He sulked, pushing food around his plate. "I was hoping to be a kept man by now, but I suppose I'll just continue delivering mail."

"Yes, I suppose you will." She leaned down and kissed him. "My prodigy thanks you for your sacrifice."

"Prodigy?" Quinn perked up. "Who are you training?"

"A very talented kid in my music program."

My interest was piqued. "One of your foster kids?"

"Yes. A drummer. I have a feeling about him."

I straightened up in my chair, my eyes now fixed on my mother as my pulse quickened. A drummer, she said? I knew a drummer like that.

"What's the feeling?" I asked, not daring to dream that the same drummer had crossed both our paths.

"He's got that something special that can't be taught, you know? I'm just building off that. Working with him on his timing and technique. He learns so fast. It's amazing no one has ever really worked with him before me."

Dots were connecting everywhere, but it couldn't be. It couldn't.

"Does the kid know who you are? That he's getting trained— for free—by the famous Michelle McKallister?"

Mom rolled her eyes. "Hardly, Scott, and he's an eighteen-year-old foster kid who's barely getting by. Do you really want me to charge him while you eat your dinner in a seven-thou-sand-square-foot home?"

"Please don't ruin my dinner."

Quinn laughed. I would have too had my heart not been racing so fast.

"Wait," I said. "You have older foster kids in your program? You never told me that. I thought they were all young. Kids and teens."

"I started two different programs, one for the younger kids and one for the older ones over at Camden Place, the housing co-op for foster kids who've aged out of the system."

What in the living hell? How had I not known this? I'd assumed Beats was too old to benefit from my mother's music class. Had I known, I would've... what? What would I have done? I wasn't sure, but it felt like I'd wasted a whole lot of time not knowing this pertinent information.

I actually whimpered my displeasure. "I wish you'd told me."

"Why?"

"I... I just like to know what you're doing."

"Really?" She quirked her brows. "Since when?"

"Since always."

"O...kay. I was under the impression you barely listened to anything I said. But I tell you what, Grace, when I get home, I'll give you a full report."

She was mocking me, of course, and I surely deserved it. She had spoken of the program occasionally, but there had never been anything to catch my attention until her drummer boy foster kid paralleled my own. What were the chances it was the same guy we were both talking about? There had to be plenty of prodigy drummers in the dream capital of the world. Although how many of them were eighteen-year-olds in foster care?

Wait. Was it really such a coincidence? I was the one who'd encouraged my mother to start her music program in the first place—*because of Beats*. I'd thought maybe she might be able to help heal talented musicians like him, like she'd healed Jake. I'd just never thought it would be Beats himself. It had never occurred to me that programs existed to house fosters who aged out of the system. Beats had never mentioned it to me, although a lot had been left unsaid, considering we'd only had twenty-four hours together. So, if I really thought about it, her happening upon him wasn't that much of a coincidence after all.

"If he's that good, ask him if he wants to join my new band," Quinn said, only half joking.

"You already have a band. Are you abandoning the Dude Pack?"

"Grace, don't make me feel bad. They can't hang, and you know it."

I did, but I was still sad for them all the same. Music was what they lived for, and Quinn was the only one who could take them to that place, and now he never would.

"Well, someone's going to snatch this kid up," Mom said. "So it might as well be you."

"Then ask him for me. I'm serious."

"I will, once he's ready. Like I said, he's raw. He's trained almost exclusively on paint buckets."

The fork dropped from my hand, clanging onto the plate and bouncing over the edge of the table. The mewl that escaped my mouth drew everyone's attention.

"Grace, are you okay?"

I couldn't talk. Could barely breathe. My body flushed from top to toes. Beats. Mom was talking about Beats. It had to be. My mother. My mother knew him.

"She's choking," Dad yelled, reaching over and heroically smacking my back in an attempt to dislodge the chicken he assumed was stuck in my throat.

"I'm okay. I'm okay," I lied, nearly beaten off my chair by his punches. Righting myself, I tentatively asked, "Is his name Beats?"

"Beats?" Her forehead wrinkled. "No, who's that?"

I was forced to come up with a split-second lie. "Just a drummer on social media who plays on buckets."

"Oh, no. Not him. This kid's name is Rory. Rory Higgins."

I EXCUSED myself when my mother left the table, never so relieved that she'd forced me to share my location on her phone and vice versa. It meant I could follow her directly to Camden Place and smoke the evasive drummer right out of his hiding spot. Beats was alive and well, which meant all the crying I'd done for him was for naught. This whole time, he'd just been ghosting me. Steam squealed through my ears.

Arriving shortly after my mother, I made sure to park in a different lot to ensure confidentiality. I then turned off my tracking. I would need ample, undisturbed time to rip Beats a new one. No, not Beats. The slippery sucker was named Rory. Was that really so hard for him to admit? He could've kept his last name a secret and still given me Rory, which would have prevented me from writing his stripper name, Beats, into my diary for the past seven months. My mood soured. I wasn't sure if I was relieved he was alive or if I wanted to rekill him.

I tracked my mother to the recreation center and followed the sound of the drums through the long hallway. Peeking into the open door, I saw them in the back of the class, Beats on the stool and my mother standing just to the right of him. They seemed so in sync, so focused on a goal. Beats had put on some much-needed weight, and his hair was shorter than before, pretty boy in style, but he still maintained that same wild, edgy look I found so attractive. Observing him now, I understood why. It was the way his eyes were set, with a tired squinch in them, and added to that, the darker pigment of the skin circling them, which set them off in striking fashion.

Yet there was something different in the way he interacted with my mother. He was so relaxed, so engaged. Not looking for the nearest exit. It hit me then that the foster kid who didn't trust adults trusted my mother. Something about that spoke to me, and despite my anger at being dumped, the sweetness of the moment touched my heart.

My mother was healing him.

While they were absorbed in conversation, I slipped into the room and tucked myself behind a podium. With my head resting against the wall, I listened to my mother and Beats interacting and was struck by their familiarity. Their mutual respect. Their friendship, even.

My mom didn't always get a fair shake. Emma had resented her for her actions when Jake went missing. So had Kyle and, to an extent, Quinn too. But I understood my mother in a way that my other siblings didn't. I *was* my mother in so many ways. Both fiercely devoted to family, we'd stop at nothing to protect the ones we loved, but we could just as easily fade into the background when our strength wasn't needed. My gregarious father was like the sturdy walls of our home, but my practical mother had always been the bedrock.

Watching her now with Beats, I was so proud of her. Like me, she'd been able to look past his shield and see the broken boy behind. Even though he'd abandoned me, I still wanted the best for him, and I loved that my mother was drawing out his talent just as she'd done for Jake before him. Quinn had benefitted too, despite him not realizing his wounds also needed healing.

An hour passed, maybe more, before the two finally called it a night. When I'd heard Beats playing on the street all those months ago, I'd thought he was perfect, but now that my mother had corrected his quirks and introduced tricks to improve his timing, I was amazed. My mother had taken something that was already great and made it incredible.

I slipped out the door, exited the building, and hid behind a gathering of bushes as I waited for the unlikely pair to exit. And they did, together, making small talk as Beats walked my mom out to her car. Ah, he was making sure she got off safely. But he was still a scoundrel, and I couldn't forget that, no matter how incredibly hot he was.

It was on his way back that I stepped into the light, startling him so thoroughly that his body slammed into the brick retaining wall.

"Son of a fuck!" Beats bounced back, his hands at the ready.

"Stop!" I said, seriously concerned he might punch me.

Beats blinked, placing his right foot a step closer and examining me in the dim light. "Grace?"

He said my name in question form, steeped in disbelief.

"Yes. If you hit me, I'll kick you in the nuts."

His hands instantly dropped to his sides. "What are you doing here?"

"I think the question is, what are *you* doing here, alive and well?"

"I live here. Grace..."

Beats took a step forward. I took one back, shooting death rays from my eyes. He halted in place, smart enough to read the signs of a woman scorned. He lifted his hands in front of him like he was suddenly under attack by a rabid dog.

"Wait, are you pissed?" he asked. "You look pissed."

"Um... you know," I clenched my teeth. "I'm not super-duper happy with you right now."

"I can see that. I'm just really confused," he said, taking a tentative step forward.

I crossed my arms in front of me, accentuating the frostiness his actions had created between us. "You and me both."

Beat shook his head, still seemingly trying to wrap his head around getting caught in his lies. "What are you doing here?"

"Checking to see if it was really you. Funny story—for the past seven months, I thought you were dead, but no, you're actually very much alive. Good for you, douchebag."

"Oh shit, Grace, no. I can explain."

"No need. I've seen all I care to." I turned to leave but then thought better of it. "Actually, no. You don't get off that easy. Not that you care, but I've spent countless hours of my life worrying about you, and all this time you've been fucking fantastic. How awesome for you. Now, please excuse me, I'm going to go flog myself in the town square."

We both stood there a second, staring at each other in silence, and then I watched a smile slowly spread across his face. "Does Los Angeles even have a town square?"

The tension in my body instantly eased. "I... honestly don't know. But I suppose I could flog myself in the mall parking lot, too."

"I definitely think that seems more on brand for you," he agreed, and that charm I'd fallen head over feet for came roaring back.

"Ah, Beats." I flattened my palms on his chest and pushed him. "Why'd you have to be such a disappointment? If you didn't want me around, you could've just told me to get lost. At least I can respect that."

"Because I didn't want you to get lost. You were right to be worried about me. Something happened that night after I left your car. Something bad."

He pointed to a scar above his eye that definitely hadn't been there before. I unfolded my arms and took a step closer, touching my finger to the scar. Anger instantly transformed into concern. My beautiful drummer boy was no longer a douchebag. Hallelujah! "What happened?"

Beats launched into a retelling of that night and its aftermath. I was shocked to learn of his two-week hospital stay, followed by a months-long stint in a rehabilitation clinic. There were certain things, certain mannerisms and hesitations that convinced me I wasn't getting the whole story, but it didn't really matter. The results were the same. He'd been severely injured, and while he was lying in the hospital fighting for his life, I'd lost my faith in him.

"It wasn't that I didn't want to call you, Grace. It was that I couldn't. I lost everything. The money, my buckets and sticks, the clothes you washed for me. Your number."

"I thought..."

"I know what you thought," he said, sliding his fingers along my forearm in a move that sent my shivers tripping all over themselves. "But I wouldn't do that to you. I just wouldn't."

"I had a bad feeling that night. I should've trusted my intuition and insisted on driving you to the hotel."

"Motel." He grinned.

"What?"

"I don't think you realize they don't mean the same thing, Grace. Hotel and motel."

I blinked, unsure what he was talking about. "You rent them for the night. What's the difference?"

"Like two, three hundred dollars. Never mind. Anyway, it wouldn't have mattered whether you drove me there or not. They would've picked me off the next day or the day after."

"You're saying they targeted you?"

Beats instantly backtracked, becoming flustered. He shoved his hands in his pockets. "No, I... it was just thugs..."

He was lying. I wanted to probe him about it, but I'd just found him again and didn't want to push him away.

"Okay," I said, laying my hand on his to reassure him. "It doesn't matter. I'm just so happy you're okay, Beats. Hey, wait, can I call you Rory?"

"You know my name?"

"I do now."

"How?"

"Does it matter? I found you."

He squinted even deeper than normal, letting it be known he thought I was lying too, but like me, he didn't want to push it either. "You aren't the only one who was looking. Do you have any idea how many Graces live in LA that are on Snapchat?"

"Did you try Grace Note?"

His face dropped. "You better be fucking kidding me!"

"I am." I laughed. "Anyway, let's just agree that we both suffered, and move on from there."

"Okay," he agreed. "Although I feel like I suffered more."

"It's not a competition, Rory."

He smiled, shaking his head as if still processing the change of both of our fortunes. "Can I hug you without you sending me back to the hospital?"

"You can." I stepped forward and wrapped my arms around him. "The question is, Rory, can I hug you without you taking me to the towel hut?"

He lips rode close to my ear. "That memory has gotten me through some rough nights."

"Oh, me too."

We stared at each other, the chemistry between us pulsating. Rory leaned in, so close our lips were only a kiss apart. I could feel his breath on me and shivered despite the warmth.

"How'd you find me, really?" he whispered into my parted lips.

"That information has to be earned."

"How can I do that?" he asked, closing the tiny gap between us and ever so lightly brushing his lips over mine. So gentle. So sweet. I wasn't nearly as compassionate. Sweeping my fingers into his hair, I pulled him to me and our lips crashed into one another like a head-on collision. His hands were in my hair now too, urgent and rough, the choirboy in him taking a seat.

The heat of his touch was a reminder of the cravings he'd awakened in me in the towel hut, and now they could never be suppressed. Sex had always been something the cool kids did and something I mildly feared. What if the boy didn't find me attractive? What if I was awkward? Or if I embarrassed myself? But when Rory's hands were on me, when he was kissing my lips and taunting me with the promise of things to come, my body warmed to his touch and I lost all inhibition. With him I wasn't afraid because I knew he wanted me.

His fingers slid down over my ass, forcing a groan from somewhere deep in my throat, the desire he'd sparked in me seven months ago roaring back to life. I didn't know what to do with myself, my hands, my legs. Everything tingled, and it felt like the tiniest touch would send me over the edge. Oh god, the edge. I'd never been over it until he'd brought me there at the water park, and I hadn't been able to recreate it since. I wanted it. I wanted him. His lips left my mouth to pepper my bare neck with kisses. I felt his arm wrap around me and his hand on my lower back, pressing our bodies together.

"I miss the way you taste," he rasped, his voice raw with desire.

"Do you have a room? In this building?" I wasn't sure what I was asking or even if I could follow through with the proposal. I was running on pure lust.

"Not in this one. We have to walk. Do you want to go there?"

"We can't stay here."

He shook his head, untangling from me. "Fuck, Grace."

That was it. His entire assessment of the situation we both found ourselves in. I giggled because I couldn't put it into words any better. I just knew I'd never felt like this with anyone before, and I doubted I'd ever feel this way again.

Rory led me around the building and along a pathway that connected a series of buildings. I wondered at the change in him. The squirrely, nervous boy, his eyes darting every which way, had grown up. Or matured. Or... maybe the fight had just been beaten out of him. I squeezed his hand tighter. If that were the case, I'd need to work harder because I wasn't going to ever let him go.

Arriving at a light-blue building, Rory took a look around before tapping his key to the pad and pushing the entry door open. I followed him up a set of stairs and down a hallway until we arrived at his room.

He let me into his studio apartment, and I scanned the open space.

"Look at you with your big boy place."

He shut the door behind him, and doubt instantly crept in—not about Rory but about myself and whether I was ready to take the next step.

"It beats my last digs."

I took in his decor, trying to make sense of who he was. Not one thing in here spoke to the abandoned boy I'd met on the street. He was more subdued now than before. But *this* subdued? Everything was so neutral. So TikTok posh. My eye caught on the decorative tray with an aesthetic book and candle on his small square coffee table.

"Is that a wood-wick candle?"

"A what?"

"This," I said, picking it up. "The wick is made of wood. It crackles when it burns."

"I have no idea. I've never burned it. It's not mine."

"Sure. Right."

"I'm serious. The place came furnished."

"So, you're saying your design style is not Bohemian chic?"

"It is not. It's just hard to find gutter chic in the stores nowadays."

I laughed. Like everything else about him, Rory's humor surprised me. He was quick on the upswing, always having an answer. It made me wonder what influences had come and gone throughout his life and why none of them had stuck. How could others not have seen the goodness he hid just beneath the surface?

"This place. It's almost too good to be true."

Rory nodded, so slow I wondered what was prompting the less-than-enthusiastic response.

"*Is* it too good to be true?" I asked.

"No. It's what it appears to be. I've been sort of... lost. It's been rough since I last saw you."

"Worse than the streets?"

"Uh..." He laughed, but there was no light behind it. "Mentally worse, I guess you can say. Here, let me give you a hint."

Rory walked to the window and gently nudged the mini disco ball that hung on a string in his window. "I named her Grace."

"Hey, that's my name."

"Yeah, I know." He smiled. "It reminded me of you. Your sparkle. No shit, I sometimes talk to it."

He seemed different; more introspective and less urban cowboy. But his admission—that he talked to a little globe of light because it reminded him of me—was what ovaries were made for.

"My god, Rory, that might be the strangely nicest thing anyone has ever said to me."

"I'm not a psycho or anything," he clarified.

"No. No." I grinned. "Of course not."

"I just... I missed you."

I glided my fingers along his face, wishing there was a way to ease his pain. And maybe there was, but it would take time. Something we now had plenty of. Rory leaned into my touch, like the weight of what he'd been carrying tipped him to one side.

"I'm here now. If you'll let me be."

"If? I'm not the wild card here."

"You think I am?"

He tried to pull away, but I held tight.

"I never wavered, Rory. As far as you're concerned, I stayed right where I was the day you walked away from my car. You're the one who seems conflicted."

"Not about you. It's hard for me. Getting attached."

"Why?"

"Because it never lasts. Eventually someone hands me my bag and sends me on my way."

"I'm not going to leave you."

"Everyone leaves me, Grace. Everyone. That's why I'm here in this place now. No one ever wanted me, and now I'm eighteen. I have no family. One friend and she's like fifty. Until you surprised the shit out of me on the path outside, I was all alone. So trust me when I say, I'm not the wild card here. I'll just keep holding on and holding on"—his voice cracked—"until you leave me."

My heart broke for him and the life I could never imagine living. I'd always had places to go for my emotional healing. I don't think I could have made it on my own without. "But what if I didn't leave? What if we floated on your lazy river forever?"

"Not going to happen."

"But what if it does?"

"Then I'd be really goddamn lucky."

"Let's make a pact, then." I offered him my hooked pinkie finger. "You and me forever."

His mood shifted. "I think this requires more than a pinkie promise."

"What then? How do we seal it? A blood swap? Matching tattoos? Branding?"

"Jesus," he laughed. "You go straight for the pain. I was thinking more along the lines of pleasure."

"You weren't just playing on my emotions to get me in bed, were you?"

"No, I am actually suffering." He chuckled. "But not when I'm with you."

"Does that line actually get you laid?"

"I don't know. Let's see."

Rory stepped closer, placing one hand on my waist and the other tracing his fingers along my hairline. His gaze roamed over my eyes, hair, and mouth, as if committing it all to memory. But I didn't want that. I didn't want this to be a memory he looked back on fondly. I wanted this to be us at the very start.

Gripping his strong jaw, I placed the tiniest kiss to his mouth. And then another and another, finally letting my lips just linger there, savoring our union. Rory remained still, allowing me to take the lead. To find my bravery. And I did, hooking his bottom lip between my teeth and teasing him. Inviting his participation. He groaned, his fingers tangling in my hair as he dropped onto my open mouth, forming a seal and kissing me deeply. The velvet texture of his lips drove a shiver down my spine.

He walked me back and eased me onto the edge of the bed, dropping to his knees between my legs. The height difference between us now leveled, I wrapped my arms around his neck and our lips crashed into each other again. This kiss was hotter, promising wonders to come. Rory had used his tongue sparingly before, easing me in to the new sensation, but now it was hunting mine down. There was nowhere for it to hide, and I didn't want it to. If I'd had reservations about maintaining my virtue when I'd walked in the door, it all vanished with this kneeling kiss.

Rory broke away from the kiss long enough to flash me the hungriest look I'd ever seen on another's face. He wanted me. All of me. I pulled the shirt over my head. His eyes tracked to my breasts, his hands needing no instruction. Their warmth slid under my bra, cupping my breasts and circling the nipples with his thumbs. I bit down on my lower lip when his wet tongue joined the fingers, the combination so carnal I wrapped my legs around his kneeling body and arched my back, allowing him full access to my body. A hand slid up between my breasts, reaching to my neck and up over my parted lips. I sucked on his fingers and moaned.

The sensations rippling through my body were all new and all empowering. I wanted more, not just of this but of him. I wanted to see him naked. Feel him. I pushed back on his weight, righting myself until I was back on my ass on the edge of his bed.

"Grace," Rory rasped, his voice so caught up in lust he sounded like an old man.

"Shhh," I whispered, grasping the material of his shirt in my fists. "My turn."

My fingers freed the top button of his shirt, exposing a small area of his skin. Continuing downward, another button was gone, revealing the shallow ridge running through the middle of his breastbone. I traced the line with a fingernail and watched as Rory's body quivered and his breathing intensified. A third button gone and his lickable abdomen came into view. I parted the two sections of his shirt, exposing his stomach and the whole of his chest before taking a taste of the treasure. It was my thumbs circling his nipples and my wet tongue trailing along his skin up to his chin and into his parted lips that were now causing his ripples.

His mouth closed over mine, a violent need passing between us. I broke the kiss, unbuttoned his jeans, and exposed his pubic bone. He stood up, allowing me to shed the last barrier to his nakedness. There was no hesitation, only anticipation and nervous excitement. And then he was there, naked before me like my own personal buffet. I wasn't sure what to do with all the goodies, but I sure as hell wanted to sample them all.

Rory nearly doubled over, his body clenching almost as if in pain, when my tongue touched him. I held his hips as I got a feel and taste of him. He legs shook, guttural groans escaping from him. And then he pulled away. I blinked up at him, confused.

"You're going to have to stop," he said, leaving my side temporarily to dig through his side drawer. Holy shit. The condom. In my virginal haste, I hadn't even considered it. I watched him roll it down, my eyes widening when I realized where it was going.

He must have seen my expression. "We don't have to."

I grabbed his arm and pulled him back. "Shut up," I said, scooting up on the bed to make room for him.

He climbed on, the weight of him compressing the mattress. I drew in a sharp breath. Oh shit. Oh shit. This was happening, and I was both terrified and beyond excited.

On his hands and knees, Rory bent over me, his much shorter hair still long enough to tumble into his eyes as he stared down at me with a lustful gaze. His mouth parted, hanging there in anticipation. I lifted my head, trying to nibble him. He tipped his back, smiling. Tempting. His tongue swiped along my lower lips, and I caught him with my teeth. It was an erotic struggle, capped with my fingers finding his hardness and squeezing. His body arched like a bridge.

Breaking free of my mouth, Rory marked a trail along my body, pressing kisses down my chin, my neck, between my breasts, and then to my trembling stomach. His fingers took hold of my waistband, and slowly he slid my pants over my hips. He dipped his head between my legs, swiping his teeth over my panties. I wasn't sure when he removed them, but I was well aware of the moment they were gone and his fingers and tongue were upon me.

It was akin to an electrocution, my body convulsing with tiny pulses of electricity. I gripped the comforter, arching and moaning.

"Holy fucking shit, Grace," he remarked.

I didn't really need his commentary, just more of whatever the hell he was doing. The mattress compressed again. Rory's fingers gripped my thighs and I parted my legs wider, and in the moment, I felt no fear. No second-guessing. There would be no regrets. This was what I wanted. As it was always intended. Just me and my drummer boy.

He took it slow, allowing my body to adjust and for the pain to subside. But once I was there, pleasure skipping through my insides, Rory took no mercy. I had to cover my mouth with my hand to keep my shock and awe from reaching his neighbors. No one could keep up that pace. Rory didn't last long, his sexy body shuddering, then stalling in midair before collapsing on top of me.

I lay there a moment, both of us panting and my fingers tangled in his hair. I was still throbbing down there and unsure if it was due to pain or unquenched thirst. After a brief moment of rest, Rory slid back down my body and brought me the rest of the way there.

25

RORY: THE BANK OF TRUST

S he lay on her side, nestled in my arms. Random kisses peppered my neck and cheeks and lips. But as much as I wanted to be present for Grace, I couldn't stop myself from glancing at the door, worrying about what might burst through and punish me by hurting her. I'd only ever had myself to protect, but now I had her, and something told me Grace didn't move fast.

Maybe I shouldn't have had sex with her in my bed because now I was expected to stay. What I hadn't told her in my "nobody stays" speech was that I'd adopted the same behavior as a protective mechanism: leave before they could leave me.

It wasn't that I wanted to leave her, but I'd been trained to run. To never get attached. Sex, for me, had always been on the move. There was no lingering or talking about feelings. In and out like a fast-food drive-through. If I wanted to stay with Grace, I needed to rewire my entire thinking and learn to fine dine. But nothing in my nomadic background had taught me how.

"You okay?" she asked, tracing her finger along my chest.

I gritted my teeth. "Mm-hmm."

"That's not encouraging. You look like you just watched your cat get hit by a semi."

"I'm gonna be honest with you. If I had an ejection seat right now, I'd already have pushed the button."

"Oh." She lifted her head up to look me in the eyes. "That's not insulting at all."

She spoke with humor, but I realized how it might sound. "That came out wrong."

Propping herself on an elbow, Grace pulled her hair to the side. "You're lucky I'm a lastborn child, and very little hurts my feelings."

"Trust me when I say it's not you. You're fucking amazing, Grace. It's all me. I've got... issues."

"I know. You told me."

"I know it's contrary to our towel hut experience, but I don't like confined spaces. I don't like closed doors. I don't like being alone with people. I feel trapped, like I'm suffocating. And I know I have to find a way to deal with it or I'm going to lose you, and that stresses me out more."

"So, me stuck to you like a Band-Aid probably isn't helping with the anxiety," she said, grabbing her bra and sitting up.

"I don't mean to hurt your feelings."

"You're not hurting them," she said with no offense at all. "I know a thing or two about boundaries. I understand you didn't ask for your... issues, and that it's not what you want but what you need to breathe."

"Yes," I said, stunned she got me on the first pass. "How do you know that?"

"I grew up with someone like that. My brother. You remind me of him... a lot."

It made sense. He was the reason she'd stared at me like she had when we first met. She'd seen him in me, which made me wonder, if we were so alike, what my end fate would be. "What happened to him?"

"He became a wildly successful musician. Met a beautiful girl. They're getting married in a couple of weeks."

"Don't lie to me. What really happened to him?"

Grace sat up on her knees. "That's the truth. He struggled for years. There were suicide attempts, and he spent years isolating himself, pushing people away."

"And then what? He just magically got better?"

"There was no magically about it. I have no idea what goes through his head on a daily basis or if he's been in therapy. All I know is he survives and he thrives. His fiancée, Casey, allows him space but not too much. When he wants to blast through the roof in an ejection seat, she grabs his hand and holds him back. That's who I can be for you. If you don't feel comfortable with me cuddling up against you, tell me. If you want to go outside where there are no walls, tell me. I might get mad at you sometimes, but I'm not going to feel bad about things you can't help. And that is why"—she leaned in on all fours and kissed me—"I'm the perfect girl for you. Don't forget it."

I grabbed her face, deepening the kiss. She climbed into my lap, wrapping her arms around me, and I instantly hardened.

"Is this happening again?" She nibbled on my lower lip. "I already put my bra and panties on."

"That's half the fun."

"I really have to get home," she said between kisses. "My parents don't know where I am, and it's only a matter of time before my mom checks her phone and realizes my tracking is off."

"Fine."

I let her up and watched her get dressed. After she was done, she crawled back onto the bed and straddled me. So damn seductive.

She bit down on her lower lip, shyly smiling. "Can I ask you something?"

I brushed her hair out of her face and kissed her. "Sure."

"Will you take me to the homecoming dance?"

"What? Why?"

"Because I've always wanted to go, and it's my senior year coming up, and I only want to go with you."

"Ugh." I dropped my head into the pillow. "Of all the things you could ask me post-sex."

She laughed. "You have time to prepare. Summer just started."

"That won't be enough time."

"Stop." She lightly tapped my face. "It's not that bad. We dress up, go in, have a few dances, and then leave."

"That's actually really bad. I'd rather dry hump a porcupine."

"Really? Would you really?" Her smile slayed me.

I closed my eyes and groaned.

"Please," she whined, dipping her head into my neck and kissing me. "Pretty please."

A dance at her upscale school. I couldn't think of anything I wanted to do less, but saying no to Grace was not something I wanted to get accustomed to.

"I'll think about it."

"Yay!" She cheered, actually clapping.

"I said I'll think about it, not that I'll go."

"I know. Hey, do you have a calendar?"

"Like on the wall?"

"Anywhere. I want to pencil it in. And I'll add a few other additions. Tomorrow: sex. Tuesday: sex."

And to think I'd been worried about taking her virginity—that she might have regrets. Apparently not. It didn't seem to register with her that she'd just given it away to me and could never get it back. I just hoped she wouldn't regret it someday. At least I'd given Grace the choice, which was more consideration than I'd gotten.

"On second thought... Let's do it again."

"Right now?"

"Well, you're busy all next week."

My laugh came in a slow rumble, and hers followed a ripple away. Once combined, the bed shook from our hysterics. I wrapped her in my arms, flipped her onto her back, and hovered over her with my hands on either side of her head.

A ringing phone killed our vibe.

"Oh my god," Grace moaned. "My mother."

"How do you know it's her?"

"It's her. Almost like the woman has a chastity meter that just went off."

"She's a little late. Might need some batteries in it."

Grace climbed off my lap and crawled across the bed to retrieve her phone. I could see the black FaceTime screen come up with a large-lettered mood killer written across the screen. 'Mom.'

"Oh shit!" I said, scrambling off the bed. "Don't get that."

I retrieved my jeans off the floor and hurriedly dragged them up my bare legs.

"I wasn't planning on it," she laughed. "My god, you're quick on the draw."

"Yeah, well, I don't need to know your mother to know seeing her seventeen-year-old daughter naked in bed with an eighteen-year-old street kid has all the makings of a Shake-spearean tragedy."

"Former," she corrected. "Former street kid."

"Do you really think the correct tense will matter to her?" I said, pointing to her phone. "Get your finger away from the accept button."

"It's nowhere near it." She giggled. "Dude, chill. You're making me miss vulnerable Rory who wanted to catapult out of the ceiling a minute ago. Look." She held up her phone. "The FaceTime request disconnected."

I leaned over to confirm the black screen while struggling to right my shirt and get it over my head. It took several tries.

"I need to call her back. Can I count on you to be cool?"

"Yeah," I said, rummaging through a drawer to grab some socks. Even though I hadn't been wearing them before, I felt the need for them now. I jumped on one foot, slipping one sock on and then the other. "I'll be quiet."

She looked me over, amused. "Are you going somewhere?"

"No. Call her back." I pulled a beanie over my head. "Make sure you don't accidently FaceTime."

Grace shook her head and pushed the call button. "Hey, sorry I missed the call."

There was a pause as Grace got an earful and then began a one-sided conversation. "I told you I was going out. Yes, I did. Just as you were leaving. I mean, maybe you didn't hear me. At the movie theater. Just hanging out. I know. The reception's really bad. I can't even send texts."

Grace was a horrible liar. I'd seen three-year-olds with a better command of deception. Her mother was never going to buy this shit. My pulse was spinning like a record player.

I grabbed a sweatshirt.

There was a long period of silence as Grace listened. I assumed her mother was relating how disappointed she was in her daughter. Wasn't that how it went in real families? Disappointment was the strongest discipline. Grace reacted appropriately—not the least bit concerned. And why should she be? Disappointment wasn't followed by fists.

I watched her twirl a strand of hair as she listened. At one point, she glanced up at me and rolled her eyes. This was a whole other world to me.

"Okay. Okay, Mom. Yes. I'm sorry. I won't do it again. I'm leaving soon."

I shoved my feet into a pair of shoes.

"Yes, Mom. *Soon* means now. Okay. Oh my god. Relax."

Another pause. "I love you too."

Grace hung up and then flung herself onto her back, her arms and legs flailing in an adorable fit. Then she laughed, covering her face.

I arrived at the edge of the bed dressed like a ski lift operator.

She got a load of my outfit and her eyes rounded. "What's going on here?"

"I'm prepared to flee."

"Where are you going?"

"Anywhere your mother is not. What did she say?"

"She said that she would very much like for me to come home because, according to her, I didn't ask to go out."

"You didn't ask, though."

"No. But I told her I did."

"And she bought that?"

"Yes, Rory. It's called trust."

"But you lied to her."

"I know. Here's how it works. You bank the trust, so then when you really need to lie, you skim a little out of savings. Get it?"

I shook my head. "You and I grew up very differently. There are no trust banks in foster care."

"What happened if you lied?"

I swept my hair to the side to reveal a two-inch scar just above my right ear.

Her playful demeanor disintegrated on impact.

"Don't," I said.

Grace didn't shy away, pushing my hand away and pulling my hair back. "Who did this to you?"

"Does it really matter now? I was twelve."

"Yes, it does... to me."

"Grace, you're stressing me the fuck out, and I'm about to have heatstroke. Get your shoes on. I'm walking you to your car. We can have story time on one of your next scheduled appointments."

She stretched up on her knees and kissed my scar before she got herself ready, and then we were out the door. It wasn't until we reached her car that I noticed the change in her demeanor.

"Is everything okay?"

"I have something to tell you, and you're probably not going to like it, but the good news is, you have no clothes left, so..."

"Just tell me."

"My mother is Mrs. M."

The words she spoke bounced around in my brain for a few seconds before they fully registered.

"Wait, what? How?"

"I'm the one who, unintentionally, sent her to you."

"Mrs. M? You're Mrs. M's daughter?"

She nodded.

I shook my head, pissed and I wasn't even sure why.

"Just let me explain."

And she did. Grace documented the series of events that led her mother to my doorstep. I listened, intently, struggling with every single word. Mrs. M was my ticket out of here. My chance at a better life. If she found out what I'd done with her daughter...

My heart hammered in my chest. There was no plausible scenario where I didn't pay the price. Like the time in that foster home playing chase with the family's biological son. We broke a lamp, both of us, but I was the one who stood staring at a wall for hours.

Grace was just as guilty as me, but she had trust banked. I did not.

"It's not like I was holding this back from you. I just found out today. I only came to confront you, maybe even punch you in the gut. I didn't expect any of this, so don't look at me like I catfished you or something."

I leaned against her car, feeling defeated.

Grace hugged me. "Nothing bad is going to happen. My mother loves you."

"She did... before I deflowered her daughter."

"Rory, I'm going to fix this. I already have a plan. I'm going to 'volunteer' for the next class as your emotional support fuck buddy, and that's how we'll 'meet' for the first time."

I glared at her.

"Too soon?" She smiled up at me. "Don't be mad."

The tension slowly eased. "Is there anything else I need to know before I go flog myself in the town square?"

She laughed. "Just one. M stands for McKallister."

My brain was not connecting the dots.

"Mrs. M is Michelle McKallister."

Nope. Nothing.

"Rory, the night we met, you saw me go into the VIP entrance at my brother's concert. McKallister."

That was when it registered. "Jake?"

She nodded.

"You're his *sister*?" I asked, the hair on my arms peaking to attention. If I reminded her of Jake McKallister, the kid who'd spent over a month in what could only be described as a living hell, then she assumed something similarly sinister had happened to me. She wasn't wrong, but I didn't like her thinking I wasn't whole.

"Yes. Younger by nine years."

"And your mom..."

"...is his mother, and the woman who trained a superstar. And now she has her sights set on you."

26

GRACE: RED DELICIOUS

If there was such a thing as too much chemistry, Rory and I had it. My plan to "meet" him for the first time in the class my mother taught was a solid one—in my head—but in person was a different matter altogether. There were seven days between our reunion and his next class. And of those seven days, I'd snuck off to Camden Place and had sex with Rory on every one of those. It was safe to say we had a solid connection.

Hopefully no one in class noticed. The hour flew by. Our goodbye lingered. And as he walked off, my eyes dropped to his ass and followed it all the way out the door.

"Grace." My mother startled me, her gaze alternating between me and Rory's exiting frame. That expression on her face, like she was fighting back the stomach flu, gave me pause. Shit, did she know? In hindsight, maybe Rory and I had gone too fast during class—from "Nice to meet you" to me practically sitting on his lap. My bad. I couldn't get enough of him. I couldn't. I really had tried to keep it in check during our first official meet and greet, but my fluttering heart refused to obey. I'd been all giggles and teasing and touching.

And my mother was no dummy.

"Help me get everything packed," she said in a clipped tone.

She and I worked in silence until the car was packed and the door was closed. Only then did she turn to me, eyes blazing.

"You know him."

"No, I don't. I just met him tonight."

"How do you know Rory?" she repeated, only this time I knew the bank of trust had just gone under.

"I told you—I just met him tonight."

"Grace Lucia McKallister, don't you dare lie to me. I'm going to ask you one more time. How do you know, Rory?"

I held my ground. "I don't."

"Fine." She pulled her phone out of her purse and began texting.

"What are you doing?"

My mother didn't answer, furiously one-finger texting.

"Mom. Mom!" I screeched, reaching for her phone. "What are you doing?"

She switched the phone to her other hand, playing keep away. "I just texted Rory."

"Mom! Oh my god." I flung my body back onto the seat. "You're ridiculous."

"If you won't tell me, then he will."

"You're going to freak him out if you summon him here."

"How would you know?" she asked, the fury in her eyes burning a hole through me. "I thought you didn't know him."

"Text him back, Mom. Text him back and tell him not to come."

"Too late," she replied, gesturing with her eyes. I looked up to find Rory walking our way, his head down in solemn prayer. He'd obviously been hanging out near the parking lot because it had taken him less than a minute to arrive at the driver's side window from the time he got the text.

My mother greeted him with a frosty stare. "Get in."

~

WE DROVE in silence to a Denny's down the street. Without a word, Mom got out and slammed the door. Rory and I sat there, unsure what to do.

"Are we eating?" I asked.

"I don't know. She's your mother."

"Don't remind me. I'm so mortified. I can't believe she's doing this."

"What do we do?" he asked. Since when had he picked up my habit of nail biting? "Do you think we should tell the truth?"

"And give her the satisfaction? I don't think so."

"Grace, she knows. There's no way to lie our way out of this."

My mother summoned us from the Denny's front stoop. "Now!"

Both Rory and I jumped, exiting the vehicle in unison.

I turned to him. "Well, it was nice knowing you."

"If we don't survive," he said, "it's been fun. You're a bad-ass chick."

~

MY MOTHER HAD ALREADY DISAPPEARED into the restaurant and was seated when Rory and I entered, him dragging several steps behind. It was in that moment that I made the decision. Rory was right. There was no way to lie our way out of this. The only thing we could do now was own it.

To the horror of our audience of one glaring at us from the booth, I grabbed my guy's face and grafted a defiant open-mouthed kiss, with tongue, onto his tasty lips.

~

My mother didn't speak to either one of us until after the waitress had come to take our order. Rory and I sat side by side on our bench, my mother on the other. A medieval interrogation.

"How long has this been going on?" she asked.

"I met him seven months ago."

"Seven months?" She looked between the two of us. "You've been lying to me for *seven months*?"

"Mrs. M..."

"You!" Mom waved a finger at Rory. "I don't want to hear from you right now."

And so, I went into the whole story of how we'd met on the street and how he had given me the idea for the class and how I'd only found out she was training him last week. She listened intently, only occasionally butting in to ask a question here or there.

"Okay, now you," she said to Rory. "What are your intentions toward my daughter?"

"I...uh..." He looked my way and then back at her. "I really like your daughter, and my intentions would be, you know, to keep getting to know her."

"Me too," I agreed. "I was going to ask him if he would go to the homecoming dance with me. Rory, what do you say? You wanna be my date?"

Mom's eyes fluttered as she looked away, irritated. I'd just hijacked the conversation for my own selfish gain, but it was Homecoming, and I really wanted to go.

"Well, I, um... I'm not much of a dancer."

"We don't have to dance. We can just hang out. It would mean so much."

Rory's eyes narrowed in on me, knowing full well what I was doing. I smiled innocently back. His head twisted between my mother and me, looking for an out that wasn't in his future.

Without an ounce of enthusiasm, he said, "Um, sure."

"Yes!" I lit up, almost bouncing up and down in my seat before sealing his promposal, such as it was, with a kiss.

My mother pursed her lips, clearly not appreciating the direction this conversation was going. She sucked in a deep breath and went for the kill. "It's clear the two of you are having sex."

"Oh my god, Mom!" My face turned the brightest shade of Red Delicious apple. "You're so embarrassing. I cannot believe you just said that."

She put her hand up to stop me. "I don't want to hear it. I have eyes. And that little display when you walked in was all I needed to see. Have you at least been using protection?"

The horror of it all was complete. I wanted to slither under the booth, a pile of bones, to join all the other greasy, grimy remains below.

"Yes," Rory finally answered for both of us. "We've been careful."

"Well, hallelujah for that," she mumbled. Mom looked away. Then back at us. Then toward the restaurant's bar-style kitchen. Preparing for a difficult conversation, she smoothed out her napkin and arranged the sugar packets by color. The whole time Rory and I sat there like little ice sculptures frozen in time. We both instinctively knew to let her work through the fact that her musical prodigy had just admitted to having sex with her underage daughter. I could appreciate it wasn't an easy thing to hear, and I had some sympathy. However, if my mother planned to forbid us from seeing each other, well then, that was where I'd draw the line.

"Mrs. M," Rory finally broke the silence. "Can I just say how sorry I am? When we met, I had no idea you were Grace's mom. You've been so nice to me, and the training you've given me... it's more than I ever could've asked for. I promise none of this was meant to disrespect you."

The waitress approached the table, and we all fell back like slices from an apple corer. Once our drinks had been dropped off, Mom seemed to have gathered the strength of mind to speak again.

"Obviously, the two of you are tight." She winced at the word 'tight.' My god, she hadn't just tied the loss of my virginity to it, had she? Yes. Yes, she had. My cheeks burned.

"I meant"—she sighed—"you're very clearly in a relationship, and there would be no point in my forbidding it because, god knows, I can't have you two sneaking around. Grace, I am all kinds of disappointed. You put yourself in danger by wandering around the streets like that. And after all the talks we had, I'm hurt you didn't tell me about Rory. I could have maybe helped him. And then you outright lied to me about coming over here. You are going to have to earn back my trust. And Rory... I know you're a good kid, and that's why I'm giving you the benefit of the doubt. So, here's what's going to happen. There will be no more meetups at Rory's apartment. From now on, you will come to our house if you want to see Grace. Starting tomorrow for dinner. And Grace, your father does not need to know about any of your extracurricular activities. Speaking of which, there will be no more hooking up between the two of you until this girl is on birth control."

I opened my mouth to protest, but my utter mortification prevented any words from exiting.

My mother wagged a finger in my face. "Ah! Silence. And, Mr. Higgins, that does not mean you get a free ride. Even after my daughter is on birth control, you will continue to wrap it up tight. Am I clear?"

Numbly, we nodded our agreement.

And that was how my mother discovered I had a boyfriend.

27

RORY: ALL IN THE FAMILY

"Don't give me that side-eye, Higgins."

I gave it to her anyway. How could I not? Grace was entering her residence through a security gate powered by facial recognition technology.

"I'm not even looking in your direction, Caviar."

"What do you think side-eye means?"

Keeping my eyes straight ahead, I fought to suppress a smile. If she was embarrassed by her wealth, far be it from me to make her feel better.

"All the security is because of Jake. His fans have been known to scale the walls. This tends to slow them down."

"I thought you said he doesn't live here."

"He doesn't. That's the jacked-up part. He bought the place for my parents when he was still a teenager, but he's never actually lived here, except maybe during that first year or two when he'd stay between tours. But the celebrity sightseeing buses still drive by here multiple times a day hoping to spot him."

Who could blame them? This was definitely a home base worthy of a rock star. When Nikki and I dreamed of our matching mansions on the hill, this right here was the shit we were talking about. Spanish style, circular driveway, two-story white exterior, emerald-green window shutters, clay tile roof. And it was huge—the size of two or three large houses combined.

"Just know," Grace said, trying to play down her swanky digs, "the house is fancy. The people are not."

Yeah, sure, I thought, looking down at my jeans and t-shirt and suddenly feeling way out of place. I'd grown up on the edges of society, and whether people wanted to admit it or not, there was a stigma attached. Grace seemed unaffected by it, but that didn't mean her family would be. "I feel like I should be wearing a suit and tie."

"That's only because you haven't met my dad yet. Once you do, you'll understand why formality is neither required nor appreciated. Honestly, the best I can hope for is that he's wearing a shirt with coffee stains on it. The worst is that he'll be walking around bare-chested in board shorts and flip-flops. Mom promised to rein him in tonight, but who knows."

It didn't matter to me what the man wore. All I cared about was that he didn't corner and question me about my intentions toward his daughter. I didn't have any. My only plan at this point was to hold on to her for as long as I reasonably could. There were no illusions; I knew this wouldn't last. She'd outgrow me and trade up. I glanced at her house. Way up.

The security gate roared to life, and Grace inched her car forward until there was enough room to pass. Once through the gate, Grace reached up and pushed a button in her car, which stopped the gate and sent it back in the direction it had come. It was only then I felt my pulse tick up. From the outside, waiting dormant in its locked position, the large metal gate seemed harmless, but when it slid into action, the deep clanging of the metal caused the hairs on my arms to rise to attention. Ever since the flyer had been left on my door, I had been seeing threats everywhere. I rotated in my seat, and suddenly I was in the back seat of Hartman's car, the gate closing, locking behind me, sealing my fate. My heart raced, and my hands started twitching. I blinked in quick succession.

Grace witnessed my transformation, her eyes growing in alarm as they bounced between me and the rearview mirror.

"What is it? What do you see?" Following my stare, a light bulb clicked on in her head. "Is it the *gate*?"

How had she learned to read my cues so easily? Of all the people who'd passed through my life, no one had picked up on the anxiety that manifested in my hands and feet, and my facial tics. They'd been quick to put a label on me: hyperactive. But it wasn't that. It was stress and fear, misdiagnosed and then left unmanaged. Yet Grace had figured me out the first night we met. All those experts missing the signs made me wonder if they'd even been looking.

"I don't like being locked in," I said.

Had I already told her that trigger? I'd rattled off a few the day we got back together, but there were more where those came from. So many more. I'd omitted them to keep from over-whelming and freaking her out, but the list was long. I didn't like walls. I didn't like excessive touch. I didn't like mirrors or gates or cameras. God, I was so damn weak.

"There's a door on the right side of the gate," she said. "You don't need a code to get out. You're not trapped, Rory. You can leave anytime you want."

I acknowledged her explanation despite my senses still being on high alert. Righting myself in the seat, we drove the short distance to the house. Once she parked, Grace placed a hand over mine, squeezing the jitters out. No words, just a soothing assist.

"Sorry," I said, willing my agitations away. "Just give me a sec."

"Of course." Her hand continued to hold mine tightly. "I got you, babe."

Something in Grace's easy vibe relaxed me. She never probed for details or made a big deal out of my quirks. Grace acknowledged the issue and moved on, proving that not everything needed an evaluation or scheduled meeting. I understood I wasn't normal. I didn't need a team of professionals pointing it out and slapping a label on my forehead to carry with me like a weighted backpack for the rest of my life.

I looked out the windshield, noticing for the first time a guy sitting on the porch, and did a double take.

"Is that...?"

"No," Grace said. "Not Jake. I know he looks a lot like him. That's Quinn, the one I told you about."

"The overprotective one?"

"Yes. He'll try to intimidate you, but he's really just a big talker. You could easily take him, if it came to that."

Whoa, hold on. She never told me to come prepared for a brawl.

"Will it come to that?" I asked.

"Um..." She hesitated. "No."

"That doesn't sound encouraging."

"He enjoys scaring the guys away. It's kind of his thing. On the plus side, it's probably why I was still a virgin for you."

"Okay, well, I never asked for you to be one."

"I know, I'm just saying. Anyway, back to militant Quinn. When we were kids, he assigned himself my protector, and now that I've grown up, he's having a little trouble moving on. Just don't take his bait and you'll be fine. Once we get by him, the rest of the brothers will be a breeze."

As if I wasn't nervous enough, now I had to deal with the overprotective gatekeeper who'd want to smash my face in. But Quinn gave me no choice. He stood as we walked up, blocking the path with a wide, hostile stance. I might not have been a match for Hartman, a trained heavy, but the hell if my street urchin ass couldn't take the win against a kid who'd grown up in a castle sipping Perrier by the pool.

Remaining neutral in posture, I waited for Quinn to conduct his thorough head-to-toe scan. In the process, he frowned and squinted and cocked his head, all while formulating an opinion. Finally, he looked me in the eyes and offered a quick up-nod. "Cool. You wanna join my band?"

I rocked back in surprise, the confident smirk on his face in direct contrast to the prickly, overprotective brother Grace had spoken of. The same guy who'd threatened the lives of all those who came before me had just as easily tossed his baby sister's welfare aside for his own selfish gain.

Now that was a front man.

"Hell yeah, I wanna join."

～

"EVERYONE, LISTEN UP," Quinn called out as we walked into the kitchen. A small gathering of people looked up from their conversations. "This is my new drummer, Rory. Can we all give him a warm welcome?"

There was a smattering of applause.

"He's also the first boyfriend I've ever had in my whole life, all because Quinn is such a misogynist asshole," Grace said, to no applause at all. "No? Okay. Apparently finding a quality drummer is more important to this family than finding lasting love."

Her choice of words—*boyfriend* and *love*—drew curious glances in my direction. Considering they'd only become aware of me today with Michelle's dinner invitation, I could under-stand their surprise. It seemed Grace was an emotional communicator. If she thought it, she said it. Like the whole homecoming thing—I'd been blackmailed. She knew what she was doing at the Denny's, giving me no choice in front of her mother without making me look like a prick.

Grace had operated with that same boldness from the start, referring to me as her boyfriend shortly after we'd had sex in my studio apartment. We'd never had the discussion, nor had Grace asked me to confirm our relationship status. At this point, the time to correct her had come and gone, but I figured, hey, if a girl like her wanted a boyfriend like me, who was I to complain?

Greeted by a man wearing a casual t-shirt, I knew instantly it was Grace's father from the prominent coffee stain splattered across the front. He embraced me. "Welcome, Rory. I'm Quinn's father, Scott. I can't tell you how long we've waited for this special day. Such a dream come true. Our son has finally found his drummer. I think we'd all sort of given up hope. But look at you."

A shaggy-haired dude stepped in front of me. "Quick—spell gonorrhea."

"Kyle!" Mrs. M gasped.

He ignored her, motioning for me to answer.

"Um..." Of all the days for my limited schooling to fail me. "*G-O-N-E-R-E-A?*"

Kyle patted me on the shoulder. "You're good. Make yourself at home."

Another of the brothers laughed. "What the fuck was that?"

"Keith," Mrs. M groaned. "Language. We have a guest. Can you all at least pretend to have manners?"

"That's what you're worried about? Not Kyle giving your guest an STD spelling bee?"

"It wasn't a spelling bee. It was a test. I would never trust anyone dating my little sister who can spell *gonorrhea* right on the first try."

I wasn't sure how to respond, so I laughed. It seemed the only response to an STD ice-breaker. And that was just the opening act. It went down the line from there.

"I'm Emma, Quinn's older sister."

"I'm Finn, Quinn's older sister's boyfriend."

"I'm Kenzie, the gonorrhea guy's girlfriend."

"We weren't properly introduced. I'm Keith. Welcome to the band."

Mrs. M put a hand on my shoulder. "Two of Grace's older brothers weren't able to make it on such short notice, but you'll meet them another time."

I didn't understand the hospitality. There was no reason for it. They weren't getting paid to take care of me. There was nothing in it for them at all. And yet, they all engaged me. These people were not who I'd thought they would be. The big fancy house I'd viewed from outside the gate was a smokescreen for the laid-back bunch inside. The way they'd all seamlessly shifted their humor to fit the new Quinn-based narrative, to the amused detriment of their youngest born, was what convinced me the McKallisters were a breed all their own. I'd worried I would suffer through the night, but not after all that.

"Mom, less chatting. More cooking," Quinn said.

"Actually, the pizzas are ready for the toppings to go on, but!" She raised her voice. "I'm warning all of you. If I see blood this time, it'll be our last homemade pizza night."

"Yeah, yeah." Kyle reached across me to grab a raw red onion. "How many times have we heard that?"

She tried again. "Just don't act like heathens in front of our guest."

"No, sorry," Quinn said. "I haven't been fighting for every handful of cheese since I was five to play nice now. If Rory can't hang, he can't eat."

"Just tell him the rules, and let's get a move on," Emma said.

There were rules to pizza night?

It fell on Grace to spell them out. "We each get to design our half—to be eaten by all—but there's only a finite amount of the good stuff, and you will be mercilessly judged if yours displeases the others."

"She's not kidding," Finn said. "I was almost tossed out on my first McKallister pizza night. It's all about making deals and quick decisions; otherwise, you'll be left with nothing but pineapple and tears."

"And don't even think of plain cheese pizza. We have to share these, and that's just selfish to the rest of us. If you have no imagination, you deserve to pick mushrooms off your pizza. Got it?" Keith said.

I nodded.

"I'm gonna need a verbal there, bud. We take this shit seriously."

"I got it." I laughed, leaning over to whisper in Grace's ear, "Is it just me, or does this pizza night have more hurt feelings than most?"

"Rory, come over here with me. We'll make this one together," Scott said, patting the stool beside him. "Don't be scared."

Objections were immediately raised as to Scott's nefarious intentions.

"It's a trap," Grace warned.

"Don't look him in the eye."

"He's using your newness against you," Finn cautioned.

Scott groaned. "Don't listen to them, Rory. This has nothing to do with stealing your ingredients. Just because you're young and inexperienced and don't know any different doesn't mean a thing. This is about me wanting to bond with my new drum-in-law. If that's wrong, I don't want to be right."

A smile crossed my face as I took in all the warring factions. It was all happiness, bickering, laughter, and love. Everything I'd ever wanted in a family and more. I'd been placed in a couple of families with similar dynamics, but they'd never made room for me despite them pretending I was part of the tribe. This was different. The McKallisters embraced me like I'd been born into their inner circle. Or maybe I was so starved for belonging that I'd attached myself to the first family who'd pulled up a stool.

I'd gone into this relationship with Grace with the mindset to hold on for as long as she'd allow me to, but after sampling her family, I didn't want to just get by, like I'd been doing my whole life. I had to fight if I wanted to secure the girl, the future, and the family I'd always wanted.

I'D BARELY OPENED the door when Grace pushed her way in, panting and sweaty like she'd run the whole way from the parking lot to my apartment. And I knew she had.

"Hurry," she said, kicking the door shut while removing her shirt and bra. "We've got seven minutes."

She didn't need to tell me twice. My shirt was off in an instant, and I closed the short gap between us. Wrapping my hand around the back of her neck, I hauled Grace to me, my lips crashing into hers. Our mouths parted. Our tongues tousled. Her fingers buried in my hair. We were a jumble of tangled, groping, needy limbs.

"I drove the back way. Maps showed less traffic. Bought us three extra minutes." Each sentence she spoke was between ravenous kisses. Groaning, I used my one free hand to slip fingers into her waistband and drop her short shorts to the floor.

"Best. Girlfriend. Ever," I said, walking her back until her legs hit the bed, and I tossed her onto it. When her back hit the mattress, Grace bounced, but I caught her on the upswing, my body crash-landing on top of her. With no time to spare, I heaved her further up on the bed and dipped between her trembling legs. Her body bowed, fingers ripping through my hair, and she whimpered in that raspy voice I'd come to love.

Thankfully, Grace didn't require a whole lot of tender loving care. Or foreplay. My girl came prepared, typically having listened to a sizzling audiobook on the car ride over. She was like an instant hot water recirculating system: always hot, always wet, and always ready when you turned on the tap. Not only that but the girl was built for speed, making my job exceptionally easy. Sixty seconds on her trigger spot and my thoroughbred was crossing the finish line. And a few seconds after that, I was rolling on a rubber and busting through the starting gate.

This was what we'd been reduced to—traffic-dependent quickie junkies. It couldn't be good for our developing brains. We were young. Habits were forming. What was all this saying to our subconscious minds? Speed—good. Tiny enclosed spaces —fine. Lovemaking—Huh? Aftercare—what the fuck was that?

As part of the deal Grace and I had made with Michelle, we kept our relationship almost entirely under her roof. That meant I spent most of my spare time on the McKallister property, with its pool and basketball court and cool people and soundproof music room. Not a bad trade-off for the sex we weren't supposed to be having. Under her watchful eye, Michelle thought she had us under control with her clearly defined rules. No closed doors. No going off on our own for extended periods of time; no hands on each other's bodies. But all the restrictions had done was drive us underground. Speed us up. Make us savvier.

Grace especially. To my surprise, she was a sneaky little bitch, and I goddamn loved her for it. Her bank of trust was just the tip of the iceberg. As the youngest and most unassuming member of her family, Grace had learned to operate under the radar. She'd also become the perfect spy. She regularly charted the comings and goings of her entire family, and calculated the amount of time between when one would leave and another would come back. She knew how long her father worked out in the home gym, right down to the equipment he used on any given day. She knew when Quinn showered, when he left and came back from his part-time job, and when her other siblings would be visiting. If there was, say, a five-minute or longer gap in time, we would bang out quickies in various places around her house. In her bedroom. In her bathroom. In the backyard shed. Even her old Little Tikes fairy princess castle.

To be fair, there weren't a lot of five-minute gaps at her house, so ninety-nine percent of the sex we weren't supposed to be having was taking place to and from my apartment. With no car of my own, Grace regularly picked me up and took me home. The round-trip drive was thirty minutes, depending on traffic. Michelle knew exactly how much time it would take and tracked her daughter's phone throughout the journey. That was where my girlfriend's most meticulous charting came into play. Grace devised a schedule based entirely on Michelle's schedule, the idea being that the busier she was, the less time she had to focus on how much time Grace was lingering at my place. Grace had it down to a science, and her calculations had yet to let us down.

I moved inside Grace, our rutting grunts arriving in perfect unison. No talk, no loving kisses, no awkward giggles. We had sex like we were a hidden menu item at a popular burger joint— animal style. Picking up speed, every time-sensitive thrust brought us closer together. She was everything to me. Everything. Grace gripped me tight, her heavy, raspy panting bringing me to the edge of sanity. Hitting the crescendo, I went rigid. She arched her back. The world stopped, if only for a split second, and then we collapsed back onto the mattress, spent and fully satisfied, with two minutes left.

With time to spare, I leaned on my elbow and pushed a strand of hair out of her eyes, both of us still working to catch our breaths. She looked up at me with such trust. Such affection. I traced her soft pink lips, her smile shaping wherever my finger touched. God, she was so beautiful, that flushed skin against my white sheets. I'd once thought Grace was too good for me, that I wasn't worthy of a girl like her, but not anymore. She was making me better. Worthy of her.

I remembered as a child lying in bed and wondering how I'd be able to identify love for myself. If I didn't know what it looked like or what it felt like, how would I even know if I found it? But lying here with Grace, I knew it had finally come for me. I still couldn't explain what it was, but that feeling inside me—my heart beating only for her—proved that we were more than a passing infatuation. We were end game love.

"I love you," I whispered, testing the words out for size.

A smile skipped across her face as carefree as a schoolgirl's.

"I love you too," she said, almost like it was an afterthought. As if she'd loved me way longer than it had taken me to figure out that I loved her back.

She lifted her head and kissed my lips. "Now, get off me. We've got to go."

THE WEEKS SPENT with Grace and the McKallisters were the best of my life. It wasn't like I'd had many great experiences to begin with, but this would've topped them all no matter what. If I could, I would've spent every minute of my day with her and them, but my free time was limited to afternoons and evenings. As part of the deal living at Camden Place, I was required to work a minimum of eighty hours a month, and I did so busing tables at a breakfast café a block away. In addition to the work, they also required us to participate in therapy sessions and life skills classes. I got the reasoning behind it, but that didn't mean I had to like it. Although I might have been the only one. My fellow residents seemed to love talking about their feelings, which told me they really didn't have anything shocking to hide, like I did. Not that I was complaining about their emotional dumps, which allowed me to just sit in the circle with my mouth shut until the session was over.

The life skills classes were better because, unlike therapy, they were on subjects I could actually use, like driver's training, meal prep, and budget planning. But time was quickly running out for Grace and me before she went back to school in a few weeks, and despite her reassurances, I knew things were going to drastically change. There would be no more lazy afternoons by the pool. No more stolen kisses behind the shed. No more family game nights.

Life on this side of the gate felt like a whole other world, like I'd stepped into an alternate universe where I was safe and where people treated me like one of their own. But as much as I loved being around Grace and her family, there was always that nagging voice in my head reminding me that all this was too good to be true. That life was never this kind to me. But then, Grace would curl up next to me on the couch, her soft hair tickling my neck, or Quinn would wrap an arm around my shoulder and whisper the world's most inappropriate joke in my ear. Or Michelle would make my favorite dinner. Yes, I already had one.

But nothing spoke more of family than Scott taking me under his wing. I'd never had any role models or people to look up to, so I had no choice but to follow or get left behind. Scott effortlessly slipped into the role of father figure, showing me more in the last few weeks than I'd learned from all the men who'd passed through my life put together. Thanks to him, I'd been taught how to barbecue, play poker, build Legos, and open the door for his daughter. And then there were the less tangible things, like the importance of a firm handshake, how to speak up for myself, and the value of looking others in the eye. Such instruction might seem insignificant to some, but for me, it was a revelation, and I soaked it up like a sponge. Scott was teaching me how to stand on my own two feet. How to be a man.

THE ONLY MCKALLISTER I hadn't connected with was Jake. For one, I hadn't made the best first impression. Hours before he came around for the first time, I'd lost a bet with Quinn and the guys in our new ragtag band. I was too new to understand the seriousness with which they took lost wagers. The three of them pinned me down and spiked my hair with cement gel before spray-painting it blue. Grace was not amused; nor, did it seem, was Jake. He barely spoke three sentences to me that day.

Unlike the other members of his family, Jake was not welcoming. He never engaged me. The only time there was any interaction with him was when I caught him staring at me, but then he'd quickly look away. I wanted to confront him, but I didn't dare. It was his house. His family. His right to hate my guts. So I kept my distance, careful to clear out before there were only the two of us left in a room together.

"... the first couple of slices went down fine," Casey giggled, tears sliding down her cheeks as she told the tale of the German chocolate cake she and Jake had flushed down the toilet in their honeymoon suite. "But we got cocky. Started feeding bigger slices into the toilet."

She halted her lively storytelling, dissolving into a fit of hysterics that set off the rest of us.

Jake picked up the tale where Casey left off. "German chocolate cake is already the ugly duckling of the cake world, so you can imagine what it looked like coming back up from the bowels of hell. When it crested, and the first bits and pieces began to drain over the sides of the bowl, Casey's like, 'Do something!' I'm like, 'What do you want me to do?' and she's like, 'Plunge it' and I'm like, 'With my hands?'"

I'd never seen Jake so animated and alive. The times I'd been around him, he'd always been subdued, but today, playing off his outgoing wife, Jake was every bit as entertaining as the rest of his family. It was the first time I saw the similarities between us. I'd always kept to myself, lost in the murkiness of my mind, until Grace came along and dragged me into the light. Now I couldn't imagine not basking in her sun.

Casey recovered enough to put the finishing touches on the German chocolate cake story. "We had to call maintenance to come plunge the toilet. He totally thought it had come out of Jake's ass."

"Only because this traitor"—Jake hooked his arm around the back of his wife's neck and playfully dragged a giggling Casey to his chest—"went and hid behind the drapes and left me to deal with the whole thing. The poor guy was throwing up in his mouth. But what was I supposed to do, tell him we were flushing cake down the pipes?"

Honeymoon-related conversation continued until Casey announced she had pictures of their wedding on her laptop in the other room. The girls left with her, as did Finn. He'd been given no choice. But the other guys left one by one, lured away by dessert. I didn't realize until it was too late that it was just Jake and me out on the porch. I froze, not sure if I should stay or go.

"Relax," he said. "I'm not going to hurt you. I swear you and Grace are like skittish rabbits around me."

"Why is Grace skittish with you?"

"I don't know. You're tight with her. You tell me."

"You overestimate my ability to effectively communicate."

Jake laughed. "So, this whole thing isn't an act?"

"The skittish rabbit thing? No, it's no act. I'm always looking over my shoulder."

Slowly, he dragged his eyes over me, sizing me up. I shouldn't have mentioned that last part. It suggested I had something to hide; which was true, but he didn't need to know.

"What happened to the blue spiky hair?" Jake finally spoke. "I thought that was your signature look."

"No." I grinned. "I lost a bet to your brother that day. Retribution was swift."

"Oh, I'm sure it was. Quinn takes competition to a whole new level."

The way it was said sounded more like a diss, so I kept my mouth shut, not wanting to get between two rival brothers.

"So, what's your story?" Jake asked.

"What have you been told?"

He smiled. "Good thinking. Get the lowdown before you answer."

"Do you give your life story to everyone who asks?"

"Don't have to. Everyone already knows."

I raised my brows, surprised he'd go there. He was a notoriously private person, probably because he had to deal with the entire world knowing the worst parts of his life. At least my secret was mine.

"All right. Here's what I've been told. You're a foster kid," he said. "My sister met you at the music class my mom has been tutoring you at. I heard the reason you're coming over here every day is so Grace won't go over there. That's about it."

"And you don't believe that?"

"Should I?"

I laughed, tossing his line back at him. "Good thinking. Get the lowdown before you answer."

"Why are you in foster care?" he asked.

"Standard reason. I don't have parents."

"What happened to them?"

"I don't know."

"You don't know?" he responded, skeptical. "I'm trying to trust that you are who you say you are, but here's the problem. You appear out of nowhere, and suddenly you're dating my sister and playing in a band with my brother... oh, and you just so happen to be a tour-quality drummer... who's never toured. If you were trying to advance your career, this would be a fairly cushy way to do it."

He had a point. I must look sketchy as hell to him.

"You think I'm using Grace?"

"I think you genuinely like her, and she likes you back. I'm just trying to figure out what came first, the chicken or the egg."

"Well, which one is Grace?"

"Huh?"

"Is Grace the chicken or the egg?"

"I don't know," he chuckled, then took a random guess. "The egg?"

"Don't look at me." I joined in the laughter. "It's your analogy."

His lighthearted banter turned on a dime, and his eyes lasered into me. "Are you playing my sister?"

My nerves ticked up at his pinpoint bluntness. "No."

"Why did you start blinking?"

"I do that when I get nervous."

"Or when you're lying?"

"Yes, that too. But I'm not lying right now. Grace is to me what Casey is to you."

"And what is that?"

"Everything that makes you good."

28

GRACE: TAKE ME HOME

The summer sailed by. Despite the bulk of it being spent inside our property line, it didn't bother either one of us. Rory seemed happiest at my house anyway. He came every day after work, and we sunned and swam and went for walks, played and talked and napped. Family dinners or game nights were a near daily affair, where Rory hung with the rest like he'd always been around. He'd even managed to win Jake over in a late-play move that stunned us all.

All good things must come to an end, and so it did for the summer of Grace and Rory. I would go back to school, severely cutting into our time together. He'd still come over to train with my mom, pal around with my dad, and practice with the band—working name Grace Note. Quinn wasn't so pleased with that, reminding me often not to get too attached to it because he planned to change it just as soon as a better name—literally any other name—came along. But it had been nearly three months, and it was still Grace Note.

We'd told ourselves our time together would continue uninterrupted, but of course, that was wishful thinking. School took up a huge chunk of my time, as did filling out and mailing in college applications. The plan had always been to move away to a four-year college. That was what I'd always said I wanted—someplace far away where I could forge my own path separate from my famous last name. But that was before Rory. Before I fell madly and wholeheartedly in love. I could no longer imagine my life without him.

My list of colleges changed, my top choices now all in the Southern California area. This upset my mother, who didn't want me to sideline my life for a boy. But she didn't understand. His life was my life, and I would go where he was to support him.

My stubbornness caused issues at home, which landed me in house arrest more than once. My punishment became Rory's. When I was in trouble, he couldn't come over, and I knew he hated it. We fought sometimes over that, him almost always taking my mother's side and urging me to go away to college. I relented and sent out applications to my former top schools, but I didn't plan to go if accepted. My parents could say what they wanted, but this was my life and I chose Rory.

If I wanted to be totally honest, my main reason for staying was that I feared once their band started booking gigs, Rory would have temptations he'd never experienced before. Away at college, I'd be out of sight and out of mind. The thought never crossed my mind that I might meet someone too because I knew it would never happen. I had blinders on. That much was clear just from the interactions I was having at school.

"Hi, Grace," a girl called to me, walking the opposite way down the hall. I gave her a friendly wave and continued on my way.

A funny thing happened in the transition from junior to senior year—I was no longer a pariah. I'd narrowed down the reason to one of three things. The nepo baby mean girls had graduated, and without their constant badgering, others were allowed to form their own opinions about me. Number two: now that I was no longer in Quinn's shadow, people could actually see *me* and were no longer shying away. But the most likely reason was that falling in love with Rory had changed me. I no longer had to chase adoration because I had it now in the palm of my hand. I was stronger and more confident, and it showed.

Boys surrounded me, and I had more Homecoming invitations than I knew what to do with, but I was never tempted, not once, because I already had the real thing. And it wasn't just the boys with a newfound interest in me. On the first day of senior year, I found myself the center of attention. My classmates gathered around me like timidly curious woodland creatures. I was invited into all of the relevant friend groups, floating between them as I struggled to build lasting bonds.

Some days, I just didn't feel like trying, and like my sister before me, I found myself in the library at lunchtime, nibbling on my food and working on homework so I wouldn't have so much to do when Rory came around.

Every time I lunched in the library, I took a spot at the same table, a few seats down from the only other person sitting there. Her name was a mystery. I'd introduced myself when I'd first sat at her table, but it was immediately clear the girl was painfully shy. She mumbled her name back to me.

Rea? I attempted to clarify. She mumbled again. *Shea? Renee? Margaret?* Like a trooper, the whisper-girl just kept trying until finally, it was so awkward I just smiled and nodded and said *Ohhh, okay,* like I knew what she had said.

To this day, I didn't know what her name was, and we'd reached that point in our relationship where it would be too embarrassing to ask. Despite that, we'd become friends in an odd, comforting way. My friend with no name didn't dress like the other kids. Instead of trendy labels, she wore baggy pants and a long-sleeved shirt. Her hair was long and dark, often uncombed, and reached all the way to her waist. One day her hair was bright and shiny, and I told her how pretty it was, and she got lost in the layers of bashfulness, her cheeks blooming, but once she thought my attention was diverted, a tiny smile transformed her neutral face.

My phone buzzed on the table, startling both of us. I glanced at the number, didn't recognize it, and sent it straight to voicemail. My bookish friend smiled at me. I smiled back, and we resumed our work. A minute later, my phone rang again. Same number. I looked up at the girl. Her forehead furrowed as my phone interrupted her work a second time. *Oops, my bad*, I gestured, then smiled. She grimaced. I sent the call to voicemail.

Packing up at the end of lunch, my phone rang for the third time. Same number. Now I wasn't sure what to do. As a general rule, I never picked up unknown numbers. If someone I knew was bleeding out and needed my assistance, that person better call me from a number in my contacts or he/she/they would surely die. I checked on my silent seat partner to get her opinion. Her brow was lifted, eyes shifting back and forth between me and the phone as if to say, *Are you going to pick that up?*

"Should I?"

She mumbled something that I took to mean yes.

"Okay," I said. Our code seemed to work for us.

I kept my voice low so as not to disturb others. "Hello?"

"Is Rory there?" the female caller asked.

This got my attention, which must have registered on my face because my table partner mirrored my surprised expression. Scooting upright in my chair, questions started whirling. Why was she calling me asking for Rory?

"Who's this?"

"It doesn't matter."

She sounded older, seasoned.

"Actually, it does," I said, already feeling that pinprick jealousy rear up inside me.

Her tone shortened. "Just put him on."

Mine shortened even more. "How about you give me your name, and I'll consider it?"

"Look, little girl, I don't have time for your shit. Tell Rory that Martin and Co. know all about his new Patty, and they're coming for a chat real soon. Like real soon."

"I don't understand any of this."

"You're not supposed to because the message isn't for you." She was so condescending that I wanted to hang up on her over and over and over. "Just tell him what I said. I'll wait."

"I can't. He's not here."

"Where is he?"

"I don't know. I'm at school."

"At school? I didn't realize Rory was dating a child."

A child? Anger rippled through me, yet I could not summon one comeback.

"Just give me his phone number," the woman said.

"I'm not going to do that."

She swore, and then the line went dead.

"Hello?"

I pulled the phone from my ear and looked at the screen and then at my friend. She stared at me, a question in her gaze. I shrugged. She shrugged. I called the number back, but it only rang. No voicemail picked up.

It wasn't that I wanted to talk to her again, after how rude she'd been, but something about the conversation didn't sit right. This woman seemed to know Rory. But how? Pulling out my notebook, I jotted down the phone number and what she'd said before googling "Martin and Co." No place of business came up.

GRACE

> Do you know some woman who works for
> Martin and Co.? She said they're coming to talk
> to you.

I sent the text off to Rory, knowing he was at work still and wouldn't answer me until he was off, but if this truly was as urgent as she made it seem, I wanted him to know.

Shoving the phone in my pocket, I waved at my oddly awesome friend and went off to class.

I was in sixth period when the first call came in. Phones weren't allowed out of backpacks, but I took a peek and saw it was Rory calling. And then, like the woman before him, he called and called again. It wasn't until class was over that I could text him back.

GRACE

> Sorry I was in class

His response arrived a split second after mine was sent.

RORY

> Meet me out front by the flagpole

Wait, Rory was here? At my school? My heart sped up at just the thought of our worlds crossing. I wanted to share him, but he was skittish about school and didn't want to go anywhere near it. I speed walked through the hallways, my heart soaring until I realized he hadn't come for me. He'd come because of the message from the bitchy woman who'd called me a little girl.

Rory was right where he said he'd be, in a black t-shirt that hugged him tight and a pair of faded jeans. His hair was a flyaway mess, and he held the sticks in his hands, banging them against the flagpole in a rousing beat. He had the attention of everyone who passed him by. Not that he noticed. He was stressed, more than I'd seen him in a long time. I could see it in his body movements and in the deep grooves of his forehead. Something had been bothering him for a while now, and despite our long conversations about nothing, I'd never been able to pull that information out of him.

Rory stopped the impromptu drumming when he saw me. He walked over, taking the stairs two at a time. God, he was so handsome, eye candy for the musically inclined. I imagined him making it to the top of the steps, picking me up, and kissing me in front of all my jealous classmates. But as he approached, the expression on his face told me there would be no magical movie moment. Rory was more than stressed; he was panicked. He grabbed my hand and guided me down the steps in a caveman move I really wasn't digging.

"Rory," I said, "slow down."

He wasn't listening, instead just dragging me along.

"Rory!" This time, I added the brakes. "Stop. Tell me what's going on, or I'm not going with you."

Eyes swiveled in our direction. My classmates whispered behind their hands at the scene we were making.

"Not here, Grace."

"Did I do something wrong? I didn't give her your number. I didn't think you'd want me too unless..." I halted, my face souring. He wasn't seeing this woman, was he?

"What do you know about her?" he said, raising my suspicions more.

My lips flattened. "Am I not supposed to know about her?"

Rory glanced around. More people were watching now. It wasn't every day a hot drummer showed up and pounded out a tune on the flagpole. It was even less common that he was talking to Jake McKallister's little sister. My classmates assumed he was someone. And they weren't wrong. He would be theirs one day. But first he was mine.

"Please," he pleaded. "Let's just go to your car."

Rory and I didn't speak on the way there. It wasn't until we were in my car that I asked, "Who's Patty?"

He stiffened. "Where did you hear that?"

"The bitchy woman said they knew about your new Patty."

"Grace," he stopped me, the horrified look on his face giving me pause. "You have to tell me exactly what she said."

I pulled my notebook out and read it to him exactly as she said it to me. "She said, and I quote, '*Look little girl, I don't have time for your shit. Tell Rory that Martin and Co. know all about his new Patty, and they're coming for a chat real soon. Like real soon.*'"

The color drained from his face. The message she'd sent made no sense to me, but it sure did to Rory. He looked like he might actually pass out.

I grabbed his hand, abandoning the jealousy in my veins to help him through whatever crisis he was experiencing. "What is it?"

He sat back in his seat, and I could see the wheels turning. "It's nothing."

"Nothing? It doesn't look like nothing. Who is she?"

"Not now, Grace."

"If not now, when?"

"How about never?"

"That won't work for me."

"Grace, please. I can't."

The fear in his eyes was real. I wanted to push, but I wasn't sure how far I could without breaking him, so I softened my approach.

"Let's go back to your place for a while. I'll turn off my tracking, so Mom can't find me. I'll just be the two of us, and then we can talk."

Rory twisted his head, like he was in some horror movie. "No."

"No? Why not?"

"I don't want to go back there. Not right now. Take me home."

"That's what I just said."

"No. Not to Camden Place." He caught my eye. "Home."

Home. He meant mine. My home had become his home.

THAT NIGHT RORY asked my mother if he could spend the night. Something was definitely wrong. Something about the phone call had spooked him enough that he didn't want to go home. When I tried to visit him in the room my mom had made up for him, he refused me entry. It took some effort on my part just to get him to go outside to the firepit, where I hoped to get some clarity.

"What's going on, Rory?"

"I didn't want to disrespect your mother for letting me stay."

"Not that. Why don't you want to go home? What did that message mean?"

He sighed, and I could feel the heaviness he carried. I wrapped my arms around him and held him as tightly as my arms allowed me. I wanted to squeeze out his pain because I knew that was what this was. Something from his past was surfacing, and it was hurting him enough to drive a wedge between us.

Gently, I kissed his neck. His chin. His cheek. His nose.

"I'm here for you. You know that, right?"

"I know."

"And I love you and you love me, right?"

He nodded.

"So, anything you tell me is in confidence. It's safe with me, and I will never judge you. I don't care what happened in the past. I don't care if you went to jail for punching a koala, although it would definitely pain me. The point is nothing you can say to me would make me not love you. And if you suffered some sort of past abuse that's messing with your head, you know I'll be right here for you."

"Grace, please."

"Please what? I'm trying to understand. I want to be there for you. What did that message mean? Why don't you want to go home?"

He was silent a long time, but I didn't dare speak. I needed an answer to at least one of those questions.

"There are things you don't know about me. Things that happened to me as a kid. All I want is for it to go away. That message... Those people, they won't let me forget."

"Who won't let you? That woman? Who is she?"

"Her name is Nikki. She's my foster sister."

"And Patty?"

"A former foster mom."

"And Martin and Co.?"

His walls went up. Rory shot to his feet, pacing back and forth like a nervous caged lion.

"Are they the people who won't let you forget?"

"Her. Them. And then the others. Everyone wants something from me. Everyone. I just want..." Rory slammed his hands down on the retaining wall, angry tears escaping him. "I just want..."

I jumped up, grabbing him, holding his restless body steady. "What do you want?"

"To be with you. That's all I want."

"You have me."

He wrangled free of my arms. "Don't you get it, Grace? They'll never let me keep you."

RORY LEFT me stunned and confused at the firepit that night. What could possibly have happened to him to warrant retaliation? Could the beating the night I'd left him in the parking lot be tied to all this? None of it made sense, and Rory wasn't talking. The next day he pretended nothing had happened. I knew he wanted me to leave it be, but there was something wrong. I could feel the shift in our relationship. Nikki held some power over him, but he wouldn't tell me what. It made me realize how little I knew about him. I'd always tried to be respectful of his life, knowing there were things he didn't want to tell me, but maybe I'd been giving him too much leeway. If we were going to make a life together, shouldn't I know?

The next evening, with Rory and the band practicing, I tapped my sister-in-law, Casey, on the shoulder.

"Can I talk to you?"

"Sure," she said, grabbing a carrot stick and dipping it in ranch. She crunched nearly the whole way through her veggie before her eyes rounded. "Oh, you mean privately?"

I nodded, leading her down the hallway, up the stairs, and into my bedroom. I could hear her licking the ranch off her fingers as she walked.

"Wow, you get exercise every time you go to your bedroom," she said, wiping the rest of the ranch onto her jeans.

"I need to talk to you," I said, shutting the door behind us.

"Okay, but if this is about Jake, I really can't say anything."

"Wait. What? Is there something going on with Jake?"

"No." Her eyes shifted to the rug, like a child caught in a lie.

"Whoa, hold on. What's happening with Jake?"

"Nothing," she lied. "What did you want to ask me?"

Momentarily stunned, I wasn't sure which wounded boy I should be concerned about.

"Rory." I redirected my thoughts. "I think he was abused as a child."

Casey didn't seem to be the least bit surprised. "Jake said the same thing."

"He did?"

"Yes. He's sensitive to that. Said he saw it in his eyes. Whatever that means."

"What else did he say?"

"Grace, I can't. You need to talk to Jake if you want to know."

Again, I got the impression not all was well in their newlywed world. "Is everything okay?"

"It's fine. Jake's been dealing with some demons since the wedding and it's been"—tears welled in her eyes—"difficult."

"Oh. I'm sorry. If you don't want to talk right now, it's okay."

"No. Go on."

"Something is upsetting Rory. Something big and he won't tell me. I keep trying but he shuts me down every time. I feel like he's slipping away and I don't know how to help him."

Casey nodded as if this were an everyday occurrence in her life. "You want my advice, Grace? Don't give Rory a choice. If he wants this relationship with you—if he loves you—he owes it to you to be honest. He needs to let you know upfront what you're walking into."

"You didn't know with Jake?"

"Well... I thought I knew. It's different with Jake. The world knows what happened to him. All you have to do is type his name into a search engine and you could read for days. But all that, it just barely scratches the surface of who Jake is and what happened to him."

"And he won't tell you?"

"I know some things."

Now I was intensely curious.

"Do you know how he escaped? How he"—I dropped my voice to a bare whisper—"managed to get the knife?"

Casey bit down on her lower lip. So much turmoil going through her. I totally lost track of Rory in this conversation. My sister-in-law nodded her head, slowly at first, then with slightly more vigor. My eyes popped wide open, followed by a quick gasp. I knew she'd never tell, never break his trust in her, but holy hell. As far as I knew, no one in the family knew that part of the story. The why. The how. He'd been thirteen at the time. How had he managed to gain the upper hand?

"How did you get him to tell you?"

"Just like you, I let him choose the pace. I waited so patiently. But Grace, Rory's never going to tell you unless you give him no choice. He can't have it both ways. It's either you and him together forever, or him and his secret forever and ever."

"What if I ask him and he still won't tell me?"

"Well, Grace, the answer to that depends on how much you love him."

29

RORY: I'M YOURS

My world was closing in.

Before the call, my biggest worry had been the flyers. They kept showing up in random places: on a light pole between Camden Place; at my work; on the door of the recreation room; another one on the door of my building. There was never any written threat attached, although it was implied all the same. They were watching, reserving the right to exterminate me at their convenience.

Everything changed once Nikki's warning call came in to Grace. The threat was no longer directed specifically at me. The mention of Patty, the foster mom I'd wanted to go home to all those years ago, was Nikki's way of telling me they knew about the McKallisters and that it was no longer just me I was fighting to save. It was them, too. I needed to find Nikki. After what happened in the alleyway, I didn't trust her at all, but I couldn't afford *not* to trust her either. I called the number back, the one she'd used to contact Grace, but it went to a homeless shelter, giving me no way to track her down.

And Grace. No matter what happened now, she would get hurt. There was no way around it. She already didn't trust me,

Nikki's call having driven a wedge between us as only my foster sister could do. It killed me to see that look in her eye. She was suspicious of Nikki—jealous, even—and I really couldn't blame her. We were what I'd said we were, foster siblings, but there was more to us than that, and to tell Grace the truth about Nikki meant I would have to open up my life to her in a way I wasn't ready for. Not yet. Probably not ever.

And so, my world continued to shrink.

The threats too big to ignore, I stopped going to work. I crammed my backpack full of essentials and stopped going to my apartment. Those first two nights after the message arrived I spent at the McKallisters, making lame excuses for why I couldn't go back. The third night, I slept on the streets. Tonight, I expected, would be more of the same. It was as if I'd made a full circle, back to where I'd started, with rats nibbling at my toes.

It became clearer by the day that I would need to call Dutch and tell him everything. He might want to use me for his own benefit, but at least he had a vested interest in keeping me alive. I'd tell him about the threats and the flyers and the significance of the phrase. About Nikki's call and my connection to the McKallisters. Witness protection seemed my only way out of this. If I disappeared into another life, the McKallisters would be safe in theirs.

There was no other way. I just had to make it to Friday, and then I would call Dutch and set things in motion. With the plan in place, I intended to spend my last two days with Grace and her family, making what last memories I could with them before my whole life, my entire identity, was erased.

That was before the text came in. Before my world didn't just close down around me, it slammed the fucking door.

> We need to talk

THE TEXT WAS FROM JAKE. I didn't even know he had my number, but I supposed someone like him could easily get it. I wasn't sure which of the two messages was more chilling, Grace's call informing me that Martin was on the hunt or Jake's cryptic text message, but there was little doubt in my mind the two were connected.

Since I was at the McKallisters when his text came in, I angled my phone away from Grace and typed each letter with dread.

RORY

> About what?

JAKE

> In person. Where are you?

> At your parents' house

> Stay there. I'll text when I'm outside the gate

No part of that exchange eased my fear. Whatever he had to talk to me about was important enough that he'd interrupt his regularly scheduled program to tend to me. The gravity of the situation hit me. My old life was colliding with my new, and there would be no co-mingling.

∼

JAKE

> Here. Just you. Not Grace

I was numb; could hardly move. Whatever he had to say I wouldn't like. This was it. The end of everything. Camden Place. The band. The McKallisters. Grace. It had all been for nothing.

Slowly, I unfolded myself from Grace's arms, sliding to the edge of the sofa to allow the dread to pass through before rising to my feet.

"Where are you going?" Grace asked, her hand gliding along my arm and through my fingers before it fell off for good.

"I need to make a phone call."

"To that company?"

I could see the irritation drawing her lips into a fine line. To be clear, her issue wasn't with the 'company' itself but with its 'receptionist' Nikki. My sister had always lacked social skills, but I could only imagine how much worse they'd become since she'd taken to sucking dudes off in the streets.

"I'm not calling *her*," I replied. "Don't worry."

"Why should I be worried?" Grace asked, laughing away the suggestion of competition, but the pinched expression on her face gave her away. Grace was jealous, a trait I'd never seen in her before. But then, our relationship existed almost entirely on this property. We didn't have a lot of outside forces to contend with, and certainly none like Nikki, whose only goal seemed to be to destroy us. Aside from the quickies at my place, our love story floated around in a luxury bubble, behind a state-of-the-art security system meant to keep us safe. Leave it to Nikki to burst that bubble.

Leaning down, I whispered for Grace's ears only, "I'm yours. Never forget that."

Because of my slow exit, I jogged to the gate and let myself out. Jake wasn't waiting in front. I pulled my phone out to text him when he flashed me with his high beams from up the street. I walked to his car with a detached acceptance. Jake unlocked the door, and I opened it and slid in.

Flipping his car around in the middle of the road, he drove in the opposite direction from the house, moving out of the immediate area. A couple of minutes later, he pulled into the parking lot of an office building. There we sat looking straight ahead, the fear frothing up inside me.

"There's no easy way to say this, Rory, so I'm just going to show you." Jake passed his phone to me. "This came through in an email."

I knew what it was going to be before I even looked at the photo. The thing I feared most: my dirty secret out in the open. I'd seen the image before. Hartman had used it for blackmail to get us back in his car over and over again. In it, little kid me stared hard into the camera, the horror of my situation nearly splitting the lens in two. It was that same flat glare I saw from the boy in the mirror.

The man in the picture had been blurred to protect his identity, but I knew who he was—I knew who they all were, and I could send every last one of them to the life in prison they deserved. I didn't want to imagine what Jake thought of me. The image itself wasn't explicitly graphic, but there was no doubt what it depicted. And this was just one of hundreds, maybe thousands more. They existed on the dark web, and despite Special Agent Dutch and people like him trying to stamp them out, they would never be totally eradicated as long as deviants searching for this content existed.

With bile rising from my gut, I passed the phone back to Jake. A moment ticked by before I opened the car door and let the nastiness spew out. I wiped the spittle away with the back of my hand and glanced his way. Jake had his head tipped back on his seat like my misery was also his. I swiveled around to the open door and threw up again. And again. Emptying my insides until there was nothing left to absolve me. I'd tried so hard to bury the memories deep inside, letting my jitters do their thing when the truth got too close, but there was no point now. Grace's brother knew who I was. What I'd done. It didn't matter whether I was to blame or not; no one wanted *that* hellish baggage attached to someone they loved.

I shut the door, righting myself. "I don't know what you want me to say."

"Nothing. I debated even showing you, but what else was I supposed to do?"

"How'd you even know this was me?"

"My social media manager deals with all incoming messages. She actually thought it was me."

I flinched at the fucked-up world that put us both into the uncompromising position of having to defend our younger selves for things we had no control over. Not that her mix-up wasn't understandable, given his background.

"Hell, *I* even thought it was me for a second there when she called me in a panic. Once I pulled up the image myself, I knew it was you. Could see it in your eyes."

I shrank back, feeling sick. "What do they want?"

"150K."

"You're being blackmailed?"

I wasn't sure why I was so shocked. They were the scum of the earth, abusing children. Blackmail was almost tame for them. But I had to hand it to them, they'd gone straight to the top. Jake McKallister. The one person who couldn't afford to be messed up in this shit was now neck deep in it.

"Who else knows about this?" I asked.

"Just my social media manager, and she signed a confidentiality agreement to work for me. This isn't leaking from my end."

I took a moment to digest the information and then nodded.

"How old are you in this picture?" Jake asked.

"Ten."

His grimace said it all. No need for him to vocalize his sympathy when I knew I had it.

"Is this how you ended up in foster care?"

"No. Foster care is how I ended up there. Group homes are hunting grounds for pervs preying on kids. We're low-hanging fruit. Easy pickings. My sister was lured in first. Then me. And then"—I pointed at his phone—"that happened."

"Fuck, Rory, I'm so sorry."

I turned my head away, looking out the window into the darkness, wishing it would swallow me up into its nothingness.

"So, where do we go from here?" he asked.

"I don't know. You tell me."

"If I thought it would help you, Rory, I'd pay it but I'm assuming there are more where this came from."

I nodded, my face flaming with shame.

"As soon as I pay, they'll be back for more. You know that, right?"

I continued nodding. He was right. This was never going to stop. Never.

"The one thing I know for sure is I can't have this on my phone. Or in my email. And I definitely don't want more images coming my way. If someone sees I have this on my computer... I can't risk it. I have to turn this over to the police. It's nothing against you, but I have to protect myself and Grace and my family."

I could feel my world shrinking by the second. I didn't blame Jake for wanting to pass off this particularly scorching hot potato. Given his past, if he were to be found with images like this, it would end him. I couldn't let Grace and the McKallisters pay for my sins.

"Not the police—the FBI. They already know about this. It's in their interest to keep it secret. I'll get you the number to my contact."

His eyes widened in surprise. "You're working with the FBI?"

"Not officially, no. But they're building a case, and they want me to testify."

"Will you?"

"I don't know. I haven't decided yet."

Jake was quiet for a second, watching me. "Look, I like you, Rory. You know I do. None of this is your fault, and I'll help you in whatever way I can, but if the media finds out about this and makes the connection to Grace, the story will blow up. She's only seventeen. I don't want her to be dragged through the dirt like I was at that age."

"She won't be," I said, shoring up what little fortitude I had left. "Not if I disappear."

"What does that mean?"

"If I agree to testify, they'll have to protect me. Put me in hiding. Change my name. I'll lose everything. It's why I haven't done it yet. I don't want to lose her," I said, struggling to get through. "But I don't have much of a choice now, and at least then Grace would be free of me."

Jake gripped the steering wheel, pissed. "So fucking unfair."

Tell me about it, I thought, laying my head back on the head-rest. I willed the despair away.

"Just between us"—Jake dropped his gaze, his voice lowering —"sometimes I wish I'd let Casey go."

It hit me, the significance of what he was saying. He'd been faced with the same choice that I was now.

"Why? You and Casey seem like the perfect couple."

"She wants a normal life. Kids."

"And you don't."

"It's not that I don't want that. I don't know if I can. There's a lot of shit going on in my head that she has no idea about. I should've been honest with myself from the start and let Casey go when I had the chance, but I loved her too much. I was selfish. And now she's stuck with a guy who's too damaged to be what she deserves. I know you understand what I'm saying."

I did. Jake's message came through loud and clear. In many ways, we weren't all that different. I loved Grace. She was my salvation. Just as Casey was Jake's. But if I loved her that much, I owed her the chance at a fulfilling and safe life—without me in it.

"If I do this," I said, my voice cracking, "you can never tell her."

"If you do this, you're braver than me."

STANDING ON THE SIDEWALK, I watched Jake drive away before solemnly walking back to the gate. The decision was made. I had to leave. But how? Grace would see right through me. Nothing I said would be convincing. And if I just disappeared, she'd never move on. Grace would make it her mission in life to find me. I knew she would.

"Rory?"

The familiar voice stopped me dead in my tracks. Even though I needed to find her, I still feared what she had to say. Slowly, I turned to face my sister, half expecting her right-hand man to jump out from the bushes and murder me.

"Are you here to finish me off?" I was almost hopeful.

"Do you want me to?" Nikki replied.

"It might be easier. But maybe you just want to watch Hartman do it." It was a low blow, but I felt entitled to take it.

"Your memory fails you." She frowned. "I tried to save you."

"You left me dying in the alley."

"The police were running toward you!"

"And you were running away. Nice, Nik. Thanks a lot."

"Who do you think has been watching over you the past few

months? You've been off living the high life with your glamour girlfriend and her rich family, and I've been in hell." She dropped her voice to a gravelly whisper. "I've literally been on my fucking knees for you, so lay off the attitude."

We stood there staring, at an impasse. I couldn't tell if she was lying or playing both sides. I grabbed her arm and led her away from the security cameras.

"What do you know?"

"About?"

"Who is sending me the message—the flyers that say, *on the count of three.* Is it from them?"

"Jesus, Rory. Who did you think they're from, your kinder-garten teacher?"

"I'm on the verge of a fucking panic attack, so just tell me what's going on."

"They want you to keep your mouth shut. They know you're working with the FBI, so they can't forcibly do it for you."

"I'm not working with the FBI."

"You are. You just don't realize it. You think you got into the Camden Place—the all-inclusive Sandals retreat for foster kids —on your looks alone? News flash: you're not that attractive."

I shrugged off the insult. "What about the photograph sent to Jake? Of me. Who's blackmailing him?"

Her brows dipped, head slowly shaking. "I don't know anything about that."

I eyed her skeptically.

"I don't, but I doubt it's coming from the top. They've been trying to get rid of all their kiddie stash. If they could, they'd be flushing it down the toilets. Too bad it's all digital."

"Right. Too bad."

"Sounds to me more like a minor player looking for a payday. Someone found out you were connected to Jake, and they had the presence of mind to exploit it."

That was what scared me the most. Someone had made the connection, and it felt like this was only the beginning of an ominously dark storm coming my way. I had to leave. I had to.

"Trust me, Rory. If this gets out, he won't be the only one. The only way to stop the wave coming their way is to distance yourself from the McKallisters. They're easy targets. Especially with Jake being in the public eye and worth millions. He's ripe for blackmail."

"Because he's associated with me," I said flatly.

"What did you think was going to happen?"

"I don't know, Nik. I'm playing defense here. If you hadn't fed me to the wolves, none of this would've been an issue."

"It's not like I did it on purpose. I was a victim too. I know you blame me, but I was lured in, just like you."

My jaw tightened. As always, our versions differed.

"Why did you call Grace? Why not come to my apartment or my work and warn me? Were you trying to ruin my relationship?"

"Why would I do that?"

I could think of a few reasons, but I kept my mouth shut.

"I didn't know where you lived, Rory. All I had was her number from the note she left you that night Hartman tried to kill you. I was smart enough to pocket it before he saw it. I only found you now because I had a meeting with Dutch, and I looked through his files when he went to get me a drink."

"You're working with Dutch?"

"Why do you sound so surprised? We were both victims of the same people."

"I know, but that would require you to turn on your buddies."

"My buddies? Do you think I'm deep in with these guys? I'm a street whore, Rory, not a mastermind. I've been a virtual prisoner since I came back to Los Angeles. Hartman found me all strung out, wandering the Stroll. He got me just clean enough to send me back out on the street, so at least he could make a little money off my misery. Always thinking, that one," she said through a bitter frown, tapping her chipped fingernail to her temple. "I only hear things because they talk over me, thinking I'm too dumb to retain anything. But imagine what they would think if I flat-out asked them where you lived? They might think I had a few surviving brain cells in my head and wouldn't be so eager to plot in my presence. I've been doing the best I can, Rory, so don't you dare accuse me of being part of the boys' club."

She was visibly shaking. Although she'd claimed to be a great actress as a child, she wasn't. If this was all an act, then she deserved an Oscar. "I'm sorry, Nik. Okay? This whole this is bearing down on me, and I don't know what to do."

"I do. Come with me."

"Where?"

"Into the witness protection program. Dutch said he'd place us together. The two of us. Like old times."

My blood ran cold. Old times? Yeah, that wasn't going to happen.

Nikki misinterpreted my silence as acceptance. She reached up and gently traced her fingers along my face.

"Nikki..." I was about to tell her to back off when she abruptly pulled my head down and kissed my lips. It took my brain a second to register, but when it finally did, I jerked away like I'd touched a scalding flame.

"What'd you do that for?" I blasted angrily.

"I thought... shit... I thought you wanted me to."

"When have I ever wanted you to?" My voice ticked up, old anger rearing its head.

"I'm sorry, okay? You know I don't understand social cues. I get confused."

"There should be no confusion. You're my *sister*."

"In your mind only. We're not related."

I let her explanation simmer. "That doesn't make it right."

"I know. I'm sorry, Rory. I'm so screwed up in the head. I shouldn't have kissed you, I know that. My brain doesn't always work the way it should."

"Then I'll make it very clear for you to understand. Don't ever do that again."

Nikki shook her head. "I won't."

"I need to go," I said, turning to leave her on the sidewalk.

"You're not coming with me?"

I turned around to face her. "What part of that conversation made you think I would?"

"You have to. They're going to kill you." Nikki locked eyes with me. "Is this about her? You know you have to leave her, right?"

Just her speaking those words angered me. Mostly because I was pissed at her, but also because I knew she was right.

"I know," I sneered.

"Come with me now, then. Dutch is waiting."

I stomped back to her until I was inches from her face. "Just to be clear: we might both be going into protection, but there isn't any 'me and you.' I'm going alone, and so are you."

"Why do you have to be so mean to me all the time?"

Every tic in my body was set in motion. "You know why."

Her lip quivered, and a tear slipped down her cheek. She looked away. "Can I at least drive you there?"

"Someone gave *you* a car loan?"

"No. I stole it."

I shook my head, laughing at the absurdity of it all. "As tempting as the offer is, I can't leave until Friday."

"Why Friday?"

"It's the Homecoming dance."

30

RORY: THE END

Q uinn appeared out of nowhere, the force of his thrust knocking me to the ground.

"What the fuck?" I swore, and I got to my feet only to be shoved back down again.

Quinn threw my backpack at me. "Get out!"

Things were moving too fast to comprehend. "Dude...?"

"I saw you," he growled through clenched teeth.

"What did you see?"

"Who is she, Rory? How long have you been cheating on my sister?"

My eyes rounded in horror. "No. Quinn. That's not... no... you have it all wrong. That girl out there, she's my sister."

Quinn was not interested in the truth. He kicked me while I was already down. A foot in my face. Pain exploded through my cheek, and my head bounced off the grass on the rebound. He lunged for me, and I only barely managed to roll away and rise to my feet. My fists curled at my sides.

"You fucking liar." He jabbed his finger at me, poking into my chest. "I saw you kiss her."

"It's not what it looks like."

"It was on the lips, Rory. There's no explaining that—and if she's really your sister, then you're not only a cheat but a sick pervert too."

"She's my foster sister, dude. We're not related."

I sounded like Nikki, explaining the unexplainable away. It didn't matter, though, because Quinn was not having it. He pulled out his phone and held it at a distance, presumably so I couldn't rip it out of his hand. When he pressed play, my face instantly fell. He'd caught our exchange. Her hand on my face. The kiss. Out of context and under the glow of a streetlight, it appeared all the more intimate. It had meant nothing, but now it meant everything. I was doomed. There was nothing I could say to satisfy his rage.

The porch lights flicked on, and Grace stepped out on the landing.

"Rory? Quinn?"

She looked between us, struggling to comprehend. It was when she spotted the blood trickling from the boot print in my cheek that realization kicked in.

"Are you two fighting?" There was such disbelief in the question, and why wouldn't there be? Quinn and I had become close over the summer. Good friends. There was no reason for us to be fighting.

"Go back inside, Grace," Quinn demanded, holding his hand to keep her away as if I were the most wicked of villains.

"You're kidding, I hope," she said, racing barefoot down the stairs and across the grass until she was at my side. She'd shown her allegiance, and it was to me. God, I was going to miss her. Grace touched the blood on my cheek, her eyes flaring with anger. Whipping around, she bared her teeth and shoved Quinn back with all her might.

"What did you do?" she screamed.

"Point that finger back at your boyfriend," he said. "Ask him, Grace. Ask him what he did."

No doubt hearing the commotion from inside the house, both Scott and Michelle appeared on the porch, saw the stand-off, and both rushed into the fray.

"Ask him what?" Grace questioned.

Quinn advanced on me, stopping inches from my face. "Ask him why he was outside of the front gate kissing his foster sister. And if he tries to lie, I'm happy to provide the proof."

Grace wormed her way between the two of us and stared up at me. "What's he talking about?"

All eyes were on me. This was all wrong. Everyone hating me. It wasn't how I wanted to say goodbye. I wanted Grace to at least know how much I loved her. But then again, maybe letting that perception of me as a cheater stand was for the best. If she thought I'd been sneaking around behind her back, Grace wouldn't come looking. I could disappear into my new identity, and all of this would just be memory. My hands began to shake, followed by my legs and my feet. Pressure closed in on my chest.

"I'm sorry, Grace."

"Wait." She touched my face, willing to forgive me sight unseen. Her loyalty killed me. "What are you sorry for?"

Glancing at all the faces staring at me, I doubled down on the lie that would end Grace and me forever. I would never again take a music lesson from Michelle or make barbecue ribs with Scott or play drums in Quinn's band. I would be erased from the McKallister family for good. The only family I'd ever known.

"I cheated on you," I said, fighting back the flood of emotion. "With Nikki. The girl who called you. I'm with her. I'm sorry."

The hurt, misery, and horror that played out over Grace's

face sickened me. I wanted to grab her and tell her it was all a lie, that I loved her and only her, but our time had come. This was the end. It was time to go.

"No," she said. "You're lying."

"I'm not."

"Yes!" Her voice rose. "You're lying. Why are you lying? I *know* you. I know what's in your heart. You love me. You do."

I shook my head, bending down to pick up my bag as an errant tear slipped down my face. I wiped it away before its mutiny was discovered.

Grace caught me on my way up, placing her hands on either side of my face and forcing me to look her way. "Please, Beats. Please. Don't do this. Whatever's scaring you, I can fix it. I got you, remember?"

"Stop." I pulled away from her. "I have to go."

Michelle stepped in, grabbing her daughter's arm and pulling her back. "Grace, honey..."

"Rory." Scott raised his voice, the first time I'd ever heard him do such a thing. He was pissed. At me. "Just leave."

That was when Grace snapped, ripping her arm out of Michelle's grip and screaming. "Nooo! Nooo!"

We all froze in place, her anger like a lightning rod.

"Everyone, just go away! Go!"

Michelle, Scott, and Quinn backed up. I did too, but she fisted my shirt, forcing me to remain.

"Go!" she screamed at the others. The three of them moved to the edge of the grass. Only then did Grace lay her forehead against my chest, sobs erupting from somewhere deep inside her. I couldn't stop the tears from slipping out of my eyes. She was ripping my heart out just as I was doing to her.

A minute passed, maybe two, before she lifted her head and again placed her hands on my face, forcing our eyes to connect. "Tell me you don't love me. Tell me and I'll let you go."

I wouldn't say it. I couldn't.

Removing her hands from my face, I walked away.

Past the gate. Under the streetlight. Across the street. Down the hill.

All I could hear were Grace's screams.

PART III

THE BRIDGE

31

GRACE: SOPHOMORE SLUMP
PRESENT DAY

I was a fraud. There, I said it. My whole life I'd fancied myself a songwriter, but I wasn't. Not even close. "Promises" had been a fluke. Beginner's luck. And now everyone thought I was some high-quality musical poet when I'd be hard-pressed to write a coherent grocery list.

I laid my head back on the chair, gripping the armrest and drawing in deep breaths in an effort to slow my heart rate. If I was going to have a full-on meltdown, it wasn't going to be high above the fly-over states.

"Are you leaving or coming home?"

I glanced over at the woman seated beside me. Big eyes. Sweet face. She was trying to console me, no doubt assuming I was afraid of flying. I almost wanted to laugh. Crashing was the least of my worries. Honestly, that would be a relief. In three weeks' time, I would be on a bus touring North America with the hottest new band in town, tasked with helping them write their second album. And I had nothing. My notebook was empty save for the hundreds and hundreds of stupid, half-assed ideas I'd thought were inspired in the moment but would amount to nothing.

"Coming home." I forced a smile. "What about you?"

"Leaving. My husband and I are celebrating our ten-year anniversary. Going to do the whole touristy thing. Hollywood. Disneyland."

I looked around for this husband of hers, one that would match her sweetness and energy, but saw no one who fit the bill. "Is he on the plane?"

"In the back."

"So, you're sitting in first class, and he's in the back?"

She laughed. "It's an anniversary, not a honeymoon."

My seat partner went on to explain her husband earned the seat through mileage points from work travel, but there was only enough for one upgrade and he'd given it to her. Aw. That, right there, was love. My blood pressure leveled off. Pulling my notebook out of my backpack, I jotted down my thoughts about such marital sacrifice. You never knew what seedling could flourish into a song, and god knows, I needed a garden. It was the entire reason I'd made the trip to New York in the first place—for inspiration. To write a damn song.

My intentions were good when I dropped Elliott off at the airport and hopped on a flight of my own to New York City. The idea was to devote my days to writing, and, oh man, I was so gung ho that first day, sealing myself off in the rented tiny studio apartment, fully prepared to practice brutalizing tough love. No fun of any kind until the creativity flowed! That was my motto. It lasted one day. The rest of the time was spent staring at the empty notebook and watching HGTV. Nights were just as unproductive. I went to musicals or walked the touristy streets or visited local venues to listen to bands play—anything I could think of to spark my brain to produce something creative. But nothing happened, and my fear grew.

It had seemed so simple: tap into the magic that made "Promises" a hit, and everything would fall into place. But that was easier said than done, especially considering I hadn't written anything magical in years. I'd penned "Promises" when I was seventeen. Not that I'd told anyone that. The music industry thought I was a contemporary songwriter with fresh ideas, not a has-been who stole songs from the old notebooks of a teenage girl.

Like Rory had predicted, I'd found my muse in Ray Davis, the man who lived in my head. But those songs were dark and personal, with no commercial value. My current songs were lighter but had no bite. "Promises" had been a happy medium between the two, and that was what I was trying—and failing miserably—to recreate now. The clock was ticking. If I screwed up my big break, I feared there would be no second chance.

Certainly not with Sketch Monsters, who were going to fall into the dreaded sophomore slump all because of me. The curse of the second album was real, and widely feared in the industry. The first album gave a glimpse of a band's artistry, but it was the follow-up record that either cemented them as a force to be reckoned with or one whose days were numbered. Sketch Monsters was going to slump, and it would all be my fault. My pulse raced at just the thought of being the reason for their fall.

Stop! I was putting way too much pressure on myself... as well as credit. I hadn't been hired to write Sketch Monsters' new album. My job was to work side by side with Quinn to help bring *his* ideas to life, not mine. I wasn't that damn important. I had to keep reminding myself. *Grace. You don't mean shit.*

"I hope you don't mind me asking this," the wife beside me said. "But are you related to *the* McKallisters? I overheard the flight attendant call you Miss McKallister. I didn't really think that much about it until I realized you do actually look like you could be one of them."

One of 'them'? Like we were a species all our own. Most families of celebrities existed in the background, but we were a

special case. It had to do a lot with the kidnapping and the notoriety that came with it, but there were other things. Kyle's turn
on a survival reality show. Emma marrying actor Finn Perry.
Quinn's unexpected rise to fame. Then there was the exposé a
few years back—a reporter digging into my mother's past discovered that her maiden name matched that of one of the wealth-
iest hotel moguls in America, and a juicy story of disownment
followed. All of which had combined to make "McKallister" a
household name, and that was why my seat partner was now
staring at me expectantly. I considered lying, but why bother? If
my New York trip was any indication, my last name would
forever be my only claim to fame.

"I'm the baby sister. Grace," I said.

Her excitement was palpable, but to her credit, she kept it
under control.

"You must have had the most interesting life."

I wanted to laugh until I cried because I was feeling pretty
damn miserable. Yes, I'd grown up backstage, hanging out with
musicians. I went to awards shows and movie sets and had
homemade pizza night with some pretty famous faces. But the
thing I craved most had no monetary or status-enhancing value.
I wanted what she had—a man who'd sit in the back of the
plane for my comfort. Some might say I'd thrown him away in
Elliott, but it wasn't true. Elliott wasn't the one. I'd had the one,
and he was gone.

It was in that moment I realized what I had to do to bring
back my muse. I had to finally face the devastation Rory had
dealt to my young heart. Only then could I write my songs from
the place inside me where the darkness dwelt.

"Pretty interesting," I agreed.

～

AFTER COLLECTING my luggage and giving the anniversary couple the number for Angel Line Tours, Jess's "Map of the Stars" bus tour so they could drive by my family's house to take pictures, I ordered an Uber bound for Quinn, whom I'd tracked to a nearby rehearsal studio. It was actually perfect. I could watch the band practice and get a feel for their post-tragedy style. So much had happened since the shooting that I felt like I'd lost track of Sketch Monsters. Had their vibe on stage changed? Should I be writing more emotional songs, or did they prefer to stay closer to their heavy rock roots? I'd need to know all this so I could tailor my crappy songs to their energy.

Grace, I scolded myself, *we talked about this.*

Besides, I'd promised Quinn that he'd be my first stop once I got home. I assumed he wanted the lowdown on the breakup, as did everyone else in the family, judging by the number of calls I'd sent straight to voicemail. The texts were worse. Hundreds of them, most left unanswered. I just didn't have anything to say, and I certainly wasn't going to defend my decision. I did not love by committee.

It was easy talking my way past security at the studio. All it took was my ID, some strategic Jake talk, and a family Christmas photo that I already had cued up on my phone after my hours-long chitchat with Claudia while her husband John sat in the back.

The door to Studio Four was propped open, and I could hear my brother's voice as I approached, rolling my suitcase behind me. Laughter erupted, and I smiled. Quinn was holding court, just like old times. He sounded stronger now, more in control. Hearing him made me excited for the tour. I couldn't wait to reconnect with him after so many months of him sticking close to his girl. Jess would be joining the tour with her school-age son during summer break, but until then, Quinn was all mine.

Knocking on the open door to announce myself, I ducked into the studio with the smile still on my face. "Hey, guys!"

Silence. And lots and lots of the whites of eyeballs. I looked around at all the sweaty bodies and surprised faces. Quinn shot to his feet.

"Grace. Um... hey," he stuttered. "What... uh... what are you doing here? Why didn't you call first? Let me know you were coming?"

"Nice to see you too," I replied, confused by the less-than-enthusiastic welcome as I glanced around the studio and waved my greetings to all the Monsters. Matty the bassist. Mike the guitarist. Rory the drummer. My head snapped back, doing a comedic double take. *Rory the drummer?* It was then my brain caught up. Rory the fucking drummer!

The room was so quiet I could hear Quinn's traitorous heart-beat. I blinked, trying to make sense of it all. Rory was here. And he looked like his old scorching hot self again—hair cut to shoulder length, his face clean-shaven, captivating eyes staring back at me.

Rotating my head toward Quinn, I shot daggers his way. He didn't say a word, just stood there looking as terrified as a bushy-tailed cat in a room full of rocking chairs. What the hell was going on? Slowly, I turned my scalpel glare to Rory. His eyes wide, he sat there on his stool, sticks suspended over the skins almost like he'd been frozen in time.

And then it hit me: all the guilty faces. Quinn had hired his old band mate. My old boyfriend. The destroyer of my teenaged heart. But that wasn't even the worst part. He'd lied to me. Oh god, the betrayal. I was going to pass out. Right here. Straight-away. How could he do this to me?

Rory suddenly defrosted and stood up, rounding the drum kit. "Grace."

Quinn, the bushy-tailed backstabber, walked toward me too.

Both approached cautiously, and so they should. I felt positively murderous at the moment. Not interested in a reunion, I slipped out of the door and swung my suitcase into its opening, knocking both boys over like bowling pins as I dashed down the hall, out of the studio, and into the streets of Los Angeles where I got lost in a crowd of people.

ONCE THE SUN WENT DOWN, I made my trek across the powdery sand to my refuge for the night, the beach house Jake owned. I could have just crashed at a hotel, but I was looking for emotional comfort tonight, and this place held special significance to me. It was here I'd crafted my first sand castles. Here where I'd learned to swim with the sharks. And here where a young, naive Grace had built a rickety bridge with a boy who was barely hanging on. It was that bridge I was counting on now. *Come on, Jake, don't let me down.*

The closer I got to my oasis, the heavier my steps became. Nothing was as it should be. There was no spring in my step, no joy from being in my happy place along the coastline. I was irrationally angry and not sure why. It wasn't even Rory I was mad at. He was the mistress in this pairing; Quinn was the cheater. The only McKallister text messages I hadn't left unopened. He'd had his chance to tell me then. I would've listened. I might even have encouraged the pairing, because, despite everything, all I'd ever wanted was the best for both of them.

But there had been no communication. No one had said a word. Not Quinn. Not Jess. Not anyone in my family. And I had a feeling they all knew and had chosen Quinn's well-being over mine. *He suffered. He's lucky to be alive.* Well, guess what? So was I. Did everyone forget I'd been in that arena too? Like Kyle before me, my suffering had been overshadowed by someone else's greater suffering and then been canceled out completely. And like the "greater good" kind of girl I was, I'd just let it go.

My family took my stability for granted. They saw me only as the sturdy rock that others came to rest upon. I listened. I loved. And when the time was right, I wiped the tears and dispensed the hugs. Even after the shooting, when my own life was rocked to the core, I'd been there for others. For Quinn. For Jess. For my mom and dad. Yet, no one fretted over *my* well-being. Sure, they asked how I was doing, but they didn't look past my wilted smile and my faked reassurances. Did no one understand that even the most precious of stones would come apart if enough pressure was applied? That was what had happened. Cruel, unbinding pressure, and today, I'd finally shattered.

Spotting the house up ahead, I trudged forward, noting how different it looked from the shoreline instead of from the exclusive enclave's front security gates. Normally, I would get a code from Jake, and none of this sneaking around would be necessary, but contacting him meant the whole family would know where I was, and I had no interest in seeing any one of them tonight.

I shone my phone's flashlight onto the underbelly of the deck, and it illuminated the long pillars that dropped from the building above into the sand to create the pier-like setting under which I now stood. I headed for the stairs, though I knew I'd never get to the top because of the state-of-the-art security gate up there. With no key and no code, the only way into this fortress was through a long-ago promise, and if Jake had forgotten, I'd be spending the night sleeping in the sand.

With my foot on the bottom rung, I began counting the steps. *Eight up.* That was what he'd said to me all those years ago: *Eight stairs up, under the small awning.* Following his long-ago directions, I stopped on the seventh rung and reached my hand under number eight. *Please, Jake. Please remember.* But there was nothing there. My heart sank. I felt stupid to have believed it in the first place. We'd been kids. He'd been destroyed. Keeping past promises to his five-year-old sister couldn't have been high on Jake's priority list when he'd bought the place years later as a famous musician.

I checked again, just to be sure, ducking my head and shining my light under the eighth stair. Nothing. He'd forgotten. Dejected, I laid my head down on the step, rewinding the events of the day as I fought off frustrated tears. Stretching out my tired body, I slipped my hands under the ninth step above my head. I shot straight up. There was something under there. *Eight up.* I palmed my forehead. I'd been looking under the eighth step, not above. Math had never been my strong suit. Shining my light, I dipped my head lower to look under the step, and I spotted a tiny, oblong canister tucked into a wedge in the concrete. Pulling it free of its hiding spot, the first thing I saw was my name etched onto the aluminum canister.

Jake had left me the key.

~

Grace, five years old

"You don't have to be afraid of me, you know?" Jake tells me, standing over me and covering up the sun. I don't like that he takes my light away. I don't believe him when he says I don't need to be scared.

"Why did you go out in the water?" I ask him.

"I don't know."

"You could've drowned."

"But I didn't."

"But you could have. Mommy said so," I remind him.

Jake looks at the sea before sitting down beside me. "Why don't you go out in the water?"

"I don't want to get eaten by sharks," I say.

"There are worse things than getting eaten by sharks."

I pat the wet sand with my shovel. "No, there's not."

"Yes, there are," he says, forming a pile of sand with his hands. "Way worse."

"But if you get eaten by a shark, you die."

"That's the point."

I don't understand why he says things like that. He's not right, and that's why he scares me. "I don't like when you say mean things," I tell him.

"I wasn't being mean. I was being honest. Why do you care? You hate me anyway."

I go back to playing with my sand castle and wish he would go away. Not far away like last time, but far enough so he doesn't scare me. Jake waits for my answer, but I don't give him one.

"Do you know what today is, Grace?"

"No."

"It's the anniversary of the day he took me," Jake says.

I feel scared of that man and scared of Jake. I want to run away from my brother, but he's too close. He'll grab me.

Jake is silent for a long time before he lies down in the sand. I hope we don't have to talk anymore.

"Someday, Gracie, you're going to hear things about me... really bad things. And they're probably going to be true, but just remember that I didn't ask for this. He was like a shark, ripping me up piece by piece. I had to try and get away, right? I had to stop the attack. You would've done the same, right?"

I don't understand what he's saying, but I don't want him to be sad either. I reach up and wipe the tears off his face with my sandy fingers. I kiss Jake's cheek and whisper in his ear, "That's why I don't go in the water."

Jake blinks at me. "You don't understand anything I'm saying, do you?"

I shake my head.

He laughs through his tears.

"Jake?" I say, wiping more of his tears away. "When are you going to be okay again?"

"I don't know, but I feel better being here on the beach," he says.

"Maybe we should move here," I say, "where you can feel better all the time."

"Yeah, maybe someday."

"How come not now?" I ask.

"Because I don't have millions of dollars to buy this place."

"Maybe someday you will have lots of money, and then you can be happy forever."

"Sure," he replies. "Maybe someday."

I flop back into the sand, happy with the plan. "And maybe someday I'll need a place like this to be happy forever too."

Jake smiles at me. "I hope you never need that, Grace."

"But what if I get sad and need to come here?" I ask him.

He sits up and looks at the beach house, then points to the stairs that lead up to the back deck. "If I ever buy this place, and you need to come here because you feel sad, count eight stairs up and look under the small awning."

I tilt my head and ask, "Why?"

"Because that's where I'll keep a key for you."

~

32

GRACE: GOLDILOCKS

Technology had evolved since Jake made his promise. Physical keys were now almost as extinct as dinosaurs. The canister tucked into the awning had only a note inside, from Jake. A clue. Genius, really, because no one outside of immediate family would ever guess the answer, but everyone inside would know it instantly.

What does Keith want to be when he grows up?

I entered "pirate" into the touchpad, and Jake's beach house was mine for the night. After lighting the place up, I went straight for the liquor cabinet. I wasn't a huge drinker, but sometimes nothing else dulled the senses. From the looks of his extensive alcohol selection, it looked like Jake did this himself from time to time. Hmm... what to choose? I needed something that would go straight to work. I selected a drink I'd never tried before—bourbon whiskey—because its formidable black bottle with gold writing screamed intoxication. I was right. Two oversized glasses of that warmed my insides right up. Soon even bad decisions seemed good, and I easily finished off an entire box of questionably expired crackers.

Leaving my whiskey friend for later, I took a shower and

wandered the house in a towel, looking for the best spot to sleep. There were four rooms to choose from, but in my bourbonated state, I decided it was perfectly fine to bunk in Jake's master suite and borrow some clothes from the dresser. Slipping under the sheets of my big brother's bed, I fell fast asleep.

I couldn't tell you how far into dreamtime I was when I heard my name whispered in conjunction with the shaking of my shoulder. My eyes shot open and I flailed wildly, trying to dislodge the world's most downy-soft bedding. Somehow it had wrapped itself around me like a high-end swaddle. With one last swing of my legs, I kicked the comforter off and flipped onto my butt.

Jake was standing beside the bed, looking both alarmed and amused.

I peered up at him, my sleepy eyes crossed.

"Nice hair," he said.

"You scared me," I whined, suddenly very aware that I was in a t-shirt and panties in front of my superstar brother; and not just any t-shirt and panties, but *his* t-shirt and his *wife's* panties.

Smoothing down my mane, I cursed myself for choosing not to dry my hair after showering. The thought had been to deal with the aftermath in the morning when I woke up alone... without Jake.

"What are you doing here?" I asked.

"Me?" His voice elevated in surprise. "That's my bed you're sleeping in, Goldilocks."

"I know, but I tried the one down the hall and it was too soft, and then I tried a bed in the kids' bunkroom but it was too small. So I made my way down the hall and lay in your bed and it was *just right*."

"I see you helped yourself to my bottle of bourbon, too. Did you know that was a gift from the crown prince of Abu Dhabi?"

My eyes rounded in horror. "Oh my god. Seriously?"

"No. But it was fucking expensive, so I hope you enjoyed it."

"Well, I've never had bourbon whiskey before so I wouldn't know the difference."

He remained silent, forcing me to backtrack.

"It tasted great. Best I've ever had."

A lopsided grin decorated his face. I always thought he was so handsome when there was a lightness in his eyes.

"How did you find me?" I asked.

"I followed the crumb trail."

"Those crackers were expired, I hope you know. You need to do a better job of stocking your pantry."

"Right, because I want my trespassers to feel welcome and full."

"Don't snack shame me," I said, lifting the sheet over my face. "I've had a shitty day, Jake."

"You wanna tell me about it?"

"Where to begin? Quinn lied to me. The family hates me. I'm about to go on tour with my ex-boyfriend. And you were out of my favorite shampoo in the bathroom."

"My god." He grinned. "How do you go on?"

Jake, with his *real* problems, probably thought I was such a silly little girl. The truth was his good days were probably worse than my bad.

"Get dressed," he said. "Meet me on the deck. I'll make you another drink, and we'll talk."

I nodded, but added, "Jake, I'd prefer a coffee instead. Maybe the CEO of Starbucks gifted you some?"

He waved me off, laughing as he walked out.

By the time I joined him out on the deck in a pair of leggings and a sweatshirt borrowed from his wife, with my hair pulled into a messy bun, he had the firepit on and two coffees steaming in their cups.

"Your wife's short," I commented, sitting beside him and

lifting my leg to show him the indisputable capri-length proof of my claim. "You can tell her that for me."

"Or... I could just tell Casey you said thank you for loaning her clothes to you in your time of need?"

"Yes." I chuckled, taking a sip of my coffee. "That's what I meant."

"So, you wanna tell me why everyone is looking for you?"

"Like you don't know."

"I actually don't. I've been busy all week and only got bits and pieces of the drama."

"Cut the bullshit, Jake. I know you know. I know the whole family knows because gossip runs rampant. You, and everyone else, purposely withheld Quinn's deceit from me."

"Wrong!" Jake game-show gonged me out. "I didn't even know you were in New York until today."

I scoffed. "Thanks for caring, Jake."

"You can't have it both ways. Either you're pissed that I knew or pissed that I didn't."

"I can be pissed at you any way I want."

Jake rolled his eyes.

I was being unreasonable, but my brother wasn't taking offense, so I continued down the spicy path. "How'd you know I came here?"

"Well, like I said, I heard you were on the lam. Then my security alerted me to an intruder, and I put two and two together. I'm smart like that."

I laughed. "Yes, you are."

"And I get why you're pissed," he said. "I would be too."

"Right? I hate everyone! Maybe not you."

"Thank you."

Settling back into my chair, I gave a sigh, long and heavy. "You think I'm overreacting, don't you?"

"About the family not telling you? That's for you to decide.

But if you're talking about Rory joining Sketch Monsters, then yes. He's a great drummer, and he's a perfect fit for them. Quinn made a business decision. Can't fault him for that."

"So, you're telling me Casey would be totally fine if you hired your ex-girlfriend as a backup singer?"

"Krista is a pop star, so she probably wouldn't be my backup singer..."

"That's not the point," I snapped back, all sassy-like.

Jake's smile faded as the next words tumbled out of his mouth. "As far as *your* ex... Rory's been through a lot. He deserves a break."

I sat up. "How do you know what he's been through?"

Jake averted his gaze. "I don't."

But something in the way he said it gave me pause. "You know something."

"No, I don't."

"Yes, you do. How do you know he's been through a lot? I never told you that."

Now my brother was squirming.

"Jake? Tell me or I'm going to hit you."

He scooted his chair back. I scooted mine closer.

"He was a foster kid," Jake said as if that explained everything.

"So?"

"So I was assuming the worst. That's all."

Jake was definitely lying, and I intended to get to the bottom of it. "What. Do. You. Know?"

He shook his head. "Nothing."

I hit him. Not too hard, just enough to get him going. He swatted me away.

"Okay, look. There are things you don't know about Rory, all right? That's all I'm saying."

"And you do?"

Just based on his split-second indecision, I knew the answer was yes.

I wasn't sure if I wanted to slap him again or press him for details. I was furious and curious and totally undecided on what emotion I wanted to unleash on him. "Tell me."

"I can't. You need to ask him."

I gasped, realization hitting me like a head-on collision. "You know why he left, don't you?"

"No."

"Yes, you do!" I raised my voice. "Tell me!"

"Grace, quiet. The neighbors are going to hear you."

"Do you think I care about the neighbors? You lied to me. You let me suffer." I stopped in mid-fume, the worst-case scenario popping into my head. "Oh my god, Jake, did you have something to do with him leaving?"

"No," he said, but there was some hesitation. "Look, all I will tell you is Rory wasn't cheating on you."

Tears instantly flooded my eyes. Jake reached over to comfort me, but I jerked away. "How do you know that?"

"I was with him that night just before it all went down. I called him out to the street to talk."

"Why?"

"Because someone from his past was blackmailing me."

"Was it his sister?"

"I don't know. Maybe. Whoever it was had also been threatening him. He left to protect you, Grace."

"Then why not *tell* me that? Why make up a whole story about his foster sister?"

"That's a question for Rory. And now that you'll be traveling with him on the tour bus, you'll have plenty of time to beat it out of him."

"And you haven't seen him since?"

My brother hesitated again.

"Oh my god. You're worse than Quinn."

"I saw him at the hospital. Right after you left the bathroom, I went in. We exchanged a few words, and then I left."

I sighed, beckoning for the next part with my fingers. He knew the drill by now.

"I told him he owed it to himself to start playing again... and he might have expressed a desire to get back together with you."

I kicked his chair. "And you're just telling me this now?"

"Don't you get all righteous with me, Grace. I didn't see you running to Elliott and telling him you were in the bathroom with your ex. You're no innocent when it comes to keeping secrets, so back off."

"What's that supposed to mean?"

He paused, then lifted his eyes to mine. "The Reindeer Man?"

I gasped. Full-on horror movie worthy. "You were awake?"

"In the loosest of terms, yes. Things from that time are blurry, but I definitely remember you whispering that in my ear."

"Why didn't you say anything then?"

"Because you didn't want me to know."

"Yes, I did."

"No, you didn't. You said you'd never tell me if I was awake. And then when you came in to see me in my room later, you were so freaked out, sliding against the walls. Just like when you were a little girl. It's why I never told you."

"Told me what?"

"Grace, I've always known your Reindeer Man was Ray."

"What? How?" I stuttered.

"Ray told me."

"He... the Reindeer Man told you?"

"I didn't call him that, but yes."

"What did he say?"

"Basically what you told me. He thought it was funny."

"No." A lump formed in my throat. "No, it wasn't. It wasn't funny."

Jake took my hands. "I know. He did it to terrorize you. When I came home, I didn't know what you remembered. I tried to talk to you about it, to make sure you were all right, but you were so scared of me. You'd scream and run away anytime I got near. I wasn't sure if you were afraid of me or of what Ray had said to you, but your reaction was freaking Mom out, so I just stayed away."

"Why was it freaking her out?"

"She thought I was going to hurt you, or maybe that I already had. I was barely sane back then. Even I was confused. I thought maybe I had done something to you. It's why she wouldn't leave us alone in a room together unless others were in there with us. Why you went to a child psychologist. Why, to this day, I avoid being alone with you unless there's a witness present."

We sat in silence, both of us processing in our own ways.

"I am so sorry," I said, my soft voice cutting through the quiet of the night. "I could've stopped it. I could've saved you."

Jake pulled me to him, holding me tight. "This was never your fight to begin with. Why do you think Ray told you? Why do you think he chose to whisper in your ear and not Quinn's or Kyle's? Because he knew you couldn't stop it. He knew you were too young to understand. You were dealing with a serial killer, Twinkle. There was nothing you or anyone else could've done to save me."

I buried my head in his chest, my tears dissolving in his shirt. Jake had been my ally all along; I just never knew it. This felt like a turning point for us. A chance for us to start our relationship anew.

"And you can't save Rory either," he said, as if instinctively knowing that was what had attracted me to him in the first place. A chance to right a wrong, though I'd failed him too. "Only he can do that. But..."

Pulling free of the hug, I blinked up at him. "But what?"

"You can love him—like Casey loves me."

"I do love him."

"Then tell him. You both want each other, so stop wasting time."

Jake was right. Rory and I had wasted way too much time. I needed to talk to him. He needed to know I still loved him. It wasn't too late for us... as long as he loved me too.

"Hello?" A voice from inside the house halted our conversation.

"Are you expecting company?" I asked, looking Jake's way.

"My guess: it's the three bears, home at last."

"Jake"—I lengthened his name like a mother scolding her child—"what have you done? Did you invite Satan here?"

"If you mean Quinn, yes."

Quinn stepped forward, his hands up in surrender. "Before you say anything, I come with peace offerings."

"Huh." I fought off a grin. "You think bribing me will absolve you of guilt?"

"Well, let's allow the offerings a chance to work their magic before you decide. First, I have a Sephora gift card."

"How much?"

"Fifty dollars."

I dropped my gaze, disappointed.

"I meant fifty dollars times four," he tried again.

My smile broadened. Now he was talking.

"And then I got you a heated blanket."

He tossed it at me, and I immediately rubbed it against my cheek, purring.

"And here are the obligatory flowers. Lilies, your favorite."

"Okay." I nodded, willing to entertain the possibility of forgiveness.

"Finally, the donuts from the shop open nights with the line that goes down the block. I had to whore myself out to the group of girls at the front of the line to buy these for you... but it was worth feeling all dirty inside because you deserve them."

He handed over the box with a gallant bow.

"Oh, and I got a dozen in case you wanted to share them."

"I don't."

"I just thought because there were a dozen..."

I hit him with a glare.

"Alrighty," he laughed. "That would be a no."

His expression shifted. "I'm sorry, Grace. It was so shitty of me not to tell you. I didn't want you to say no, so I went behind your back. And then for some reason, my brain thought it was completely reasonable to tell you when you got home. It never once occurred to me that you might happen upon my deceit before I had a chance to explain myself. I'm not very smart. You know that. And don't be mad at Jake or anyone else in the family. They're all mindless enablers. They know not what they do."

"I didn't do shit," Jake said.

"Shush," Quinn silenced him before turning back to me. "This is one hundred percent my fault and if you don't want to share a donut with me, I'll understand."

"I don't."

"Oh, okay. I thought maybe you changed your mind after my heartfelt apology, but that's fine."

"I forgive you, but only because I know Dad dropped you on your head as a kid."

"So many times." He nodded.

"All right," I sighed, holding my arms out to him. "You may hug me now."

"That's it?" he asked, bending down to give me a squeeze,

plopping a kiss on my cheek. "Jesus, that was way easier than I thought."

"Only because I softened her up before you got here," Jake said. "So if anyone gets a donut, it should be me."

"You can have one." I opened the box for Jake. "But only because I drank your royal bourbon."

Jake bit into the doughy pastry and made a show of its excellence for Quinn.

Looking between my two brothers, I was struck by their combined star power, both so handsome and talented and in demand. They had better things to do with their time than to tend to their little sister, yet here they were, coming to my rescue when I needed them most.

I opened my arms to both of them. "Come here, you two."

~

Grace, four years old

He waves. I giggle and wave back at him.

Then he smiles, and I smile too!

He comes over all sneaky-like, tiptoeing and putting his finger on his lips. But he is smiling so big, so I giggle and smile back at him again!

He is so silly. I like the reindeer on his hat. Then he pats my head and leans over, his breath so warm that it tickles my neck! He whispers something in my ear.

"I'm going to kill your brother."

~

33

RORY: HUDDLE UP

I wished Quinn had never told me. It would've been so much less stress if I hadn't known Grace was coming to rehearsals, and we'd just happened upon each other instead. We'd do the customary awkward dance around the issue, and that would be that. But no, Quinn had to make a huge ordeal about me getting to practice early so I could talk privately with her. About what? Me leaving the band? I didn't think so. Quinn had asked me to join, not the other way around. As far as I was concerned, this was a family matter, and they could leave me the fuck out of it.

Besides, it wasn't my job that was on the line, especially not now that I knew the set inside and out and had been solidly embraced by the other members of the band. As long as my head didn't spontaneously explode, I was going on tour with them, so Grace needed to get on board real damn fast. Only problem was, I couldn't tell her about the chastity pact I'd made with Tucker. Somehow I didn't think she'd appreciate the nitty-gritty details, nor the fact that Tucker considered me a more valuable asset than her. She had a hit song under her belt, yet she would have to yield to me, a drummer with zero touring experience. I could only imagine how that would go down. No, it was up to me to keep our relationship strictly above the belt. There would be no side-by-side couch cuddles. No enclosed spaces. No seven-minute breaks. All we had to do was keep it professional and we'd both have the careers we'd always desired.

The only real wild card here was Grace herself and whether she'd come in here guns a-blazing, demanding I quit the band. And maybe I would have, back in my bleeding-heart days where I put everyone before myself, but I was done living my life to accommodate others. I'd come this far, on the verge of my stadium dream coming true, and I wasn't going to quit for anyone. Not even for her. Really, she should think of this as on-the-job training. Grace was a songwriter, and thus it was her job to deal with dickhead musicians, so if she couldn't find common ground with me, maybe she needed to rethink her own professional goals.

Speaking of being a professional, she was late. I sat on my stool, spinning around. The metal frame didn't move; it was me doing the spinning. At times like this I sort of wished I still had my tics. In many ways they had been comforting, my feet and hands bobbing like a jackhammer. But anxiety medication had largely taken them away once I'd become Rory Robinson. He was respectable, after all. He even took fictional family vacations. Couldn't have the Boy Scout of the Year suffering from little dog shaker syndrome.

My god, where was she? I just wanted to get this over with.

On my fourteenth spin around, she appeared in the doorway —my Nantucket dream girl, her arms crossed in front of her, an amused look on her face. All my bravado faded away. The desperate promise I'd made to Tucker seemed foolish now. How the hell was I going to stay away from her?

"That looks fun," she said.

"It is."

"Are you self-powered, or do you have an engine in there I never knew about?"

Gah, she was trying to kill me with cuteness. "I was entertaining myself because you were late."

"Yes, well, you try telling time by the placement of the sun and the moon."

Using my lines back on me. Made me wonder what else she remembered about our time together. If she was anything like me, it was everything. I'd had my fair share of hookups over the years, even one short-lived relationship, but none ever sparked like Grace and I had.

"I hear you want to talk to me in private."

"I do," she said. "Can I come in?"

"Did you go through the metal detector downstairs?"

She opened her arms. "I didn't beep once."

"Good for me."

"Yes." She smiled. "Good for you."

There was a weird vibe in the room—an incredible familiarity, yet at the same time, I didn't really know her at all. Five years she'd lived her life away from me, and time had changed her. *I* had changed her. She seemed more cautious now, no longer the impulsive girl who led with her heart.

"Can I just say one thing before we get started?" I asked.

"Sure."

"I need for this to be clear. None of this was my doing. Quinn came to me. I was all set to join another band, and then he knocked on my door and offered me the world. I couldn't turn it down."

"I know," she said, wandering over to me. "Relax."

Relax? Did she have any idea what her presence did to me?

"Quinn explained everything to me."

"That's it? You're not pissed?"

"Not about that, no."

I didn't need to ask what she was still pissed about. She'd made her feelings very clear in the bathroom at the hospital. And while I'd play nice for the tour, keeping my distance, that didn't mean I wasn't still angling to win her back.

"But we can put all that behind us because"—she paused, sliding a strand of hair behind her ear just as she had as an insecure girl—"at the end of the day, we want the same thing, right?"

"Yes." I rose from the stool. "Exactly."

Her face lit up. "Oh my god. I was so nervous. I wasn't sure where your head was at. But you agree?"

"A hundred thousand percent, I agree. We have the same goal, Grace. Our careers come first. Both of us benefit if this Sketch Monsters tour succeeds. Just because we have a past doesn't mean we can't keep our relationship now totally professional."

She blinked, looking flustered. "Professional?"

"Is that not what you were talking about?"

"No, it was." She turned away from me. "Totally professional."

I sensed tension. "You all right?"

"Uh-huh."

She wasn't okay. She was definitely pissed. I wasn't sure what I'd done wrong, but Grace wasn't making eye contact, so it was clearly something.

"So, what do you suggest we do to keep it professional?" she asked, on the move. Crossing the room.

The vibe was way off now, but that didn't change the fact that I'd made Tucker a promise—to save *her* job.

"Oh, okay," I said, pulling my talking points from the list I'd already created in my head. "About the tour. We'll be traveling in tight quarters, so we should probably have someone between us at all times."

She blinked. "Like an old grandma chaperone from the fifties?"

"I mean, sure, if we can find an old grandma chaperone from the fifties who wants to go on tour with us. But I was more thinking along the lines of the other band members."

"So, let me just be clear. I can't sit next to you?"

"I think it's best for both of us if we keep our distance. Do our own thing. Be friends."

"Hmm. That doesn't sound very friendly to me."

"Well, what do you suggest we do, Grace? Get back together and blow up the entire tour?"

Her eyes widened to ungodly proportions. "That's what you think will happen?"

"We don't have a great track record."

"*You*, Rory. You don't have a great track record. I've never faltered."

She was on the other side of the room now, pressed against the wall.

"By the way," she called from very far away. "I forgot to ask. How's Nikki?"

Okay, I'd totally misread the situation. She was actually furious. I took another spin on the stool. Damn the medication! I would've been halfway through a toe-tap solo right now without it.

"She's fine," I said, although I had no idea how she was. Hadn't seen her in years. She'd skipped out way before the trial started, leaving me to testify on my own, so we weren't on the best of terms. "We're not together."

"Mm-hmm," Grace replied, flat-lipped. "I don't care."

"No, I wasn't saying you did. I was just telling you."

Grace laughed, but, oh lord, it wasn't a happy sound—more like a wounded animal with its foot caught in a trap.

"Since we're doing story time right now," she bristled, "I'm not together with Elliott anymore either."

To which I replied, for no apparent reason, "I'm single."

"Just shut up, Rory." She rolled her eyes. "There's absolutely no reason for me to know your dating status. We're friends, remember?"

"You said you weren't with Elliott, so I was reciprocating."

"No, you said you weren't with Nikki, so I was reciprocating. Now you're just being redundant."

Letting it all sink in, I stared at Grace. "This friend thing isn't going to work, is it?"

"That all depends."

"On?"

"Whether or not you'll be bringing women back and banging them in the bunk room."

"Me?" I protested. "What about you?"

"I don't bang women."

"You know what I mean."

"I'm not the problem, Rory. I think you underestimate the appeal of being in a popular rock band. You'll walk into the green room after the show and have your pick." Giving her best Oprah impression, Grace pointed out imaginary women in the audience. "You can fuck me. And you can fuck me. And you can fuck me."

"That's not going to happen."

"Yes, Rory. That's very much going to happen. I may not have feelings for you anymore..." She paused, almost as if catching her breath. "But I certainly don't want to watch you fall in love, either. My friendship has its limits."

"Okay, if we're making demands, then I don't want to watch you fall in love either."

"I can assure you, I have no interest in trolling the pit for a lover."

"I don't either."

"It won't matter whether you want to or not. You will. And you know how I know? You left me for another girl. Stood me up at Homecoming. I never got to go to the damn dance, you dickhead. Argh," she groaned. "Just promise me you'll bang the groupies when I'm not around."

Flustered, the words slipped out of my mouth before I could stop them. "I promise."

"Fuck you, Beats!"

Grace stormed out.

Oh, yeah. Tucker had called it. Grace and I were both going to lose our jobs.

As it turned out, we didn't need an old 50's granny to work as a chaperone. Grace wanted nothing to do with me. In fact, she made a point of avoiding me to the extreme, cutting wide swaths or waiting until I was halfway down the corridor before filing in behind me. Really, she'd barely said any words to me at all in the two weeks leading up to our first concert date. On the flight to our first venue, she sat with Quinn. It was crickets. Somehow, she'd taken my call for friendship to mean we were never going to speak to each other again. Up until now, it had been easy to avoid her, but that wouldn't be the case tonight when we moved into the tour bus for the first time. How was I supposed to avoid her if we were all sharing the same bathroom and sleeping in bunks within a few feet of each other?

At least I was fulfilling my promise to Tucker. I'd successfully friend-zoned Grace to the point her frostiness worried me. The plan had always been to finish off the tour and then pursue her with everything I had but now I feared I was losing her one missed opportunity at a time.

"Huddle up," Quinn said.

Mike and Matty joined him in the hall within eyeshot of the stage. I stepped forward too but stayed on the outskirts of their circle. It seemed the place for me. I was officially a member of the band now, but not really. I'd proven nothing, and until I did, I wasn't worthy of a huddle. Really, at this point I wasn't even sure if my legs would carry me onto the stage. After the sound check, I'd been feeling the nerves. I'd never been on a stage before—at least nothing even close to this one—and right about now, it was really hitting me hard. The screams of the crowd; the trembling beneath my feet. The stadium was electrified. And they were all here to see Sketch Monsters. Quinn, Matty, Mike, and their ghost drummer Brandon. I didn't belong up there with them. I hadn't paid my dues. The only reason I was standing here now was because I'd met a pretty girl on the sidewalk when I was a homeless runaway, and she'd refused to let me go.

I looked over to see Grace standing a few feet back. She'd been watching me. Our eyes met, mine rapidly blinking, and she knew I was panicking. She'd talked me through this many times before. *Run*, my brain was telling me. *Run away*. My heart sped up, and sweat prickled my skin. Grace rushed to my side.

"Is everything okay?" Quinn asked.

"I need…" I couldn't breathe. I stumbled backward.

"Whoa." Mike grabbed one arm, Matty the other.

Tucker swooped in. "Goddammit. Take him back to the greenroom. Let the stage manager know we're going to be delayed."

"No." Grace stood up to him. "He'll be fine. Bring him over here, and everyone back off."

They shuttled me into a storage room a few feet away, and I slid down the wall to the ground, now gasping for air.

"Give me a second," she said, pushing Quinn and Tucker and everyone else out of the tiny space and shutting the door.

Grace was instantly on her knees, holding my face. "Slow down. Take a deep breath in through your nose, and exhale out through your mouth."

I kept my eyes focused on hers as we breathed together. A minute passed, maybe two. She checked my pulse.

"Still fast. A few more breaths, slow and deep."

I focused on her lips speaking those words over and over. She was so beautiful. I'd never not want her. How was I going to keep up this friendship façade—especially when she didn't want to be my friend? I wanted to steal a kiss right here in the middle of my panic attack. Tell her the friend zone was a sham. But I couldn't risk her job. I needed her here, whether she was talking to me or not.

The muffled sound of the announcer filtered through the door.

"Oh, shit!" I jumped to my feet, the quick ascent dizzying me. "I have to be on stage!"

Grace scrambled to her feet and pushed me against the wall, steadying me. "Yes, you do, but your heart is still racing."

"I'm okay."

"No, you're not. What's happening? I've never seen you nervous like this before you play."

"It's not about the drumming. It's about watching those guys together like a winning team... I didn't earn this. I only got the job because of my affiliation with the McKallister family, and everyone knows it. I don't belong in their huddle. Those people out there—they're here for Sketch Monsters, for Brandon. How am I supposed to live up to that? I never should've joined this band."

All the feelings that had sent me into the storage room swarmed back.

"No, you're not going back to that place," Grace said, grabbing my face and forcing me to look her in the eyes. "Just because you got this break doesn't mean you didn't earn it. Do you really think you got the job through nepotism? I can assure you, my brother is not that principled. I watched Quinn clear-cut his best friend from high school to make room for you in Grace Note, based solely on the fact that my mother called you a prodigy. If Quinn asked you to join Sketch Monsters, it's because he thinks you're the best fit for the band. If anything, every strike was against you. You slept with his sister. Hell, you slept with *your* sister. And then you broke my heart. If that doesn't prove you earned your spot through talent alone, nothing does."

"She's not my real sister."

"That's not the point."

"And I didn't sleep with her."

"That shouldn't even need to be said. And yet..." She smiled.

Grace smiled! My pulse slowed. Maybe we could still be friends... or more. My breathing evened. I gripped the back of her neck and placed my forehead against hers. We hung there a second, hot breath passing back and forth as regret swept over me.

"I'm sorry."

"Don't," she said, finally drawing back.

Her hesitation pained me. "I'm sorry, Grace. For everything. This is not the way I wanted things to be."

Grace lifted her head, looking deep into my eyes. "I know."

"Do you? Because the tension between us..."

She cut me off. "Rory, I appreciate you trying to make things right with me, but you're actually supposed to be on that stage right now. So, how about we focus on that, and save the apologies for *after* opening night?"

I nodded.

"Now, go out there and put yourself on the team. Here's what's going to happen. You're going to walk out on the stage with that same swagger I saw from you the very first night we met. You're going to take your seat and imagine you're on the sidewalk and you've got your bucket drums all around you. And then you're going to play like you did the night I met you, with passion and ferocity and a determination to win. Your head will be thrashing and your hands and feet will be moving at the speed of light. You'll be in your element, and the people in the audience will cheer for you, and you're going to be flippin' great. It's how I met you, Beats. I fell in love with you that night. And now you're going to go out there and make them fall in love with you too."

Her faith in me was contagious. And she was right. This was an opportunity; the start of a new chapter in my life. I had to make it count. Feeling the energy of her words, I turned for the door.

"And Rory?"

I looked over my shoulder.

"Turn every minute out there into a memory."

I swooped in, grabbed the sides of her neck, and planted a deep kiss on her lips, then let her go. I pointed at her. "That was for luck."

Grace touched her lips. The smile on her face was the first moment I was turning into a memory, and there would be a whole lot more where that came from.

I opened the door to a choir of terrified faces. No doubt they thought opening night would be taking place tomorrow. Quinn stood there, open-mouthed, holding my sticks like some delivery man.

I glanced from one person to the next before snagging them from his hands. "Okay," I said. "I'm ready."

His eyes widened. "Are you sure? You don't need me to stab you with an EpiPen or anything?"

"I think that's for allergies. But no worries. It was just nerves. Grace talked me down. Everything's fine. Let's go."

We all stood there a second before Quinn said, "All right, then, huddle back up."

Matty and Mike got into the circle, but again, I hung back. Once I proved myself worthy, I'd join them. Then three sets of arms reached over and grabbed handfuls of my shirt and dragged me in.

34

GRACE: HI. WHO'S THIS?

Hi

The text from an unknown number popped onto my screen while I was lying on the top bunk of the tour bus. It was late, too late for random text messages from strangers. The after-party had started in the green room after the show and spilled onto the tour bus afterward. It was our first night traveling together, and so far, it was all I'd imagined it to be: the music, the excitement, the screaming fans. And as the tires rolled along the open road on our way to another show, the boys partied like a proper rock band. That wasn't to say I didn't get caught up in the action, enough that I forgot I'd been friend-zoned by Rory, and I had a sinking suspicion that I'd accidentally groped him on the makeshift dance floor that was the narrow aisle that ran the length of the bus. God, I hoped he didn't remember that.

Chances are he wouldn't. Rory had had an eventful day, to say the least. Opening night was huge. No one, including security, had been expecting the kind of crowds that greeted the freshman band, but months of media focus after the shooting and several hit songs had created a frenzied atmosphere, prompting security to escort the members of Sketch Monsters to the bus while holding fans back behind hastily erected barricades. It was safe to say, the first stop on their stadium tour had gone off better than expected.

Well...

I smiled. Except maybe for Rory and his full-on breakdown seconds before the show began. Although you'd never know it from the way he recovered on stage. After the huddle broke, Rory made his way to the darkened stage, the pulse of the excited crowd vibrating at his feet. I couldn't imagine what he must have been feeling in that moment, or the courage it had to have taken. But he did it, exactly as I'd said he would. He took his spot at the drums, twirled his sticks into oblivion, then tapped them together twice before kicking off the first beat of the first song of the rest of his life. The crowd roared as the others joined in, and the lights went up on the house.

Rory Higgins had arrived.

I was so proud of him. The significance of the moment could not be understated. He'd fought so hard to get here, from that kid on the street barely surviving to a rising star. If his teenage self could see him now! I frowned. Why did I think of him as two people—the Rory I'd once known and the man he was now? The five years of separation seemed an almost insurmountable hurdle. Or... I sighed. Maybe it was me not wanting to leave behind the boy I'd loved and embrace the man he'd become.

To be fair, I'd tried during that meeting Quinn had arranged between us weeks ago, but then Rory went and drew the line. A professional relationship? Yeah, not gonna happen. There was no middle ground. We were either lovers, or I hated him. And up until tonight, I hated him. Not just in words either. As with any unhealthy relationship, I tried to find special ways to show him how much I loathed him every single day. Small acts of hostility went a long way in conveying how I felt about his call for professionalism.

But then, tonight... he'd tipped everything on its head. The ill-timed apology. The kiss for luck. And the spray of light emanating from his drum kit. I'd been watching the show from the side of the stage, where the occasional sparkle would flash before my eyes. I observed it for several minutes, intrigued, until the stage manager passed and I waved him down. The man removed his earpiece.

"What's the light coming off the drum kit?" I'd screamed over the pounding beat.

"Drummer's got a mini disco ball hanging off his kick drum. I told him to remove it, but he insisted."

It took a second for the stage manager's words—and their immense meaning—to populate in my head, but when they did, I was like a lovesick turtledove ready to mate for life. Rory had kept my namesake, the disco ball, hanging in his window from Camden Place. The one he'd admitted talking to when he was missing me. He'd hung it on his kit, to remind him... of me. That was when I knew Rory was lying about only wanting to be my friend. The dickhead still loved me. Sorry, still a little tipsy.

GRACE

Who's this?

Move your curtain and look to your right

I smiled so wide I thought my lips would fall off. Pushing the privacy curtain aside, I was rewarded with Rory's handsomeness staring back at me, a cocktail of expressions on his face. A spritz of inebriation, a splash of pride, a squirt of amusement, and a drizzle of hotness that hurt my eyes. I wanted to drink him down. In a shot glass. Followed by a chaser.

His fingers moved over his phone.

> Will you be my friend?

> I already have a lot of friends. What makes you special?

He smiled, so cocky.

> Because I just rocked the house. And I'm gonna be a star

> Yawn

> Oh. Right. Forgot I was talking to a McKallister where stars grew up in every other bedroom

> Exactly. I need more

Matty's drunken snore from below rocked my bunk. Rory raised his brows at the exact same time I did, which set off a rippling of muffled giggles.

More snores. A fart. More partially stifled giggles.

"Shut up!" Tucker grumbled. "It's like sleeping in a porta-potty."

And that, right there, was the reason Rory and me were texting our conversation from four feet away. The bunkroom had eight beds, with six of them occupied. Quinn, Matty, and Mike had claimed three of the four bottom bunks for themselves. Tucker, who would normally be traveling either by plane or in the crew bus behind, took the band's offer to sleep in their bus because of his still-healing injuries. He'd taken the last bottom bunk. That left the two at the top for Rory and me. And since we couldn't have a back-and-forth conversation without waking our roommates, texting it would have to be.

All right, then, what can I do to earn your friendship?

My eyes fluttered up to meet his. Oh, so much suggestion! And we both knew my Rory-induced thing for quick public fornication.

GRACE

Show me some skin

No hesitation whatsoever as he lifted his shirt.

Higher

He obliged. I swallowed.

When did you get a tattoo?

I have a bunch of them

No you don't

Yes I do

Since when?

Since I had five years to fill them in

Huh. I did not know this about you. What else don't I know?

He looked up from his phone, through strands of hair. The look on his face. The conflict. The promise of answers to come. A full-body flush hit me in all the feels. I'd never wanted anyone but him. And I never would.

I blinked first, redirecting my attention on the screen.

> GRACE
>
> Do you have any tattoos of me?

As a matter of fact...

> Nooo...

I silently squealed, sending a barrage of laughing, blushing emojis.

Yep, a big ol' picture of your face on my ass

My excitement waned.

> Ah, man. You got me all excited. Show me what you got

Rory pulled his shirt up and over his head.
My eyes. Oh, my eyes.

> Yeah, baby!

But wait. That wasn't all. Rory rolled over and pulled his sweatpants down, exposing his Graceless butt.

> GRACE
>
> Okay fine. You win. I'll be your friend

~

RORY
Hi

> GRACE
>
> Who's this?

. . .

> Move your curtain and look to your right

SHIRTLESS. Made sense. Tonight he was skipping right over the flirting part and going straight for the drool. You see why I was having difficulty believing his friendship proclamation? The man was like a mullet—professional by day, giving no fucks by night. Talk about confusing. Either he wanted me or he didn't. Until he made up his mind, I was playing hard to get.

Rory twisted his long body, arms overhead, as if in a yawn, but I knew what he was doing—tempting me in an effort to awaken the teenage nymph of yore who could ride him to climax in sixty seconds flat. That was definitely not me anymore. Poor Elliott had had to work like a soiled miner to chip one out of me, and even then, I'd often had to close my eyes and think of another. And by *another...*

I drew in a breath and ran my eyes over his smooth, naturally muscled chest. Why not objectify him? It was what he wanted. But as my gaze traveled upward, I caught the oddly expectant look in his eyes. *Uh, yeah, I don't think so, bud.* I pointed to my oversized sweatshirt to emphasize how disappointed he was going to be if he thought I was going to fuck him with my brother and boss in the bunk below.

GRACE

> Not happening. We're strictly colleagues, remember? Put your shirt back on, Mr. Higgins

> This is how I sleep

> No, it's not. I never saw you sleep without a shirt on

> You never saw me sleep period. Beds were not for sleeping when we were together

He had a point. Our relationship back then did not even involve cuddling. I blushed at my randy younger self, flopping back on the bed. He did the same.

> Oh my god, Rory, we were so bad

> The worst. Your poor mother. She had to know we were in heat twenty-four seven. And you were the worst. I was trying so hard to be respectful of her and then I'd feel movement and you'd have your hand down my pants

We both muffled our laughs, me covering mine with a pillow.

> What can I say? You turned me on... and on and on

Rory shifted to his side, the smile on his face fading.

> God, I miss those days, Grace

> Me too

There was a wistfulness to the next words he typed.

> We were so good together

I reached out my hand. He stretched his across the aisle. Our fingers laced into each other like they'd never left. Like we were still floating down the lazy river on the cusp of a love that would last and last.

∼

RORY

Hi

GRACE

Who's this?

TEN DAYS HAD PASSED, but our routine hadn't varied much.

Move your curtain and look to your right

I peek-a-booed from behind my curtain. Rory was posed on his side, arm overhead, legs open and crossed... and so very naked, save for a sheet slung precariously over his junk. I squeaked, clamping my hand over my mouth to keep the sound in.

This was us. Every night. Every single night. Show or travel day. Rain or shine. Alcohol or apple cider. Rory and me, we had our text talks. Sometimes we just talked. But other times, usually when the liquid courage was flowing, we got our frisk on. Thanks to noise-reducing earplugs that had showed up on every bunk after that first night when Matty's snores kept everyone awake, I wasn't as worried about the others hearing my hushed squeals and giggles.

Plus, Tucker had moved out of the bus, after entering the bathroom on day five following an incident where Mike had dropped a deuce in the communal toilet. Tucker stumbled out, gagging. *Jesus Christ!* he'd screamed. *It looks like a peanut M&M blew its head off in there.*

That was when Tucker opted to spend his own money on flights and hotels over having to endure the indignities of bus living. Apparently, those were perks he'd negotiated into the contract when he was manager of AnyDayNow, but Sketch Monsters wasn't big enough to warrant such expenses. Yet.

The tour blew past the three-week mark. We'd started our travels with a flight to Vancouver and had been zigzagging our way through the Western states, hitting the biggest cities along the way. A downward trek through California would culminate in back-to-back shows in Los Angeles before our tour hung a sharp left and took us through the heartland.

I turned my focus back on Rory. His flirty vibe was doing something for me.

RORY

Your turn

GRACE

What do you want to see?

I'm not picky

Hooking a finger in my sleep shirt, I pulled it down to reveal the rise of my bosoms, adding a sexy tongue to my show.

Yawn

Ah. Rude. You said you weren't picky

I showed you mine. Give me something

Tipping my head over the bunk, I checked for any lights in the bunks below me. Everyone appeared tucked in tight for the night. I pulled my shirt up to expose one breast.

Rory held two fingers up. He wanted them both. I gave it to him. But he wasn't satisfied. He twirled his fingers, wanting me to play with them. I circled my breasts, using my fingertips to arouse them. My breathing increased as my hips moved to the sensation. Rory was rapt with attention, and when I slid my tongue over a nipple, he reached down with one hand and grasped his bulge.

With the other one, he wrote

> Down further

A lip trapped under my teeth, I gave his direction as much thought as those blended margaritas at the Mexican restaurant we'd closed down tonight would afford me, which was oh so very little. Two fingers slipped under the waistband of my sleep shorts, finding wetness straightaway. Locking eyes on Rory, I circled the swollen flesh, desire instantly overwhelming me. He was hungry—predatory, even—and as he watched me, Rory took to satisfying his own aching want.

We were moving in unison, keeping time with each other as we came ever closer to release, still mindful of the precarious situation we were in. One tiny moan and we were done for. We were living in the post-apocalyptic world of the movie "A Quiet Place," our lives depending on a totally mute and motionless orgasm. No sound. No movement above the necessary. And when it roared through me, I arched my lower half to reduce the threat of shaking the bunk, silently bringing myself where my body screamed to go. The pained expression on Rory's face confirmed the two of us were a matching pair.

∼

RORY

> Hi

GRACE

> Who's this?

Move your curtain and look to your right

No. I don't trust you anymore

Me?

HE ASKED, as if some innocent lamb.

What did I do?

You make me do bad things

I make you do nothing. I'm four feet away. I haven't touched you

We had text sex! With my brother one bunk over! Like how dumb are we? Really, seriously. We're so stupid they're going to study our brains after we die

You're not that dumb, Grace

Plural, Rory

Come on. Open your curtain. I have a surprise

If it's your dick on a stick, I'm not interested

My what? Hahaha. Do you want to see my surprise or what?

He knew I couldn't pass up a surprise. But I had to be more careful. He was where all my bad decisions went to die.

Grace, don't make come over there

I slid the curtain aside. Rory was on his knees on the bunk, with his shirt off. His waistband was pulled dangerously low to reveal a newly placed, still red and raw tattoo of what looked like a half-opened curtain just to the right of those sexy sculpted lines of his abdominal V. Written atop the curtain was my name in bright-pink ink: Grace Note.

35

RORY: WELCOME TO FAME

There are things they don't tell you about fame. Things that could easily be jotted down and assembled into a handbook. *Welcome to Fame: The Do's and Don'ts.* But no, they keep it a secret, forcing us newbies to figure it out through trial and error.

First, and probably the most important—*don't* make eye contact unless you plan to back it up with conversation. Second, and really, it goes hand in hand with the first—*don't* stop walking, again unless you want to be surrounded and forced to have that conversation you were trying to avoid. Third, and I like this one, *do* absolutely accept the perks that come with fame, because it's fleeting, and you never know how long the back door entrance at popular restaurants will stay open for you.

The fourth rule? Well, I learned that one today on the bus when it was stopped in traffic through a narrow highway passageway on the 101 freeway in the Southern California area. We were on our way to Los Angeles for an extended weekend and two shows, before heading east and away on tour for months. I couldn't wait. Every night I played was a good one. I even liked the traveling part, except when Grace was working, which was pretty much anytime I wasn't. It made sense. She could only go so far on her own before she needed Quinn and his undivided attention. During those times, she swatted me away like a pesky fly. But I kept coming back because she was the only solid surface I wanted to land on.

I watched her now, guitar in hand, pencil in her mouth. Words and sounds were speaking to her and when they came, she jotted them down before returning the pencil to her teeth. Was it wrong that I wanted to be that pencil and the tough love it was receiving? Even bad attention was better than none at all. At night, the two of us in our separate bunks. Yeah. That was when my girl was friendly. All other times, not so much, making me wonder how Grace could so easily discard me when I could barely breathe when she was near.

I got it. She wasn't traveling with the band to be my girl-friend. She was traveling to work and build a career outside of the connections that had gotten her on the bus. We spoke a lot about that in our nightly talks—her desire to make a name for herself through her own talent and drive.

Glancing over at her now, I could tell Grace was irritated. Quinn wasn't digging a line in one of the songs they were working on, though according to her, it was perfect. They argued a lot. Not like throwing shit around the room, just bickering all day, every day. Was this what it was like having a sibling? With Nikki, she'd told me what to do and I just did it. No discussion. No arguing. The only time I made my stand was the last time we ever lived together.

"So, what you're saying is this verse is dog shit?" she asked.

"No. There's a halfway point between Grammy-worthy and dog shit. That's where we're at now."

"Says the guy who wrote, 'You are the sun in my life... now get ninety-three million miles away from me.'"

"I actually like that one," Matty said.

Quinn bumped fists with him.

"Ah, Rory? I think you have an admirer," Mike said, looking out the window.

I perked up from the other side of the bus. "It's about fucking time."

"She wrote your name across her breasts."

He had me at breasts. "Why didn't you say that in the first place?"

I crossed the aisle to his side and checked things out for myself. It had become a parking lot in the middle of the 101 freeway and would remain this way until they removed the over-turned big rig up ahead and disposed of the thousands of pounds of newly harvested tomatoes that had spilled out onto the roadway. You knew it was bad when people started getting out of their cars and pissing on the guardrails. But the bachelorette party in the convertible limo beside us was in full swing. I had to hand it to them. If you have to be stuck in a standstill, this was the way to do it.

With the crew bus directly behind us, we took up the space of ten cars, and those around us began to notice. With our all-black coaches, sleek tinted windows, and no company identifiers on the exterior, our traffic neighbors seemed to understand the buses were carrying more than a group of foreign tourists. Leave it to the drunken girls in the limo to crack the code. They guessed correctly that we were a touring band, even coming around to knock on the door, asking to be let in to use the bathroom.

I would have let them in, being a newbie and all, but Tucker —on the bus for this short leg—said no. He was being a dick, and wouldn't even let us open the windows for a little back and forth communication. He said they might try to get in, which was bullshit because the women would have to be World War Z zombies to scale the sides of these monster buses. Even with Tucker's precautions, though, our identity didn't stay a secret for long. Probably because the bus behind us didn't have Tucker on it. Their door opened for the women—of course it did—and our buddies on the other bus poured out onto the freeway like ants. The women surrounded them, and in a few seconds they were screaming our names. "It's Sketch Monsters!"

"Rory, get away from the window," Tucker instructed, but I didn't heed the warning. I had a fan waiting. A topless one. It would be rude not to respond. Sliding the window down as far as it would go, I propped my arms onto the rim and hung out like an overeager unpopular kid who'd suddenly become popular. A chorus of screams erupted, causing my ego to blast through the roof. The other guys didn't get it. They were more accustomed to fame after having taken a sharp upward turn to notoriety. Although they'd barely been a band before the shooting, afterward they were one of the most recognizable names in the industry. They'd already learned the rules of fame that I was now unraveling.

"Who's getting married?" I asked the ladies, hoping it wasn't the woman with my name written in Sharpie on her chest.

"Karine," they all yelled in unison. Yep, it was her. Good luck with the happily ever after.

"Congrats," I said. "When's the wedding?"

"Three weeks," Karine said. "But I'll dump him for you."

Damn. I felt sorry for her dude.

"Let me in your bus and I'll show you."

I laughed, enjoying the attention, until I looked back at Grace. Her focus was on me, with way more interest in my conversation with the bride-to-be than in beating her brother to the ground.

"Sorry, I can't let you in. My manager says no."

"Get away from the window," Tucker barked.

I ignored him.

"Can you come out, then? Talk to us?"

Removing my upper body from the window, I got a look at Tucker's murderous face and then returned to my enthusiastic audience. "Um, I can't."

"Why not?"

"Because my manager thinks you're going to devour me, and drummers are hard to find."

"Ah, baby. We'll take good care of you."

I laughed, chuckling alongside Mike and Matty, who were both now hanging out the windows talking to their own admirers. Again I checked on Grace. She was no longer working, the words and music no longer flowing creatively through her mind. No, she looked pretty pissed. I was going to be hearing about this tonight during our text talk.

I turned back to my admirers. "Sorry, I can't."

There were cries and pouts all around, but even I realized the stupidity of stepping off the bus.

"Well, can you sign something for us, then?" Karine asked.

"Sure, what do you want me to sign?"

"Do you have a guitar pick?"

"I'm a drummer, so no."

"Dude." Matty spoke to me out of his window. "You should always carry toothpicks to hand out."

"Why would I do that?"

"Because they're like dollhouse drumsticks. It would be funny."

I gawked at our guitarist. "No, they would just be toothpicks. How am I even supposed to sign them?"

"You could probably get one of those etching machines."

"No offense, Matty, but if I handed out machine-etched toothpicks to my fans, I wouldn't have any left."

"Fine. It was just an idea," he said, all bent out of shape that I didn't think it was his best ever. "You don't have to be a dick."

Karine tried again. "Do you have a headshot you can sign?"

"What's that?"

The woman blinked up at me.

"He's new to all this," Mike explained.

Undeterred, Karine asked, "Well, what do you have in the bus that you can sign and throw out?" she asked.

I popped my head back into the bus and looked around.

Quinn was now watching me, amused, his guitar tucked in the crook of his arm. I got off the couch and searched for something, anything better than toothpicks. Snagging a Sharpie off the desk, I rummaged through the drawers in the small kitchen until I came upon the first flat surface to write my name on and carried it back to the window.

"The spatula?" Mike laughed.

Quinn's head spun around. "Dude, put it back. That's my favorite spatula."

I stopped in surprise. "You have a favorite spatula?"

"Yes. I use it to make eggs every morning. Put it back where you found it."

"Ugh," I groaned, walking Quinn's favorite spatula back and shoving it, now with my signature scribbled across it, back into the drawer. "What am I supposed to sign then?"

That brought me to the fourth rule of my do's and don'ts handbook. *Don't give fans the shirt off your back.*

36

RORY: THE REAL THING

By the time the bus finally pulled into the parking lot at the arena, we were all packed and ready to go. With the five-day extended stay in Los Angeles, the others had friends, family, and girlfriends waiting. I didn't have anyone or anyplace to be. I'd let the lease run out on my apartment in the weeks leading up to the tour and stayed in a cheap motel until it was time to fly to Vancouver to start the rest of my life. The tour bus was my home now. The band and the crew and Grace, they'd become my friends and family. So, while everyone was preparing to enjoy a fun weekend with loved ones, I would spend it alone in a hotel.

In no hurry, I waited for everyone to exit the bus before I lay back on the couch and pulled out my phone. Until the driver kicked me off, I planned to stay.

Grace popped her head back in the door. "You coming?"

"I'll be leaving soon," I answered.

Climbing the stairs, she walked over to me, her bag slung over her shoulder and guitar in hand. Grace nudged me with her knee. "Let's go."

I thought she meant for me to vacate the bus, so I stood up and grabbed my bag.

"I called us a ride."

"Us?"

"You're coming home with me. My parents are having a barbecue."

I dropped my bag. "No."

"Yes."

"Grace. Your family does not want me there."

"How do you know? Did you talk to them?"

"I don't need to talk to them to know I'm not welcome."

"Wrong. I texted my mom earlier, and she was excited to see you."

"Uh-huh."

"I'm serious. I told her you're a good boy now and that you even tattooed my name dangerously close to your gonads to say you were sorry. She was like, 'Oh, well in that case bring him over.'"

I grinned. "How generous of her."

"Right?"

Taking a look around for spies and seeing none, I gathered Grace in my arms for a quick hug. "Thank you for the offer, but I'm fine. I'm planning on getting my tan on at the hotel pool."

"Or... you can bronze up in my pool."

I wanted to go—she knew I did—but there was no going back. Once families were gone, they were gone. I'd learned that the hard way in foster care. Over and over again. The McKallisters were the last on a long list of burned bridges. "You know I can't go."

"Why not?"

"Your family hates me. That look on your father's face when he told me to leave that night—it's seared into my brain for eternity."

"My parents know we're friends again."

"Friends?"

"Yes. We're not dating. You're free to painfully flirt with whoever you please."

"Painfully? That was some of my best work back there."

"Ooh." She flinched. "Good thing you're in a popular band then. No wooing required. Look, Rory. We're friends with texting benefits; it doesn't have to be more complicated than that."

There was no hiding my disappointment.

"Don't give me that look," she said. "That's all we are, right?"

I winced.

"Right?" she repeated, eyeing me suspiciously. "Beats?"

"Tucker made me," I blurted out, tattling like a two-year-old.

"He made you what?"

"He made me tell you I only wanted to be friends, in order to stay on the tour."

Grace grabbed my arm and dragged me further back in the bus.

"He threatened to kick you off the tour?" she whispered.

"No, Grace, he threatened to kick *you* off the tour."

Shit. It just slipped out, and I instantly regretted it. Grace went through all the stages of fury from disbelief to simmering hatred to full-on steam rising from her ears.

"Why me? Because I'm a girl?"

"No. I mean, maybe, but more likely because you weren't in the band. He needed a drummer more than..." I let that thought trail right off after seeing her unhappy, to say the least, reaction.

"The nepo baby little sister who thinks she's a skilled song-writer but nobody else does. I got it."

"Grace." I grabbed her shoulders. She shook me off.

"Does Quinn know?" She spat the words out, already convinced he did.

"No, I promise, he has no idea. Maybe I should have told

you, but I'm the new kid on the block. When Tucker came to me, I was one day into practice. I was still trying to claw my way in. I knew how important it was for both of us. I thought we could have it all."

"Right—but you're wanted. I'm expendable."

Grace paced back and forth like a wild animal locked in a cage.

"All right," she said, coming to some agreement with herself. "Fine. If that's how Tucker wants to play, game on."

I cringed. Grace was known to be unpredictable when backed into a corner. "What are you going to do?"

No response. Instead, she turned and stalked out of the bus.

I didn't question her; I just followed her down the stairs. The others were gathered just outside, waiting on their own transportation.

Without warning, Grace pushed me back against the bus, grabbed my face, and smashed a kiss to my lips, aggressive and possessive, her tongue slipping into my mouth before I had a chance to reciprocate.

My eyes swiveled to the left to see if any others saw what was happening. As it turned out, they all had, and every one of their mouths was agape. Who could blame them? Up until just now, none of them had had any clue Grace didn't vehemently hate me.

Just as swiftly, her lips were gone, and with flat of her palm against my chest, she held me against the bus.

"Tell me why you have my namesake disco ball hanging off your kick drum," she demanded.

She already knew the answer.

"Why do you think?" I asked.

"I think it's because you still love me."

I let her hang there, knowing our audience was close by, and if I revealed the truth, the pact with Tucker would be null and void. But Grace's quickly deteriorating confidence changed my mind.

"And you'd be right. I love you, Grace. I always have."

I cupped her neck and swooped in, kissing my girl for all to see.

They all appeared sufficiently stunned.

Except for Tucker. "Well, fuck."

OUR DRIVER DID a double take when we pulled in front of the McKallister mansion, his eyes first landing on Grace and then on me.

"You live here?" he asked to no one in particular. "What do you do for a living?"

"He's a rock star," Grace said matter-of-factly as she climbed out.

The driver ogled me, no doubt trying to figure out who I was as we walked to the side security gate and Grace scanned her thumb.

"Why'd you tell him that? Now he thinks I'm someone."

"Exactly. And when he comes back to kidnap someone for ransom, he'll pick you and not me."

"Oh." A smile swept over me. "Who's going to pay my ransom?"

"I don't know. Maybe Tucker?"

"Great. So you're saying I'm going to die."

As we walked up the long driveway, memories of the last time I was here nearly brought me to my knees. I could still hear Grace's screams ringing vividly in my ears. To be back here now, with her, and all be forgiven seemed unreal. How many nights had I lain in my bed in exile, imagining my return to the McKallister house? In that make-believe world, I wasn't the villain who'd eviscerated their youngest born but a cherished, returning son. They'd gather around and welcome me home.

Reading my distress, Grace grabbed my hand. "Hey, you're going to be fine."

I wasn't so sure about that, and the sick feeling in my stomach only intensified.

"Where's your hand right now?" she asked.

I glanced down. "Holding yours."

"That's right. If I can forgive you, so can they."

In theory, yes, but I'd been softening Grace up for weeks. The other McKallisters hadn't had time to prepare, and they might very well still be living in the past.

The door swung open, and Michelle peeked her head out, only to scream out in surprise. She slapped a hand to her chest.

"I was not expecting you two to be standing right here. But now that you are..." Michelle stepped out onto the landing and pulled Grace into a hug before turning her attention to me.

In more of an apology than a greeting, I lowered my head and said, "Hey, Mrs. M."

"Get over here."

Taking me by total surprise, Michelle dragged me forward and wrapped me in her embrace. Any worries I'd had walking up the stairs were instantly eased when Michelle let go of her emotions and cried on my shoulder. Those were not the reactions of a woman who hated.

"Oh my god," Grace said by our side. "I'm going to cry."

Michelle broke the hug and placed a hand on my cheek. Her eyes were flooded with tears.

"Finally," she said. "You found your way home."

Her arms wrapped around me again, and this time, I tucked my head into her neck. The relief. The gratitude. I didn't hold back, releasing the pain I'd been holding on to for so long. I didn't think Michelle realized how much her support and friendship had meant to me as a young musician. She'd seen something special in me when no one else had, and then she'd backed it up with guidance and patience and love. She was the mother I'd never had, and when I walked away that day, I didn't just lose Grace, I lost my mother and my father and my brothers and sisters. It was such a lonely life after them. They were the reason I couldn't live another minute as Rory Robinson. Because even the perfect fake family could not live up to the real thing.

Coming up from below, Grace wedged herself into our embrace, kissing her mom's face and then mine in the seconds before the door blew open and the next surprised member of the family stumbled out.

Keith froze upon seeing our team huddle. "What's happening here?"

"Rory's home," Michelle said, wiping her tears away while tucking her shirt back in place.

He smacked my shoulder with the back of his hand. "About time."

"Where are you going?" Michelle asked.

"Gotta go to the store. Your husband is making burgers but forgot the buns. He then suggested we wrap them in lettuce as if we were some sort of herbivores. I'm sorry, but if you people want me to come over for free food, you've got to do better."

"I'll have a talk with management," she agreed.

Keith jogged down the stairs. "Oh, and Rory? Tell the guys to wait until I get back to start the beating. And if it's not too much, ask them to save a bat for me too."

Michelle rolled her eyes, pushing me through the front door. "Don't listen to him. He's kidding. Come on in. Your biggest fan is waiting. Now, I'm not going to say Scott is excited to see you, but he did cut the seal off an adult Lego set that he's been saving for a special occasion."

"Nooo," I laughed. "I still have nightmares about the Millennium Falcon."

"I heard that," Scott yelled from down the hall. "Come on. I have a stool ready for you. Don't be afraid."

The final bits of stress I'd been holding on to evaporated. Why had I ever doubted this family? They'd welcomed me in as one of their own once, and from everything I knew of them, they didn't abandon one another. No matter how bad things got, no matter what mistakes its individual members made, they stuck together and showed each other grace. Maybe this wasn't unique to them. Maybe this was how all loving families operated. They fought and fumed, but at the end of the day, they came back together and always forgave. My whole life, I'd thought my ultimate dream was to be on stage, banging it out on a drum kit of my very own, but now I knew better. Nothing beat this feeling of being part of something bigger than myself. Of being loved just for being me.

I rounded the corner where the rest of my family was gathered, and they reached out and pulled me into their huddle.

37

GRACE: LITTLE BOY LOST

We stepped out of the Uber in front of the hotel, and a doorman rushed to grab our bags.

Whispering into Rory's ear, I teased, "Is this a motel or a hotel?"

I knew the difference now, having googled it years ago after he'd corrected me, but he didn't need to know that.

"Now, my rich little friend, *this* is a hotel."

I grabbed his arm and gasped. "Rory!"

He followed my eyes, his widening at the same time as mine. Music from down the street had caught our attention.

"Can you hold our bags?" he asked the doorman. "We'll be back in a few minutes."

"Certainly, Mr. Higgins."

Rory did a double take. "How do you know who I am?"

"Drummer. Sketch Monsters. Big fan."

Rory would have stood there all day taking in the compliment had I not dragged him away.

"This can't be happening," he said, shaking his head. "How does anyone outside of the arena know who I am?"

"This is only the beginning," I said. Rory underestimated the interest his replacing Brandon had generated. He was on a collision course with fame, and I didn't think he fully understood that yet.

Minutes later, we arrived at a familiar patch of sidewalk. Under the streetlights and against the tall, slick, black building was the place I'd first seen him drum. Where I'd instantly fallen in love. Someone else was there now, a woman playing a violin, performing right where Rory once had. He squeezed my hand tighter. I couldn't imagine what this moment must be like for him, in the place where his two vastly different lives collided. If ever there was a déjà vu moment, it was now.

"Are you all right?"

"Yeah, it just hit me. Like really hit me. I can't believe this was once me. How did I survive?"

"I honestly don't know. You acted like it was no big deal, but I can't imagine the bravery it must have taken to walk these streets alone every night."

I stood quietly by his side while Rory lost himself in the memories. Several minutes passed before he let go of my hand to retrieve some money from his wallet and drop it in her violin case.

Returning to me, he asked, "Are you up for a walk? I want to show you something."

Did he even need to ask? I would go anywhere with him even if it meant half jogging like I was now to keep up with his brisk pace. Rory routed us on lighted streets, but the further we went, the sketchier our surroundings got. He seemed to realize it too, his reflexes on full alert as his eyes scanned the perimeter. Old Rory was back.

"Are you sure this is safe?" I asked.

"No. But it's just up ahead, and then we'll get out of here, I promise."

A block ahead, he stopped and pointed up at the sign.

Higgins Street. Um. Okay. Rory risked life and limb to take me here to show me a sign with his last name on it? I tried to summon up the required excitement.

"Same last name." I nodded, humoring him.

He shook his head, his brows furrowed. "This is where they found me."

My skin prickled at the ominous tone of his voice. "What do you mean? Who found you?"

"The police. I was two years old, wandering the streets barefoot in dirty, soiled pajamas."

Tears jumped to my eyes. "Oh, Rory."

"There was a search for my parents. My picture was in the news, but no one ever reported me missing. People called in from all over the world offering either tips or to adopt me, but because of my special circumstances, I lingered in foster care for years, waiting for someone to claim me. No one ever did. Finally, when I was eight years old, they cleared me for adoption. But by then I was too old, too disruptive, and my file was too bulky for anyone to want me."

"You never discovered what happened to your parents?"

"When the police found me, I was caked in dirt and mud. It had rained the night before, and runoff water was flowing through a homeless encampment at the bottom of a dry concrete creek bed. It didn't flood and wash people away, but it was enough to displace all the heavy drug users who lived there. They think I might have been separated from my mother somehow, and that given her probable drug use, she either didn't or couldn't come claim me."

I nodded silently, encouraging his words to flow. It was the most he'd ever revealed to me, and I didn't dare interrupt him now.

"When police asked my name, I guess I roared like an animal so they started called me Rory. Get it? And then I got slapped with Higgins for the street sign I was found under. So imaginative of them. Fitting, though. I was probably born on these streets, and up until you found me, I was probably going to die on them. You saved me."

"Drumming saved you."

"No. Before you..." Rory's voice cracked. "I was invisible. People would gather around and watch me play. They'd drop money in my bucket. But they never *saw* me. And as soon as the music ended, they were gone. No one cared that I was struggling. They looked right past me like I didn't matter. Like I didn't exist. But not you, Grace. You looked me in the eye when no one else would. I have no idea what you saw in me that night on the sidewalk, but I think maybe I'd been sent my own personal angel. Once I understood that someone like you could love me, it changed my whole life. You saved me, Grace. In every way."

"Damn," Rory exhaled, dropping his bag and walking straight out onto the balcony overlooking the city.

Following him out, I maneuvered myself until I was standing by his side against the railing, his arm slung over my shoulder. This right here was all I ever wanted. Rory and me, standing side by side. Equals in life, growing and learning together. We felt a bit reckless and wild, like a gust of wind would pick up and blow us both away, but I couldn't want for anything else. This was the life I wanted to live, whether in a motel or a hotel. I just wanted to be with him.

"I could get used to this," he said.

"There's going to be so much more. You're going to places beyond your wildest dreams. Just promise me you'll never take it for granted. That you'll never climb so high that you forget to be grateful for all of this."

"Then stay by my side and remind me."

"That's all I've ever wanted."

We stood there taking in the awesomeness of the moment before I broke the silence. "I'm going to take a shower. It's been almost three weeks since I've been able to move my arms over my head without banging my elbows into the bus walls."

"Okay, I'm gonna grab a drink from the mini bar and sit out here for a while."

"I imagine it's a bittersweet moment for you."

Palming my jaw with his strong hand, Rory planted a kiss on my lips. "Only sweet, Grace Note."

GRACE

Hi

RORY

Who's this?

Come in the bathroom and see

HE DIDN'T TAKE LONG, pushing the door open a few seconds after I'd sent the text. I was waiting for him in the jetted tub, a leg suggestively propped to give him a peek of what was to come. Rory didn't need to be asked nicely. Didn't require wining or dining. He'd been trained to be ready at a moment's notice. The instant bulge of his jeans proved it. Cutting across the expansive bathroom, Rory's shirt was off before he reached the tub. My lips parted in anticipation as he slipped his hands through my hair and hooked them around the back of my neck. He pulled me to him with the urgency I desired, and his lips crashed into mine, then his tongue thrashed against my tongue. I groaned, and my body instantly heated up, remembering the thrill of being with him.

I slid my wet hand along the ridges of his stomach, something I'd wanted to do since he'd flashed me skin on our first text talk. Rory wasn't jacked. His genetically lanky physique carried very little body fat, but the physicality of drumming had toned every inch of him, from his strong arms to his toned abs to the tips of his tapping toes. He had always been perfection to me, the kind of sexy that cast away all my inhibitions. With Rory, I didn't think. I just did. The wild and sexy girl who lived inside my lascivious body always thanked me in the morning.

As he gripped the sides of the tub, his hair fell forward. I brushed it away and nipped at his lower lip. He nipped back. Ours was a game with no losers.

"What is it with you in confined spaces?" he asked.

I grabbed the denim waistband and jerked him forward, nearly pulling him into the water with me. "With you, I like the urgency."

"But not with everyone?" he asked, jealousy rearing its head. I squashed it quickly. The last thing either of us needed was thinking about the others that came between the bumps in our road.

"Only with you."

Popping the buttons on his jeans, I tugged them over his slim hips and pulled them down as far as my reach would allow. Rory took over from there, removing the remnants of his clothing before stepping into the tub. Straddling me, he flinched when the porcelain dug into his knees. I wrapped my arms around his back and maneuvered our bodies until we'd flipped, with him sitting atop the porcelain and me sitting on top of him.

"Better," I whispered.

His answer was to run a hand down my body, enfolding the

swelling of my breasts before sliding ever further down and slipping his middle finger into me. I let out a tiny gasp and bore down, trying to push it even deeper. I moved with his hand, grunting at the sensations he brought out of me. It was too good. Too soon.

"No," I panted. "Not yet."

He removed his finger, letting me rest, but not for long. Grabbing my ass with both hands, Rory positioned me over his hardness. Slowly I lowered myself down, my body remembering every inch of him as I took his entire length. Only when our bodies were flush did I sway my hips to the waves of the sloshing water. Rory laid his head back on the tub's rim, his body splayed out in such a sensual pose I felt like I needed to stop again just to prolong the moment.

His hands grasped my waist, holding me firmly as I fought off the orgasm wanting to take me. Tipping his head forward, he circled my nipples with his lips, drawing a gasp from mine as I arched my back. He thrust from below, forcing my body up and causing tiny explosions to rip through my lower body.

"So fucking sexy!" he said, fingers slicing through my wet hair, taking a handful and forcing me to look him in the eyes before placing his mouth to mine in a long, slow, deep kiss. My tongue searched out the corners of his mouth and I wrapped my arms around his neck, bracing myself for the surge that was rippling through my body. My breathing deepened, and I moaned. Grabbing a fistful of his hair, I wriggled about, my legs jerking as I cried out.

Rory's body tensed, and he emitted low, grunting pants as he rode it out with me. I bucked atop him until the orgasm passed, continuing to rock back and forth to coax every last bit of the feeling out of this moment I'd waited so long for. And then I collapsed into his arms, wanting to cry. After so much time apart, Rory and I were finally back.

RORY LEFT for the arena around two in the afternoon the next day for a planned meet and greet, followed by sound check. I hung back at the hotel for some quiet time, forgetting how nice it was to just be. As much as I loved traveling with the guys, they overwhelmed me with their energy at times. Sometimes a girl needed a good daytime talk show to clear the testosterone from the mind.

My phone buzzed on the table beside me, and I spun it toward me to check the caller ID. Unknown. I let it go to voicemail. Less than twenty seconds later, the second call came through. The hairs on my arms prickled. The pattern of the calls. Could it be her? I answered the call on the third ring.

"Grace?"

My heart dropped to the floor. Even after all these years, I hadn't forgotten her voice. I should have hung up right then and there but this woman held some power over Rory, and I feared if I cut her off, she'd find another way to him. And suddenly, he'd be gone again.

"Is this Nikki?"

"Good memory."

It felt scandalous to talk to her, like I was betraying Rory's trust after only just yesterday pledging my allegiance. "How do you have my number?"

"I held on to it."

"For five years?"

"Has it been that long?"

"Almost six, actually."

"Jesus. Can't believe no one's killed me yet."

This woman was a vessel of negativity. I wondered if she'd always been this way, or if it was a more recent development.

"Are you looking for Rory?" I asked.

"No. Not Rory," she said. "Just you. Can we talk?"

"We are talking."

"In person."

I bit down on my lower lip. "I don't know."

"It's important. I'll go wherever you want."

Don't do it, I warned myself. *Don't do it*. But my god, curiosity got the best of me. "When?"

"Now."

I checked the time, calculating the activities of the afternoon and evening to figure out if it was even feasible. All the Monsters family members were gathering backstage for a dinner before the concert tonight. I was the one planning it, though Tucker had been the one to get it bankrolled. No, I absolutely did not have time for this.

"Come to the lobby of the Grand Villa Hotel at four."

"They won't let me in there."

"Why?"

"I'm a street whore. That's why."

Good thing she couldn't see my face over the phone. I was appropriately stunned. Clearing my throat, I said, "I'll let the doorman know I'm expecting you. What do you look like?"

"Skinny. Long, dark hair. Vacant stare. Picture *Pretty Woman* on opioids."

I raised my brow. Was she kidding?

"Four, then?" Nikki confirmed.

"I'll be there."

NIKKI WALKED STRAIGHT toward me after passing through the entrance. Interesting. She knew what I looked like, and considering I wasn't a public figure like my brothers, that meant she'd done some digging. I watched her approach, and she hadn't been kidding. With her heavily drawn makeup and drop neck, skintight dress resting at her upper thighs, Nikki looked the part of a strung out prostitute. Clearly, she'd seen the worst humanity had to offer and had not dealt with it appropriately.

She seemed opposite of Rory in every way, yet they shared a past that had ultimately sent him into hiding. The question was why. I couldn't tell by looking at Nikki if she was the victim or the villain in Rory's life story, but I was sure she was the key to unraveling it.

She cast me a hard stare upon approach. Why did it feel like we were rivals? If she was his sister, why the competitive glare? Unsteady in her gait, Nikki used the edges of the table to slide into place across from me. It was easy to see she was being propelled by narcotics. Once settled into her seat, Nikki pulled her long hair to one side, revealing extensions in varying stages of falling away.

"I feel like I should bow to you or something," she said.

"Bow?"

"Royalty. The famed McKallister family. Good for you." Her compliment was steeped in contempt. She hated me and couldn't contain it. "How Rory managed to snag you, I'll never understand."

"I feel like I'm the lucky one."

She looked me up and down. "Uh-huh."

"What's that supposed to mean? Rory's an amazing guy."

"Oh, I know. That much isn't in dispute. I just can't figure out how the two of you ever crossed paths."

"He didn't tell you?"

She smiled, but under her heavy makeup, it looked almost predatory. "How much do you know about our favorite guy?"

"Enough."

"But not everything? That's why you agreed to meet me, right? You want to know?"

"Know what?"

"Why he left you."

Oh, god. She'd hit the nerve. Rory and I had just reconnected, and while I planned to get the story out of him someday, I knew I was in for an uphill battle. Rory held his secrets tight. But Nikki... She was open to negotiation.

"I'd be lying if I said I wasn't curious."

"Good," Nikki said. "That's what I was betting on. We both have something the other wants."

"And what do you want, Nikki?"

"A ticket."

I blinked. "Like to the show?"

"Yes."

"Why can't you buy one yourself?"

"They're sold out."

"Scalper?"

"I'm broke, Grace. Look at me. I'm begging you."

"Why do you want to go so bad?"

Her eyes shifted to the cocktail table, one broken nail tracing the imperfections in the wood. "It's something I've always dreamed—to see him perform on a big stage. A victory for the forgotten."

When she looked back up, there were tears in her eyes, and instinctively, I understood this broken woman was telling me the truth.

"What do I get in return?"

Her back straightened, and her lips flattened into a straight line. "Ask me anything. I've got nothing left to hide."

38

RORY: THE RIGHT APOLOGY

G race's text came in during sound check.

GRACE

Nikki wants a favor

I didn't get the message until just before four, the time she'd planned to meet with my foster sister in the hotel lobby. It was too late to stop the head-on collision from happening, so instead, I caught a ride to the hotel with a security guard, wringing my hands the entire seven-minute drive. There was no scenario where this ended well. My two halves did not make a whole, and if I didn't get there in time, Nikki would light me up.

I hurried through the doors, instantly zeroing in on my targets. They were sitting there so calmly. Grace saw me coming and waved me over, which prompted Nikki to look over her shoulder and then back at Grace as I dropped into a chair beside her.

"What did I miss?" I asked, trying to remain calm while casting daggers at Nikki.

"You told him?" Nik protested, as if Grace owed her

anything at all. "Let me guess—you two don't have any secrets." Nikki's eyes settled on me. "I find that hard to believe."

An uncomfortable silence settled in the space between us. Nikki might not have meant it as a threat, but it was—her way of telling me that she reserved the right to destroy me at her convenience. I could picture her going to the media, selling our story. I realized then that I'd never be able to shelter in place with my secrets, not with unstable Nikki holding every single one of them. I had no choice but to flip the narrative and put Nikki in charge of my fate.

"Why don't you tell her, then? Go ahead. Give her every last detail. And don't forget to go all the way back."

I was calling her bluff, knowing she wouldn't act on it because for her to take a stroll down memory lane meant she'd have to reconcile things she'd never admit to doing.

Nikki dropped her head. "I don't want to fight with you, Rory. I'm too tired."

"You're tired?"

"Yes, Rory. I'm tired. I'm struggling. Just trying to get through every day."

"Boo-fucking-hoo."

The glare that passed between us would burn up anyone in its path.

"What do you want from me?" Nik asked. "Another apology?"

"Another?" I asked in disbelief. "Not once, in our entire lives, have you apologized for what you did."

"Seriously? Sorry is all I ever say to you!" she protested, so loudly people around us turned to stare. "You never forgive me. I'm sorry. I'm sorry. How many times do you want me to apologize? You can hate me all you want, but I was a victim too. They fooled me just like they fooled you."

I slammed my hand down. "I'm not talking about that, and you know it!"

Now we did have an audience. Grace laid a hand on my arm, but I shook her off, too pissed to take her or anyone around us into consideration. If Nikki was going to come here asking for favors, the least she could do was apologize for the right thing.

It was as if the dam had burst, and Nikki broke into sobs.

Grace shifted uncomfortably, understanding full well she wasn't part of the conversation but not knowing how to extract herself without making an even bigger scene. I avoided Grace, knowing if I even looked her way, I'd lose my nerve. Nikki had to atone for her sins. There was no other way.

"I did it, okay," Nikki said, her whispered words spoken to the floor.

I leaned in, inches from her face. "What did you do?"

More sobs.

"I thought that's what love was. And I loved you so much."

"What did you do, Nik?" I kept pushing, forcing her to admit it.

"I touched you."

"Where?"

"In places I shouldn't have. I made you do things to me. I didn't know it was wrong, I swear."

"Liar."

"Rory, please. I didn't."

"You did know it was wrong. You told me I could never tell anyone."

"It was what my stepfather used to say to me. If I told anyone, they'd take me away. And they did. A teacher reported it and they took me away. I never got to see my mom or Jerry again. And I know it's so warped, but Jerry never hurt me in the physical sense. He made me feel loved, and because I loved you, I thought..."

I closed my eyes, and a pained exhalation followed. This right here was why I'd always had such conflicted feelings about Nikki. Her wires were all crossed, to a point where she actually thought her stepfather hadn't hurt her, and every choice she'd made from that point forward was through the lens of a wounded child. The abused had become the abuser. It was my fate to shatter.

"I was eight," she said. "I know it's no excuse. But I was terrified if you told anyone, they'd separate us. I couldn't lose you because you were the only good thing in my life. I was selfish. I know that now."

"You manipulated me, Nik, telling me you were the only one who would ever love me. You made me afraid I'd be alone forever. For five years you made me beg the social workers not to separate us, and during all that time you continued to abuse me. If I tried to leave, you threatened to kill yourself. You trapped me in your miserable hell. Those five years, I could have been adopted into a family, but you made us a package deal. Two broken kids for the price of one. What perspective parent would take that losing bet? You turned me into you. Damaged and unadoptable."

"I know," she sobbed between words. "What else can I say to you but I'm sorry. Every bad thing that has ever come your way has been because of me. My mind likes to pretend it was because of Martin and Hartman and the others, but it wasn't. It was me. I stole your innocence way before they ever got you in their clutches. Look at me, Rory. Please."

Slowly, I leveled my gaze.

"I'm sorry. And this time for the real reason. I'm sorry for abusing you. I'm sorry for ruining your chances of a family of your own. I'm sorry for making you susceptible to the hunters. I'm sorry for sentencing you to a life of foster care and abuse and homelessness. I'm sorry for all of it. You were right. It was all me."

I lowered my head to the table, at a loss for words. Nicola Aldana had finally confessed to her sins. It was what I'd always wanted; what the boy in the mirror had demanded in order for me to live free from his judgment. But now what? Did I forgive her? Did I want to? I understood she was a victim too, but where did it stop? When did the cycle of abuse end? It was easy to hate Martin and his men, the ruthless monsters behind, and in front of, the camera. It was harder, though, to hate the monster you actually loved. Because somewhere inside I still did love Nikki, even though I knew I needed to let her go for my own sake.

"Why did you come here?" I asked without looking up. "What do you want from me?"

"She wants a ticket to tonight's show," Grace intervened, running her fingers through my hair in an attempt to console me.

I lifted my head, staring. "That's all you want—a ticket?"

"One show, and then I'll walk away," Nikki said, her voice breaking like shards of glass tumbling to the floor. "You promised me, Rory, remember?"

I remembered; I'd just never understood why it was so important to her. This had always been Nikki's dream—to watch me perform on stage. To see me succeed. Those nights we'd lain awake, dreaming of being something more—her a famous actress and me a professional drummer—and when our make-believe was over, she'd make me promise to give her a ticket to my show. I did, every single time. And now she'd come to collect.

"Why has this always been so important to you?" I asked.

"Because only when I see you up on stage, living your dream, will I know for sure that you survived me."

NIKKI GOT HER TICKET. Later that night, she sent Grace a video of her in a seat smiling through the tears. She then flipped the camera in the direction of the stage and recorded me slamming down a drum solo with a crazy smile on my face. She captioned the video "Best night of my life" and followed it up with the text.

NIK

Tell Rory I'm so proud of the man he's become. Tell him he's going to have it all. Everything he's ever dreamed of. That mansion in the hills. The pedigree girl—treat him right, Grace. But most of all, tell him he never has to run again. I love you, Rory, even if you don't believe me

By morning, Nikki was dead.

39

GRACE: THE PHOENIX

"Rory?"

I stepped into the hotel room and looked around, calling his name again. No response. I checked the bathroom and the balcony, but he wasn't here. I pulled out my phone. No text. I sent one off, then checked his location. It was off. I considered the possibilities. Where could he have gone?

Hours earlier, I'd left him on the couch in a half-comatose state to meet my mom for dinner. He said he was going to order room service and just chill in front of the TV. It was a well-deserved break, considering the punishing schedule he and the boys were operating under. Six months. Eighty-three shows. Of which they were now at the halfway point, but with plans for a European and Asian extension of the tour already in the works, Sketch Monsters could see themselves on the road for over a year.

This week, though, we were back home for a scheduled mid-tour break. I hadn't gone home, choosing to stay with Rory in the same hotel we'd had the night we officially got back together. The weekend we'd walked to his street sign. The weekend his foster sister had ended her life. The death certificate listed it as an unintentional overdose, but Rory and I knew the truth. She had planned it, the ticket to the show serving as her last meal. Going through her phone for recent contacts, the police had called me, and I was the one who was forced to break the news to Rory.

He didn't flinch. Didn't say a word. Just nodded and walked away. Of course, I tried to talk to him about her death, but he wasn't interested, insisting he was fine and that it was a relief. Certainly, it didn't seem to affect his work any. He played with both precision and charisma, his popularity rising with every show. Quinn was the first one to be surrounded by excited mobs, but Rory wasn't too far behind. And he took his newfound celebrity in stride, exuding a childlike excitement for any new experience that came his way.

To the naked eye, he was fine—great, even—playing every concert and going to every meet-and-greet with a smile on his face. But I knew Rory. Something wasn't right. Some of his tics had returned despite the medicine he took to control his anxiety. Granted, much of it could be explained by the stressors of his hectic life. But there was something else, something only I would notice. The grace notes were gone. The subtle embellishments to a song that he added without even thinking that made each song, each performance, unapologetically his own.

GRACE

Hey do you know where Rory is?

QUINN

No why?

Can't find him. He's not in the room where I left him

> He's not a dog. He doesn't stay where you leave him

> I realize that. But he turned off his location and hasn't answered my text

Quinn's non-answer meant he was thinking like a guy, assuming Rory had something to hide. If he did, he'd be a magician because the two of us rarely left each other's sides. It wasn't that I didn't give him his space, it was just there was no space to take. We worked together and lived together and traveled together. No space. But if he'd wanted some, why didn't he just tell me?

I walked down to the lobby and then to the bar. No Rory. I even asked the doorman, who hadn't seen him, or if he had, he wasn't talking. Something felt off, and I chewed on my lower lip as I returned to the room. Where could he be? I opened the balcony door and stepped out into the warm evening air. Pressing my body to the railing, I looked down. So many floors. It was then I heard the faint sound of a pounding rhythm.

Beats.

I FOLLOWED THE MUSIC, instinctively knowing those buckets were set up on the sidewalk where I'd first seen him drum. I was right. He was there, a small crowd circled around him. I was surprised it wasn't a mob. Rory was recognizable now. Not a household face or name like Jake, but to music fans, he was well known. Although, when I got a closer view, I understood why he'd been able to blend in. Rory had disguised himself—not enough to fool a hard-core fan but enough for the casual

onlooker not to recognize him. His hair was tucked into a baseball cap with a fake mullet attached to the back, and a pair of
phony glasses completed his undercover efforts.

Stripped to the basics in a tank top and shorts, sweat rained
down his body. I wondered how long he'd been out here, but
more curious than that, what had made him revisit this sidewalk
and play for his life like he had so many times before. Rory kept
his focus down, not engaging the audience like he had when he
was dependent on tips. I wasn't sure if it was to keep him from
being noticed or if the weight he was carrying prevented him
from lifting his head.

At one point, he did look up, scanning the crowd until his
eyes landed on me. He seemed almost too tired and beaten
down to be surprised. Oh god, how had I not seen this before?
He was sad. I choked up. Rory looked away, despondent. If he
was struggling, why hadn't he told me? Why come down onto
the streets and take it out on the buckets when he had me, the
woman he loved, who had proven she'd support him every step
of the way?

Rory performed one last song before wrapping up the set. I
waited off to the side for the crowd to disperse. Only when he
was alone did I walk up to him.

"How did you find me?" he asked.

"I heard you from the hotel balcony."

A faint smile appeared. "Shit, no wonder people hated when
I played out here."

"I, for one, loved it," I said dreamily, remembering the wild
kid he'd been. "Why'd you come down here, Rory?"

He nestled his buckets into each other before dragging the
tip bucket over. He counted out his cash and shoved it in his
pocket.

"Needed to make some extra money."

"Ah," I said, walking over to the building with the sleek black siding that worked like air-conditioned walls and slid down on my butt. I patted the concrete beside me. "Come sit."

Rory grabbed his stuff and joined me on the ground. We'd come full circle to the day we'd met. Only now, all promises had been met and both our dreams were coming true, his on stage and mine in words, ones that were now flowing freely. Rory had been the missing piece all along. Once he was returned to my puzzle, I was complete and I couldn't write fast enough. Jake's kidnapper didn't stand a chance with this new and confident me. Now when he bent down to whisper in my ear, I punched back. I emasculated him in my mind and eviscerated him in song. He'd once been the place inside me that scared the hell out of me, but now he was my muse: dark, light, and everything in between. I would smear his name until death came for me, and in the process of evening the score, my own insecurities fell away. Ray Davis had picked me to dump his confession on because he thought I had no voice. Oh, how wrong he was!

But Rory seemed not to have reached his ah-ha moment as I had. Nikki's death had sent him into a sideways spiral, and I needed to help him figure out why.

"Why'd you come down here?" I repeated.

There was a long pause before he said, "The streets were calling me."

"Why?"

He shook his head. "You wouldn't understand."

"Try me."

A long sigh was followed by the truth. "I feel safer out here. Nobody knows who I am. No one cares."

"But isn't that what you wanted? For people to know who you are? To get off the streets? To be safe?"

"It was... It is. It's just... nothing good lasts. Trust me, I know."

"But this will. You've gotten to a place where no one can take this away from you now."

He dropped his head, unconvinced. "Someone can. Someone will. You have no idea what's lurking out there. I'm living in a house of cards. The question isn't *if* it's coming down but *when*."

"What does that mean?"

"Too many people know too many things about me, and it's only a matter of time before I'm buried under my past."

"So what? This is your solution? Run away? Disappear into the streets? You promised me you'd never run again. You promised."

"I know. I'm not going to leave you. I'm not going to leave the band. I just... I'm scared, and out here, *this* is a scared I understand. The streets don't care what I did. It's like a river of catfish out here—the smellier and more decaying, the better."

"Does it really matter, Rory? If your past is exposed? I'm not trying to diminish your suffering, but so what? It's not like the people who love you are going to abandon you. You're part of a family now. We stand by each other's sides. And your fans—they'll rally around you. Honestly, the smellier and more decaying your story is, the more they're going to embrace you. Everyone loves an underdog."

"Oh, pretty sure they won't love this one."

"I do. I love you."

"Because you don't know."

I wanted to crawl into a hole, knowing what I had to reveal. My guilt.

"Rory, I know."

The shift in his expression was swift. From despondent to furious.

"Nikki told me. In exchange for the concert ticket, she said I could ask her anything. I wasn't going to. I didn't want to. But I did. I asked her why you disappeared that night. And she gave me so much more."

"What did she tell you?" Just by the horror on his face, I could tell he already knew the answer.

"What happened at the ranch house. The pictures and videos. The abuse. Hartman trying to murder you the night of the water park. The kiss outside my front gate. The witness protection program. The trial. I know all of it. Even that you wanted to wait until Friday so you could take me to Homecoming."

Rory rose to his feet, pacing back and forth, grabbing his hair as he swore and kicked the wall.

"Nikki, you fucking bitch!" he screamed up into the darkened sky. "That wasn't yours to tell!"

Then he picked his buckets up and threw them in a fit of anger. They smashed against the building before hitting the ground and rolling every which way.

"Rory!" I yelled at him. "Stop! Get yourself under control now!"

Or else was the unspoken ultimatum. He stopped raging.

"Now get back over here and face the thing inside that scares you. If you tell me yours, I'll tell you mine. I'll tell you what I found when I dug deep, and the reason I stared at you the way I did the day we met."

Panting, he turned to me, suddenly more curious than angry.

"Sit," I demanded.

He slunk back over and dropped to the ground, crossing his legs as he faced me.

"Thank you," I said, before adding, "Psycho."

A smile, a real one, surfaced. "Sorry."

I reached over and touched his face.

"No, I'm sorry, Rory. It was wrong of me to go behind your back."

"You think?

"I asked Nikki because you wouldn't trust me with the truth."

Rory tapped his fingers on the sidewalk, his eyes blinking. I laid a hand on his to steady him, but he moved it away. "It's not that I don't trust you. You don't understand the chunk carved out of me when I swore to tell the truth in court. To have to admit to things I'd buried long ago. I don't tell you not because I don't trust you, but because it physically hurts me to talk about it. After testifying... I wasn't... I wasn't sure I wanted to go on. I almost didn't make it out of that period of my life. The medicine I take isn't just for my anxiety and tics. It's to keep me from doing what Nikki did. And now..."

I grabbed his hands in mine.

"It's coming, Grace."

He was rambling, and I was struggling to keep up with his train of thought. "What's coming?"

"The end of me. And when it comes, it'll take all of you down with me, no matter what I do to try and stop it. It's why I came out here tonight. I can breathe. Safety in anonymity."

"Is it Martin Lindell you're afraid of?" I asked, assuming he was Rory's Reindeer Man.

"I'm not afraid of him or his posse of pervs, Grace. I buried them so deep behind bars, they're never getting out."

"Then what?"

"The fame. The media interest. I feel like the virus has already been unleashed, and it's now silently spreading. That's what's going to bury me."

"It didn't bury Jake. He knew what the infamy of his past would do to his fame. He chose this life."

"Because what else was he going to do? His secret is wide open. Mine's not. *Yet.* But it will be. It's only a matter of time before explicit pictures of me as a kid are being whack-a-moled off the internet. Think about it. If Nikki was talking to you, who else was she sharing her story with? One oxy pill and I'm sure she was singing like a bird. And the worst... the worst of it."

Rory struggled to get the words out. "After Nik died, I was lying in the bunk and trying to remember the good moments with her. And there were moments. She wasn't all bad, you know? It wasn't until we went our separate ways, and I was suddenly on my own in the system, that I realized how much she'd protected me. Let's just say my fear of four walls happened after we were separated. Anyway, lying in my bunk after she died, I asked myself what the best thing she'd ever done for me was. And my answer? She died."

Rory tipped his head back against the building and covered his eyes with his hands. "I can't even cry for her, Grace. I've spent my whole life holding my breath, waiting for the next horrible thing to happen. And Nikki, whether she was directly responsible or not, was the link to my past that I feared. Would she betray me to Martin and his men? Would she leave me to testify alone? Would she sell me out to the media and blow up my life? Would she somehow turn you against me? She was the link to it all, and when I found out she was dead, I was flooded with relief. All I could think was it's over. I'm finally free."

"And that makes you feel guilty?"

"It makes me feel like a shitty person. Do you know I never picked up her ashes? Nikki's sitting on a shelf somewhere all by herself, while I'm out there living my dream."

"It's not much of a dream if all you're doing is waiting for it to implode at any minute."

He nodded. "You see why the streets are looking better and better?"

"I see, but there's a better way to fight this. If it's coming, get in front of it. Reveal the truth on your own terms and take away their power."

Rory allowed the idea time to populate in his head. "Maybe you're right. If everyone knows the story, no one can profit from it."

"Exactly. And I will be standing right there by your side, as will the Monsters, my parents, and Jake. We've all got you. We won't let you fall."

Taking hold of my hand, Rory kissed the back of it. "You never do."

"That's right," I said, gliding my fingers along his face. "No one messes with my man."

"Not even Tucker," he said.

Especially not Tucker. After I'd shown him that Rory and I were in a nonnegotiable relationship, he backed down... without even a fight. It was at that moment we became an official couple.

"Your turn," he said. "What did you find when you looked inside?"

"The Reindeer Man."

He rubbed his chin, considering. "You're afraid of Santa?"

A smile jumped to my face. "Not quite."

I told him the story of Ray Davis coming to me as a kid. What he'd whispered in my ear. How Jake said he'd purposely done it to terrorize me. The guilt I felt for not telling anyone. For not saving Jake. And then I told him what it was I'd seen in him that day.

"When Jake came home after the kidnapping, there was this look in his eyes, like someone had scooped out his insides and left him a broken shell. I'd never seen that in any other soul until I met you on the sidewalk with Hudson. I was so drawn to you, and I think it was because I knew what you needed. I knew how to repair you. I'd watched my mother heal Jake, day by day, piece by piece. I used to hide behind furniture and listen to them practice just like I did the night I discovered she was training you. She restored his faith in humanity, and I wished I could do the same for you. Of course, I never thought I'd see you again. And then there you were on the street! Don't you see, Rory? You're my redemption. I couldn't save Jake, but I'll be damned if I don't save you. So you need to find a better way to deal with your house of cards because I'm not letting you go, and I'm sure as hell not living out on the streets with you."

Rory stood up and offered me a hand. "You wouldn't last a night."

Once on my feet, I wrapped my arms around his neck and kissed him. "No, I wouldn't. Let's go home."

"Speaking of that, I don't want to live in a hotel when I come back here. I want to buy that mansion in the hills."

"I like that. Can I come over and visit?"

"No."

"No?" I laughed. "You have a whole mansion and you won't let me enjoy it?"

"You don't need an invitation, Grace. Because you're going to live there with me." Rory grabbed his buckets.

"You're bringing those with you?"

"Yeah. I paid good money to have these Instacarted to me. Plus they'll fit nicely in my new garage."

Walking back to the hotel, we came upon a teenage boy close in age to what Rory was when I'd met him. He was skinny and dirty and stood on the sidewalk with a guitar in hand. Rory stopped.

The kid's eyes widened when he realized who was standing in front of him. "Are you...?"

Rory put his finger to his lips, then nodded. "What's your name?"

"Flash."

"Flash, huh? Doesn't look like you're all that fast," Rory said, gesturing to the teen's black eye.

"I'm fast, but dumb. Ran myself right into a corner."

"Ah." Rory winced. "I've made that mistake before. Can you keep a secret?"

The teen nodded.

"I used to live on the streets just like you. Busked right over there."

"I know."

"You do?"

"Everyone does. You're the Phoenix."

"What are you talking about?"

"That's what everyone calls you out here. The street kid who rose from the ashes. The Phoenix."

Rory's hand trembled in mine, and I gripped tighter. He looked at me, a flood of emotion filling his eyes. Those tears he hadn't been able to shed for Nikki came for this boy and for the symbol of hope he'd become. His past wouldn't be his downfall; it would be his legacy. What was it Nikki had called it?

A victory for the forgotten.

The Phoenix.

And I'd been the one to repair his broken shell from the blueprint my mother had modeled for me.

"Can you spare some change?" the boy asked.

"Oh, Flash," Rory said. "I can do a whole lot more than that."

40

RORY: COMING HOME

I climbed an incline at the back of my newly purchased property, then sat on a patch of groundcover at the top of the hill and took it all in. A jumble of emotions hit me in the feels: pride, shock, gratitude. My house. It wasn't a sprawling estate like what Jake bought for his parents, but it was still everything Nikki and I would lie awake at night imagining as kids. A two-story Spanish-style house with a clay tile roof and a pool that made me giddy to look at. There was no lazy river, but it had waterslides and rock grottos and waterfalls all in a tropical oasis.

Despite having had plenty of time to get used to the idea of being a first-time homeowner, through the long process of quali-fying, searching, and finally closing on the property, nothing had prepared me for this incredible accomplishment. The ulti-mate measure of success: a home of my very own. I hadn't gotten here alone. The safety net I'd lacked my whole life had come alive the day I met Grace, and together we were unstoppable. This place was proof of our collective power.

"I made it, Nik," I said, subdued in tone and pitch. "I wish you could see it. It's everything we ever dreamed of."

I went on to describe the place to her. In the eight months

since her death, I'd worked my way through my conflicting feelings and had come to a place of peace and acceptance. The forgiveness part was still a work in progress, but I was getting there. Understanding that she was a victim too helped in the healing process. If Nikki had found her own grace, maybe she could have been saved like me.

"I'm sorry I left you on the shelf for so long," I said, holding her urn gently in my hands. On the front was Nikki's full name and the dates of both her birth and her death. Dignity. It was all I could offer her now. "But I've got you now. I've got you."

Prying the lid off, I released her ashes and watched as the light wind picked them up and sprinkled them along the hillside.

She finally got her mansion in the hills.

FROM MY PERCH, I saw Grace walk out onto the patio, shielding her eyes as she looked for me. I let out a bird whistle to get her attention.

"Is there a reason you're perched up there?" Walking past the pool, Grace started up the hill.

"I wouldn't," I said.

"Why?"

I held up the empty urn. "Nikki."

Grace squealed and jogged back down. "I swear to god, Rory. You need to be better socialized."

"What? I told you I was going to scatter her ashes."

"I know, but I thought you were going to rent a boat or take a hike or something, not fertilize our backyard with her. What if the wind picks up?"

"You know, Grace," I said, standing up and making my way

down to join her, "your compassion is one of the things I love most about you."

She smiled. "Well, excuse me if I don't want your sister blowing onto my salad. Now hurry. The car is coming to pick us up in forty-five minutes. Go hop in the shower. We don't want Nikki coming with us."

THE RIBBON EXTENDED across two posts in front of the entrance to the newly renovated apartment complex. Once a run-down eyesore a few blocks from Camden Place, this was its sister complex, set to house foster kids who'd aged out of the system. The three buildings formed a U-shape and opened out into a large interior green space where we were gathered today. And we'd do it again in about a year's time when another complex, currently under construction, opened down the street. Once completed, the three complexes would serve upwards of a thousand displaced and aged-out foster kids, offering them the support they needed to rise from the ashes of a life that had never been their choosing.

Although I'd donated to the cause, it wasn't my victory we'd come to celebrate. It was Michelle's. She'd been working tirelessly with community leaders and other volunteers to raise money for the renovations, her son being one of the project's biggest donors. But what was special about this place for me was that it had been inspired by my struggles in the system. This project had begun six years ago, not long after my disappearance. Her concern for me had prompted Michelle to spearhead the efforts that eventually led to this ribbon-cutting ceremony.

Grace beamed up at me with that freshness I'd always loved. She looked stunning in her light-yellow gown, her hair curled and swept back on one side with a sparkly clip. She was radiant.

So polished and perfect. I'd once thought I wasn't worthy of her, but she'd made me. She'd filled my broken shell full and made me worthy.

I bent down and whispered in her ear, "This is all because of you."

"Me?" She laughed. "My monetary contribution might've bought that tree over there."

"This is more than donations, Grace. You were the spark that started this whole thing. If you hadn't stopped and talked to me on the street that night, hadn't tried to save me, hadn't planted the seed in your mother to start her music program for foster kids, none of us would be standing here today."

"Let's be honest. Altruism had nothing to do with it. I was a teenage girl; you were hot. And then there was the towel hut. End of story."

I shook my head, smiling. "Maybe don't share your version of events with the donors at dinner."

"Ugh, don't remind me. I'm going to be beating all those rich ladies off you tonight." An idea came to her in that moment. She grabbed my face, placing a lipstick kiss to my cheek. "There, now you're mine."

"I've always been yours."

Quinn groaned. "You two are irritating the shit out of me. And I swear to god, I better never know what happened in that towel hut."

I looked down the line of McKallisters and their significant others who'd come to support Michelle in her worthy cause. Every member of Sketch Monsters was also here, as well as Tucker and Bodhi Beckett and RJ Contreras, former members of the boy band AnyDayNow that he'd managed before us. The star power had come out in force tonight, with one notable exception. But based on the cheers and screams coming from out on the street, he'd just arrived.

Jake and Casey walked across the grass, managing to drop the jaws of even the most seasoned of millionaire donors. His fame brought an authenticity to the proceedings, a reason to pull out the checkbook and keep on giving. As he approached our lineup, he dropped Casey's hand and wrapped his arms around me, slapping a hug onto my back.

"You sure know how to bring it on," he said, the inside joke meant for my ears only.

He moved on from me, slipping into our line beside Scott and Michelle before bending down and kissing his mother on the cheek.

"Proud of you, Mom," I heard him whisper.

The mayor stepped forward and said a few words about the project before instructing those of us with scissors to step up to the ribbon, which was pretty much anyone who was famous or had been a major donor. Michelle stood on one side of me, Jake on the other. We cut the ribbon, allowing the wrap over the sign to fall away, revealing the name of the building complex that would support former foster kids like me for years to come.

The Phoenix.

"Are we there yet?" Grace asked for the hundredth time.

"No. Almost."

"You said that the last time," she protested.

"I know, but then we got stuck in traffic. Now we are almost there for real."

She propped open one eye. "I think maybe you're trying to be romantic, but you're being the opposite. Like, I actually want to hurt you."

"I know." I laughed. "Thank you for your restraint. Now close your eyes."

But instead of obeying, her other eye joined the mutiny, and she used them both to glare at me. "If there isn't a room with puppies or a wading pool full of skin care products, then you will have failed to impress me."

"We'll see about that," I said, reaching over and closing her eyes myself. "The driver is pulling in now. Keep them shut."

Damn, her impatience had no limits. I'd been battling her from the start of this surprise trip. Just getting her out of the donor's dinner early had been a chore, making me wonder if I'd miscalculated and this whole thing was a giant mistake. It was a grand gesture, for sure. Grace and I had never been big on over-the-top displays of love. We showed our affection for each other in different ways: the disco ball that still hung from my drum kit; the texts we had sitting right beside one another; the single she'd written for Sketch Monsters, "House of Cards," that shot all the way to the top of the charts.

But this wasn't just a grand gesture; it was an unrealized promise.

"Pull in here," I said to the driver. "All the way to the front."

Coordinating these two major events had not been not easy. I'd had to share my idea with Michelle early on so she could plan the ribbon cutting around it. It was the only way I could think of to get Grace all fancied up without giving it all away.

The car came to a stop. The noise of the crowds outside drew her attention.

"Now?" she asked.

"No."

The driver got out and walked around the car and opened the door. The whoosh of air prompted another impatient question.

"Now?"

"No." I grabbed her hand. "I'm going to help you out. Keep your eyes shut. I'm going to walk you to your surprise."

She groaned, but there was a smile on her face. Grace was intrigued. Excited whispers created a buzz in the air as those around us realized who we were and what we were doing here. For security purposes, only staff had been made aware of our attendance tonight, so the surprised reaction of the crowd now was understandable. People called out my name, catching me off guard, though I should have expected it. This was Quinn's old stomping ground. He was a legend here, and so was Sketch Monsters. Everybody knew my name by association alone.

With a finger pressed to my lips, I pleaded with the onlookers to keep my secret just before stopping in front of the open double doors. Music blared from inside.

"Now?" she tried again.

"Now."

It took a moment for the significance of it to register, but when it did, she gasped.

The music. The photo booth. The archway made of balloons.

"Grace Note. Will you go to Homecoming with me?"

It was Friday night, and my girl finally got her dance.

∾

The End

ALSO BY J. BENGTSSON

Cake: A Love Story

The Theory Of Second Best

Fiercely Emma

Cake: The Newlyweds

Rogue Wave

Hunker Down

Like The Wind

Next In Line

Ripple Effect

Grace Note

Visit jbengtssonbooks.com for signed paperback copies of the Cake
Series